DARWIN 977881

Poe   in 1830,
livir   uce did
not   himself
dish   his aunt

Mrs Clemms in Baltimore, where he began to publish stories in magazines. When 'MS. Found in a Bottle' won a short-story competition one of the judges helped secure him a job as an editor on the *Southern Literary Messenger*. During his time with the periodical he did much to increase its readership, but he was eventually sacked because of his excessive drinking. In 1836 Poe married his thirteen-year-old cousin, Virginia Clemms. Much of his early work went unnoticed and only in 1840 was *Tales of the Grotesque and Arabesque* published in two volumes, which included his famous story 'The Fall of the House of Usher'. Plans for starting his own magazine did not lead to much and he continued to work as a magazine editor for various publications. His *Tales* and *The Raven and Other Poems* (1845) did bring him some recognition, but unfortunately it was not enough to sustain his family financially. Mrs Clemms and Virginia nearly starved to death one winter. After his wife's death in 1847 Poe became increasingly unstable and his dependence on drink and drugs increased. Depressed and erratic, he attempted suicide in 1848. He died tragically in 1849, five days after being found in a delirious and semi-conscious condition in Baltimore. His reputation has grown steadily since his death and he has been much admired by writers such as R. L. Stevenson, Hart Crane and Baudelaire.

A companion volume to Poe's *Selected Tales*, also published in Penguin Popular Classics, *Spirits of the Dead: Tales and Poems* contains much of his classic poetry, such as *The Raven* and *Lenore*, as well as a selection of his lesser-known but equally chilling short stories.

PENGUIN POPULAR CLASSICS

SPIRITS OF THE DEAD: TALES AND POEMS

EDGAR ALLAN POE

PENGUIN BOOKS

PENGUIN BOOKS

Published by the Penguin Group
Penguin Books Ltd, 27 Wrights Lane, London w8 5tz, England
Penguin Books USA Inc., 375 Hudson Street, New York, New York 10014, USA
Penguin Books Australia Ltd, Ringwood, Victoria, Australia
Penguin Books Canada Ltd, 10 Alcorn Avenue, Toronto, Ontario, Canada m4v 3b2
Penguin Books (NZ) Ltd, 182–190 Wairau Road, Auckland 10, New Zealand

Penguin Books Ltd, Registered Offices: Harmondsworth, Middlesex, England

This collection published in Penguin Popular Classics 1997
1 3 5 7 9 10 8 6 4 2

Printed in England by Clays Ltd, St Ives plc

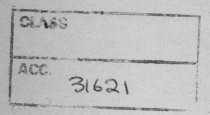

CONTENTS

CONTENTS

POEMS PUBLISHED BEFORE 1845

THE HAPPIEST DAY, THE HAPPIEST HOUR

[Tamerlane and other Poems, 1827.]

THE happiest day—the happiest hour
  My sear'd and blighted heart hath known,
The highest hope of pride and power,
  I feel hath flown.

Of power! said I? yes! such I ween;
  But they have vanish'd long, alas!
The visions of my youth have been—
  But let them pass.

And, pride, what have I now with thee?
  Another brow may even inherit   10
The venom thou hast pour'd on me—
  Be still, my spirit!

The happiest day—the happiest hour
  Mine eyes shall see—have ever seen,
The brightest glance of pride and power,
  I feel—have been:

But were that hope of pride and power
  Now offer'd, with the pain
Even *then* I felt—that brightest hour
  I would not live again: 20

For on its wing was dark alloy,
  And, as it flutter'd—fell
An essence—powerful to destroy
  A soul that knew it well.

STANZAS

[*Tamerlane and other Poems*, 1827.]

How often we forget all time, when lone
Admiring Nature's universal throne ;
Her woods—her wilds—her mountains—the intense
Reply of HERS to OUR intelligence !

[BYRON, *The Island.*]

1

IN youth have I known one with whom the Earth
In secret communing held—as he with it,
In daylight, and in beauty from his birth :
Whose fervid, flickering torch of life was lit
From the sun and stars, whence he had drawn forth
A passionate light—such for his spirit was fit—
And yet that spirit knew not, in the hour
Of its own fervour, what had o'er it power.

2

Perhaps it may be that my mind is wrought
To a fever by the moonbeam that hangs o'er,   10
But I will half believe that wild light fraught
With more of sovereignty than ancient lore
Hath ever told—or is it of a thought
The unembodied essence, and no more,
That with a quickening spell doth o'er us pass
As dew of the night-time o'er the summer grass ?

3

Doth o'er us pass, when, as th' expanding eye
To the loved object—so the tear to the lid
Will start, which lately slept in apathy ?
And yet it need not be—(that object) hid   20
From us in life—but common—which doth lie
Each hour before us—but *then* only, bid
With a strange sound, as of a harp-string broken,
To awake us—'Tis a symbol and a token

4

Of what in other worlds shall be—and given
In beauty by our God, to those alone
Who otherwise would fall from life and Heaven
Drawn by their heart's passion, and that tone,
That high tone of the spirit which hath striven,
Tho' not with Faith—with godliness—whose throne 30
With desperate energy 't hath beaten down ;
Wearing its own deep feeling as a crown.

EVENING STAR

[Tamerlane and other Poems, 1827.]

'Twas noontide of summer,
   And mid-time of night ;
And stars, in their orbits,
   Shone pale, thro' the light
Of the brighter, cold moon,
   'Mid planets her slaves,
Herself in the Heavens,
   Her beam on the waves.
      I gazed awhile
      On her cold smile ;   10
Too cold—too cold for me—
   There pass'd, as a shroud,
   A fleecy cloud,
And I turn'd away to thee,
   Proud Evening Star,
   In thy glory afar,
And dearer thy beam shall be ;
   For joy to my heart
   Is the proud part
Thou bearest in Heaven at night,   20
   And more I admire
   Thy distant fire,
Than that colder, lowly light.

DREAMS

[*Tamerlane and other Poems,* 1827.]

Oh ! that my young life were a lasting dream !
My spirit not awakening, till the beam
Of an Eternity should bring the morrow.
Yes ! tho' that long dream were of hopeless sorrow,
'Twere better than the cold reality
Of waking life, to him whose heart must be,
And hath been still, upon the lovely earth,
A chaos of deep passion, from his birth.
But should it be—that dream eternally
Continuing—as dreams have been to me   10
In my young boyhood—should it thus be given,
'Twere folly still to hope for higher Heaven.
For I have revell'd, when the sun was bright
I' the summer sky, in dreams of living light
And loveliness,—have left my very heart
In climes of my imagining, apart
From mine own home, with beings that have been
Of mine own thought—what more could I have seen ?
'Twas once—and only once—and the wild hour
From my remembrance shall not pass—some power   20
Or spell had bound me—'twas the chilly wind
Came o'er me in the night, and left behind
Its image on my spirit—or the moon
Shone on my slumbers in her lofty noon
Too coldly—or the stars—howe'er it was
That dream was as that night-wind—let it pass.

I *have been* happy, tho' in a dream.
I have been happy—and I love the theme :
Dreams ! in their vivid colouring of life,
As in that fleeting, shadowy, misty strife   30
Of semblance with reality, which brings
To the delirious eye, more lovely things
Of Paradise and Love—and all our own !
Than young Hope in his sunniest hour hath known.

SPIRITS OF THE DEAD

[*Al Aaraaf, Tamerlane, and Minor Poems,* 1829.]

THY soul shall find itself alone
'Mid dark thoughts of the grey tomb-stone ;
Not one, of all the crowd, to pry
Into thine hour of secrecy.

Be silent in that solitude,
    Which is not loneliness—for then
The spirits of the dead, who stood
    In life before thee, are again
In death around thee, and their will
Shall overshadow thee ; be still.   10

The night, though clear, shall frown,
And the stars shall not look down
From their high thrones in the Heaven
With light like hope to mortals given,
But their red orbs, without beam,
To thy weariness shall seem
As a burning and a fever
Which would cling to thee for ever.

Now are thoughts thou shalt not banish,
Now are visions ne'er to vanish ;   20
From thy spirit shall they pass
No more, like dew-drop from the grass.

The breeze, the breath of God, is still,
And the mist upon the hill
Shadowy, shadowy, yet unbroken,
Is a symbol and a token.
How it hangs upon the trees,
A mystery of mysteries !

TO M——

[*Al Aaraaf, Tamerlane, and Minor Poems,* 1829.]

O ! I care not that my earthly lot
   Hath little of Earth in it,
That years of love have been forgot
   In the fever of a minute :

I heed not that the desolate
   Are happier, sweet, than I,
But that you meddle with my fate
   Who am a passer by.

It *is* not that my founts of bliss
   Are gushing—strange ! with tears—   10
Or that the thrill of a single kiss
   Hath palsied many years—

'Tis not that the flowers of twenty springs
   Which have wither'd as they rose
Lie dead on my heart-strings
   With the weight of an age of snows.

Not that the grass—O ! may it thrive !
   On my grave is growing or grown—
But that, while I am dead yet alive
   I cannot be, lady, alone.   20

THE RAVEN AND OTHER POEMS
1845

TO THE NOBLEST OF HER SEX—

TO THE AUTHOR OF

' THE DRAMA IN EXILE '—

TO MISS ELIZABETH BARRETT BARRETT,

OF ENGLAND,

I DEDICATE THIS VOLUME,

WITH THE MOST ENTHUSIASTIC ADMIRATION

AND WITH THE MOST SINCERE ESTEEM.

E. A. P.

PREFACE

THESE trifles are collected and republished chiefly with
a view to their redempt on from the many improvements
to which they have been subjected while going at random
' the rounds of the press '.   If what I have written is to
circulate at all, I am naturally anxious that it should
circulate as I wrote it.   In defence of my own taste, nevertheless, it is incumbent upon me to say, that I think nothing
in this volume of much value to the public, or very credit-
able to myself.   Events not to be controlled have prevented
me from making, at any time, any serious effort in what,
under happier circumstances, would have been the field
of my choice.   With me poetry has been not a purpose,
but a passion ; and the passions should be held in reverence ; they must not—they cannot at will be excited with
an eye to the paltry compensations, or the more paltry
commendations, of mankind.

E. A. P.

THE RAVEN

ONCE upon a midnight dreary, while I pondered, weak
and weary,
Over many a quaint and curious volume of forgotten lore,
While I nodded, nearly napping, suddenly there came
a tapping,
As of some one gently rapping, rapping at my chamber
door.
' 'Tis some visitor,' I muttered, ' tapping at my chamber
door—
Only this, and nothing more.'

Ah, distinctly I remember it was in the bleak December,
And each separate dying ember wrought its ghost upon
the floor.
Eagerly I wished the morrow ;—vainly I had sought
to borrow
From my books surcease of sorrow—sorrow for the lost
Lenore— 10
For the rare and radiant maiden whom the angels name
Lenore—
Nameless here for evermore.

And the silken sad uncertain rustling of each purple
curtain
Thrilled me—filled me with fantastic terrors never felt
before ;
So that now, to still the beating of my heart, I stood
repeating,
' 'Tis some visitor entreating entrance at my chamber
door—
Some late visitor entreating entrance at my chamber
door ;—
This it is, and nothing more.'

Presently my soul grew stronger ; hesitating then
no longer,
' Sir,' said I, ' or Madam, truly your forgiveness I implore ; 20

But the fact is I was napping, and so gently you came
    rapping,
And so faintly you came tapping, tapping at my chamber
    door,
That I scarce was sure I heard you '—here I opened wide
    the door ;—
        Darkness there, and nothing more.

Deep into that darkness peering, long I stood there
    wondering, fearing,
Doubting, dreaming dreams no mortals ever dared to dream
    before ;
  But the silence was unbroken, and the stillness gave no
    token,
  And the only word there spoken was the whispered word,
    ' Lenore ! '
This I whispered, and an echo murmured back the word,
    ' Lenore ! '—
        Merely this, and nothing more.   30

Back into the chamber turning, all my soul within me
    burning,
Soon again I heard a tapping somewhat louder than before.
  ' Surely,' said I, ' surely that is something at my window
    lattice :
  Let me see, then, what thereat is, and this mystery
    explore—
Let my heart be still a moment and this mystery explore ;—
        'Tis the wind and nothing more.'

Open here I flung the shutter, when, with many a flirt
    and flutter,
In there stepped a stately raven of the saintly days of
    yore ;
  Not the least obeisance made he ; not a minute stopped
    or stayed he ;
  But, with mien of lord or lady, perched above my
    chamber door—   40
Perched upon a bust of Pallas just above my chamber
    door—
        Perched, and sat, and nothing more.

Then this ebony bird beguiling my sad fancy into
    smiling,
By the grave and stern decorum of the countenance it wore.
  ' Though thy crest be shorn and shaven, thou,' I said,
      ' art sure no craven,
    Ghastly grim and ancient raven wandering from the
      Nightly shore—
Tell me what thy lordly name is on the Night's Plutonian
      shore ! '
              Quoth the Raven, ' Nevermore '.

Much I marvelled this ungainly fowl to hear discourse
    so plainly,
Though its answer little meaning—little relevancy bore ; 50
    For we cannot help agreeing that no living human being
    Ever yet was blest with seeing bird above his chamber
      door—
Bird or beast upon the sculptured bust above his chamber
      door,
              With such name as ' Nevermore '.

But the raven, sitting lonely on the placid bust, spoke
    only
That one word, as if his soul in that one word he did out-
    pour.
    Nothing further then he uttered—not a feather then he
      fluttered—
    Till I scarcely more than muttered, ' other friends have
      flown before—
On the morrow *he* will leave me, as my hopes have flown
      before.'
              Then the bird said, ' Nevermore '.   60

Startled at the stillness broken by reply so aptly spoken,
' Doubtless ', said I, ' what it utters is its only stock and
    store,
    Caught from some unhappy master whom unmerciful
      Disaster
    Followed fast and followed faster till his songs one
      burden bore—
Till the dirges of his Hope that melancholy burden bore
              Of " Never—nevermore ".'

But the Raven still beguiling all my fancy into smiling,
Straight I wheeled a cushioned seat in front of bird, and
bust and door ;
   Then upon the velvet sinking, I betook myself to
   linking
   Fancy unto fancy, thinking what this ominous bird
   of yore—   70
What this grim, ungainly, ghastly, gaunt and ominous
bird of yore
          Meant in croaking ' Nevermore '.

This I sat engaged in guessing, but no syllable expressing
To the fowl whose fiery eyes now burned into my bosom's
core ;
   This and more I sat divining, with my head at ease
   reclining
   On the cushion's velvet lining that the lamplight gloated
   o'er,
But whose velvet violet lining with the lamplight gloating
o'er,
          She shall press, ah, nevermore !

Then methought the air grew denser, perfumed from
an unseen censer
Swung by Seraphim whose footfalls tinkled on the tufted
floor.   80
   ' Wretch,' I cried, ' thy God hath lent thee—by these
   angels he hath sent thee
   Respite—respite and nepenthe, from thy memories of
   Lenore !
Quaff, oh quaff this kind nepenthe and forget this lost
Lenore ! '
          Quoth the Raven, ' Nevermore '.

' Prophet ! ' said I, ' thing of evil !—prophet still, if
bird or devil !—
Whether Tempter sent, or whether tempest tossed thee
here ashore,
   Desolate yet all undaunted, on this desert land enchanted—
   On this home by horror haunted—tell me truly, I
   implore—

Is there—*is* there balm in Gilead ?—tell me—tell me,
    I implore ! '
           Quoth the Raven, ' Nevermore '.   90

' Prophet ! ' said I, ' thing of evil—prophet still, if bird
    or devil !
By that Heaven that bends above us—by that God we
    both adore—
    Tell this soul with sorrow laden if, within the distant
        Aidenn,
    It shall clasp a sainted maiden whom the angels name
        Lenore—
Clasp a rare and radiant maiden whom the angels name
    Lenore.'
           Quoth the Raven, ' Nevermore '.

' Be that word our sign in parting, bird or fiend,' I
    shrieked, upstarting—
' Get thee back into the tempest and the Night's Plutonian
    shore !
    Leave no black plume as a token of that lie thy soul
        hath spoken !
    Leave my loneliness unbroken !—quit the bust above
        my door !   100
Take thy beak from out my heart, and take thy form from
    off my door ! '
           Quoth the Raven, ' Nevermore '.

And the Raven, never flitting, still is sitting, still is
    sitting
On the pallid bust of Pallas just above my chamber door ;
    And his eyes have all the seeming of a demon's that is
        dreaming,
    And the lamplight o'er him streaming throws his shadow
        on the floor ;
And my soul from out that shadow that lies floating on
    the floor
           Shall be lifted—nevermore !

THE VALLEY OF UNREST

ONCE it smiled a silent dell
Where the people did not dwell ;
They had gone unto the wars,
Trusting to the mild-eyed stars,
Nightly, from their azure towers,
To keep watch above the flowers,
In the midst of which all day
The red sunlight lazily lay.
Now each visitor shall confess
The sad valley's restlessness.   10
Nothing there is motionless—
Nothing save the airs that brood
Over the magic solitude.
Ah, by no wind are stirred those trees
That palpitate like the chill seas
Around the misty Hebrides !
Ah, by no wind those clouds are driven
That rustle through the unquiet Heaven
Uneasily, from morn till even,
Over the violets there that lie   20
In myriad types of the human eye—
Over the lilies there that wave
And weep above a nameless grave !
They wave :—from out their fragrant tops
Eternal dews come down in drops.
They weep :—from off their delicate stems
Perennial tears descend in gems.

BRIDAL BALLAD

THE ring is on my hand,
  And the wreath is on my brow ;
Satin and jewels grand
Are all at my command,
  And I am happy now.

And my lord he loves me well ;
  But, when first he breathed his vow,
I felt my bosom swell—
For the words rang as a knell,

And the voice seemed *his* who fell 10
In the battle down the dell,
  And who is happy now.

But he spoke to re-assure me,
  And he kissed my pallid brow,
While a reverie came o'er me,
And to the church-yard bore me,
And I sighed to him before me,
Thinking him dead D'Elormie,
  ' Oh, I am happy now ! '

And thus the words were spoken, 20
  And this the plighted vow,
And, though my faith be broken,
And, though my heart be broken,
Here is a ring, as token
  That I am happy now !

Would God I could awaken !
  For I dream I know not how !
And my soul is sorely shaken
Lest an evil step be taken,—
Lest the dead who is forsaken 30
  May not be happy now.

THE SLEEPER

AT midnight, in the month of June,
I stand beneath the mystic moon.
An opiate vapour, dewy, dim,
Exhales from out her golden rim,
And, softly dripping, drop by drop,
Upon the quiet mountain top,
Steals drowsily and musically
Into the universal valley.
The rosemary nods upon the grave ;
The lily lolls upon the wave ; 10
Wrapping the fog about its breast,
The ruin moulders into rest ;
Looking like Lethe, see ! the lake

A conscious slumber seems to take,
And would not, for the world, awake.
All Beauty sleeps!—and lo! where lies
Irene, with her Destinies!

O, lady bright! can it be right—
This window open to the night?
The wanton airs, from the tree-top,   20
Laughingly through the lattice drop—
The bodiless airs, a wizard rout,
Flit through thy chamber in and out,
And wave the curtain canopy
So fitfully—so fearfully—
Above the closed and fringèd lid
'Neath which thy slumb'ring soul lies hid,
That, o'er the floor and down the wall,
Like ghosts the shadows rise and fall!
Oh, lady dear, hast thou no fear?   30
Why and what art thou dreaming here?
Sure thou art come o'er far-off seas,
A wonder to these garden trees!
Strange is thy pallor! strange thy dress,
Strange, above all, thy length of tress,
And this all solemn silentness!

The lady sleeps! Oh, may her sleep,
Which is enduring, so be deep!
Heaven have her in its sacred keep!
This chamber changed for one more holy,   40
This bed for one more melancholy,
I pray to God that she may lie
For ever with unopened eye,
While the pale sheeted ghosts go by!

My love, she sleeps! Oh, may her sleep
As it is lasting, so be deep!
Soft may the worms about her creep!
Far in the forest, dim and old,
For her may some tall vault unfold—
Some vault that oft has flung its black   50
And wingèd panels fluttering back,

Triumphant, o'er the crested palls,
Of her grand family funerals—
Some sepulchre, remote, alone,
Against whose portal she hath thrown,
In childhood, many an idle stone—
Some tomb from out whose sounding door
She ne'er shall force an echo more,
Thrilling to think, poor child of sin !
It was the dead who groaned within.   60

THE COLISEUM

Type of the antique Rome ! Rich reliquary
Of lofty contemplation left to Time
By buried centuries of pomp and power !
At length—at length—after so many days
Of weary pilgrimage and burning thirst,
(Thirst for the springs of lore that in thee lie,)
I kneel, an altered and an humble man,
Amid thy shadows, and so drink within
My very soul thy grandeur, gloom, and glory !

Vastness ! and Age ! and Memories of Eld !   10
Silence ! and Desolation ! and dim Night !
I feel ye now—I feel ye in your strength—
O spells more sure than e'er Judaean king
Taught in the gardens of Gethsemane !
O charms more potent than the rapt Chaldee
Ever drew down from out the quiet stars !

Here, where a hero fell, a column falls !
Here, where the mimic eagle glared in gold,
A midnight vigil holds the swarthy bat !
Here, where the dames of Rome their gilded hair   20
Waved to the wind, now wave the reed and thistle !
Here, where on golden throne the monarch lolled,
Glides, spectre-like, unto his marble home,
Lit by the wan light of the hornèd moon,
The swift and silent lizard of the stones !

But stay ! these walls—these ivy-clad arcades—
These mouldering plinths—these sad and blackened shafts—
These vague entablatures—this crumbling frieze—
These shattered cornices—this wreck—this ruin—
These stones—alas ! these grey stones—are they all—   30
All of the famed, and the colossal left
By the corrosive Hours to Fate and me ?

' Not all '—the Echoes answer me—' not all !
Prophetic sounds and loud, arise forever
From us, and from all Ruin, unto the wise,
As melody from Memnon to the Sun.
We rule the hearts of mightiest men—we rule
With a despotic sway all giant minds.
We are not impotent—we pallid stones.
Not all our power is gone—not all our fame—   40
Not all the magic of our high renown—
Not all the wonder that encircles us—
Not all the mysteries that in us lie—
Not all the memories that hang upon
And cling around about us as a garment,
Clothing us in a robe of more than glory.'

LENORE

AH, broken is the golden bowl ! the spirit flown forever !
Let the bell toll !—a saintly soul floats on the Stygian river ;
And, Guy de Vere, hast *thou* no tear ?—weep now or nevermore !
See ! on yon drear and rigid bier low lies thy love, Lenore !
Come ! let the burial rite be read—the funeral song be sung !—
An anthem for the queenliest dead that ever died so young—
A dirge for her the doubly dead in that she died so young.

'Wretches ! ye loved her for her wealth and hated her for her pride,
And when she fell in feeble health, ye blessed her—that she died !

How *shall* the ritual, then, be read ?—the requiem how
  be sung   10
By you—by yours, the evil eye,—by yours, the slanderous
  tongue
That did to death the innocence that died, and died so
  young ? '

Peccavimus ; but rave not thus ! and let a Sabbath song
Go up to God so solemnly the dead may feel no wrong.
The sweet Lenore hath ' gone before ', with Hope, that
  flew beside,
Leaving thee wild for the dear child that should have
  been thy bride—
For her, the fair and *debonair*, that now so lowly lies,
The life upon her yellow hair but not within her eyes—
The life still there, upon her hair—the death upon her
  eyes.

  ' Avaunt ! avaunt ! from fiends below, the indignant
    ghost is riven—   20
From Hell unto a high estate far up within the Heaven—
From grief and groan, to a golden throne, beside the King
  of Heaven !
Let no bell toll, then,—lest her soul, amid its hallowed
  mirth,
Should catch the note as it doth float up from the damnèd
  Earth !
And I !—to-night my heart is light !—no dirge will I
  upraise,
But waft the angel on her flight with a Paean of old days ! '

CATHOLIC HYMN

> At morn—at noon—at twilight dim—
> Maria ! thou hast heard my hymn !
> In joy and woe—in good and ill—
> Mother of God, be with me still !
> When the hours flew brightly by,
> And not a cloud obscured the sky,
> My soul, lest it should truant be,
> Thy grace did guide to thine and thee ;

Now, when storms of Fate o'ercast
Darkly my Present and my Past,   10
Let my Future radiant shine
With sweet hopes of thee and thine !

ISRAFEL

And the angel Israfel, whose heart-strings are a lute, and who has
the sweetest voice of all God's creatures.—*Koran*.

In Heaven a spirit doth dwell
    ' Whose heart-strings are a lute ' ;
None sing so wildly well
As the angel Israfel,
And the giddy stars (so legends tell),
Ceasing their hymns, attend the spell
    Of his voice, all mute.

Tottering above
    In her highest noon,
    The enamoured moon   10
Blushes with love,
    While, to listen, the red levin
    (With the rapid Pleiads, even,
    Which were seven,)
    Pauses in Heaven.

And they say (the starry choir
    And the other listening things)
That Israfeli's fire
Is owing to that lyre
    By which he sits and sings—   20
The trembling living wire
    Of those unusual strings.

But the skies that angel trod,
    Where deep thoughts are a duty—
Where Love's a grown-up God—
    Where the Houri glances are
Imbued with all the beauty
    Which we worship in a star.

Therefore thou art not wrong,
   Israfeli, who despisest   30
An unimpassioned song ;
To thee the laurels belong,
   Best bard, because the wisest !
Merrily live, and long !

The ecstasies above
   With thy burning measures suit—
Thy grief, thy joy, thy hate, thy love,
   With the fervour of thy lute—
   Well may the stars be mute !

Yes, Heaven is thine ; but this   40
   Is a world of sweets and sours ;
   Our flowers are merely—flowers,
And the shadow of thy perfect bliss
   Is the sunshine of ours.

If I could dwell
Where Israfel
   Hath dwelt, and he where I,
He might not sing so wildly well
   A mortal melody,
While a bolder note than this might swell   50
   From my lyre within the sky.

DREAMLAND

By a route obscure and lonely,
Haunted by ill angels only,
Where an Eidolon, named NIGHT,
On a black throne reigns upright,
I have reached these lands but newly
From an ultimate dim Thule—
From a wild weird clime that lieth, sublime,
        Out of SPACE—out of TIME.

Bottomless vales and boundless floods,
And chasms, and caves, and Titan woods,
With forms that no man can discover   10
For the tears that drip all over ;

Mountains toppling evermore
Into seas without a shore ;
Seas that restlessly aspire,
Surging, unto skies of fire ;
Lakes that endlessly outspread
Their lone waters—lone and dead,—
Their still waters—still and chilly
With the snows of the lolling lily.   20

By the lakes that thus outspread
Their lone waters, lone and dead,—
Their sad waters, sad and chilly
With the snows of the lolling lily,—
By the mountains—near the river
Murmuring lowly, murmuring ever,—
By the grey woods,—by the swamp
Where the toad and the newt encamp,—
By the dismal tarns and pools
        Where dwell the Ghouls,—   30
By each spot the most unholy—
In each nook most melancholy,—
There the traveller meets aghast
Sheeted Memories of the Past—
Shrouded forms that start and sigh
As they pass the wanderer by—
White-robed forms of friends long given,
In agony, to the Earth—and Heaven.

For the heart whose woes are legion
'Tis a peaceful, soothing region—   40
For the spirit that walks in shadow
'Tis—oh, 'tis an Eldorado !
But the traveller, travelling through it,
May not—dare not openly view it !
Never its mysteries are exposed
To the weak human eye unclosed ;
So wills its King, who hath forbid
The uplifting of the fringèd lid ;
And thus the sad Soul that here passes
Beholds it but through darkened glasses.   50

By a route obscure and lonely,
Haunted by ill angels only,
Where an Eidolon, named NIGHT,
On a black throne reigns upright,
I have wandered home but newly
From this ultimate dim Thule.

SONNET—TO ZANTE

FAIR isle, that from the fairest of all flowers,
   Thy gentlest of all gentle names dost take !
How many memories of what radiant hours
   At sight of thee and thine at once awake !
How many scenes of what departed bliss !
   How many thoughts of what entombèd hopes !
How many visions of a maiden that is
   No more—no more upon thy verdant slopes !
No more ! alas, that magical sad sound
   Transforming all ! Thy charms shall please *no more*— 10
Thy memory *no more !* Accursèd ground
   Henceforth I hold thy flower-enamelled shore,
O hyacinthine isle ! O purple Zante !
       ' Isola d'oro ! Fior di Levante ! '

THE CITY IN THE SEA

Lo ! Death has reared himself a throne
In a strange city lying alone
Far down within the dim West,
Where the good and the bad and the worst and the best
Have gone to their eternal rest.
There shrines and palaces and towers
(Time-eaten towers that tremble not !
Resemble nothing that is ours.
Around, by lifting winds forgot,
Resignedly beneath the sky   10
The melancholy waters lie.

No rays from the holy heaven come down
On the long night-time of that town ;

But light from out the lurid sea
Streams up the turrets silently—
Gleams up the pinnacles far and free—
Up domes—up spires—up kingly halls—
Up fanes—up Babylon-like walls—
Up shadowy long-forgotten bowers
Of sculptured ivy and stone flowers—   20
Up many and many a marvellous shrine
Whose wreathèd friezes intertwine
The viol, the violet, and the vine.
Resignedly beneath the sky
The melancholy waters lie.
So blend the turrets and shadows there
That all seem pendulous in air,
While from a proud tower in the town
Death looks gigantically down.

There open fanes and gaping graves   30
Yawn level with the luminous waves ;
But not the riches there that lie
In each idol's diamond eye—
Not the gaily-jewelled dead
Tempt the waters from their bed ;
For no ripples curl, alas !
Along that wilderness of glass—
No swellings tell that winds may be
Upon some far-off happier sea—
No heavings hint that winds have been   40
On seas less hideously serene.

But lo, a stir is in the air !
The wave—there is a movement there !
As if the towers had thrust aside,
In slightly sinking, the dull tide—
As if their tops had feebly given
A void within the filmy Heaven.
The waves have now a redder glow—
The hours are breathing faint and low—
And when, amid no earthly moans,   50
Down, down that town shall settle hence,
Hell, rising from a thousand thrones,
Shall do it reverence.

TO ONE IN PARADISE

THOU wast all that to me, love,
　For which my soul did pine—
A green isle in the sea, love,
　A fountain and a shrine,
All wreathed with fairy fruits and flowers,
　And all the flowers were mine.

Ah, dream too bright to last !
　Ah, starry Hope ! that didst arise
But to be overcast !
　A voice from out the Future cries,　　　　10
' On ! on ! '—but o'er the Past
　(Dim gulf !) my spirit hovering lies
Mute, motionless, aghast !

For, alas ! alas ! with me
　The light of Life is o'er !
　' No more—no more—no more— '
(Such language holds the solemn sea
　To the sands upon the shore)
Shall bloom the thunder-blasted tree
　Or the stricken eagle soar !　　　　20

And all my days are trances,
　And all my nightly dreams
Are where thy grey eye glances,
　And where thy footstep gleams—
In what ethereal dances,
　By what eternal streams.

EULALIE—A SONG

I DWELT alone
In a world of moan,
And my soul was a stagnant tide,
Till the fair and gentle Eulalie became my blushing bride—
Till the yellow-haired young Eulalie became my smiling
bride.

Ah, less—less bright
The stars of the night
Than the eyes of the radiant girl !
And never a flake
That the vapour can make   10
With the moon-tints of purple and pearl,
Can vie with the modest Eulalie's most unregarded curl—
Can compare with the bright-eyed Eulalie's most humble
and careless curl.

Now Doubt—now Pain
Come never again,
For her soul gives me sigh for sigh,
And all day long
Shines, bright and strong,
Astarté within the sky,
While ever to her dear Eulalie upturns her matron eye— 20
While ever to her young Eulalie upturns her violet eye.

TO F——S S. O——D

[Mrs. Frances Sargent Osgood.]

THOU wouldst be loved ?—then let thy heart
From its present pathway part not !
Being everything which now thou art,
Be nothing which thou art not.
So with the world thy gentle ways,
Thy grace, thy more than beauty,
Shall be an endless theme of praise,
And love—a simple duty.

TO F——

[F—— is, presumably, Mrs. Frances Sargent Osgood.]

BELOVED ! amid the earnest woes
  That crowd around my earthly path—
(Drear path, alas ! where grows
Not even one lonely rose)—
  My soul at least a solace hath
In dreams of thee, and therein knows
An Eden of bland repose.

And thus thy memory is to me
  Like some enchanted far-off isle
In some tumultuous sea—   10
Some ocean throbbing far and free
  With storms—but where meanwhile
Serenest skies continually
  Just o'er that one bright island smile.

SONNET—SILENCE

THERE are some qualities—some incorporate things,
  That have a double life, which thus is made
A type of that twin entity which springs
  From matter and light, evinced in solid and shade.
There is a two-fold *Silence*—sea and shore—
  Body and soul. One dwells in lonely places,
  Newly with grass o'ergrown ; some solemn graces,
Some human memories and tearful lore,
Render him terrorless : his name 's ' No More '.
He is the corporate Silence : dread him not !   10
  No power hath he of evil in himself ;
But should some urgent fate (untimely lot !)
  Bring thee to meet his shadow (nameless elf,
That haunteth the lone regions where hath trod
No foot of man,) commend thyself to God !

THE CONQUEROR WORM

Lo ! 'tis a gala night
  Within the lonesome latter years !
An angel throng, bewinged, bedight
  In veils, and drowned in tears,
Sit in a theatre, to see
  A play of hopes and fears,
While the orchestra breathes fitfully
  The music of the spheres.

Mimes, in the form of God on high,
  Mutter and mumble low,   10
And hither and thither fly—
  Mere puppets they, who come and go
At bidding of vast formless things
  That shift the scenery to and fro,
Flapping from out their Condor wings
  Invisible Woe !

That motley drama—oh, be sure
  It shall not be forgot !
With its Phantom chased for evermore,
  By a crowd that seize it not,   20
Through a circle that ever returneth in
  To the self-same spot,
And much of Madness, and more of Sin,
  And Horror the soul of the plot.

But see, amid the mimic rout
  A crawling shape intrude !
A blood-red thing that writhes from out
  The scenic solitude !
It writhes !—it writhes !—with mortal pangs
  The mimes become its food,   30
And seraphs sob at vermin fangs
  In human gore imbued.

Out—out are the lights—out all !
  And, over each quivering form,
The curtain, a funeral pall,
  Comes down with the rush of a storm,

While the angels, all pallid and wan,
  Uprising, unveiling, affirm
That the play is the tragedy, ' Man ',
  And its hero the Conqueror Worm.   40

THE HAUNTED PALACE

In the greenest of our valleys
  By good angels tenanted,
Once a fair and stately palace—
  Radiant palace—reared its head.
In the monarch Thought's dominion—
  It stood there !
Never seraph spread a pinion
  Over fabric half so fair !

Banners yellow, glorious, golden,
  On its roof did float and flow,   10
(This—all this—was in the olden
  Time long ago,)
And every gentle air that dallied,
  In that sweet day,
Along the ramparts plumed and pallid,
  A wingèd odour went away.

Wanderers in that happy valley,
  Through two luminous windows, saw
Spirits moving musically,
  To a lute's well-tunèd law,   20
Round about a throne where, sitting
  (Porphyrogene !)
In state his glory well-befitting,
  The ruler of the realm was seen.

And all with pearl and ruby glowing
  Was the fair palace door,
Through which came flowing, flowing, flowing,
  And sparkling evermore,
A troop of Echoes, whose sweet duty
  Was but to sing,   30
In voices of surpassing beauty,
  The wit and wisdom of their king.

But evil things, in robes of sorrow,
   Assailed the monarch's high estate.
(Ah, let us mourn !—for never morrow [1]
   Shall dawn upon him desolate !)
And round about his home the glory
   That blushed and bloomed,
Is but a dim-remembered story
   Of the old time entombed.   40

And travellers, now, within that valley,
   Through the red-litten windows see
Vast forms, that move fantastically
   To a discordant melody,
While, like a ghastly rapid river,
   Through the pale door
A hideous throng rush out forever
   And laugh—but smile no more.

---

[1] The 1845 text has 'sorrow' for morrow.   But this is obviously
a misprint.—ED.

SCENES FROM 'POLITIAN'

AN UNPUBLISHED DRAMA

DRAMATIS PERSONAE

POLITIAN, Earl of Leicester.
DI BROGLIO, a Roman Duke.
COUNT CASTIGLIONE, his son.
BALDAZZAR, Duke of Surrey,
    Friend to Politian.

A MONK.
LALAGE.
ALESSANDRA, betrothed to Casti-
    glione.
JACINTA, maid to Lalage.

The Scene lies in Rome.

SCENES FROM 'POLITIAN'

AN UNPUBLISHED DRAMA

I

Rome.—*A Hall in a Palace.*

Alessandra *and* Castiglione.

ALESSANDRA.

Thou art sad, Castiglione.

CASTIGLIONE.

Sad !—not I.
Oh, I'm the happiest, happiest man in Rome !
A few days more, thou knowest, my Alessandra,
Will make thee mine. Oh, I am very happy !

ALESSANDRA.

Methinks thou hast a singular way of showing
Thy happiness !—what ails thee, cousin of mine ?
Why didst thou sigh so deeply ?

CASTIGLIONE.

Did I sigh ?
I was not conscious of it. It is a fashion,
A silly—a most silly fashion I have
When I am *very* happy. Did I sigh¦?   9
                                        (*Sighing.*)

ALESSANDRA.

Thou didst. Thou art not well. Thou hast indulged
Too much of late, and I am vexed to see it.
Late hours and wine, Castiglione,—these
Will ruin thee ! thou art already altered—
Thy looks are haggard—nothing so wears away
The constitution as late hours and wine.

CASTIGLIONE (*musing*).

Nothing, fair cousin, nothing—not even deep sorrow—
Wears it away like evil hours and wine.
I will amend.

ALESSANDRA.

Do it ! I would have thee drop
Thy riotous company, too—fellows low born—   20

Ill suit the like with old Di Broglio's heir
And Alessandra's husband.

CASTIGLIONE.

> I will drop them.

ALESSANDRA.

Thou wilt—thou must. Attend thou also more
To thy dress and equipage—they are over plain
For thy lofty rank and fashion—much depends
Upon appearances.

CASTIGLIONE.

> I'll see to it.

ALESSANDRA.

Then see to it !—pay more attention, sir,
To a becoming carriage—much thou wantest
In dignity.

CASTIGLIONE.

> Much, much, oh ! much I want
In proper dignity.

ALESSANDRA (haughtily).

> Thou mockest me, sir.   30

CASTIGLIONE (abstractedly).

Sweet, gentle Lalage !

ALESSANDRA.

> Heard I aright ?
I speak to him—he speaks of Lalage !
Sir Count ! (<i>places her hand on his shoulder</i>) what art thou
      dreaming ? (<i>aside</i>) He's not well !
What ails thee, sir ?

CASTIGLIONE (starting).

> Cousin ! fair cousin !—madam !
I crave thy pardon—indeed I am not well—
Your hand from off my shoulder, if you please.
This air is most oppressive !—Madam—the Duke !

Enter DI BROGLIO.

DI BROGLIO.

My son, I've news for thee !—hey ?—what's the matter ?
      (<i>observing Alessandra.</i>)
I' the pouts ? Kiss her, Castiglione ! kiss her,
You dog ! and make it up, I say, this minute !   40

I've news for you both.   Politian is expected
Hourly in Rome—Politian, Earl of Leicester !
We'll have him at the wedding.   'Tis his first visit
To the imperial city.

ALESSANDRA.
     What !   Politian
Of Britain, Earl of Leicester ?

DI BROGLIO.
        The same, my love.
We'll have him at the wedding.   A man quite young
In years, but grey in fame.   I have not seen him,
But Rumour speaks of him as of a prodigy
Preëminent in arts and arms, and wealth,
And high descent.   We'll have him at the wedding. 50

ALESSANDRA.
I have heard much of this Politian.
Gay, volatile and giddy—is he not ?
And little given to thinking.

DI BROGLIO.
       Far from it, love.
No branch, they say, of all philosophy
So deep abstruse he has not mastered it.
Learned as few are learned.

ALESSANDRA.
       'Tis very strange !
I have known men have seen Politian
And sought his company.   They speak of him
As of one who entered madly into life,
Drinking the cup of pleasure to the dregs.   60

CASTIGLIONE.
Ridiculous !   Now *I* have seen Politian
And know him well—nor learned nor mirthful he.
He is a dreamer, and a man shut out
From common passions.

DI BROGLIO.
      Children, we disagree.
Let us go forth and taste the fragrant air
Of the garden.   Did I dream, or did I hear
Politian was a *melancholy* man ?   (*Exeunt.*)

II

ROME.—*A Lady's apartment, with a window open and looking into a garden.* LALAGE, *in deep mourning, reading at a table on which lie some books and a hand mirror. In the background* JACINTA (*a servant maid*) *leans carelessly upon a chair.*

LALAGE.

Jacinta, is it thou ?

JACINTA (*pertly*).
                    Yes, ma'am, I'm here.

LALAGE.

I did not know, Jacinta, you were in waiting.
Sit down !—let not my presence trouble you—   70
Sit down !—for I am humble, most humble.

JACINTA (*aside*).
                    'Tis time.

(JACINTA *seats herself in a side-long manner upon the chair, resting her elbows upon the back, and regarding her mistress with a contemptuous look.* LALAGE *continues to read.*)

LALAGE.

' It in another climate, so he said,
' Bore a bright golden flower, but not i' this soil ! '
            (*pauses—turns over some leaves, and resumes.*)
' No lingering winters there, nor snow, nor shower—
' But Ocean ever to refresh mankind
' Breathes the shrill spirit of the western wind.'
O, beautiful !—most beautiful !—how like
To what my fevered soul doth dream of Heaven !
O happy land ! (*pauses.*) She died !—the maiden died !   80
O still more happy maiden who couldst die !
Jacinta !

(JACINTA *returns no answer, and* LALAGE *presently resumes.*)

Again !—a similar tale
Told of a beauteous dame beyond the sea !
Thus speaketh one Ferdinand in the words of the play—
' She died full young '—one Bossola answers him—
' I think not so—her infelicity

'Seemed to have years too many'—Ah luckless lady!
Jacinta! (*still no answer.*)
            Here's a far sterner story,
But like—oh, very like in its despair—   90
Of that Egyptian queen, winning so easily
A thousand hearts—losing at length her own.
She died. Thus endeth the history—and her maids
Lean over her and weep—two gentle maids
With gentle names—Eiros and Charmion!
Rainbow and Dove!——Jacinta!

JACINTA (*pettishly*).
              Madam, what *is* it?

LALAGE.
Wilt thou, my good Jacinta, be so kind
As go down in the library and bring me
The Holy Evangelists?

JACINTA.
          Pshaw!   (*Exit.*

LALAGE.
             If there be balm   100
For the wounded spirit in Gilead it is there!
Dew in the night-time of my bitter trouble
Will there be found—'dew sweeter far than that
Which hangs like chains of pearl on Hermon hill.'
    (*Re-enter* JACINTA, *and throws a volume on the table.*)
There, ma'am, 's the book. Indeed she is very trouble-
     some.   (*Aside.*)

LALAGE (*astonished*).
What didst thou say, Jacinta? Have I done aught
To grieve thee or to vex thee?—I am sorry.
For thou hast served me long and ever been
Trustworthy and respectful.   (*resumes her reading.*)

JACINTA (*aside*).
             I can't believe
She has any more jewels—no—no—she gave me all.   110

LALAGE.
What didst thou say, Jacinta? Now I bethink me
Thou hast not spoken lately of thy wedding.
How fares good Ugo?—and when is it to be?
Can I do aught?—is there no farther aid

Thou needest, Jacinta ?

JACINTA.

Is there no *farther* aid !

That 's meant for me (*aside*).   I'm sure, madam, you need not
Be always throwing those jewels in my teeth.

LALAGE.

Jewels ! Jacinta,—now indeed, Jacinta,
I thought not of the jewels.

JACINTA.

Oh ! perhaps not !

But then I might have sworn it.   After all,   120
There 's Ugo says the ring is only paste,
For he 's sure the Count Castiglione never
Would have given a real diamond to such as you ;
And at the best I'm certain, madam, you cannot
Have use for jewels *now*.   But I might have sworn it. (*Exit.*)
        (LALAGE *bursts into tears and leans her head upon*
            the table—after a short pause raises it.)

LALAGE.

Poor Lalage !—and is it come to this ?
Thy servant maid !—but courage !—'tis but a viper
Whom thou hast cherished to sting thee to the soul !
                            (*Taking up the mirror.*)
Ha ! here at least 's a friend—too much a friend
In earlier days—a friend will not deceive thee.   130
Fair mirror and true ! now tell me (for thou canst)
A tale—a pretty tale—and heed thou not
Though it be rife with woe.   It answers me.
It speaks of sunken eyes, and wasted cheeks,
And Beauty long deceased—remembers me
Of Joy departed—Hope, the Seraph Hope,
Inurnèd and entombed :—now, in a tone
Low, sad, and solemn, but most audible,
Whispers of early grave untimely yawning
For ruined maid.   Fair mirror and true—thou liest not ! 140
Thou hast no end to gain—no heart to break—
Castiglione lied who said he loved—
Thou true—he false !—false !—false !
            (*While she speaks, a monk enters her apartment,*
                and approaches unobserved.)

MONK.

Refuge thou hast,
Sweet daughter, in Heaven.   Think of eternal things !
Give up thy soul to penitence, and pray !

LALAGE (*arising hurriedly*).
I *cannot* pray !—My soul is at war with God !
The frightful sounds of merriment below
Disturb my senses—go ! I cannot pray—
The sweet airs from the garden worry me !   150
Thy presence grieves me—go !—thy priestly raiment
Fills me with dread—thy ebony crucifix
With horror and awe !

MONK.
Think of thy precious soul !

LALAGE.
Think of my early days !—think of my father
And mother in Heaven ! think of our quiet home,
And the rivulet that ran before the door !
Think of my little sisters !—think of them !
And think of me !—think of my trusting love
And confidence—his vows—my ruin—think—think
Of my unspeakable misery !—begone !   160
Yet stay ! yet stay !—what was it thou saidst of prayer
And penitence ? Didst thou not speak of faith
And vows before the throne ?

MONK.
I did.

LALAGE.
'Tis well
There *is* a vow were fitting should be made—
A sacred vow, imperative, and urgent,
A solemn vow !

MONK.
Daughter, this zeal is well

LALAGE.
Father, this zeal is anything but well !
Hast thou a crucifix fit for this thing ?
A crucifix whereon to register   169
This sacred vow ?   (*He hands her his own.*)

Not that—Oh ! no !—no !—no !

(Shuddering.)

Not that ! Not that !—I tell thee, holy man,
Thy raiments and thy ebony cross affright me !
Stand back ! I have a crucifix myself,—
I have a crucifix ! Methinks 'twere fitting
The deed—the vow—the symbol of the deed—
And the deed's register should tally, father !

(Draws a cross-handled dagger, and raises it on
high.)

Behold the cross wherewith a vow like mine
Is written in Heaven !

MONK.

           Thy words are madness, daughter,
And speak a purpose unholy—thy lips are livid—   180
Thine eyes are wild—tempt not the wrath divine !
Pause ere too late !—oh, be not—be not rash !
Swear not the oath—oh, swear it not !

LALAGE.

'Tis sworn !

III

An apartment in a Palace. POLITIAN and BALDAZZAR.

BALDAZZAR.

——Arouse thee now, Politian !
Thou must not—nay indeed, indeed, thou shalt not
Give way unto these humours. Be thyself !
Shake off the idle fancies that beset thee,
And live, for now thou diest !

POLITIAN.

Not so, Baldazzar

Surely I live.

BALDAZZAR.

Politian, it doth grieve me

To see thee thus.

POLITIAN.

          Baldazzar, it doth grieve me   190
To give thee cause for grief, my honoured friend.
Command me, sir ! what wouldst thou have me do ?
At thy behest I will shake off that nature

Which from my forefathers I did inherit,
Which with my mother's milk I did imbibe,
And be no more Politian, but some other.
Command me, sir !

BALDAZZAR.
To the field, then—to the field—
To the senate or the field.

POLITIAN.
Alas ! alas !
There is an imp would follow me even there !
There is an imp *hath* followed me even there !   200
There is——what voice was that ?

BALDAZZAR.
I heard it not.
I heard not any voice except thine own,
And the echo of thine own.

POLITIAN.
Then I but dreamed.

BALDAZZAR.
Give not thy soul to dreams : the camp—the court,
Befit thee—Fame awaits thee—Glory calls—
And her, the trumpet-tongued, thou wilt not hear
In hearkening to imaginary sounds
And phantom voices.

POLITIAN.
It *is* a phantom voice !
Didst thou not hear it *then* ?

BALDAZZAR.
I heard it not.

POLITIAN.
Thou heardst it not !—Baldazzar, speak no more   210
To me, Politian, of thy camps and courts.
Oh ! I am sick, sick, sick, even unto death,
Of the hollow and high-sounding vanities
Of the populous Earth ! Bear with me yet awhile !
We have been boys together—schoolfellows—
And now are friends—yet shall not be so long—
For in the eternal city thou shalt do me
A kind and gentle office, and a Power

A Power august, benignant and supreme—
Shall then absolve thee of all further duties   220
Unto thy friend.

BALDAZZAR.

Thou speakest a fearful riddle
I *will* not understand.

POLITIAN.

Yet now as Fate
Approaches, and the Hours are breathing low,
The sands of Time are changed to golden grains,
And dazzle me, Baldazzar. Alas ! alas !
I *cannot* die, having within my heart
So keen a relish for the beautiful
As hath been kindled within it.   Methinks the air
Is balmier now than it was wont to be—
Rich melodies are floating in the winds—   230
A rarer loveliness bedecks the earth—
And with a holier lustre the quiet moon
Sitteth in Heaven.—Hist ! hist ! thou canst not say
Thou hearest not *now*, Baldazzar ?

BALDAZZAR.

Indeed I hear not.

POLITIAN.

Not hear it !—listen now !—listen !—the faintest sound
And yet the sweetest that ear ever heard !
A lady's voice !—and sorrow in the tone !
Baldazzar, it oppresses me like a spell !
Again !—again !—how solemnly it falls
Into my heart of hearts ! that eloquent voice   240
Surely I never heard—yet it were well
Had I *but* heard it with its thrilling tones
In earlier days !

BALDAZZAR.

I myself hear it now.
Be still !—the voice, if I mistake not greatly,
Proceeds from yonder lattice—which you may see
Very plainly through the window—it belongs,
Does it not ? unto this palace of the Duke ?
The singer is undoubtedly beneath
The roof of his Excellency—and perhaps

Is even that Alessandra of whom he spoke 250
As the betrothed of Castiglione,
His son and heir.

POLITIAN.

Be still !—it comes again !

VOICE (*very faintly*).

' And is thy heart so strong
As for to leave me thus
Who hath loved thee so long
In wealth and woe among ?
And is thy heart so strong
As for to leave me thus ?
    Say nay—say nay ! ' 260

BALDAZZAR.

The song is English, and I oft have heard it
In merry England—never so plaintively—
Hist ! hist ! it comes again !

VOICE (*more loudly*).

' Is it so strong
As for to leave me thus
Who hath loved thee so long
In wealth and woe among ?
And is thy heart so strong
As for to leave me thus ?
    Say nay—say nay ! ' 270

BALDAZZAR.

'Tis hushed and all is still !

POLITIAN.
    All *is not* still !

BALDAZZAR.

Let us go down.

POLITIAN.
    Go down, Baldazzar, go !

BALDAZZAR.

The hour is growing late—the Duke awaits us,—
Thy presence is expected in the hall
Below. What ails thee, Earl Politian ?

VOICE (*distinctly*).
'Who hath loved thee so long
In wealth and woe among,
And is thy heart so strong ?
            Say nay—say nay ! '

BALDAZZAR.
Let us descend !—'tis time. Politian, give   280
These fancies to the wind. Remember, pray,
Your bearing lately savoured much of rudeness
Unto the Duke. Arouse thee ! and remember !

POLITIAN.
Remember ? I do. Lead on ! I *do* remember.
                                    (*Going.*)

Let us descend. Believe me I would give,
Freely would give the broad lands of my earldom
To look upon the face hidden by yon lattice—
' To gaze upon that veiled face, and hear
Once more that silent tongue.'

BALDAZZAR.
                    Let me beg you, sir,
Descend with me—the Duke may be offended.   290
Let us go down, I pray you.

VOICE (*loudly*).
            Say nay !—say nay !

POLITIAN (*aside*).
'Tis strange !—'tis very strange—methought the voice
Chimed in with my desires, and bade me stay !
                        (*Approaching the window.*)
Sweet voice ! I heed thee, and will surely stay.
Now be this Fancy, by Heaven ! or be it Fate,
Still will I not descend. Baldazzar make
Apology unto the Duke for me ;
I go not down to-night.

BALDAZZAR.
                Your lordship's pleasure
Shall be attended to. Good-night, Politian.

POLITIAN.
Good-night, my friend, good-night.   300

IV

The gardens of a Palace—Moonlight.

LALAGE *and* POLITIAN.

LALAGE.

And dost thou speak of love
To *me*, Politian ?—dost thou speak of love
To Lalage ?—ah, woe—ah, woe is me !
This mockery is most cruel—most cruel indeed !

POLITIAN.

Weep not ! oh, sob not thus !—thy bitter tears
Will madden me. Oh, mourn not, Lalage—
Be·comforted ! I know—I know it all,
And *still* I speak of love. Look at me, brightest
And beautiful Lalage !—turn here thine eyes !
Thou askest me if I could speak of love,   310
Knowing what I know, and seeing what I have seen.
Thou askest me that—and thus I answer thee—
Thus on my bended knee I answer thee.   (*Kneeling*.)
Sweet Lalage, *I love thee—love thee—love thee ;*
Thro' good and ill—thro' weal and woe I *love thee*.
Not mother, with her first-born on her knee,
Thrills with intenser love than I for thee.
Not on God's altar, in any time or clime,
Burned there a holier fire than burneth now
Within my spirit for *thee*.   And do I love ?   320
                                                 (*Arising*.)
Even for thy woes I love thee—even for thy woes—
Thy beauty and thy woes.

LALAGE.
                      Alas, proud Earl,
Thou dost forget thyself, remembering me !
How, in thy father's halls, among the maidens
Pure and reproachless of thy princely line,
Could the dishonoured Lalage abide ?
Thy wife, and with a tainted memory—
My seared and blighted name, how would it tally
With the ancestral honours of thy house,
And with thy glory ?

POLITIAN.

Speak not to me of glory !   330

I hate—I loathe the name ; I do abhor
The unsatisfactory and ideal thing.
Art thou not Lalage and I Politian ?
Do I not love—art thou not beautiful—
What need we more ? Ha ! glory !—now speak not of it.
By all I hold most sacred and most solemn—
By all my wishes now—my fears hereafter—
By all I scorn on earth and hope in heaven—
There is no deed I would more glory in,
Than in thy cause to scoff at this same glory   340
And trample it under foot. What matters it—
What matters it, my fairest, and my best,
That we go down unhonoured and forgotten
Into the dust—so we descend together.
Descend together—and then—and then, perchance—

LALAGE.

Why dost thou pause, Politian ?

POLITIAN.

And then, perchance

Arise together, Lalage, and roam
The starry and quiet dwellings of the blest,
And still——

LALAGE.

Why dost thou pause, Politian ?

POLITIAN.

And still *together—together*.

LALAGE.

Now Earl of Leicester !   350

Thou *lovest* me, and in my heart of hearts
I feel thou lovest me truly.

POLITIAN.

Oh, Lalage !
(*Throwing himself upon his knee.*)

And lovest thou *me* ?

LALAGE.

Hist ! hush ! within the gloom

Of yonder trees methought a figure past—
A spectral figure, solemn, and slow, and noiseless—

Like the grim shadow Conscience, solemn and noiseless.
              (*Walks across and returns.*)
I was mistaken—'twas but a giant bough
Stirred by the autumn wind. Politian !

POLITIAN.

My Lalage—my love ! why art thou moved ?
Why dost thou turn so pale ? Not Conscience' self,   360
Far less a shadow which thou likenest to it,
Should shake the firm spirit thus. But the night wind
Is chilly—and these melancholy boughs
Throw over all things a gloom.

LALAGE.
                        Politian !
Thou speakest to me of love. Knowest thou the land
With which all tongues are busy—a land new found—
Miraculously found by one of Genoa—
A thousand leagues within the golden west ?
A fairy land of flowers, and fruit, and sunshine,
And crystal lakes, and over-arching forests,   370
And mountains, around whose towering summits the winds
Of Heaven untrammelled flow—which air to breathe
Is Happiness now, and will be Freedom hereafter
In days that are to come ?

POLITIAN.
                  O, wilt thou—wilt thou
Fly to that Paradise—my Lalage, wilt thou
Fly thither with me ? There Care shall be forgotten,
And Sorrow shall be no more, and Eros be all.
And life shall then be mine, for I will live
For thee, and in thine eyes—and thou shalt be
No more a mourner—but the radiant Joys   380
Shall wait upon thee, and the angel Hope
Attend thee ever ; and I will kneel to thee
And worship thee, and call thee my beloved,
My own, my beautiful, my love, my wife,
My all ;—oh, wilt thou—wilt thou, Lalage,
Fly thither with me ?

LALAGE.
              A deed is to be done—
Castiglione lives !

POLITIAN.

And he shall die !   (*Exit.*)

LALAGE (*after a pause*).

And—he—shall—die !——alas !
Castiglione die ? Who spoke the words ?
Where am I ?—what was it he said ?—Politian !   390
Thou *art* not gone——thou art not *gone*, Politian !
I *feel* thou art not gone—yet dare not look,
Lest I behold thee not ; thou *couldst* not go
With those words upon thy lips—O, speak to me !
And let me hear thy voice—one word—one word,
To say thou art not gone,—one little sentence,
To say how thou dost scorn—how thou dost hate
My womanly weakness. Ha ! ha ! thou *art* not gone—
O speak to me ! I *knew* thou wouldst not go !
I knew thou wouldst not, couldst not, *durst* not go.   400
Villain, thou *art* not gone—thou mockest me !
And thus I clutch thee—thus !——He is gone, he is gone—
Gone—gone.   Where am I ?——'tis well—'tis very well !
So that the blade be keen—the blow be sure,
'Tis well, 'tis *very* well—alas ! alas !

V

The suburbs. POLITIAN *alone.*

POLITIAN.

This weakness grows upon me. I am faint,
And much I fear me ill—it will not do
To die ere I have lived !—Stay, stay thy hand,
O Azrael, yet awhile !—Prince of the Powers
Of Darkness and the Tomb, O pity me !   410
O pity me ! let me not perish now,
In the budding of my Paradisal Hope !
Give me to live yet—yet a little while :
'Tis I who pray for life—I who so late
Demanded but to die !—what sayeth the Count ?

Enter BALDAZZAR.

BALDAZZAR.

That knowing no cause of quarrel or of feud
Between the Earl Politian and himself,
He doth decline your cartel.

POLITIAN.
                    What didst thou say ?
What answer was it you brought me, good Baldazzar ?
With what excessive fragrance the zephyr comes   420
Laden from yonder bowers !—a fairer day,
Or one more worthy Italy, methinks
No mortal eyes have seen !—*what* said the Count ?

BALDAZZAR.
That he, Castiglione, not being aware
Of any feud existing, or any cause
Of quarrel between your lordship and himself,
Cannot accept the challenge.

POLITIAN.
                    It is most true—
All this is very true.   When saw you, sir,
When saw you now, Baldazzar, in the frigid
Ungenial Britain which we left so lately,   430
A heaven so calm as this—so utterly free
From the evil taint of clouds ?—and he did *say* ?

BALDAZZAR.
No more, my lord, than I have told you, sir :
The Count Castiglione will not fight,
Having no cause for quarrel.

POLITIAN.
                    Now this is true—
All very true.   Thou art my friend, Baldazzar,
And I have not forgotten it—thou'lt do me
A piece of service ; wilt thou go back and say
Unto this man, that I, the Earl of Leicester,
Hold him a villain ?—thus much, I prythee, say   440
Unto the Count—it is exceeding just
He should have cause for quarrel.

BALDAZZAR.
                    My lord !—my friend !——
POLITIAN (*aside*).
'Tis he !—he comes himself ?   (*aloud.*) Thou reasonest well.
I know what thou wouldst say—not send the message—
Well !—I will think of it—I will not send it.
Now prythee, leave me—hither doth come a person

With whom affairs of a most private nature
I would adjust.

BALDAZZAR.

    I go—to-morrow we meet,
Do we not ?—at the Vatican.

POLITIAN.

      At the Vatican.
     (*Exit* BALDAZZAR.)
   Enter CASTIGLIONE.

CASTIGLIONE.

The Earl of Leicester here !   450

POLITIAN.

I *am* the Earl of Leicester, and thou seest,
Dost thou not ? that I am here.

CASTIGLIONE.

     My lord, some strange,
Some singular mistake—misunderstanding—
Hath without doubt arisen : thou hast been urged
Thereby, in heat of anger, to address
Some words most unaccountable, in writing,
To me, Castiglione ; the bearer being
Baldazzar, Duke of Surrey. I am aware
Of nothing which might warrant thee in this thing,
Having given thee no offence. Ha !—am I right ? 460
'Twas a mistake ?—undoubtedly—we all
Do err at times.

POLITIAN.

  Draw, villain, and prate no more !

CASTIGLIONE.

Ha !—draw ?—and villain ? have at thee then at once,
Proud Earl !   (*Draws.*)

POLITIAN (*drawing*).

  Thus to the expiatory tomb,
Untimely sepulchre, I do devote thee
In the name of Lalage !

CASTIGLIONE (*letting fall his sword and recoiling to the
      extremity of the stage*).

     Of Lalage !
Hold off—thy sacred hand !—avaunt, I say !
Avaunt—I will not fight thee—indeed I dare not.

POLITIAN.

Thou wilt not fight with me didst say, Sir Count ?
Shall I be baffled thus ?—now this is well ;   470
Didst say thou *darest* not ? Ha !

CASTIGLIONE.

I dare not—dare not—
Hold off thy hand—with that beloved name
So fresh upon thy lips I will not fight thee—
I cannot—dare not.

POLITIAN.

Now by my halidom
I do believe thee !—coward, I do believe thee !

CASTIGLIONE.

Ha !—coward !—this may not be !
(*Clutches his sword and staggers towards* POLITIAN,
*but his purpose is changed before reaching him,
and he falls upon his knee at the feet of the Earl.*)
Alas ! my lord,
It is—it is—most true. In such a cause
I am the veriest coward. O pity me !

POLITIAN (*greatly softened*).

Alas !—I do—indeed I pity thee.

CASTIGLIONE.

And Lalage——

POLITIAN.

Scoundrel !—arise and die !   480

CASTIGLIONE.

It needeth not be—thus—thus—O let me die
Thus on my bended knee. It were most fitting
That in this deep humiliation I perish.
For in the fight I will not raise a hand
Against thee, Earl of Leicester. Strike thou home—
(*Baring his bosom.*)
Here is no let or hindrance to thy weapon—
Strike home. I *will not* fight thee.

POLITIAN.

Now, s' Death and Hell !
Am I not—am I not sorely—grievously tempted
To take thee at thy word ? But mark me, sir,
Think not to fly me thus. Do thou prepare   490

For public insult in the streets—before
The eyes of the citizens. I'll follow thee—
Like an avenging spirit I'll follow thee
Even unto death. Before those whom thou lovest—
Before all Rome I'll taunt thee, villain,—I'll taunt thee,
Dost hear ? with *cowardice*—thou *wilt not* fight me ?
Thou liest ! thou *shalt !*   (*Exit.*

CASTIGLIONE.
                        Now this indeed is just !
Most righteous, and most just, avenging Heaven !

POEMS WRITTEN IN YOUTH

POEMS WRITTEN IN YOUTH

[Private reasons—some of which have reference to the sin of plagiarism, and others to the date of Tennyson's first poems—have induced me, after some hesitation, to republish these, the crude compositions of my earliest boyhood. They are printed *verbatim*—without alteration from the original edition—the date of which is too remote to be judiciously acknowledged.—E. A. P.]

SONNET—TO SCIENCE

SCIENCE ! true daughter of Old Time thou art !
  Who alterest all things with thy peering eyes.
Why preyest thou thus upon the poet's heart,
  Vulture, whose wings are dull realities ?
How should he love thee ? or how deem thee wise,
  Who wouldst not leave him in his wandering
To seek for treasure in the jewelled skies,
  Albeit he soared with an undaunted wing ?
Hast thou not dragged Diana from her car ?
  And driven the Hamadryad from the wood   10
To seek a shelter in some happier star ?
  Hast thou not torn the Naiad from her flood,
The Elfin from the green grass, and from me
The summer dream beneath the tamarind tree ?

AL AARAAF

PART I

O ! NOTHING earthly save the ray
(Thrown back from flowers) of Beauty's eye,
As in those gardens where the day
Springs from the gems of Circassy—
O ! nothing earthly save the thrill
Of melody in woodland rill—
Or (music of the passion-hearted)
Joy's voice so peacefully departed
That like the murmur in the shell,
Its echo dwelleth and will dwell—   10

Oh, nothing of the dross of ours—
Yet all the beauty—all the flowers
That list our Love, and deck our bowers—
Adorn yon world afar, afar—
The wandering star.

'Twas a sweet time for Nesace—for there
Her world lay lolling on the golden air,
Near four bright suns—a temporary rest—
An oasis in desert of the blest.
Away—away—'mid seas of rays that roll   20
Empyrean splendour o'er th' unchained soul—
The soul that scarce (the billows are so dense)
Can struggle to its destin'd eminence,—
To distant spheres, from time to time, she rode
And late to ours, the favour'd one of God—
But, now, the ruler of an anchor'd realm,
She throws aside the sceptre—leaves the helm,
And, amid incense and high spiritual hymns,
Laves in quadruple light her angel limbs.

Now happiest, loveliest in yon lovely Earth,   30
Whence sprang the ' Idea of Beauty ' into birth,
(Falling in wreaths thro' many a startled star,
Like woman's hair 'mid pearls, until, afar,
It lit on hills Achaian, and there dwelt)
She looked into Infinity—and knelt.
Rich clouds, for canopies, about her curled—
Fit emblems of the model of her world—
Seen but in beauty—not impeding sight
Of other beauty glittering thro' the light—
A wreath that twined each starry form around,   40
And all the opal'd air in colour bound.

All hurriedly she knelt upon a bed
Of flowers : of lilies such as rear'd the head
On the fair Capo Deucato, and sprang
So eagerly around about to hang
Upon the flying footsteps of——deep pride—
Of her who lov'd a mortal—and so died.
The Sephalica, budding with young bees,
Upreared its purple stem around her knees :—

And gemmy flower, of Trebizond misnam'd— 50
Inmate of highest stars, where erst it sham'd
All other loveliness :—its honied dew
(The fabled nectar that the heathen knew)
Deliriously sweet, was dropp'd from Heaven,
And fell on gardens of the unforgiven
In Trebizond—and on a sunny flower
So like its own above that, to this hour,
It still remaineth, torturing the bee
With madness, and unwonted reverie :
In Heaven, and all its environs, the leaf 60
And blossom of the fairy plant in grief
Disconsolate linger—grief that hangs her head,
Repenting follies that full long have fled,
Heaving her white breast to the balmy air,
Like guilty beauty, chasten'd and more fair :
Nyctanthes too, as sacred as the light
She fears to perfume, perfuming the night :
And Clytia, pondering between many a sun,
While pettish tears adown her petals run :
And that aspiring flower that sprang on Earth, 70
And died, ere scarce exalted into birth,
Bursting its odorous heart in spirit to wing
Its way to Heaven, from garden of a king :
And Valisnerian lotus, thither flown
From struggling with the waters of the Rhone :
And thy most lovely purple perfume, Zante !
Isola d'oro !—Fior di Levante !
And the Nelumbo bud that floats for ever
With Indian Cupid down the holy river—
Fair flowers, and fairy ! to whose care is given 80
To bear the Goddess' song, in odours, up to Heaven :

      ' Spirit ! that dwellest where,
        In the deep sky,
     The terrible and fair,
        In beauty vie !
    Beyond the line of blue—
       The boundary of the star
    Which turneth at the view
       Of thy barrier and thy bar—

Of the barrier overgone   90
  By the comets who were cast
From their pride and from their throne
  To be drudges till the last—
To be carriers of fire
  (The red fire of their heart)
With speed that may not tire
  And with pain that shall not part—
Who livest—*that* we know—
  In Eternity—we feel—
But the shadow of whose brow   100
  What spirit shall reveal ?
Tho' the beings whom thy Nesace,
  Thy messenger hath known
Have dream'd for thy Infinity
  A model of their own—
Thy will is done, O God !
  The star hath ridden high ·
Thro' many a tempest, but she rode
  Beneath thy burning eye ;
And here, in thought, to thee—   110
  In thought that can alone
Ascend thy empire and so be
  A partner of thy throne—
By wingèd Fantasy,
My embassy is given,
Till secrecy shall knowledge be
  In the environs of Heaven.'

She ceas'd—and buried then her burning cheek
Abash'd, amid the lilies there, to seek
A shelter from the fervour of His eye ;   120
For the stars trembled at the Deity.
She stirr'd not—breath'd not—for a voice was there
How solemnly pervading the calm air !
A sound of silence on the startled ear
Which dreamy poets name ' the music of the sphere '.
Ours is a world of words : Quiet we call
' Silence '—which is the merest word of all.
All Nature speaks, and ev'n ideal things
Flap shadowy sounds from visionary wings—

But ah ! not so when, thus, in realms on high   130
The eternal voice of God is passing by,
And the red winds are withering in the sky :—

  ' What tho' in worlds which sightless cycles run,
Linked to a little system, and one sun—
Where all my love is folly and the crowd
Still think my terrors but the thunder cloud,
The storm, the earthquake, and the ocean-wrath—
(Ah ! will they cross me in my angrier path ?)
What tho' in worlds which own a single sun
The sands of Time grow dimmer as they run,   140
Yet thine is my resplendency, so given
To bear my secrets thro' the upper Heaven !
Leave tenantless thy crystal home, and fly,
With all thy train, athwart the moony sky—
Apart—like fire-flies in Sicilian night,
And wing to other worlds another light !
Divulge the secrets of thy embassy
To the proud orbs that twinkle—and so be
To ev'ry heart a barrier and a ban
Lest the stars totter in the guilt of man ! '   150

  Up rose the maiden in the yellow night,
The single-moonèd eve !—on Earth we plight
Our faith to one love—and one moon adore—
The birth-place of young Beauty had no more.
As sprang that yellow star from downy hours
Up rose the maiden from her shrine of flowers,
And bent o'er sheeny mountains and dim plain
Her way, but left not yet her Therasaean reign.

PART II

HIGH on a mountain of enamell'd head—
Such as the drowsy shepherd on his bed   160
Of giant pasturage lying at his ease,
Raising his heavy eyelid, starts and sees
With many a mutter'd ' hope to be forgiven '
What time the moon is quadrated in Heaven—
Of rosy head that, towering far away
Into the sunlit ether, caught the ray

Of sunken suns at eve—at noon of night,
While the moon danc'd with the fair stranger light—
Uprear'd upon such height arose a pile
Of gorgeous columns on th' unburthen'd air,　　170
Flashing from Parian marble that twin smile
Far down upon the wave that sparkled there,
And nursled the young mountain in its lair.
Of molten stars their pavement, such as fall
Thro' the ebon air, besilvering the pall
Of their own dissolution, while they die—
Adorning then the dwellings of the sky.
A dome, by linkèd light from Heaven let down,
Sat gently on these columns as a crown—
A window of one circular diamond, there,　　180
Look'd out above into the purple air,
And rays from God shot down that meteor chain
And hallow'd all the beauty twice again,
Save, when, between th' Empyrean and that ring,
Some eager spirit flapp'd his dusky wing.
But on the pillars Seraph eyes have seen
The dimness of this world : that greyish green
That Nature loves the best for Beauty's grave
Lurk'd in each cornice, round each architrave—
And every sculptur'd cherub thereabout　　190
That from his màrble dwelling peerèd out,
Seem'd earthly in the shadow of his niche—
Achaian statues in a world so rich !
Friezes from Tadmor and Persepolis—
From Balbec, and the stilly, clear abyss
Of beautiful Gomorrah ! O, the wave
Is now upon thee—but too late to save !

Sound loves to revel in a summer night :
Witness the murmur of the grey twilight
That stole upon the ear, in Eyraco,　　200
Of many a wild star-gazer long ago—
That stealeth ever on the ear of him
Who, musing, gazeth on the distance dim,
And sees the darkness coming as a cloud—
Is not its form—its voice—most palpable and loud ?

But what is this ?—it cometh, and it brings
A music with it—'tis the rush of wings—
A pause—and then a sweeping, falling strain
And Nesace is in her halls again.
From the wild energy of wanton haste   210
   Her cheeks were flushing, and her lips apart ;
And zone that clung around her gentle waist
   Had burst beneath the heaving of her heart.
Within the centre of that hall to breathe,
She paused and panted, Zanthe ! all beneath,
The fairy light that kiss'd her golden hair
And long'd to rest, yet could but sparkle there.

   Young flowers were whispering in melody
To happy flowers that night—and tree to tree ;
Fountains were gushing music as they fell   220
In many a star-lit grove, or moon-lit dell ;
Yet silence came upon material things—
Fair flowers, bright waterfalls and angel wings—
And sound alone that from the spirit sprang
Bore burthen to the charm the maiden sang :

      ' 'Neath the blue-bell or streamer—
         Or tufted wild spray
      That keeps, from the dreamer,
         The moonbeam away—
      Bright beings ! that ponder,   230
         With half closing eyes,
      On the stars which your wonder
         Hath drawn from the skies,
      Till they glance thro' the shade, and
         Come down to your brow
      Like——eyes of the maiden
         Who calls on you now—
      Arise ! from your dreaming
         In violet bowers,
      To duty beseeming   240
         These star-litten hours—
      And shake from your tresses
         Encumber'd with dew

The breath of those kisses
    That cumber them too—
(O ! how, without you, Love !
    Could angels be blest ?)
Those kisses of true Love
    That lull'd ye to rest !
Up !—shake from your wing   250
    Each hindering thing :
The dew of the night—
    It would weigh down your flight
And true love caresses—
    O, leave them apart !
They are light on the tresses,
    But lead on the heart.

Ligeia ! Ligeia !
    My beautiful one !
Whose harshest idea   260
    Will to melody run,
O ! is it thy will
    On the breezes to toss ?
Or, capriciously still,
    Like the lone Albatross,
Incumbent on night
    (As she on the air)
To keep watch with delight
    On the harmony there ?

Ligeia ! wherever   270
    Thy image may be,
No magic shall sever
    ·Thy music from thee.
Thou hast bound many eyes
    In a dreamy sleep—
But the strains still arise
    Which *thy* vigilance keep—
The sound of the rain,
    Which leaps down to the flower—
And dances again   280
    In the rhythm of the shower—
The murmur that springs
    From the growing of grass

Are the music of things—
    But are modell'd, alas !—
Away, then, my dearest,
    Oh ! hie thee away
To the springs that lie clearest
    Beneath the moon-ray—
To lone lake that smiles,   290
    In its dream of deep rest,
At the many star-isles
    That enjewel its breast—
Where wild flowers, creeping,
    Have mingled their shade,
On its margin is sleeping
    Full many a maid—
Some have left the cool glade, and
    Have slept with the bee—
Arouse them, my maiden,   300
    On moorland and lea—
Go ! breathe on their slumber,
    All softly in ear,
Thy musical number
    They slumbered to hear—
For what can awaken
    An angel so soon,
Whose sleep hath been taken
    Beneath the cold moon,
As the spell which no slumber   310
    Of witchery may test,
The rhythmical number
    Which lull'd him to rest ? '

Spirits in wing, and angels to the view,
A thousand seraphs burst th' Empyrean thro',
Young dreams still hovering on their drowsy flight—
Seraphs in all but ' Knowledge ', the keen light
That fell, refracted, thro' thy bounds, afar,
O Death ! from eye of God upon that star :
Sweet was that error—sweeter still that death—   320
Sweet was that error—even with *us* the breath
Of Science dims the mirror of our joy—
To them 'twere the Simoom, and would destroy—

For what (to them) availeth it to know
That Truth is Falsehood—or that Bliss is Woe ?
Sweet was their death—with them to die was rife
With the last ecstasy of satiate life—
Beyond that death no immortality—
But sleep that pondereth and is not ' to be '—
And there—oh ! may my weary spirit dwell—   330
Apart from Heaven's Eternity—and yet how far from
        Hell !
What guilty spirit, in what shrubbery dim,
Heard not the stirring summons of that hymn ?
But two : they fell : for Heaven no grace imparts
To those who hear not for their beating hearts.
A maiden-angel and her seraph-lover—
O ! where (and ye may seek the wide skies over)
Was Love, the blind, near sober Duty known ?
Unguided Love hath fallen—'mid ' tears of perfect moan '.

He was a goodly spirit—he who fell :   340
A wanderer by moss-y-mantled well—
A gazer on the lights that shine above—
A dreamer in the moonbeam by his love :
What wonder ? for each star is eye-like there,
And looks so sweetly down on Beauty's hair—
And they, and ev'ry mossy spring were holy
To his love-haunted heart and melancholy.
The night had found (to him a night of woe)
Upon a mountain crag, young Angelo—
Beetling it bends athwart the solemn sky,   350
And scowls on starry worlds that down beneath it lie.
Here sat he with his love—his dark eye bent
With eagle gaze along the firmament :
Now turn'd it upon her—but ever then
It trembled to the orb of EARTH again.

' Ianthe, dearest, see—how dim that ray !
How lovely 'tis to look so far away !
She seem'd not thus upon that autumn eve
I left her gorgeous halls—nor mourn'd to leave.
That eve—that eve—I should remember well—   360
The sun-ray dropp'd in Lemnos, with a spell

On th' arabesque carving of a gilded hall
Wherein I sate, and on the draperied wall—
And on my eyelids—O the heavy light !
How drowsily it weigh'd them into night !
On flowers, before, and mist, and love they ran
With Persian Saadi in his Gulistan :
But O that light !—I slumber'd—Death, the while,
Stole o'er my senses in that lovely isle
So softly that no single silken hair   370
Awoke that slept—or knew that he was there.

' The last spot of Earth's orb I trod upon
Was a proud temple call'd the Parthenon ;
More beauty clung around her column'd wall
Than ev'n thy glowing bosom beats withal,
And when old Time my wing did disenthral
Thence sprang I—as the eagle from his tower,
And years I left behind me in an hour.
What time upon her airy bounds I hung,
One half the garden of her globe was flung   380
Unrolling as a chart unto my view—
Tenantless cities of the desert too !
Ianthe, beauty crowded on me then,
And half I wish'd to be again of men.' .

' My Angelo ! and why of them to be ?
A brighter dwelling-place is here for thee—
And greener fields than in yon world above,
And woman's loveliness—and passionate love.'

' But, list, Ianthe ! when the air so soft
Fail'd, as my pennon'd spirit leapt aloft,   390
Perhaps my brain grew dizzy—but the world
I left so late was into chaos hurl'd—
Sprang from her station, on the winds apart,
And roll'd, a flame, the fiery Heaven athwart.
Methought, my sweet one, then I ceased to soar
And fell—not swiftly as I rose before,
But with a downward, tremulous motion thro'
Light, brazen rays, this golden star unto !
Nor long the measure of my falling hours,
For nearest of all stars was thine to ours—   400

Dread star ! that came, amid a night of mirth,
A red Daedalion on the timid Earth.'

' We came—and to thy Earth—but not to us
Be given our lady's bidding to discuss :
We came, my love ; around, above, below,
Gay fire-fly of the night we come and go,
Nor ask a reason save the angel-nod
She grants to us, as granted by her God—
But, Angelo, than thine grey Time unfurl'd
Never his fairy wing o'er fairier world !   410
Dim was its little disk, and angel eyes
Alone could see the phantom in the skies,
When first Al Aaraaf knew her course to be
Headlong thitherward o'er the starry sea—
But when its glory swell'd upon the sky,
As glowing Beauty's bust beneath man's eye,
We paused before the heritage of men,
And thy star trembled—as doth Beauty then ! '

Thus, in discourse, the lovers whiled away
The night that waned and waned and brought no day.   420
They fell : for Heaven to them no hope imparts
Who hear not for the beating of their hearts.

NOTES BY POE TO AL AARAAF

PART I

Title] *Al Aaraaf*. A star was discovered by Tycho Brahe which
appeared suddenly in the heavens—attained, in a few days, a brilliancy
surpassing that of Jupiter—then as suddenly disappeared, and has
never been seen since.

1. 44. *On the fair Capo Deucato.* On Santa Maura—olim Deucadia.

1. 47. *Of her who lov'd a mortal—and so died.* Sappho.

1. 50. *And gemmy flower, of Trebizond misnamed.* This flower is
much noticed by Lewenhoeck and Tournefort. The bee, feeding upon
its blossom, becomes intoxicated.

1. 68. *And Clytia, pondering between many a sun.* Clytia—the
Chrysanthemum Peruvianum, or, to employ a better-known term, the
turnsol—which turns continually towards the sun, covers itself, like
Peru, the country from which it comes, with dewy clouds which cool
and refresh its flowers during the most violent heat of the day.—B. DE
ST. PIERRE.

1. 70. *And that aspiring flower that sprang on Earth.* There is cultivated in the king's garden at Paris, a species of serpentine aloes without

prickles, whose large and beautiful flower exhales a strong odour of the vanilla, during the time of its expansion, which is very short. It does not blow till towards the month of July—you then perceive it gradually open its petals—expand them—fade and die.—St. PIERRE.

l. 74. *And Valisnerian lotus, thither flown.* There is found, in the Rhone, a beautiful lily of the Valisnerian kind. Its stem will stretch to the length of three or four feet—thus preserving its head above water in the swellings of the river.

l. 76. *And thy most lovely purple perfume, Zante.* The Hyacinth.

ll. 78–9. *And the Nelumbo bud that floats for ever*
With Indian Cupid down the holy river—

It is a fiction of the Indians, that Cupid was first seen floating in one of these down the river Ganges—and that he still loves the cradle of his childhood.

l. 81. *To bear the Goddess' song, in odours, up to Heaven.* And golden vials full of odours, which are the prayers of the saints.—REV. St. JOHN.

l. 105. *A model of their own.* The Humanitarians held that God was to be understood as having really a human form.—*Vide* CLARKE'S *Sermons*, vol. i, p. 26, fol. edit.

The drift of Milton's argument leads him to employ language which would appear, at first sight, to verge upon their doctrine ; but it would be seen immediately, that he guards himself against the charge of having adopted one of the most ignorant errors of the dark ages of the church.—Dr. SUMNER'S *Notes on Milton's Christian Doctrine.*

This opinion, in spite of many testimonies to the contrary, could never have been very general. Andeus, a Syrian of Mesopotamia, was condemned for the opinion, as heretical. He lived in the beginning of the fourth century. His disciples were called Anthropomorphites.— *Vide* DU PIN.

Among Milton's minor poems are these lines :

> ' Dicite sacrorum presides nemorum Deae, &c.
> Quis ille primus cujus ex imagine
> Natura solers finxit humanum genus ?
> Eternus, incorruptus, aequaevus polo,
> Unusque et universus, exemplar Dei.'

And afterwards—

> ' Non cui profundum Caecitas lumen dedit
> Dircaeus augur vidit hunc alto sinu,' &c.

l. 114. *By wingèd Fantasy.*

> *Fantasy.* Seltsamen Tochter Jovis
> Seinem Schosskinde,
> Der Phantasie.—GOETHE.

l. 133. *What tho' in worlds which sightless cycles run.* Sightless— too small to be seen.—LEGGE.

l. 145. *Apart—like fire-flies in Sicilian night.* I have often noticed a peculiar movement of the fire-flies ;—they will collect in a body, and fly off, from a common centre, into innumerable radii.

l. 158. *Her way, but left not yet her Therasaean reign.* Therasaea, or Therasea, the island mentioned by Seneca, which, in a moment, arose from the sea to the eyes of astonished mariners.

PART II

11. 174–5.   *Of molten stars their pavement, such as fall*
                  Thro' the ebon air.

Some star, which from the ruin'd roof
Of shaked Olympus, by mischance, did fall.—MILTON.

1. 194.   *Friezes from Tadmor and Persepolis.*   Voltaire, in speaking of Persepolis, says, ' Je connois bien l'admiration qu'inspirent ces ruines—mais un palais érigé au pied d'une chaîne de rochers stériles, peut-il être un chef-d'œuvre des arts ? '

1. 196.   *Of beautiful Gomorrah ! O, the wave.*   Ula Deguisi is the Turkish appellation; but, on its own shores, it is called Bahar Loth, or Almotanah. There were undoubtedly more than two cities engulfed in the ' Dead Sea '.   In the valley of Siddim were five—Admah, Zeboin, Zoar, Sodom and Gomorrah.   Stephen of Byzantium mentions eight, and Strabo thirteen (engulfed)—but the last is out of all reason.

It is said [Tacitus, Strabo, Josephus, Daniel of St. Saba, Nau, Maundrell, Troilo, D'Arvieux] that after an excessive drought, the vestiges of columns, walls, &c., are seen above the surface.   At *any* season, such remains may be discovered by looking down into the transparent lake, and at such distances as would argue the existence of many settlements in the space now usurped by the ' Asphaltites '.

1. 200.   *That stole upon the ear, in Eyraco.*   Eyraco—Chaldea.

1. 205.   *Is not its form—its voice—most palpable and loud ?*   I have often thought I could distinctly hear the sound of the darkness as it stole over the horizon.

1. 218.   *Young flowers were whispering in melody.*   Fairies use flowers for their charactery.—*Merry Wives of Windsor.*

1. 229.   *The moonbeam away.*   In Scripture is this passage—' The sun shall not harm thee by day, nor the moon by night.'   It is perhaps not generally known that the moon, in Egypt, has the effect of producing blindness to those who sleep with the face exposed to its rays, to which circumstance the passage evidently alludes.

1. 265.   *Like the lone Albatross.*   The albatross is said to sleep on the wing.

1. 282.   *The murmur that springs.*   I met with this idea in an old English tale, which I am now unable to obtain, and quote from memory : —' The verie essence and, as it were, springeheade and origine of all musiche is the verie plesaunte sounde which the trees of the forest do make when they growe.'

1. 299.   *Have slept with the bee.*   The wild bee will not sleep in the shade if there be moonlight.

The rhyme in this verse, as in one about sixty lines before, has an appearance of affectation.   It is, however, imitated from Sir W. Scott, or rather from Claude Halcro—in whose mouth I admired its effect :

' Oh ! were there an island
    Though ever so wild,
Where woman might smile, and
    No man be beguiled,' &c.

1. 331.   *Apart from Heaven's Eternity—and yet how far from Hell !*

With the Arabians there is a medium between Heaven and Hell, where men suffer no punishment, but yet do not attain that tranquil and even happiness which they suppose to be characteristic of heavenly enjoyment.

> Un no rompido sueño,
> Un dia puro, alegre, libre quiero ; . . .
> Libre de amor, de zelo,
> De odio, de esperanzas, de recelo.
>
> LUIS PONCE DE LEÓN.

Sorrow is not excluded from ' Al Aaraaf ', but it is that sorrow which the living love to cherish for the dead, and which, in some minds, resembles the delirium of opium. The passionate excitement of Love and the buoyancy of spirit attendant upon intoxication are its less holy pleasures—the price of which, to those souls who make choice of ' Al Aaraaf ' as their residence after life, is final death and annihilation.

1. 339. *Unguided Love hath fallen—'mid ' tears of perfect moan '.*

> There be tears of perfect moan
> Wept for thee in Helicon.—MILTON.

1. 373. *Was a proud temple call'd the Parthenon.* It was entire in 1687—the most elevated spot in Athens.

1. 375. *Than ev'n thy glowing bosom beats withal.*

Shadowing more beauty in their airy brows
Than have the white breasts of the Queen of Love.—MARLOWE.

1. 390. *Fail'd as my pennon'd spirit leapt aloft.* Pennon—for pinion. —MILTON.

TAMERLANE

ADVERTISEMENT

[This Poem was printed for publication in Boston, in the year 1827, but suppressed through circumstances of a private nature.—Note to ' 1829 ' edition.]

KIND solace in a dying hour !
  Such, father, is not (now) my theme—
I will not madly deem that power
  Of Earth may shrive me of the sin
  Unearthly pride hath revell'd in—
I have no time to dote or dream :
You call it hope—that fire of fire !
It is but agony of desire :
If I *can* hope—Oh God ! I can—
  Its fount is holier—more divine—   10
I would not call thee fool, old man,
  But such is not a gift of thine.

Know thou the secret of a spirit
  Bow'd from its wild pride into shame.
O yearning heart! I did inherit
  Thy withering portion with the fame,
The searing glory which hath shone
Amid the jewels of my throne,
Halo of Hell! and with a pain
Not Hell shall make me fear again—   20
O craving heart, for the lost flowers
And sunshine of my summer hours!
The undying voice of that dead time,
With its interminable chime,
Rings, in the spirit of a spell,
Upon thy emptiness—a knell.

I have not always been as now:
The fever'd diadem on my brow
  I claim'd and won usurpingly—
Hath not the same fierce heirdom given   30
    Rome to the Caesar—this to me?
      The heritage of a kingly mind,
And a proud spirit which hath striven
    Triumphantly with human kind.

On mountain soil I first drew life:
  The mists of the Taglay have shed
  Nightly their dews upon my head,
And, I believe, the wingèd strife
And tumult of the headlong air
Have nestled in my very hair.   40

So late from Heaven—that dew—it fell
  ('Mid dreams of an unholy night)
Upon me with the touch of Hell,
  While the red flashing of the light
From clouds that hung, like banners, o'er,
  Appeared to my half-closing eye
  The pageantry of monarchy,
And the deep trumpet-thunder's roar
  Came hurriedly upon me, telling
    Of human battle, where my voice,   50

My own voice, silly child !—was swelling
   (O ! how my spirit would rejoice,
And leap within me at the cry)
The battle-cry of Victory !

The rain came down upon my head
   Unshelter'd—and the heavy wind
   Rendered me mad and deaf and blind.
It was but man, I thought, who shed
   Laurels upon me : and the rush—
The torrent of the chilly air   60
   Gurgled within my ear the crush
Of empires—with the captive's prayer—
The hum of suitors—and the tone
Of flattery 'round a sovereign's throne.

My passions, from that hapless hour,
   Usurp'd a tyranny which men
Have deem'd, since I have reach'd to power,
     My innate nature—be it so :
   But father, there liv'd one who, then,
Then—in my boyhood—when their fire   70
     Burn'd with a still intenser glow,
(For passion must, with youth, expire)
   E'en *then* who knew this iron heart
   In woman's weakness had a part.

I have no words—alas !—to tell
The loveliness of loving well !
Nor would I now attempt to trace
The more than beauty of a face
Whose lineaments, upon my mind,
Are——shadows on th' unstable wind :   80
Thus I remember having dwelt
   Some page of early lore upon,
With loitering eye, till I have felt
The letters—with their meaning—melt
   To fantasies—with none.

O, she was worthy of all love !
   Love—as in infancy was mine—
'Twas such as angel minds above
   Might envy ; her young heart the shrine

On which my every hope and thought   90
  Were incense—then a goodly gift,
    For they were childish and upright—
Pure—as her young example taught :
  Why did I leave it, and, adrift,
    Trust to the fire within, for light ?

We grew in age—and love—together,
  Roaming the forest, and the wild ;
My breast her shield in wintry weather—
  And when the friendly sunshine smil'd,
And she would mark the opening skies,   100
I saw no Heaven—but in her eyes.

Young Love's first lesson is—the heart :
  For 'mid that sunshine, and those smiles,
When, from our little cares apart,
  And laughing at her girlish wiles,
I'd throw me on her throbbing breast,
  And pour my spirit out in tears—
There was no need to speak the rest—
  No need to quiet any fears
Of her—who ask'd no reason why,   110
But turn'd on me her quiet eye !

Yet *more* than worthy of the love
My spirit struggled with, and strove,
When, on the mountain peak, alone,
Ambition lent it a new tone—
I had no being—but in thee :
  The world, and all it did contain
In the earth—the air—the sea—
  Its joy—its little lot of pain
That was new pleasure—the ideal,   120
  Dim vanities of dreams by night—
And dimmer nothings which were real—
  (Shadows—and a more shadowy light !)
Parted upon their misty wings,
  And, so, confusedly, became
  Thine image, and—a name—a name !
Two separate—yet most intimate things.

I was ambitious—have you known
  The passion, father ? You have not :
A cottager, I mark'd a throne   130
Of half the world as all my own,
  And murmur'd at such lowly lot—
But, just like any other dream,
  Upon the vapour of the dew
My own had past, did not the beam
  Of beauty which did while it thro'
The minute—the hour—the day—oppress
My mind with double loveliness.

We walk'd together on the crown
Of a high mountain which look'd down   140
Afar from its proud natural towers
  Of rock and forest, on the hills—
The dwindled hills ! begirt with bowers,
  And shouting with a thousand rills.

I spoke to her of power and pride,
  But mystically—in such guise
That she might deem it nought beside
  The moment's converse ; in her eyes
I read, perhaps too carelessly—
  A mingled feeling with my own—   150
The flush on her bright cheek, to me
  Seem'd to become a queenly throne
Too well that I should let it be
  Light in the wilderness alone.

I wrapp'd myself in grandeur then,
  And donn'd a visionary crown—
    Yet it was not that Fantasy
    Had thrown her mantle over me—
But that, among the rabble—men,
  Lion ambition is chained down—   160
And crouches to a keeper's hand—
Not so in deserts where the grand—
The wild—the terrible conspire
With their own breath to fan his fire

Look 'round thee now on Samarcand !
   Is not she queen of Earth ? her pride
Above all cities ? in her hand
   Their destinies ? in all beside
Of glory which the world hath known
Stands she not nobly and alone ?   170
Falling—her veriest stepping-stone
Shall form the pedestal of a throne—
And who her sovereign ? Timour—he
   Whom the astonished people saw
Striding o'er empires haughtily
   A diadem'd outlaw !

O, human love ! thou spirit given
On Earth, of all we hope in Heaven !
Which fall'st into the soul like rain
Upon the Siroc-wither'd plain,   180
And, failing in thy power to bless,
But leav'st the heart a wilderness !
Idea ! which bindest life around
With music of so strange a sound,
And beauty of so wild a birth—
Farewell ! for I have won the Earth.

When Hope, the eagle that tower'd, could see
   No cliff beyond him in the sky,
His pinions were bent droopingly—
   And homeward turn'd his soften'd eye.   190
'Twas sunset : when the sun will part
There comes a sullenness of heart
To him who still would look upon
The glory of the summer sun.
That soul will hate the ev'ning mist,
So often lovely, and will list
To the sound of the coming darkness (known
To those whose spirits hearken) as one
Who, in a dream of night, *would* fly
But *cannot* from a danger nigh.   200

What tho' the moon—the white moon
Shed all the splendour of her noon,
Her smile is chilly, and *her* beam,
In that time of dreariness, will seem

(So like you gather in your breath)
A portrait taken after death.
And boyhood is a summer sun
Whose waning is the dreariest one—
For all we live to know is known,
And all we seek to keep hath flown—   210
Let life, then, as the day-flower, fall
With the noon-day beauty—which is all.

I reach'd my home—my home no more
    For all had flown who made it so.
I pass'd from out its mossy door,
    And, tho' my tread was soft and low,
A voice came from the threshold stone
Of one whom I had earlier known—
    O, I defy thee, Hell, to show
    On beds of fire that burn below,   220
    A humbler heart—a deeper woe.

Father, I firmly do believe—
    I *know*—for Death, who comes for me
        From regions of the blest afar,
Where there is nothing to deceive,
        Hath left his iron gate ajar,
    And rays of truth you cannot see
    Are flashing thro' Eternity——
I do believe that Eblis hath
A snare in every human path—   230
Else how, when in the holy grove
I wandered of the idol, Love,
Who daily scents his snowy wings
With incense of burnt offerings
From the most unpolluted things,
Whose pleasant bowers are yet so riven
Above with trellis'd rays from Heaven,
No mote may shun—no tiniest fly—
The lightning of his eagle eye—
How was it that Ambition crept,   240
    Unseen, amid the revels there,
Till growing bold, he laughed and leapt
    In the tangles of Love's very hair ?

A DREAM

In visions of the dark night
  I have dreamed of joy departed—
But a waking dream of life and light
  Hath left me broken-hearted.

Ah ! what is not a dream by day
  To him whose eyes are cast
On things around him with a ray
  Turned back upon the past ?

That holy dream—that holy dream,
  While all the world were chiding,
Hath cheered me as a lovely beam
  A lonely spirit guiding.

What though that light, thro' storm and night,
  So trembled from afar—
What could there be more purely bright
  In Truth's day-star ?

ROMANCE

Romance, who loves to nod and sing,
With drowsy head and folded wing,
Among the green leaves as they shake
Far down within some shadowy lake,
To me a painted paroquet
Hath been—a most familiar bird—
Taught me my alphabet to say—
To lisp my very earliest word
While in the wild wood I did lie,
A child—with a most knowing eye.

Of late, eternal Condor years
So shake the very Heaven on high
With tumult as they thunder by,
I have no time for idle cares
Through gazing on the unquiet sky.
And when an hour with calmer wings
Its down upon my spirit flings—

That little time with lyre and rhyme
To while away—forbidden things !
My heart would feel to be a crime   20
Unless it trembled with the strings.

FAIRY-LAND

Dim vales—and shadowy floods—
And cloudy-looking woods,
Whose forms we can't discover
For the tears that drip all over !
Huge moons there wax and wane—
Again—again—again—
Every moment of the night—
Forever changing places—
And they put out the star-light
With the breath from their pale faces.   10
About twelve by the moon-dial,
One more filmy than the rest
(A kind which, upon trial,
They have found to be the best)
Comes down—still down—and down,
With its centre on the crown
Of a mountain's eminence,
While its wide circumference
In easy drapery falls
Over hamlets, over halls,   20
Wherever they may be—
O'er the strange woods—o'er the sea—
Over spirits on the wing—
Over every drowsy thing—
And buries them up quite
In a labyrinth of light—
And then, how deep !—O, deep !
Is the passion of their sleep.
In the morning they arise,
And their moony covering   30
Is soaring in the skies,
With the tempests as they toss,
Like——almost anything—
Or a yellow Albatross.

They use that moon no more
For the same end as before—
Videlicet, a tent—
Which I think extravagant :
Its atomies, however,
Into a shower dissever,   4o
Of which those butterflies .
Of Earth, who seek the skies,
And so come down again,
(Never-contented things !)
Have brought a specimen
Upon their quivering wings.

TO ———

THE bowers whereat, in dreams, I see
     The wantonest singing birds,
Are lips—and all thy melody
     Of lip-begotten words—

Thine eyes, in Heaven of heart enshrined,
     Then desolately fall,
O God ! on my funereal mind
     Like starlight on a pall—

Thy heart—*thy* heart !—I wake and sigh,
     And sleep to dream till day   1o
Of the truth that gold can never buy—
     Of the baubles that it may.

TO THE RIVER ———

FAIR river ! in thy bright, clear flow
     Of crystal, wandering water,
Thou art an emblem of the glow
         Of beauty—the unhidden heart—
     The playful maziness of art
In old Alberto's daughter ;

But when within thy wave she looks—
  Which glistens then, and trembles—
Why, then, the prettiest of brooks
  Her worshipper resembles ;   10
For in his heart, as in thy stream,
  Her image deeply lies—
His heart which trembles at the beam
  Of her soul-searching eyes.

THE LAKE—TO ——

In spring of youth it was my lot
To haunt of the wide world a spot
The which I could not love the less—
So lovely was the loneliness
Of a wild lake, with black rock bound,
And the tall pines that towered around.

But when the Night had thrown her pall
Upon that spot, as upon all,
And the mystic wind went by
Murmuring in melody—   10
Then—ah then I would awake
To the terror of the lone lake.

Yet that terror was not fright,
But a tremulous delight—
A feeling not the jewelled mine
Could teach or bribe me to define—
Nor Love—although the Love were thine.

Death was in that poisonous wave,
And in its gulf a fitting grave
For him who thence could solace bring   20
To his lone imagining—
Whose solitary soul could make
An Eden of that dim lake.

SONG

I saw thee on thy bridal day—
  When a burning blush came o'er thee,
Though happiness around thee lay,
  The world all love before thee :

And in thine eye a kindling light
  (Whatever it might be)
Was all on Earth my aching sight
  Of Loveliness could see.

That blush, perhaps, was maiden shame—
  As such it well may pass—
Though its glow hath raised a fiercer flame
  In the breast of him, alas !

Who saw thee on that bridal day,
  When that deep blush *would* come o'er thee,
Though happiness around thee lay ;
  The world all love before thee.

10

TO HELEN

[' Helen ' was Mrs. Stannard, whose death also inspired ' Lenore '.]

Helen, thy beauty is to me
  Like those Nicean barks of yore,
That gently, o'er a perfumed sea,
  The weary, wayworn wanderer bore
  To his own native shore.

On desperate seas long wont to roam,
  Thy hyacinth hair, thy classic face,
Thy Naiad airs have brought me home
  To the glory that was Greece
And the grandeur that was Rome.

10

Lo ! in yon brilliant window-niche
  How statue-like I see thee stand,
  The agate lamp within thy hand !
Ah, Psyche, from the regions which
  Are Holy Land !

FROM WORKS OF THE LATE
EDGAR ALLAN POE
(Griswold, 1850)
AND 'ALONE'

TO M. L. S——

[Mrs. Marie Louise Shew.]

OF all who hail thy presence as the morning—
Of all to whom thine absence is the night—
The blotting utterly from out high heaven
The sacred sun—of all who, weeping, bless thee
Hourly for hope—for life—ah! above all,
For the resurrection of deep-buried faith
In Truth—in Virtue—in Humanity—
Of all who, on Despair's unhallowed bed
Lying down to die, have suddenly arisen
At thy soft-murmured words, 'Let there be light!'   10
At the soft-murmured words that were fulfilled
In the seraphic glancing of thine eyes—
Of all who owe thee most—whose gratitude
Nearest resembles worship—oh, remember
The truest—the most fervently devoted,
And think that these weak lines are written by him—
By him who, as he pens them, thrills to think
His spirit is communing with an angel's.

AN ENIGMA

'SELDOM we find,' says Solomon Don Dunce,
  'Half an idea in the profoundest sonnet.
Through all the flimsy things we see at once
  As easily as through a Naples bonnet—
  Trash of all trash!—how *can* a lady don it?
Yet heavier far than your Petrarchan stuff—
Owl-downy nonsense that the faintest puff
  Twirls into trunk-paper the while you con it.'
And, veritably, Sol is right enough.
The general tuckermanities are arrant   10
Bubbles—ephemeral and *so* transparent—
  But *this* is, now—you may depend upon it—
Stable, opaque, immortal—all by dint
Of the dear names that lie concealed within 't.

[To find the name, read the first letter in the first line, the second in
the second, and so on—SARAH ANNA LEWIS.]

A VALENTINE

FOR her this rhyme is penned, whose luminous eyes,
  Brightly expressive as the twins of Leda,
Shall find her own sweet name, that nestling lies
  Upon the page, enwrapped from every reader.
Search narrowly the lines !—they hold a treasure
  Divine—a talisman—an amulet
That must be worn *at heart*. Search well the measure—
  The words—the syllables ! Do not forget
The trivialest point, or you may lose your labour !
  And yet there is in this no Gordian knot   10
Which one might not undo without a sabre,
  If one could merely comprehend the plot.
Enwritten upon the leaf where now are peering
  Eyes scintillating soul, there lie *perdus*
Three eloquent words oft uttered in the hearing
  Of poets, by poets—as the name is a poet's, too.
Its letters, although naturally lying
  Like the knight Pinto—Mendez Ferdinando—
Still form a synonym for Truth.—Cease trying !
  You will not read the riddle, though you do the best you
    can do.   20

[To find the name, read the first letter in the first line, the second in
the second, and so on—FRANCES SARGENT OSGOOD.]

ANNABEL LEE

IT was many and many a year ago,
    In a kingdom by the sea,
That a maiden there lived whom you may know
    By the name of ANNABEL LEE ;
And this maiden she lived with no other thought
    Than to love and be loved by me.

I was a child and she was a child,
    In this kingdom by the sea ;
But we loved with a love that was more than love—
    I and my Annabel Lee ;   10
With a love that the wingèd seraphs of heaven
    Coveted her and me.

And this was the reason that, long ago,
    In this kingdom by the sea,
A wind blew out of a cloud, chilling
    My beautiful Annabel Lee ;
So that her highborn kinsman came
    And bore her away from me,
To shut her up in a sepulchre
    In this kingdom by the sea.   20

The angels, not half so happy in heaven,
    Went envying her and me—
Yes !—that was the reason (as all men know,
    In this kingdom by the sea)
That the wind came out of the cloud by night,
    Chilling and killing my Annabel Lee.

But our love it was stronger by far than the love
    Of those who were older than we—
    Of many far wiser than we—
And neither the angels in heaven above,   30
    Nor the demons down under the sea,
Can ever dissever my soul from the soul
    Of the beautiful Annabel Lee.

For the moon never beams without bringing me dreams
    Of the beautiful Annabel Lee ;
And the stars never rise but I feel the bright eyes
    Of the beautiful Annabel Lee ;
And so, all the night-tide, I lie down by the side
Of my darling—my darling—my life and my bride,
    In the sepulchre there by the sea,   40
    In her tomb by the sounding sea.

THE BELLS

I

Hear the sledges with the bells—
    Silver bells !
What a world of merriment their melody foretells !
    How they tinkle, tinkle, tinkle,
      In the icy air of night !

While the stars that oversprinkle
All the heavens, seem to twinkle
With a crystalline delight ;
Keeping time, time, time,
In a sort of Runic rhyme,   10
To the tintinabulation that so musically wells
From the bells, bells, bells, bells,
Bells, bells, bells—
From the jingling and the tinkling of the bells.

II

Hear the mellow wedding bells,
Golden bells !
What a world of happiness their harmony foretells !
Through the balmy air of night
How they ring out their delight !
From the molten-golden notes,   20
And all in tune,
What a liquid ditty floats
To the turtle-dove that listens, while she gloats
On the moon !
Oh, from out the sounding cells,
What a gush of euphony voluminously wells !
How it swells !
How it dwells
On the Future ! how it tells
Of the rapture that impels   30
To the swinging and the ringing
Of the bells, bells, bells,
Of the bells, bells, bells, bells,
Bells, bells, bells—
To the rhyming and the chiming of the bells !

III

Hear the loud alarum bells—
Brazen bells !
What a tale of terror, now, their turbulency tells !
In the startled ear of night
How they scream out their affright !   40
Too much horrified to speak,
They can only shriek, shriek,
Out of tune,

In a clamorous appealing to the mercy of the fire,
In a mad expostulation with the deaf and frantic fire,
      Leaping higher, higher, higher,
      With a desperate desire,
    And a resolute endeavour,
    Now—now to sit or never,
  By the side of the pale-faced moon.   50
      Oh, the bells, bells, bells !
     What a tale their terror tells
        Of Despair !
  How they clang, and clash, and roar !
   What a horror they outpour
On the bosom of the palpitating air !
   Yet the ear it fully knows,
      By the twanging,
      And the clanging,
   How the danger ebbs and flows :   60
  Yet the ear distinctly tells,
      In the jangling,
      And the wrangling,
  How the danger sinks and swells,
By the sinking or the swelling in the anger of the bells—
       Of the bells—
   Of the bells, bells, bells, bells,
     Bells, bells, bells—
  In the clamour and the clangour of the bells !

           IV

   Hear the tolling of the bells—   70
       Iron bells !
What a world of solemn thought their monody compels !
     In the silence of the night,
     How we shiver with affright
At the melancholy menace of their tone !
    For every sound that floats
   From the rust within their throats
      Is a groan.
   And the people—ah, the people—
   They that dwell up in the steeple,   80
      All alone,

And who, tolling, tolling, tolling,
  In that muffled monotone,
Feel a glory in so rolling
  On the human heart a stone—
They are neither man nor woman—
They are neither brute nor human—
    They are Ghouls:
  And their king it is who tolls;
  And he rolls, rolls, rolls,   90
    Rolls
    A paean from the bells!
And his merry bosom swells
  With the paean of the bells!
And he dances, and he yells;
Keeping time, time, time,
In a sort of Runic rhyme,
  To the paean of the bells—
    Of the bells:
Keeping time, time, time,   100
In a sort of Runic rhyme,
  To the throbbing of the bells—
Of the bells, bells, bells—
  To the sobbing of the bells;
Keeping time, time, time,
  As he knells, knells knells,
In a happy Runic rhyme,
  To the rolling of the bells—
Of the bells, bells, bells:
  To the tolling of the bells,   110
Of the bells, bells, bells, bells—
  Bells, bells, bells—
To the moaning and the groaning of the bells.

ELDORADO

  Gaily bedight,
  A gallant knight,
In sunshine and in shadow,
    Had journeyed long,
    Singing a song,
In search of Eldorado.

But he grew old—
This knight so bold—
And o'er his heart a shadow
Fell as he found   10
No spot of ground
That looked like Eldorado.

And, as his strength
Failed him at length,
He met a pilgrim shadow—
'Shadow,' said he,
'Where can it be—
This land of Eldorado ? '

'Over the Mountains
Of the Moon,   20
Down the Valley of the Shadow,
Ride, boldly ride,'
The shade replied—
'If you seek for Eldorado ! '

ULALUME

THE skies they were ashen and sober ;
The leaves they were crisped and sere—
The leaves they were withering and sere ;
It was night in the lonesome October
Of my most immemorial year ;
It was hard by the dim lake of Auber,
In the misty mid region of Weir—
It was down by the dank tarn of Auber,
In the ghoul-haunted woodland of Weir.

Here once, through an alley Titanic,   10
Of cypress, I roamed with my Soul—
Of cypress, with Psyche, my Soul.
These were days when my heart was volcanic
As the scoriac rivers that roll—
As the lavas that restlessly roll
Their sulphurous currents down Yaanek
In the ultimate climes of the pole—
That groan as they roll down Mount Yaanek
In the realms of the boreal pole.

Our talk had been serious and sober,   20
    But our thoughts they were palsied and sere—
    Our memories were treacherous and sere—
For we knew not the month was October,
    And we marked not the night of the year—
    (Ah, night of all nights in the year !)
We noted not the dim lake of Auber—
    (Though once we had journeyed down here),
Remembered not the dank tarn of Auber,
    Nor the ghoul-haunted woodland of Weir.

And now, as the night was senescent,   30
    And star-dials pointed to morn—
    As the star-dials hinted of morn—
At the end of our path a liquescent
    And nebulous lustre was born,
Out of which a miraculous crescent
    Arose with a duplicate horn—
Astarte's bediamonded crescent
    Distinct with its duplicate horn.

And I said—' She is warmer than Dian :
    She rolls through an ether of sighs—   40
    She revels in a region of sighs :
She has seen that the tears are not dry on
    These cheeks, where the worm never dies,
And has come past the stars of the Lion,
    To point us the path to the skies—
    To the Lethean peace of the skies—
Come up, in despite of the Lion,
    To shine on us with her bright eyes—
Come up through the lair of the Lion,
    With love in her luminous eyes.'   50

But Psyche, uplifting her finger,
    Said—' Sadly this star I mistrust—
    Her pallor I strangely mistrust :—
Oh, hasten !—oh, let us not linger !
    Oh, fly !—let us fly !—for we must.'
In terror she spoke, letting sink her
    Wings until they trailed in the dust—

In agony sobbed, letting sink her
    Plumes till they trailed in the dust—
    Till they sorrowfully trailed in the dust.   60

I replied—' This is nothing but dreaming :
    Let us on by this tremulous light !
    Let us bathe in this crystalline light !
Its Sybilic splendour is beaming
    With Hope and in Beauty to-night :—
    See !—it flickers up the sky through the night !
Ah, we safely may trust to its gleaming,
    And be sure it will lead us aright—
We safely may trust to a gleaming
    That cannot but guide us aright,   70
    Since it flickers up to Heaven through the night.'

Thus I pacified Psyche and kissed her,
    And tempted her out of her gloom—
    And conquered her scruples and gloom ;
And we passed to the end of the vista,
    But were stopped by the door of a tomb—
    By the door of a legended tomb ;
And I said—' What is written, sweet sister,
    On the door of this legended tomb ? '
    She replied—' Ulalume—Ulalume—   80
    'Tis the vault of thy lost Ulalume ! '

Then my heart it grew ashen and sober
    As the leaves that were crisped and sere—
    As the leaves that were withering and sere—
And I cried—' It was surely October
    On *this* very night of last year
    That I journeyed—I journeyed down here—
    That I brought a dread burden down here—
    On this night of all nights in the year,
    Ah, what demon has tempted me here ?   90
Well I know, now, this dim lake of Auber—
    This misty mid region of Weir—
Well I know, now, this dank tarn of Auber,
    This ghoul-haunted woodland of Weir.'

[Helen was Mrs. Whitman.]

I SAW thee once—once only—years ago :
I must not say *how* many—but *not* many.
It was a July midnight ; and from out
A full-orbed moon, that, like thine own soul, soaring,
Sought a precipitate pathway up through heaven,
There fell a silvery-silken veil of light,
With quietude, and sultriness, and slumber,
Upon the upturned faces of a thousand
Roses that grew in an enchanted garden,
Where no wind dared to stir, unless on tiptoe—   10
Fell on the upturn'd faces of these roses
That gave out, in return for the love-light,
Their odorous souls in an ecstatic death—
Fell on the upturn'd faces of these roses
That smiled and died in this parterre, enchanted
By thee, and by the poetry of thy presence.

Clad all in white, upon a violet bank
I saw thee half reclining ; while the moon
Fell on the upturn'd faces of the roses,
And on thine own, upturn'd—alas, in sorrow !   20

Was it not Fate, that, on this July midnight—
Was it not Fate, (whose name is also Sorrow,)
That bade me pause before that garden-gate,
To breathe the incense of those slumbering roses ?
No footstep stirred : the hated world all slept,
Save only thee and me. (Oh, Heaven !—oh, God !
How my heart beats in coupling those two words !)
Save only thee and me. I paused—I looked—
And in an instant all things disappeared.
(Ah, bear in mind this garden was enchanted !)   30

The pearly lustre of the moon went out :
The mossy banks and the meandering paths,
The happy flowers and the repining trees,
Were seen no more : the very roses' odours
Died in the arms of the adoring airs.
All—all expired save thee—save less than thou :
Save only the divine light in thine eyes—
Save but the soul in thine uplifted eyes.

I saw but them—they were the world to me !
I saw but them—saw only them for hours,   40
Saw only them until the moon went down.
What wild heart-histories seemed to lie enwritten
Upon those crystalline, celestial spheres !
How dark a woe, yet how sublime a hope !
How silently serene a sea of pride !
How daring an ambition ; yet how deep—
How fathomless a capacity for love !

But now, at length, dear Dian sank from sight,
Into a western couch of thunder-cloud ;
And thou, a ghost, amid the entombing trees   50
Didst glide away. *Only thine eyes remained ;*
They *would not* go—they never yet have gone ;
Lighting my lonely pathway home that night,
They have not left me (as my hopes have) since ;
They follow me—they lead me through the years.
They are my ministers—yet I their slave.
Their office is to illumine and enkindle—
My duty, *to be saved* by their bright light,
And purified in their electric fire,
And sanctified in their elysian fire.   60
They fill my soul with Beauty (which is Hope),
And are far up in Heaven—the stars I kneel to
In the sad, silent watches of my night ;
While even in the meridian glare of day
I see them still—two sweetly scintillant
Venuses, unextinguished by the sun !

TO —— ——

[Mrs. Marie Louise Shew.]

NOT long ago, the writer of these lines,
In the mad pride of intellectuality,
Maintained ' the power of words '—denied that ever
A thought arose within the human brain
Beyond the utterance of the human tongue :
And now, as if in mockery of that boast,
Two words—two foreign soft dissyllables—
Italian tones, made only to be murmured

By angels dreaming in the moonlit ' dew
That hangs like chains of pearl on Hermon hill ',   10
Have stirred from out the abysses of his heart,
Unthought-like thoughts that are the souls of thought,
Richer, far wilder, far diviner visions
Than even seraph harper, Israfel,
(Who has ' the sweetest voice of all God's creatures,')
Could hope to utter. And I ! my spells are broken.
The pen falls powerless from my shivering hand.
With thy dear name as text, though bidden by thee,
I cannot write—I cannot speak or think—
Alas, I cannot feel ; for 'tis not feeling,   20
This standing motionless upon the golden
Threshold of the wide-open gate of dreams.
Gazing, entranced, adown the gorgeous vista,
And thrilling as I see, upon the right,
Upon the left, and all the way along,
Amid empurpled vapours, far away
To where the prospect terminates—*thee only*.

FOR ANNIE

THANK Heaven ! the crisis—
　　The danger is past,
And the lingering illness
　　Is over at last—
And the fever called ' Living '
　　Is conquered at last.

Sadly, I know
　　I am shorn of my strength,
And no muscle I move
　　As I lie at full length—   10
But no matter !—I feel
　　I am better at length.

And I rest so composedly,
　　Now, in my bed,
That any beholder
　　Might fancy me dead—
Might start at beholding me,
　　Thinking me dead.

The moaning and groaning,
  The sighing and sobbing,   20
Are quieted now,
  With that horrible throbbing
At heart :—ah, that horrible,
  Horrible throbbing !

The sickness—the nausea—
  The pitiless pain—
Have ceased, with the fever
  That maddened my brain—
With the fever called ' Living '
  That burned in my brain.   30

And oh ! of all tortures
  That torture the worst
Has abated—the terrible
  Torture of thirst
For the naphthaline river
  Of Passion accurst :—
I have drunk of a water
  That quenches all thirst :—

Of a water that flows,
  With a lullaby sound,   40
From a spring but a very few
  Feet under ground—
From a cavern not very far
  Down under ground.

And ah ! let it never
  Be foolishly said
That my room it is gloomy
  And narrow my bed ;
For man never slept
  In a different bed—   50
And, *to sleep*, you must slumber
  In just such a bed.

My tantalized spirit
  Here blandly reposes,
Forgetting, or never
  Regretting its roses—
Its old agitations
  Of myrtles and roses :

For now, while so quietly
    Lying, it fancies   60
A holier odour
    About it, of pansies—
A rosemary odour,
    Commingled with pansies—
With rue and the beautiful
    Puritan pansies.

And so it lies happily,
    Bathing in many
A dream of the truth
    And the beauty of Annie—   70
Drowned in a bath
    Of the tresses of Annie.

She tenderly kissed me,
    She fondly caressed,
And then I fell gently
    To sleep on her breast—
Deeply to sleep
    From the heaven of her breast.

When the light was extinguished,
    She covered me warm,   80
And she prayed to the angels
    To keep me from harm—
To the queen of the angels
    To shield me from harm.

And I lie so composedly,
    Now, in my bed,
(Knowing her love)
    That you fancy me dead—
And I rest so contentedly,
    Now, in my bed,   90
(With her love at my breast)
    That you fancy me dead—
That you shudder to look at me,
    Thinking me dead.

But my heart it is brighter
   Than all of the many
Stars in the sky,
   For it sparkles with Annie—
It glows with the light
   Of the love of my Annie—   100
With the thought of the light
   Of the eyes of my Annie.

TO MY MOTHER

[His mother-in-law, Mrs. Clemm.]

BECAUSE I feel that, in the Heavens above,
   The angels, whispering to one another,
Can find, among their burning terms of love,
   None so devotional as that of ' Mother ',
Therefore by that dear name I long have called you—
   You who are more than mother unto me,
And fill my heart of hearts, where Death installed you
   In setting my Virginia's spirit free.
My mother—my own mother, who died early,
   Was but the mother of myself ; but you   10
Are mother to the one I loved so dearly,
   And thus are dearer than the mother I knew
By that infinity with which my wife
   Was dearer to my soul than its soul-life.

A DREAM WITHIN A DREAM

TAKE this kiss upon the brow !
And, in parting from you now,
Thus much let me avow—
You are not wrong, who deem
That my days have been a dream ;
Yet if hope has flown away
In a night, or in a day,
In a vision, or in none,
Is it therefore the less *gone* ?
All that we see or seem   10
Is but a dream within a dream.

I stand amid the roar
Of a surf-tormented shore,
And I hold within my hand
Grains of the golden sand—
How few ! yet how they creep
Through my fingers to the deep,
While I weep—while I weep !
O God ! can I not grasp
Them with a tighter clasp ?   20
O God ! can I not save
One from the pitiless wave ?
Is *all* that we see or seem
But a dream within a dream ?

ALONE

[*Scribner's Magazine*, September 1875.]

FROM childhood's hour I have not been
As others were ; I have not seen
As others saw ; I could not bring
My passions from a common spring.
From the same source I have not taken
My sorrow ; I could not awaken
My heart to joy at the same tone ;
And all I loved, *I* loved alone.
Then—in my childhood, in the dawn
Of a most stormy life—was drawn   10
From every depth of good and ill
The mystery which binds me still :
From the torrent, or the fountain,
From the red cliff of the mountain,
From the sun that round me rolled
In its autumn tint of gold,
From the lightning in the sky
As it passed me flying by,
From the thunder and the storm,
And the cloud that took the form   20
(When the rest of Heaven was blue)
Of a demon in my view.

OTHER TEXTS FOR SOME OF THE POEMS

SPIRITS OF THE DEAD

[*Tamerlane and other Poems*, 1827. Here called *Visit of the Dead*.]

THY soul shall find itself alone—
Alone of all on earth—unknown
The cause—but none are near to pry
Into thine hour of secrecy.
Be silent in that solitude,
Which is not loneliness—for then
The spirits of the dead, who stood
In life before thee, are again
In death around thee, and their will
Shall then o'ershadow thee—be still :   10
For the night, tho' clear, shall frown ;
And the stars shall look not down
From their thrones, in the dark heaven,
With light like Hope to mortals given,
But their red orbs, without beam,
To thy withering heart shall seem
As a burning, and a fever
Which would cling to thee forever.
But 'twill leave thee, as each star
In the morning light afar   20
Will fly thee—and vanish :
—But its *thought* thou canst not banish.
The breath of God will be still ;
And the mist upon the hill
By that summer breeze unbroken
Shall charm thee—as a token,
And a symbol which shall be
Secrecy in thee.

THE VALLEY OF UNREST

[*Poems of Edgar A. Poe*, 1831. Here called ' The Valley Nis '.]

FAR away—far away—
Far away—as far at least
Lies that valley as the day
Down within the golden east—
All things lovely—are not they
Far away—far away ?

It is called the Valley Nis.
And a Syriac tale there is
Thereabout which Time hath said
Shall not be interpreted.   10
Something about Satan's dart—
Something about angel wings—
Much about a broken heart—
All about unhappy things :
But ' the Valley Nis ' at best
Means ' the valley of unrest '.

Once it smil'd, a silent dell
Where the people did not dwell,
Having gone unto the wars—
And the sly, mysterious stars,   20
With a visage full of meaning,
O'er the unguarded flowers were leaning :
Or the sun ray dripp'd all red
Thro' the tulips overhead,
Then grew paler as it fell
On the quiet Asphodel.

Now the *unhappy* shall confess
Nothing there is motionless :
Helen, like thy human eye
There th' uneasy violets lie—   30
There the reedy grass doth wave
Over the old forgotten grave—
One by one from the treetop
There the eternal dews do drop—
There the vague and dreamy trees
Do roll like seas in northern breeze

Around the stormy Hebrides—
There the gorgeous clouds do fly,
Rustling everlastingly,
Through the terror-stricken sky,   40
Rolling like a waterfall
O'er th' horizon's fiery wall—
There the moon doth shine by night
With a most unsteady light—
There the sun doth reel by day
' Over the hills and far away '.

THE SLEEPER

[*Poems by Edgar A. Poe*, 1831.   Here called ' Irene '.]

'TIS now (so sings the soaring moon)
Midnight in the sweet month of June,
When winged visions love to lie
Lazily upon beauty's eye,
Or worse—upon her brow to dance
In panoply of old romance,
Till thoughts and locks are left, alas !
A ne'er-to-be untangled mass.

An influence dewy, drowsy, dim,
Is dripping from that golden rim ;   10
Grey towers are mouldering into rest,
Wrapping their fog around their breast :
Looking like Lethe, see ! the lake
A conscious slumber seems to take,
And would not for the world awake ;
The rosemary sleeps upon the grave—
The lily lolls upon the wave—
And million bright pines to and fro,
Are rocking lullabies as they go,
To the lone oak that reels with bliss,   20
Nodding above the dim abyss.
All beauty sleeps : and lo ! where lies
With casement open to the skies,
Irene, with her destinies !

Thus hums the moon within her ear,

'O lady sweet ! how camest thou here ?
Strange are thine eyelids—strange thy dress !
And strange thy glorious length of tress !
Sure thou art come o'er far-off seas,
A wonder to our desert trees !   30
Some gentle wind hath thought it right
To open thy window to the night,
And wanton airs from the tree-top,
Laughingly thro' the lattice drop,
And wave this crimson canopy,
Like a banner o'er thy dreaming eye !
Lady, awake ! lady, awake !
For the holy Jesus' sake !
For strangely—fearfully in this hall
My tinted shadows rise and fall !'   40

The lady sleeps : the *dead* all sleep—
At least as long as Love doth weep :
Entranc'd, the spirit loves to lie
As long as—tears on Memory's eye :
But when a week or two go by,
And the light laughter chokes the sigh,
Indignant from the tomb doth take
Its way to some remember'd lake,
Where oft—in life—with friends—it went
To bathe in the pure element,   50
And there, from the untrodden grass,
Wreathing for its transparent brow
Those flowers that say (ah, hear them now !)
To the night-winds as they pass,
'Ai ! ai ! alas !—alas !'
Pores for a moment, ere it go,
On the clear waters there that flow,
Then sinks within (weigh'd down by woe)
Th' uncertain, shadowy heaven below.

  .   .   .   .   .   .

The lady sleeps : oh ! may her sleep   60
As it is lasting so be deep—
No icy worms about her creep :

I pray to God that she may lie
For ever with as calm an eye,
That chamber chang'd for one more holy—
That bed for one more melancholy.

Far in the forest, dim and old,
For her may some tall vault unfold,
Against whose sounding door she hath thrown,
In childhood, many an idle stone—   70
Some tomb, which oft hath flung its black
And vampire-wingèd panels back,
Flutt'ring triumphant o'er the palls
Of her old family funerals.

LENORE

[Poems by Edgar A. Poe, 1831. Here called 'A Paean'.]

How shall the burial rite be read ?
    The solemn song be sung ?
The requiem for the loveliest dead,
    That ever died so young ?

Her friends are gazing on her,
    And on her gaudy bier,
And weep !—oh ! to dishonour
    Dead beauty with a tear !

They loved her for her wealth—
    And they hated her for her pride—   10
But she grew in feeble health,
    And they *love* her—that she died.

They tell me (while they speak
    Of her ' costly-broider'd pall ')
That my voice is growing weak—
    That I should not sing at all—

Or that my tone should be
    Tun'd to such solemn song,
So mournfully—so mournfully,
    That the dead may feel no wrong.   20

But she is gone above,
  With young Hope at her side,
And I am drunk with love
  Of the dead, who is my bride—

Of the dead—dead who lies
  All perfum'd there,
With the death upon her eyes,
  And the life upon her hair.

Thus on the coffin loud and long
  I strike—the murmur sent   30
Through the grey chambers to my song,
  Shall be the accompaniment.

Thou died'st in thy life's June—
  But thou didst not die too fair :
Thou didst not die too soon,
  Nor with too calm an air.

From more than friends on earth
  Thy life and love are riven,
To join the untainted mirth
  Of more than thrones in heaven—   40

Therefore, to thee this night
  I will no requiem raise,
But waft thee on thy flight,
  With a Paean of old days.

LENORE

[The *Pioneer*, 1843.]

Ah, broken is the golden bowl !
  The Spirit flown forever !
Let the bell toll !—A saintly soul
  Glides down the Stygian river !
And let the burial rite be read—
  The funeral song be sung—
A dirge for the most lovely dead
  That ever died so young !

And, Guy de Vere,
Hast *thou* no tear ?   10
   Weep now or never more !
See, on yon drear
And rigid bier,
   Low lies thy love Lenore.

' Yon heir, whose cheeks of pallid hue
  With tears are streaming wet,
Sees only, through
Their crocodile dew,
   A vacant coronet—
     False friends ! ye lov'd her for her wealth   20
      And hated her for her pride,
  And, when she fell in feeble health,
     Ye bless'd her—that she died.
       How *shall* the ritual, then, be read ?
        The requiem *how* be sung
      For her most wrong'd of all the dead
       That ever died so young ? '

Peccavimus !
But rave not thus !
  And let the solemn song   30
Go up to God so mournfully that *she* may feel no wrong !
    The sweet Lenore
    Hath ' gone before '
      With young Hope at her side,
       And thou art wild
       For the dear child
    That should have been thy bride—
      For her, the fair
      And debonair,
       That now so lowly lies—   40
     The life still there
     Upon her hair,
       The death upon her eyes.

' Avaunt !—to-night
My heart is light—
  No dirge will I upraise,

But waft the angel on her flight
  With a Paean of old days !
  Let *no* bell toll !
  Lest her sweet soul,   50
    Amid its hallow'd mirth,
      Should catch the note
      As it doth float
  Up from the damnèd earth—
    To friends above, from fiends below,
      Th' indignant ghost is riven—
      From grief and moan
      To a gold throne
    Beside the King of Heaven.'

ISRAFEL

[*Poems by Edgar A. Poe, 1831.*]

I

In Heaven a spirit doth dwell
Whose heart-strings are a lute ;
None sing so wild—so well
As the angel Israfel—
And the giddy stars are mute.

II

Tottering above
In her highest noon,
The enamoured moon
Blushes with love—
While, to listen, the red levin   10
Pauses in Heaven.

III

And they say (the starry choir
And all the listening things)
That Israfeli's fire
Is owing to that lyre
With those unusual strings.

IV

But the Heavens that angel trod,
Where deep thoughts are a duty—
Where Love is a grown god—
Where Houri glances are—   20
Stay ! turn thine eyes afar !
Imbued with all the beauty
Which we worship in yon star.

V

Thou art not, therefore, wrong
Israfeli, who despisest
An unimpassion'd song :
To thee the laurels belong,
Best bard,—because the wisest.

VI

The ecstasies above
With thy burning measures suit—   30
Thy grief—if any—thy love
With the fervour of thy lute—
Well may the stars be mute !

VII

Yes, Heaven is thine : but this
Is a world of sweets and sours :
Our flowers are merely—flowers,
And the shadow of thy bliss
Is the sunshine of ours.

VIII

If I did dwell where Israfel
Hath dwelt, and he where I,   40
He would not sing one half so well—
One half so passionately,
While a stormier note than this would swell
From my lyre within the sky.

THE CITY IN THE SEA

[*Poems by Edgar A. Poe*, 1831. Here called ' The Doomed City '.]

Lo ! Death hath rear'd himself a throne
In a strange city, all alone,
Far down within the dim West—
And the good, and the bad, and the worst, and the best,
Have gone to their eternal rest.

There shrines, and palaces, and towers
Are—not like anything of ours—
O ! no—O ! no—*ours* never loom
To heaven with that ungodly gloom !
Time-eaten towers that tremble not !   10
Around, by lifting winds forgot,
Resignedly beneath the sky
The melancholy waters lie.

A heaven that God doth not contemn
With stars is like a diadem
We liken our ladies' eyes to them—
But there ! that everlasting pall !
It would be mockery to call
Such dreariness a heaven at all.

Yet tho' no holy rays come down   20
On the long night-time of that town,
Light from the lurid, deep sea
Streams up the turrets silently—

Up thrones—up long-forgotten bowers
Of sculptured ivy and stone flowers—
Up domes—up spires—up kingly halls—
Up fanes—up Babylon-like walls—
Up many a melancholy shrine,
Whose entablatures intertwine
The mask—the viol—and the vine.   30

There open temples—open graves
Are on a level with the waves—
But not the riches there that lie
In each idol's diamond eye,

Not the gaily-jewell'd dead
Tempt the waters from their bed :
For no ripples curl, alas !
Along that wilderness of glass—
No swellings hint that winds may be
Upon a far-off happier sea :   40
So blend the turrets and shadows there
That all seem pendulous in air,
While from the high towers of the town
Death looks gigantically down.

But lo ! a stir is in the air !
The wave ! there is a ripple there !
As if the towers had thrown aside,
In slightly sinking, the dull tide—
As if the turret-tops had given
A vacuum in the filmy Heaven :   50
The waves have now a redder glow—
The very hours are breathing low—
And when, amid no earthly moans,
Down, down that town shall settle hence,
Hell, rising from a thousand thrones,
Shall do it reverence,
And Death to some more happy clime
Shall give his undivided time.

TAMERLANE

[*Tamerlane and other Poems*, 1827.]

I

I HAVE sent for thee, holy friar ;
But 'twas not with the drunken hope,
Which is but agony of desire
To shun the fate, with which to cope
Is more than crime may dare to dream,
That I have call'd thee at this hour :
Such, father, is not my theme—
Nor am I mad, to deem that power
Of earth may shrive me of the sin
Unearthly pride hath revell'd in—   10

I would not call thee fool, old man,
But hope is not a gift of thine ;
If I *can* hope (O God ! I can)
It falls from an eternal shrine.

II

The gay wall of this gaudy tower
Grows dim around me—death is near.
I had not thought, until this hour
When passing from the earth, that ear
Of any, were it not the shade
Of one whom in life I made   20
All mystery but a simple name,
Might know the secret of a spirit
Bow'd down in sorrow, and in shame.—
Shame, said'st thou ?
                Ay, I did inherit
That hated portion, with the fame,
The worldly glory, which has shown
A demon-light around my throne,
Scorching my sear'd heart with a pain
Not Hell shall make me fear again.

III

I have not always been as now—   30
The fever'd diadem on my brow
I claim'd and won usurpingly—
Ay—the same heritage hath given
Rome to the Caesar—this to me ;
The heirdom of a kingly mind—
And a proud spirit, which hath striven
Triumphantly with human kind.

In mountain air I first drew life ;
The mists of the Taglay have shed
Nightly their dews on my young head ;   40
And my brain drank their venom then,
When after day of perilous strife
With chamois, I would seize his den
And slumber, in my pride of power,
The infant monarch of the hour—

For, with the mountain dew by night,
My soul imbibed unhallow'd feeling ;
And I would feel its essence stealing
In dreams upon me—while the light
Flashing from cloud that hovered o'er,   50
Would seem to my half-closing eye
The pageantry of monarchy !
And the deep thunder's echoing roar
Came hurriedly upon me, telling
Of war, and tumult, where my voice,
My *own* voice, silly child ! was swelling
(O how would my wild heart rejoice
And leap within me at the cry)
The battle-cry of victory !

    . . . .

IV

  The rain came down upon my head   60
But barely shelter'd—and the wind
Pass'd quickly o'er me—but my mind
Was maddening—for 'twas man that shed
Laurels upon me—and the rush,
The torrent of the chilly air
Gurgled in my pleased ear the crush
Of empires, with the captive's prayer,
The hum of suitors, the mix'd tone
Of flattery round a sovereign's throne.

The storm had ceased—and I awoke—   70
Its spirit cradled me to sleep,
And as it pass'd me by, there broke
Strange light upon me, tho' it were
My soul in mystery to steep :
For I was not as I had been ;
The child of Nature, without care,
Or thought, save of the passing scene.—

V

My passions, from that hapless hour,
Usurp'd a tyranny, which men
Have deem'd, since I have reach'd to power,   80
My innate nature—be it so :

But, father, there lived one who, then—
Then, in my boyhood, when their fire
Burn'd with a still intenser glow ;
(For passion must with youth expire)
Even *then*, who deem'd this iron heart
In woman's weakness had a part.

I have no word, alas ! to tell
The loveliness of loving well !
Nor would I dare attempt to trace   90
The breathing beauty of a face,
Which even to *my* impassion'd mind,
Leaves not its memory behind.
In spring of life have ye ne'er dwelt
Some object of delight upon,
With steadfast eye, till ye have felt
The earth reel—and the vision gone ?
And I have held to memory's eye
One object—and but one—until
Its very form hath pass'd me by,   100
But left its influence with me still.

VI

'Tis not to thee that I should name—
Thou canst not—wouldst not dare to think
The magic empire of a flame
Which even upon this perilous brink
Hath fix'd my soul, tho' unforgiven,
By what it lost for passion—Heaven.
I loved—and O, how tenderly !
Yes ! she [was] worthy of all love !
Such as in infancy was mine,   110
Tho' then its *passion* could not be :
'Twas such as angel minds above
Might envy—her young heart the shrine
On which my every hope and thought
Were incense—then a goodly gift—
For they were childish, without sin,
Pure as her young example taught ;
Why did I leave it and adrift,
Trust to the fickle star within ?

VII

We grew in age and love together   120
Roaming the forest and the wild ;
My breast her shield in wintry weather,
And when the friendly sunshine smiled
And she would mark the opening skies,
I saw no Heaven but in her eyes—
Even childhood knows the human heart ;
For when, in sunshine and in smiles,
From all our little cares apart,
Laughing at her half silly wiles,
I'd throw me on her throbbing breast,   130
And pour my spirit out in tears,
She'd look up in my wilder'd eye—
There was no need to speak the rest—
No need to quiet her kind fears—
She did not ask the reason why.

The hallow'd memory of those years
Comes o'er me in these lonely hours,
And, with sweet loveliness, appears
As perfume of strange summer flowers ;
Of flowers which we have known before   140
In infancy, which seen, recall
To mind—not flowers alone—but more,
Our earthly life, and love—and all.

VIII

Yes ! she was worthy of all love !
Even such as from the accursed time
My spirit with the tempest strove,
When on the mountain peak alone,
Ambition lent it a new tone,
And bade it first to dream of crime,
My frenzy to her bosom taught :   150
We still were young : no purer thought
Dwelt in a seraph's breast than *thine* ;
For passionate love is still divine :
I loved her as an angel might
With ray of all living light

Which blazes upon Edis' shrine.
It is not surely sin to name,
With such as mine—that mystic flame,
I had no being but in thee !
The world with all its train of bright   160
And happy beauty (for to me
All was an undefined delight),
The world—its joy—its share of pain
Which I felt not—its bodied forms
Of varied being, which contain
The bodiless spirits of the storms,
The sunshine, and the calm—the ideal
And fleeting vanity of dreams,
Fearfully beautiful ! the real
Nothings of mid day waking life—   170
Of an enchanted life, which seems,
Now as I look back, the strife
Of some ill demon, with a power
Which left me in an evil hour,
All I that felt, or saw, or thought,
Crowding, confused became
(With thine unearthly beauty fraught)
Thou—and the nothing of a name.

IX

    The passionate spirit which hath known,
And deeply felt the silent tone   180
Of its own self-supremacy,—
(I speak thus openly to thee,
'Twere folly *now* to veil a thought
With which this aching breast is fraught)
The soul which feels its innate right—
The mystic empire and high power
Given by the energetic might
Of Genius, at its natal hour ;
Which knows (believe me at this time,
When falsehood were a tenfold crime,   190
There *is* a power in the high spirit
To *know* the fate it will inherit)
The soul, which knows such power, will still
Find *Pride* the ruler of its will.

Yes ! I was proud—and ye who know
The magic of that meaning word,
So oft perverted, will bestow
Your scorn, perhaps, when ye have heard
That the proud spirit had been broken,
The proud heart burst in agony   200
At one upbraiding word or token
Of her that heart's idolatry—
I was ambitious—have ye known
Its fiery passion ?—ye have not—
A cottager, I mark'd a throne
Of half the world, as all my own,
And murmur'd at such lowly lot !
But it hath pass'd me as a dream
Which, of light step, flies with the dew,
That kindling thought—did not the beam   210
Of Beauty, which did guide it through
The livelong summer day, oppress
My mind with double loveliness—

.   .   .   .   .

X
We walk'd together to the crown
Of a high mountain, which look'd down
Afar from its proud natural towers
Of rock and forest, on the hills—
The dwindled hills, whence amid bowers
Her own fair hand had rear'd around,
Gush'd shoutingly a thousand rills,   220
Which as it were, in fairy bound
Embraced two hamlets—those our own.—
Peacefully happy—yet alone—

.   .   .   .   .

I spoke to her of power and pride—
But mystically, in such guise,
That she might deem it nought beside
The moment's converse ; in her eyes
I read (perhaps too carelessly)
A mingled feeling with my own ;
The flush on her bright cheek, to me,   230
Seem'd to become a queenly throne
Too well, that I should let it be
A light in the dark wild, alone.

XI

There—in that hour—a thought came o'er
My mind, it had not known before—
To leave her while we both were young,—
To follow my high fate among
The Strife of nations, and redeem
The idle words, which, as a dream
Now sounded to her heedless ear—   240
I held no doubt—I knew no fear
Of peril in my wild career ;
To gain an empire, and throw down
As nuptial dowry—a queen's crown,
The only feeling which possest,
With her own image, my fond breast—
Who, that had known the secret thought
Of a young peasant's bosom then,
Had deem'd him, in compassion, aught
But one, whom fantasy had led   250
Astray from reason—Among men
Ambition is chain'd down—nor fed
(As in the desert, where the grand,
The wild, the beautiful, conspire
With their own breath to fan its fire)
With thoughts such feeling can command ;
Uncheck'd by sarcasm, and scorn
Of those, who hardly will conceive
That any should become ' great ', born
In their own sphere—will not believe   260
That they shall stoop in life to one
Whom daily they are wont to see
Familiarly—whom Fortune's sun
Hath ne'er shone dazzlingly upon,
Lowly—and of their own degree—

XII

I pictured to my fancy's eye
Her silent, deep astonishment,
When, a few fleeting years gone by
(For short the time my high hope lent
To its most desperate intent,)   270
She might recall in him, whom Fame

Had gilded with a conqueror's name
(With glory—such as might inspire
Perforce, a passing thought of one,
Whom she had deem'd in his own fire
Wither'd and blasted ; who had gone
A traitor, violate of the truth
So plighted in his early youth,)
Her own Alexis, who should plight
The love he plighted *then*—again,   280
And raise his infancy's delight,
The pride and queen of Tamerlane.—

XIII

One noon of a bright summer's day
I pass'd from out the matted bower
Where in a deep, still slumber lay
My Ada. In that peaceful hour
A silent gaze was my farewell.
I had no other solace—then
To awake her, and a falsehood tell
Of a feign'd journey, were again   290
To trust the weakness of my heart
To her soft thrilling voice : to part
Thus, haply, while in sleep she dream'd
Of long delight, nor yet had deem'd
Awake, that I had held a thought
Of parting, were with madness fraught ;
I knew not woman's heart, alas !
Tho' loved, and loving—let it pass.—

XIV

I went from out the matted bower,
And hurried madly on my way :   300
And felt, with every flying hour,
That bore me from my home, more gay
There is of earth an agony
Which, ideal, still may be
The worst ill of mortality.
'Tis bliss, in its own reality,
Too real, to *his* breast who lives
Nor within himself but gives

A portion of his willing soul
To God, and to the great whole—   310
To him, whose loving Spirit will dwell
With Nature, in her wild paths : tell
Of her wondrous ways, and telling bless
Her overpowering loveliness !
A more than agony to him
Whose failing sight will grow dim
With its own living gaze upon
That loveliness around : the sun—
The blue sky—the misty light
Of the pale cloud therein, whose hue   320
Is grace to its heavenly bed of blue ;
Dim ! tho' looking on all bright !
O God ! when the thoughts that may not pass
Will burst upon him, and alas !
For the flight on Earth to Fancy given,
There are no words—unless of Heaven.

XV

. . . .

Look round thee now on Samarcand,
Is she not queen of earth ? her pride
Above all cities ? in her hand
Their destinies ? with all beside   330
Of glory, which the world hath known ?
Stands she not proudly and alone ?
And who her Sovereign ? Timur, he
Whom the astonish'd earth hath seen,
With victory, on victory,
Redoubling age ! and more, I ween,
The Zinghis' yet re-echoing fame.
And now what has he ? what ! a name.
The sound of revelry by night
Comes o'er me, with the mingled voice   340
Of many with a breast as light,
As if 'twere not the dying hour
Of one, in whom they did rejoice—
As in a leader, haply—Power
Its venom secretly imparts :
Nothing have I with human hearts.

XVI

When Fortune mark'd me for her own,
And my proud hopes had reach'd a throne
(It boots me not, good friar, to tell
A tale the world but knows too well,   350
How by what hidden deeds of might,
I clamber'd to the tottering height,)
I still was young ; and well I ween
My spirit what it e'er had been.
My eyes were still on pomp and power,
My wilder'd heart was far away
In valleys of the wild Taglay,
In mine own Ada's matted bower.
I dwelt not long in Samarcand
Ere, in a peasant's lowly guise,   360
I sought my long-abandon'd land ;
By sunset did its mountains rise
In dusky grandeur to my eyes :
But as I wander'd on the way
My heart sunk with the sun's ray.
To him who still would gaze upon
The glory of the summer sun,
There comes, when that sun will from him part,
A sullen hopelessness of heart.
That soul will hate the evening mist   370
So often lovely, and will list
To the sound of the coming darkness (known
To those whose spirits hearken) as one
Who in a dream of night *would* fly,
But cannot, from a danger nigh.
What though the moon—the silvery moon—
Shine on his path, in her high noon ;
Her smile is chilly, and *her* beam
In that time of dreariness will seem
As the portrait of one after death ;   380
A likeness taken when the breath
Of young life, and the fire of the eye,
Had lately been, but had pass'd by.
'Tis thus when the lovely summer sun
Of our boyhood his course hath run :

For all we live to know—is known ;
And all we seek to keep—hath flown ;
With the noonday beauty, which is all.
Let life, then, as the day-flower, fall—
The transient, passionate day-flower,   390
Withering at the evening hour.

XVII

I reach'd my home—my home no more—
For all was flown that made it so—
I pass'd from out its mossy door,
In vacant idleness of woe.
There met me on its threshold stone
A mountain hunter, I had known
In childhood, but he knew me not.
Something he spoke of the old cot :
It had seen better days, he said ;   400
There rose a fountain once, and *there*
Full many a fair flower raised its head :
But she who reared them was long dead,
And in such follies had no part,
What was there left me *now* ? despair—
A kingdom for a broken—heart.

NOTES ON TAMERLANE

1827 TEXT

1. 1. *I have sent for thee, holy friar.* Of the history of Tamerlane
little is known ; and with that little I have taken the full liberty of
a poet.—That he was descended from the family of Zinghis Khan is
more than probable—but he is vulgarly supposed to have been the son
of a shepherd, and to have raised himself to the throne by his own
address. He died in the year 1405, in the time of Pope Innocent VII.

How I shall account for giving him ' a friar ', as a death-bed con-
fessor—I cannot exactly determine. He wanted some one to listen
to his tale—and why not a friar ? It does not pass the bounds of possibility—quite sufficient for my purpose—and I have at least good
authority for such innovations.

1. 39. *The mists of the Taglay have shed.* The mountains of Belur
Taglay are a branch of the Imaus, in the southern part of Independent
Tartary. They are celebrated for the singular wildness and beauty
of their valleys.

11. 151–2. *No purer thought Dwelt in a seraph's breast than thine.*
I must beg the reader's pardon for making Tamerlane, a Tartar of the

fourteenth century, speak in the same language as a Boston gentleman of the nineteenth ; but of the Tartar mythology we have little information.

1. 156. *Which blazes upon Edis' shrine.* A deity presiding over virtuous love, upon whose imaginary altar a sacred fire was continually blazing.

11. 258–60. *who hardly will conceive That any should become ' great ', born In their own sphere.* Although Tamerlane speaks this, it is not the less true. It is a matter of the greatest difficulty to make the generality of mankind believe that one with whom they are upon terms of intimacy shall be called, in the world, a ' great man '. The reason is evident. There are few great men. Their actions are consequently viewed by the mass of the people through the medium of distance. The prominent parts of their characters are alone noted ; and those properties, which are minute and common to every one, not being observed, seem to have no connection with a great character.

Who ever read the private memorials, correspondence, &c., which have become so common in our time, without wondering that ' great men ' should act and think ' so abominably ' ?

1. 279. *Her own Alexis, who should plight.* That Tamerlane acquired his renown under a feigned name is not entirely a fiction.

1. 327. *Look round thee now on Samarcand.* I believe it was after the battle of Angora that Tamerlane made Samarcand his residence. It became for a time the seat of learning and the arts.

1. 333. *And who her sovereign ? Timur.* He was called Timur Bek as well as Tamerlane.

1. 337. *The Zinghis' yet re-echoing fame.* The conquests of Tamerlane far exceeded those of Zinghis Khan. He boasted to have two-thirds of the world at his command.

11. 372–3. *the sound of the coming darkness (known To those whose spirits hearken).* I have often fancied that I could distinctly hear the sound of the darkness, as it steals over the horizon—a foolish fancy, perhaps, but not more unintelligible than to see music—

The mind the music breathing from her face.

1. 389. *Let life, then, as the day-flower, fall.* There is a flower (I have never known its botanic name) vulgarly called the day-flower. It blooms beautifully in the daylight, but withers towards evening, and by night its leaves appear totally shrivelled and dead. I have forgotten, however, to mention in the text, that it lives again in the morning. If it will not flourish in Tartary, I must be forgiven for carrying it thither

A ROMANCE

[*Poems by Edgar A. Poe*, 1831.   Here called ' Introduction '.]

ROMANCE, who loves to nod and sing,
With drowsy head and folded wing,
Among the green leaves as they shake
Far down within some shadowy lake,
To me a painted paroquet
Hath been—a most familiar bird—
Taught me my alphabet to say,—
To lisp my very earliest word
While in the wild-wood I did lie,
A child—with a most knowing eye.   10

Succeeding years, too wild for song,
Then roll'd like tropic storms along,
Where, tho' the garish lights that fly
Dying along the troubled sky,
Lay bare, thro' vistas thunder-riven,
The blackness of the general Heaven,
That very blackness yet doth fling
Light on the lightning's silver wing.

For, being an idle boy lang syne,
Who read Anacreon, and drank wine,   20
I early found Anacreon rhymes
Were almost passionate sometimes—
And by strange alchemy of brain
His pleasures always turn'd to pain—
His naïveté to wild desire—
His wit to love—his wine to fire—
And so, being young and dipt in folly,
I fell in love with melancholy,
And used to throw my earthly rest
And quiet all away in jest—   30
I could not love except where Death
Was mingling his with Beauty's breath—
Or Hymen, Time, and Destiny
Were stalking between her and me.

O, then the eternal Condor years
So shook the very Heavens on high,
With tumult as they thunder'd by :
I had no time for idle cares,
Thro' gazing on the unquiet sky !
Or if an hour with calmer wing   40
Its down did on my spirit fling,
That little hour with lyre and rhyme
To while away—forbidden thing !
My heart half fear'd to be a crime
Unless it trembled with the string.

But *now* my soul hath too much room—
Gone are the glory and the gloom—
The black hath mellow'd into grey,
And all the fires are fading away.

My draught of passion hath been deep—   50
I revell'd, and I now would sleep—
And after-drunkenness of soul
Succeeds the glories of the bowl—
An idle longing night and day
To dream my very life away.

But dreams—of those who dream as I,
Aspiringly, are damned, and die :
Yet should I swear I mean alone,
By notes so very shrilly blown,
To break upon Time's monotone,   60
While yet my vapid joy and grief
Are tintless of the yellow leaf—
Why not an imp the greybeard hath,
Will shake his shadow in my path—
And even the greybeard will o'erlook
Connivingly my dreaming-book.

FAIRY-LAND

[*Poems by Edgar A. Poe*, 1831.]

Sit down beside me, Isabel,
Here, dearest, where the moonbeam fell
Just now so fairy-like and well.
Now thou art dress'd for paradise !
I am star-stricken with thine eyes !
My soul is lolling on thy sighs !
Thy hair is lifted by the moon
Like flowers by the low breath of June !
Sit down, sit down—how came we here ?
Or is it all but a dream, my dear ?   10

You know that most enormous flower—
That rose—that what d'ye call it—that hung
Up like a dog-star in this bower—
To-day (the wind blew, and) it swung
So impudently in my face,
So like a thing alive you know,
I tore it from its pride of place
And shook it into pieces—so
Be all ingratitude requited.
The winds ran off with it delighted,   20
And, thro' the opening left, as soon
As she threw off her cloak, yon moon
Has sent a ray down with a tune.

And this ray is a *fairy* ray—
Did you not say so, Isabel ?
How fantastically it fell
With a spiral twist and swell,
And over the wet grass rippled away
With a tinkling like a bell !
In my own country all the way   30
We can discover a moon ray
Which thro' some tattered curtain pries
Into the darkness of a room,
Is by (the very source of gloom)

The moats, and dust, and flies,
On which it trembles and lies
Like joy upon sorrow !
O, *when* will come the morrow ?
Isabel ! do you not fear
The night and the wonders here ? 40
Dim vales ! and shadowy floods !
And cloudy-looking woods
Whose forms we can't discover
For the tears that drip all over !

Huge moons—see ! wax and wane—
Again—again—again—
Every moment of the night—
Forever changing places !
How they put out the starlight
With the breath from their pale faces ! 50

Lo ! one is coming down
With its centre on the crown
Of a mountain's eminence !
Down—still down—and down—
Now deep shall be—O deep !
The passion of our sleep !
For that wide circumference
In easy drapery falls
Drowsily over halls—
Over ruin'd walls— 60
Over waterfalls,
O'er the strange words—o'er the sea—
Alas ! over the sea !

THE LAKE

[Tamerlane and other Poems, 1827.]

IN youth's spring it was my lot
To haunt of the wide earth a spot
The which I could not love the less ;
So lovely was the loneliness
Of a wild lake, with black rock bound,
And the tall pines that tower'd around.

But when the night had thrown her pall
Upon that spot—as upon all,
And the wind would pass me by
In its stilly melody,   10
My infant spirit would awake
To the terror of the lone lake.
Yet that terror was not fright—
But a tremulous delight,
And a feeling undefined,
Springing from a darken'd mind.
Death was in that poison'd wave
And in its gulf a fitting grave
For him who thence could solace bring
To his dark imagining ;   20
Whose wildering thought could even make
An Eden of that dim lake.

THE BELLS—A SONG

[First Draft, 1848. Published in *Sartain's Union Magazine*, Dec. 1849.]

THE Bells !—hear the bells !
The merry wedding bells !
The little silver bells !
How fairy-like a melody there swells
From the silver tinkling cells
Of the bells, bells, bells !
Of the bells !

The Bells !—ah, the bells !
The heavy iron bells !
Hear the tolling of the bells !   10
Hear the knells !
How horrible a monody there floats
From their throats—
From their deep-toned throats !
How I shudder at the notes
From the melancholy throats
Of the bells, bells, bells !
Of the bells !

NOTE

The editor of *Sartain's Union Magazine* published 'The Bells', as we now have it, in November 1849; and the following month printed, as a literary curiosity, this 'First Draft' which, he says, 'came into our possession about a year since'.

'Poe wrote the first rough draft of "The Bells" at Mrs. Shew's residence. "One day he came in," she records,[1] "and said, 'Marie Louise, I have to write a poem: I have no feeling, no sentiment, no inspiration!'" His hostess persuaded him to have some tea. It was served in the conservatory, the windows of which were open, and admitted the sound of neighbouring church bells. Mrs. Shew said, playfully, "Here is paper"; but the poet, declining it, declared, "I so dislike the noise of bells to-night, I cannot write. I have no subject—I am exhausted." The lady then took up the pen, and, pretending to mimic his style, wrote, "The Bells, by E. A. Poe"; and then, in pure sportiveness, "The Bells, the little silver Bells", Poe finishing off the stanza. She then suggested for the next verse, "The heavy iron Bells"; and this Poe also expanded into a stanza. He next copied out the complete poem, and headed it, "By Mrs. M. L. Shew", remarking that it was her poem, as she had suggested and composed so much of it. Mrs. Shew continues, "My brother came in, and I sent him to Mrs. Clemm to tell her that 'her boy would stay in town, and was well'. My brother took Mr. Poe to his own room, where he slept twelve hours, and could hardly recall the evening's work." '—*Edgar Allan Poe, his Life, Letters, and Opinions*, by John H. Ingram 1880, vol. ii, pp. 155, 156.

TO —— ——

[Manuscript variation, entitled 'To Marie Louise'.]

Not long ago the writer of these lines,
In the mad pride of intellectuality,
Maintained ' the power of words '—denied that ever
A thought arose within the human brain
Beyond the utterance of the human tongue :
And now, as if in mockery of that boast
Two words—two foreign soft dissyllables—
Two gentle sounds made only to be murmured
By angels dreaming in the moon-lit dew
That hangs like chains of pearl on Hermon-hill   10
Have stirred from out the abysses of his heart
Unthought-like thoughts—scarcely the shades of thought—

---

[1] In her ' Diary '.

Bewildering fantasies—far richer visions
Than ever the seraph harper, Israfel,
Who ' had the sweetest voice of all God's creatures ',
Would hope to utter.   Ah, Marie Louise !
In deep humility I own that now
All pride—all thought of power—all hope of fame—
All wish for Heaven—is merged for evermore
Beneath the palpitating tide of passion   20
Heaped o'er my soul by thee.   Its spells are broken—
The pen falls powerless from my shivering hand—
With that dear name as text I *cannot* write—
I cannot speak—I cannot even think—
Alas ! I cannot feel ; for 'tis *not* feeling—
This standing motionless upon the golden
Threshold of the wide-open gate of Dreams,
Gazing, entranced, adown the gorgeous vista,
And thrilling as I see upon the right—
Upon the left—and all the way along,   30
Amid the clouds of glory : far away
To where the prospect terminates—*thee only*.

A DREAM WITHIN A DREAM

[*Tamerlane and other Poems*, 1827.   Here called ' Imitation '.]

A DARK unfathom'd tide
Of interminable pride—
A mystery, and a dream,
Should my early life seem ;
I say that dream was fraught
With a wild, and waking thought
Of beings that have been,
Which my spirit hath not seen,
Had I let them pass me by,
With a dreaming eye. !   10
Let none of earth inherit
That vision on my spirit ;
Those thoughts I would control,
As a spell upon his soul :
For that bright hope at last
And that light time have past,

And my worldly rest hath gone
With a sigh as it pass'd on :
I care not tho' it perish
With a thought I then did cherish.   20

A DREAM WITHIN A DREAM

[*Al Aaraaf, Tamerlane, and Minor Poems by Edgar A. Poe*, 1829.
Here called 'To ——'.]

SHOULD my early life seem
[As well it might] a dream—
Yet I build no faith upon
The king Napoleon—
I look not up afar
To my destiny in a star.

In parting from you now
Thus much I will avow—
There are beings, and have been
Whom my spirit had not seen ;   10
Had I let them pass me by
With a dreaming eye—
If my peace hath fled away
In a night—or in a day—
In a vision—or in none—
Is it therefore the less gone ?

I am standing 'mid the roar
Of a weather-beaten shore,
And I hold within my hand
Some particles of sand—   20
How few ! and how they creep
Thro' my fingers to the deep !
My early hopes ? no—they
Went gloriously away,
Like lightning from the sky
At once—and so will I.

So young ?   Ah ! no—not now—
Thou hast not seen my brow ;
But they tell thee I am proud—
They lie—they lie aloud—   30
My bosom beats with shame
At the paltriness of name
With which they dare combine
A feeling such as mine—
Nor Stoic ?   I am not :
In the terror of my lot
I laugh to think how poor
That pleasure ' to endure ! '
What !   shade of Zeus !—I !
Endure !—no—no—defy.   40

TALES

THE SYSTEM

OF

DOCTOR TARR AND PROFESSOR FETHER

DURING the autumn of 18—, while on a tour through the extreme southern provinces of France, my route led me within a few miles of a certain *Maison de Santé*, or private Mad-House, about which I had heard much, in Paris, from my medical friends. As I had never visited a place of the kind, I thought the opportunity too good to be lost ; and so proposed to my travelling companion (a gentleman with whom I had made casual acquaintance a few days before) that we should turn aside, for an hour or so, and look through the establishment. To this he objected—pleading haste, in the first place, and, in the second, a very usual horror at the sight of a lunatic. He begged me, however, not to let any mere courtesy towards himself interfere with the gratification of my curiosity, and said that he would ride on leisurely, so that I might overtake him during the day, or, at all events, during the next. As he bade me good-by, I bethought me that there might be some difficulty in obtaining access to the premises, and mentioned my fears on this point. He replied that, in fact, unless I had personal knowledge of the superintendent, Monsieur Maillard, or some credential in the way of a letter, a difficulty might be found to exist, as the regulations of these private mad-houses were more rigid than the public hospital laws. For himself, he added, he had, some years since, made the acquaintance of Maillard, and would so far assist me as to ride up to the door and introduce me ; although his feelings on the subject of lunacy would not permit of his entering the house.

I thanked him, and, turning from the main-road, we entered a grass-grown by-path, which, in half an hour, nearly lost itself in a dense forest, clothing the base of a mountain. Through this dank and gloomy wood we rode some two miles, when the *Maison de Santé* came in view. It was a fantastic *château*, much dilapidated, and indeed scarcely tenantable through age and neglect. Its aspect inspired me with absolute dread, and, checking my horse, I half resolved to turn back. I soon, however, grew ashamed of my weakness, and proceeded.

As we rode up to the gateway, I perceived it slightly open, and the visage of a man peering through. In an instant afterward, this man came forth, accosted my companion by name, shook him cordially by the hand, and begged him to alight. It was Monsieur Maillard himself. He was a portly, fine-looking gentleman of the old school, with a polished manner, and a certain air of gravity, dignity, and authority which was very impressive.

My friend, having presented me, mentioned my desire to inspect the establishment, and received Monsieur Maillard's assurance that he would show me all attention, now took leave, and I saw him no more.

When he had gone, the superintendent ushered me into a small and exceedingly neat parlour, containing among other indications of refined taste, many books, drawings, pots of flowers, and musical instruments. A cheerful fire blazed upon the hearth. At a piano, singing an aria from Bellini, sat a young and very beautiful woman, who, at my entrance, paused in her song, and received me with graceful courtesy. Her voice was low, and her whole manner subdued. I thought, too, that I perceived the traces of sorrow in her countenance, which was excessively, although to my taste, not unpleasingly pale. She was attired in deep mourning, and excited in my bosom a feeling of mingled respect, interest, and admiration.

I had heard, at Paris, that the institution of Monsieur Maillard was managed upon what is vulgarly termed the ' system of soothing '—that all punishments were avoided—that even confinement was seldom resorted to—that the patients, while secretly watched, were left much apparent liberty, and that most of them were permitted to roam about the house and grounds, in the ordinary apparel of persons in right mind.

Keeping these impressions in view, I was cautious in what I said before the young lady ; for I could not be sure that she was sané ; and, in fact, there was a certain restless brilliancy about her eyes which half led me to imagine she was not. I confined my remarks, therefore, to general topics, and to such as I thought would not be displeasing or exciting even to a lunatic. She replied in a perfectly rational manner to all that I said ; and even her original observations were marked with the soundest good sense ; but a long acquaintance with the metaphysics of *mania*, had taught me to put no faith in such evidence of sanity, and I continued to practice, throughout the interview, the caution with which I commenced it.

Presently a smart footman in livery brought in a tray with fruit, wine, and other refreshments, of which I partook, the lady soon afterwards leaving the room. As she departed I turned my eyes in an inquiring manner towards my host.

' No,' he said, ' oh, no—a member of my family—my niece, and a most accomplished woman.'

' I beg a thousand pardons for the suspicion,' I replied, ' but of course you will know how to excuse me. The excellent administration of your affairs here is well understood in Paris, and I thought it just possible, you know—'

' Yes, yes—say no more—or rather it is myself who should thank you for the commendable prudence you have displayed. We seldom find so much of forethought in young men ; and, more than once, some unhappy *contretemps* has occurred in consequence of thoughtlessness on the part of our visitors. While my former system was in operation, and my patients were permitted the privilege of roaming to and fro at will, they were often aroused to a dangerous frenzy by injudicious persons who called to inspect the house. Hence I was obliged to enforce a rigid system of exclusion ; and none obtained access to the premises upon whose discretion I could not rely.'

' While your *former* system was in operation ! ' I said, repeating his words—' do I understand you, then, to say that the " soothing system " of which I have heard so much, is no longer in force ? '

' It is now ', he replied, ' several weeks since we have concluded to renounce it forever.'

'Indeed! you astonish me!'

'We found it, sir,' he said, with a sigh, 'absolutely necessary to return to the old usages. The *danger* of the soothing system was, at all times, appalling; and its advantages have been much over-rated. I believe, sir, that in this house it has been given a fair trial, if ever in any. We did everything that rational humanity could suggest. I am sorry that you could not have paid us a visit at an earlier period, that you might have judged for yourself. But I presume you are conversant with the soothing practice—with its details.'

'Not altogether. What I have heard has been at third or fourth hand.'

'I may state the system then, in general terms, as one in which the patients were *ménagés*, humoured. We contradicted *no* fancies which entered the brains of the mad. On the contrary, we not only indulged but encouraged them; and many of our most permanent cures have been thus effected. There is no argument which so touches the feeble reason of the madman as the *reductio ad absurdum*. We have had men, for example, who fancied themselves chickens. The cure was, to insist upon the thing as a fact— to accuse the patient of stupidity in not sufficiently perceiving it to be a fact—and thus to refuse him any other diet for a week than that which properly appertains to a chicken. In this manner a little corn and gravel were made to perform wonders.'

'But was this species of acquiescence all?'

'By no means. We put much faith in amusements of a simple kind, such as music, dancing, gymnastic exercises generally, cards, certain classes of books, and so forth. We affected to treat each individual as if for some ordinary physical disorder; and the word 'lunacy' was never employed. A great point was to set each lunatic to guard the actions of all the others. To repose confidence in the understanding or discretion of a madman, is to gain him body and soul. In this way we were enabled to dispense with an expensive body of keepers.'

'And you had no punishments of any kind?'

'None.'

'And you never confined your patients?'

'Very rarely. Now and then, the malady of some individual growing to a crisis, or taking a sudden turn of fury, we conveyed him to a secret cell, lest his disorder should infect the rest, and there kept him until we could dismiss him to his friends—for with the raging maniac we have nothing to do. He is usually removed to the public hospitals.'

'And you have now changed all this—and you think for the better ? '

'Decidedly. The system had its disadvantages, and even its dangers. It is now, happily, exploded throughout all the *Maisons de Santé* of France.'

'I am very much surprised', I said, 'at what you tell me ; for I made sure that, at this moment, no other method of treatment for mania existed in any portion of the country.'

'You are young yet, my friend,' replied my host, 'but the time will arrive when you will learn to judge for yourself of what is going on in the world, without trusting to the gossip of others. Believe nothing you hear, and only one-half that you see. Now, about our *Maisons de Santé*, it is clear that some ignoramus has misled you. After dinner, however, when you have sufficiently recovered from the fatigue of your ride, I will be happy to take you over the house, and introduce to you a system which, in my opinion, and in that of every one who has witnessed its operation, is incomparably the most effectual as yet devised.'

'Your own ? ' I inquired—' one of your own invention ? '

'I am proud ', he replied, 'to acknowledge that it is—at least in some measure.'

In this manner I conversed with Monsieur Maillard for an hour or two, during which he showed me the gardens and conservatories of the place.

'I cannot let you see my patients ', he said, 'just at present. To a sensitive mind there is always more or less of the shocking in such exhibitions ; and I do not wish to spoil your appetite for dinner. We will dine. I can give you some veal *à la Menehoult*, with cauliflowers in *velouté* sauce—after that a glass of *Clos-Vougeot*—then your nerves will be sufficiently steadied.'

At six, dinner was announced ; and my host conducted

me into a large *salle à manger*, where a very numerous
company were assembled—twenty-five or thirty in all.
They were, apparently, people of rank—certainly of high
breeding—although their habiliments, I thought, were
extravagantly rich, partaking somewhat too much of the
ostentatious finery of the *vielle cour*. I noticed that at
least two-thirds of these guests were ladies ; and some of
the latter were by no means accoutred in what a Parisian
would consider good taste at the present day. Many
females, for example, whose age could not have been less
than seventy, were bedecked with a profusion of jewelry,
such as rings, bracelets, and ear-rings, and wore their
bosoms and arms shamefully bare. · I observed, too, that
very few of the dresses were well made—or, at least, that
very few of them fitted the wearers. In looking about,
I discovered the interesting girl to whom Monsieur Maillard
had presented me in the little parlour ; but my surprise
was great to see her wearing a hoop and farthingale, with
high-heeled shoes, and a dirty cap of Brussels lace, so much
too large for her that it gave her face a ridiculously diminutive expression. When I had first seen her, she was attired,
most becomingly, in deep mourning. There was an air of
oddity, in short, about the dress of the whole party, which,
at first, caused me to recur to my original idea of the
' soothing system ', and to fancy that Monsieur Maillard
had been willing to deceive me until after dinner, that I
might experience no uncomfortable feelings during the
repast, at finding myself dining with lunatics ; but I
remembered having been informed, in Paris, that the
southern provincialists were a peculiarly eccentric people,
with a vast number of antiquated notions ; and then, too,
upon conversing with several members of the company, my
apprehensions were immediately and fully dispelled.

The dining-room, itself, although perhaps sufficiently
comfortable, and of good dimensions, had nothing too
much of elegance about it. For example, the floor was
uncarpeted ; in France however, a carpet is frequently
dispensed with. The windows, too, were without curtains ;
the shutters, being shut, were securely fastened with iron
bars, applied diagonally, after the fashion of our ordinary
shop-shutters. The apartment, I observed, formed, in itself,

a wing of the *château*, and thus the windows were on three sides of the parallelogram ; the door being at the other. There were no less than ten windows in all.

The table was superbly set out. It was loaded with plate, and more than loaded with delicacies. The profusion was absolutely barbaric. There were meats enough to have feasted the Anakim. Never, in all my life, had I witnessed so lavish, so wasteful an expenditure of the good things of life. There seemed very little taste, however, in the arrangements ; and my eyes, accustomed to quiet lights, were sadly offended by the prodigious glare of a multitude of wax candles, which, in silver candelabra, were deposited upon the table, and all about the room, wherever it was possible to find a place. There were several active servants in attendance ; and, upon a large table, at the farther end of the apartment, were seated seven or eight people with fiddles, fifes, trombones, and a drum. These fellows annoyed me very much, at intervals, during the repast, by an infinite variety of noises, which were intended for music, and which appeared to afford much entertainment to all present, with the exception of myself.

Upon the whole, I could not help thinking that there was much of the *bizarre* about everything I saw—but then the world is made up of all kinds of persons, with all modes of thought, and all sorts of conventional customs. I had travelled, too, so much as to be quite an adept in the *nil admirari* ; so I took my seat very coolly at the right hand of my host, and, having an excellent appetite, did justice to the good cheer set before me.

The conversation, in the mean time, was spirited and general. The ladies, as usual, talked a great deal. I soon found that nearly all the company were well educated ; and my host was a world of good-humoured anecdote in himself. He seemed quite willing to speak of his position as superintendent of a *Maison de Santé ;* and, indeed, the topic of lunacy was, much to my surprise, a favourite one with all present. A great many amusing stories were told, having reference to the *whims* of the patients.

' We had a fellow here once,' said a fat little gentleman, who sat at my right—' a fellow that fancied himself a tea-pot ; and, by the way, is it not especially singular how often

this particular crotchet has entered the brain of the lunatic ?
There is scarcely an insane asylum in France which cannot
supply a human tea-pot. *Our* gentleman was a Britannia-
ware tea-pot, and was careful to polish himself every
morning with buckskin and whiting.'

'And then', said a tall man, just opposite, 'we had here,
not long ago, a person who had taken it into his head that
he was a donkey—which, allegorically speaking, you will
say, was quite true. He was a troublesome patient ; and
we had much ado to keep him within bounds. For a long
time he would eat nothing but thistles ; but of this idea
we soon cured him by insisting upon his eating nothing
else. Then he was perpetually kicking out his heels—
so—so—'

'Mr. De Kock ! I will thank you to behave yourself ! '
here interrupted an old lady, who sat next to the speaker.
'Please keep your feet to yourself ! You have spoiled my
brocade ! Is it necessary, pray, to illustrate a remark in so
practical a style ? Our friend, here, can surely comprehend
you without all this. Upon my word, you are nearly as
great a donkey as the poor unfortunate imagined himself.
Your acting is very natural, as I live.'

'*Mille pardons ! Mam'selle !* ' replied Monsieur De Kock,
thus addressed—' a thousand pardons ! I had no intention
of offending. Mam'selle Laplace—Monsieur De Kock will
do himself the honour of taking wine with you.'

Here Monsieur De Kock bowed low, kissed his hand with
much ceremony, and took wine with Mam'selle Laplace.

'Allow me, *mon ami*,' now said Monsieur Maillard,
addressing myself, 'allow me to send you a morsel of
this veal *à la St. Menehoult*—you will find it particularly
fine.'

At this instant three sturdy waiters had just succeeded
in depositing safely upon the table an enormous dish, or
trencher, containing what I supposed to be the ' *monstrum,
horrendum, informe, ingens, cui lumen ademptum* '. A closer
scrutiny assured me, however, that it was only a small calf
roasted whole, and set upon its knees, with an apple in its
mouth, as is the English fashion of dressing a hare.

'Thank you, no,' I replied ; 'to say the truth, I am not
particularly partial to veal *à la St.*—what is it ?—for I do

not find that it altogether agrees with me. I will change my plate, however, and try some of the rabbit.'

There were several side-dishes on the table, containing what appeared to be the ordinary French rabbit—a very delicious *morceau*, which I can recommend.

'Pierre,' cried the host, 'change this gentleman's plate, and give him a side-piece of this rabbit *au-chat*.'

'This what?' said I.

'This rabbit *au-chat*.'

'Why, thank you—upon second thoughts, no. I will just help myself to some of the ham.'

There is no knowing what one eats, thought I to myself, at the tables of these people of the province. I will have none of their rabbit *au-chat*—and, for the matter of that, none of their *cat-au-rabbit* either.

'And then,' said a cadaverous-looking personage, near the foot of the table, taking up the thread of the conversation where it had been broken off—'and then, among other oddities, we had a patient, once upon a time, who very pertinaciously maintained himself to be a Cordova cheese, and went about, with a knife in his hand, soliciting his friends to try a small slice from the middle of his leg.'

'He was a great fool, beyond doubt,' interposed some one, 'but not to be compared with a certain individual whom we all know, with the exception of this strange gentleman. I mean the man who took himself for a bottle of champagne, and always went off with a pop and a fizz, in this fashion.'

Here the speaker, very rudely, as I thought, put his right thumb in his left cheek, withdrew it with a sound resembling the popping of a cork, and then, by a dexterous movement of the tongue upon the teeth, created a sharp hissing and fizzing, which lasted for several minutes, in imitation of the frothing of champagne. This behaviour, I saw plainly, was not very pleasing to Monsieur Maillard; but that gentleman said nothing, and the conversation was resumed by a very lean little man in a big wig.

'And then there was an ignoramus', said he, 'who mistook himself for a frog; which, by the way, he resembled in no little degree. I wish you could have seen

him, sir,'—here the speaker addressed myself—' it would
have done your heart good to see the natural airs that he
put on. Sir, if that man was *not* a frog, I can only observe
that it is a pity he was not. His croak thus—o-o-o-o-gh—
o-o-o-o-gh ! was the finest note in the world—B flat ; and
when he put his elbows upon the table thus—after taking
a glass or two of wine—and distended his mouth, thus, and
rolled up his eyes, thus, and winked them with excessive
rapidity, thus, why then, sir, I take it upon myself to say,
positively, that you would have been lost in admiration
of the genius of the man.'

' I have no doubt of it,' I said.

' And then,' said somebody else, ' then there was Petit
Gaillard, who thought himself a pinch of snuff, and was
truly distressed because he could not take himself between
his own finger and thumb.'

' And then there was Jules Desoulières, who was a very
singular genius indeed, and went mad with the idea that
he was a pumpkin. He persecuted the cook to make him
up into pies—a thing which the cook indignantly refused to
do. For my part, I am by no means sure that a pumpkin
pie *à la Desoulières*, would not have been very capital
eating, indeed ! '

' You astonish me ! ' said I ; and I looked inquisitively
at Monsieur Maillard.

' Ha ! ha ! ha ! ' said that gentleman—' he ! he ! he !—
hi ! hi ! hi !—ho ! ho ! ho !—hu ! hu ! hu !—very good
indeed ! You must not be astonished, *mon ami ;* our friend
here is a wit—a *drôle*—you must not understand him to the
letter.'

' And then,' said some other one of the party, ' then
there was Bouffon Le Grand—another extraordinary
personage in his way. He grew deranged through love, and
fancied himself possessed of two heads. One of these he
maintained to be the head of Cicero ; the other he imagined
a composite one, being Demosthenes' from the top of the
forehead to the mouth, and Lord Brougham from the
mouth to the chin. It is not impossible that he was wrong ;
but he would have convinced you of his being in the right ;
for he was a man of great eloquence. He had an absolute
passion for oratory, and could not refrain from display.

For example, he used to leap upon the dinner-table thus, and—and—'

Here a friend, at the side of the speaker, put a hand upon his shoulder, and whispered a few words in his ear ; upon which he ceased talking with great suddenness, and sank back within his chair.

'And then ', said the friend, who had whispered, ' there was Boullard, the teetotum. I call him the teetotum, because, in fact, he was seized with the droll, but not altogether irrational crotchet, that he had been converted into a teetotum. You would have roared with laughter to see him spin. He would turn round upon one heel by the hour, in this manner—so—'

Here the friend whom he had just interrupted by a whisper, performed an exactly similar office for himself.

'But then,' cried an old lady, at the top of her voice, ' your Monsieur Boullard was a madman, and a very silly madman at best ; for who, allow me to ask you, ever heard of a human teetotum ? The thing is absurd. Madame Joyeuse was a more sensible person, as you know. She had a crotchet, but it was instinct with common sense, and gave pleasure to all who had the honour of her acquaintance. She found, upon mature deliberation, that, by some accident, she had been turned into a chicken-cock ; but, as such, she behaved with propriety. She flapped her wings with prodigious effect—so—so—so—and, as for her crow, it was delicious ! Cock-a-doodle-doo !—cock-a-doodle-doo– cock-a-doodle-de-doo-doo-dooo-do-o-o-o-o-o-o- ! '

'Madame Joyeuse, I will thank you to behave yourself ! ' here interrupted our host, very angrily. ' You can either conduct yourself as a lady should do, or you can quit the table forthwith—take your choice.'

The lady (whom I was much astonished to hear addressed as Madame Joyeuse, after the description of Madame Joyeuse she had just given) blushed up to the eyebrows, and seemed exceedingly abashed at the reproof. She hung down her head, and said not a syllable in reply. But another and younger lady resumed the theme. It was my beautiful girl of the little parlour !

'Oh, Madame Joyeuse *was* a fool ! ' she exclaimed ; ' but there was really much sound sense, after all, in the

opinion of Eugénie Salsafette. She was a very beautiful
and painfully modest young lady, who thought the ordinary
mode of habiliment indecent, and wished to dress herself,
always, by getting outside, instead of inside of her clothes.
It is a thing very easily done, after all. You have only to
do so—and then so—so—so—and then so—so—so—and
then—'

'Mon dieu! Mam'selle Salsafette!' here cried a dozen
voices at once. 'What *are* you about?—forbear!—that is
sufficient!—we see, very plainly, how it is done!—hold!
hold!' and several persons were already leaping from their
seats to withold Mam'selle Salsafette from putting herself
upon a par with the Medicean Venus, when the point was
very effectually and suddenly accomplished by a series of
loud screams, or yells, from some portion of the main body
of the *château*.

My nerves were very much affected, indeed, by these
yells; but the rest of the company I really pitied. I never
saw any set of reasonable people so thoroughly frightened
in my life. They all grew as pale as so many corpses, and,
shrinking within their seats, sat quivering and gibbering
with terror, and listening for a repetition of the sound. It
came again—louder and seemingly nearer—and then a third
time *very* loud, and then a fourth time with a vigour
evidently diminished. At this apparent dying away of the
noise, the spirits of the company were immediately regained,
and all was life and anecdote as before. I now ventured to
inquire the cause of the disturbance.

'A mere *bagatelle*,' said Monsieur Maillard. 'We are
used to these things, and care really very little about them.
The lunatics, every now and then, get up a howl in concert;
one starting another, as is sometimes the case with a bevy
of dogs at night. It occasionally happens, however, that
the *concerto* yells are succeeded by a simultaneous effort at
breaking loose; when, of course, some little danger is to
be apprehended.'

'And how many have you in charge?'

'At present, we have not more than ten, altogether.'

'Principally females, I presume?'

'Oh, no—every one of them men, and stout fellows, too,
I can tell you.'

'Indeed! I have always understood that the majority of lunatics were of the gentler sex.'

'It is generally so, but not always. Some time ago, there were about twenty-seven patients here ; and, of that number, no less than eighteen were women ; but, lately, matters have changed very much, as you see.'

'Yes—have changed very much, as you see,' here interrupted the gentleman who had broken the shins of Mam'selle Laplace.

'Yes—have changed very much as you see ! ' chimed in the whole company at once.

'Hold your tongues, every one of you ! ' said my host, in a great rage. Whereupon the whole company maintained a dead silence for nearly a minute. As for one lady, she obeyed Monsieur Maillard to the letter, and thrusting out her tongue, which was an excessively long one, held it very resignedly, with both hands, until the end of the entertainment.

'And this gentlewoman,' said I, to Monsieur Maillard, bending over and addressing him in a whisper—'this good lady who has just spoken, and who gives us the cock-a-doodle-de-doo—she, I presume, is harmless—quite harmless, eh ? '

'Harmless ! ' ejaculated he, in unfeigned surprise, 'why—why what *can* you mean ? '

'Only slightly touched ? ' said I, touching my head. 'I take it for granted that she is not particularly—not dangerously affected, eh ? '

'*Mon Dieu!* what *is* it you imagine ? This lady, my particular old friend, Madame Joyeuse, is as absolutely sane as myself. She has her little eccentricities, to be sure—but then, you know, all old women—all *very* old women are more or less eccentric ! '

'To be sure,' said I—'to be sure—and then the rest of these ladies and gentlemen—'

'Are my friends and keepers,' interrupted Monsieur Maillard, drawing himself up with *hauteur*—' my very good friends and assistants.'

'What! all of them ? ' I asked—'the women and all ? '

'Assuredly,' he said—'we could not do at all without

the women ; they are the best lunatic nurses in the world ; they have a way of their own, you know ; their bright eyes have a marvellous effect ;—something like the fascination of the snake, you know.'

' To be sure,' said I—' to be sure ! They behave a little odd, eh ?—they are a little *queer*, eh ?—don't you think so ? '

' Odd !—queer !—why, do you *really* think so ? We are not very prudish, to be sure, here in the South—do pretty much as we please—enjoy life, and all that sort of thing, you know—'

' To be sure,' said I—' to be sure.'

' And then, perhaps, this *Clos-Vougeot* is a little heady, you know—a little *strong*—you understand, eh ? '

' To be sure,' said I—' to be sure. By-the-by, monsieur, did I understand you to say that the system you have adopted, in place of the celebrated soothing system, was one of very rigorous severity ? '

' By no means. Our confinement is necessarily close ; but the treatment—the medical treatment, I mean—is agreeable to the patients than otherwise.'

' And the new system is one of your own invention ? '

' Not altogether. Some portions of it are referable to Professor Tarr, of whom you have, necessarily, heard ; and, again, there are modifications in my plan which I am happy to acknowledge as belonging of right to the celebrated Fether, with whom, if I mistake not, you have the honour of an intimate acquaintance.'

' I am quite ashamed to confess,' I replied, ' that I have never even heard the name of either gentleman before.'

' Good Heavens ! ' ejaculated my host, drawing back his chair abruptly, and uplifting his hands. ' I surely do not hear you aright ! You did not intend to say, eh ? that you had never *heard* either of the learned Doctor Tarr, or of the celebrated Professor Fether ? '

' I am forced to acknowledge my ignorance,' I replied ; ' but the truth should be held inviolate above all things. Nevertheless, I feel humbled to the dust, not to be acquainted with the works of these, no doubt, extraordinary men. I will seek out their writings forthwith, and peruse them with deliberate care. Monsieur Maillard, you have really—I must confess it—you have *really*—made me ashamed of myself ! '

And this was the fact.

' Say no more, my good young friend,' he said kindly, pressing my hand—' join me now in a glass of Sauterne.'

We drank. The company followed our example, without stint. They chatted—they jested—they laughed—they perpetrated a thousand absurdities—the fiddles shrieked—the drum row-de-dowed—the trombones bellowed like so many brazen bulls of Phalaris—and the whole scene, growing gradually worse and worse, as the wines gained the ascendancy, became at length a sort of Pandemonium *in petto*. In the meantime, Monsieur Maillard and myself, with some bottles of Sauterne and Vougeot between us, continued our conversation at the top of the voice. A word spoken in an ordinary key stood no more chance of being heard than the voice of a fish from the bottom of Niagara Falls.

' And, sir,' said I, screaming in his ear, ' you mentioned something before dinner, about the danger incurred in the old system of soothing. How is that ? '

' Yes,' he replied, ' there was, occasionally, very great danger, indeed. There is no accounting for the caprices of madmen ; and, in my opinion, as well as in that of Doctor Tarr and Professor Fether, it is *never* safe to permit them to run at large unattended. A lunatic may be " soothed ", as it is called, for a time, but, in the end, he is very apt to become obstreperous. His cunning, too, is proverbial, and great. If he has a project in view, he conceals his design with a marvellous wisdom ; and the dexterity with which he counterfeits sanity, presents, to the metaphysician, one of the most singular problems in the study of mind. When a madman appears *thoroughly* sane, indeed, it is high time to put him in a strait jacket.'

' But the *danger*, my dear sir, of which you were speaking —in your own experience—during your control of this house—have you had practical reason to think liberty hazardous, in the case of a lunatic ? '

' Here ?—in my own experience ?—why, I may say, yes. For example :—no *very* long while ago, a singular circumstance occurred in this very house. The " soothing system ", you know, was then in operation, and the patients were at large. They behaved remarkably well—especially so—any one of sense might have known that some devilish scheme was brewing from that particular fact, that the fellows behaved so *remarkably* well. And, sure enough, one fine morning the keepers found themselves pinioned hand and foot, and thrown into the cells, where they were attended, as if *they* were the lunatics, by the lunatics themselves, who had usurped the offices of the keepers.'

'You don't tell me so! I never heard of anything so absurd in my life!'

'Fact—it all came to pass by means of a stupid fellow—a lunatic—who, by some means, had taken it into his head that he had invented a better system of government than any ever heard of before—of lunatic government, I mean. He wished to give his invention a trial, I suppose—and so he persuaded the rest of the patients to join him in a conspiracy for the overthrow of the reigning powers.'

'And he really succeeded?'

'No doubt of it. The keepers and kept were soon made to exchange places. Not that exactly either—for the madmen had been free, but the keepers were shut up in cells forthwith, and treated, I am sorry to say, in a very cavalier manner.'

'But I presume a counter-revolution was soon effected. This condition of things could not have long existed. The country people in the neighbourhood—visitors coming to see the establishment—would have given the alarm.'

'There you are out. The head rebel was too cunning for that. He admitted no visitors at all—with the exception, one day, of a very stupid-looking young gentleman of whom he had no reason to be afraid. He let him in to see the place—just by way of variety—to have a little fun with him. As soon as he had gammoned him sufficiently, he let him out, and sent him about his business.'

'And *how* long, then, did the madmen reign?'

'Oh, a very long time indeed—a month certainly—how much longer I can't precisely say. In the mean time, the lunatics had a jolly season of it—that you may swear. They doffed their own shabby clothes, and made free with the family wardrobe and jewels. The cellars of the *château*

were well stocked with wine ; and these madmen are just
the devils that know how to drink it. They lived well, I
can tell you.'

' And the treatment—what was the particular species of
treatment which the leader of the rebels put into operation ? '

' Why, as for that, a madman is not necessarily a fool, as
I have already observed ; and it is my honest opinion that
his treatment was a much better treatment than that which
it superseded. It was a very capital system indeed—simple
—neat—no trouble at all—in fact it was delicious—it
was—'

Here my host's observations were cut short by another
series of yells, of the same character as those which had
previously disconcerted us. This time, however, they
seemed to proceed from persons rapidly approaching.

' Gracious Heavens ! ' I ejaculated—' the lunatics have
most undoubtedly broken loose.'

' I very much fear it is so,' replied Monsieur Maillard,
now becoming excessively pale. He had scarcely finished
the sentence, before loud shouts and imprecations were
heard beneath the windows ; and, immediately afterward,
it became evident that some persons outside were endeavouring to gain entrance into the room. The door was
beaten with what appeared to be a sledge-hammer, and the
shutters were wrenched and shaken with prodigious
violence.

A scene of the most terrible confusion ensued. Monsieur
Maillard, to my excessive astonishment, threw himself
under the sideboard. I had expected more resolution at his
hands. The members of the orchestra, who, for the last
fifteen minutes, had been seemingly too much intoxicated
to do duty, now sprang all at once to their feet and to their
instruments, and, scrambling upon their table, broke out,
with one accord, into ' Yankee Doodle ', which they performed, if not exactly in tune, at least with an energy
superhuman, during the whole of the uproar.

Meantime, upon the main dining-table, among the bottles
and glasses, leaped the gentleman, who, with such difficulty,
had been restrained from leaping there before. As soon as
he fairly settled himself, he commenced an oration, which,

no doubt, was a very capital one, if it could only have been heard. At the same moment, the man with the teetotum predilections set himself to spinning around the apartment, with immense energy, and with arms outstretched at right angles with his body ; so that he had all the air of a tee-totum in fact, and knocked everybody down that happened to get in his way. And now, too, hearing an incredible popping and fizzing of champagne, I discovered at length, that it proceeded from the person who performed the bottle of that delicate drink during dinner. And then, again, the frog-man croaked away as if the salvation of his soul depended upon every note that he uttered. And, in the midst of all this, the continuous braying of a donkey arose over all. As for my old friend, Madame Joyeuse, I really could have wept for the poor lady, she appeared so terribly perplexed. All she did, however, was to stand up in a corner, by the fire-place, and sing out incessantly, at the top of her voice, ' Cock-a-doodle-de-doooooh ! '

And now came the climax—the catastrophe of the drama. As no resistance, beyond whooping and yelling and cock-a-doodle-ing, was offered to the encroachments of the party without, the ten windows were very speedily, and almost simultaneously, broken in. But I shall never forget the emotions of wonder and horror with which I gazed, when, leaping through these windows, and down among us *pêle-mêle*, fighting, stamping, scratching, and howling, there rushed a perfect army of what I took to be Chimpanzees, Ourang-Outangs, or big black baboons of the Cape of Good Hope.

I received a terrible beating—after which I rolled under a sofa and lay still. After lying there some fifteen minutes, however, during which time I listened with all my ears to what was going on in the room, I came to some satisfactory *dénouement* of this tragedy. Monsieur Maillard, it appeared, in giving me the account of the lunatic who had excited his fellows to rebellion, had been merely relating his own exploits. This gentleman had, indeed, some two or three years before, been the superintendent of the establishment ; but grew crazy himself, and so became a patient. This fact was unknown to the travelling companion who intro-duced me. The keepers, ten in number, having been suddenly overpowered, were first well tarred, then carefully feathered, and then shut up in underground cells. They had been so imprisoned for more than a month, during which period Monsieur Maillard had generously allowed them not only the tar and feathers (which constituted his 'system'), but some bread and abundance of water. The latter was pumped on them daily. At length, one, escaping through a sewer, gave freedom to all the rest.

The 'soothing system', with important modifications, has been resumed at the *château* ; yet I cannot help agreeing with Monsieur Maillard, that his own 'treatment' was a very capital one of its kind. As he justly observed, it was 'simple—neat—and gave no trouble at all—not the least'.

I have only to add that, although I have searched every library in Europe for the works of Doctor *Tarr* and Professor *Fether*, I have, up to the present day, utterly failed in my endeavours at procuring an edition.

THE LITERARY LIFE OF THINGUM BOB, ESQ.

LATE EDITOR OF THE 'GOOSETHERUMFOODLE'

BY HIMSELF

I AM now growing in years, and—since I understand that Shakespeare and Mr. Emmons are deceased—it is not impossible that I may even die. It has occurred to me, therefore, that I may as well retire from the field of Letters and repose upon my laurels. But I am ambitious of signalizing my abdication of the literary sceptre by some important bequest to posterity ; and, perhaps, I cannot do a better thing than just pen for it an account of my earlier career. My name, indeed, has been so long and so constantly before the public eye, that I am not only willing to admit the naturalness of the interest which it has everywhere excited, but ready to satisfy the extreme curiosity which it has inspired. In fact, it is no more than the duty of him who achieves greatness to leave behind him, in his ascent, such landmarks as may guide others to be great. I propose, therefore, in the present paper (which I had some idea of calling 'Memoranda to serve for the Literary History of

America ') to give a detail of those important, yet feeble and tottering first steps, by which, at length, I attained the high road to the pinnacle of human renown.

Of one's *very* remote ancestors it is superfluous to say much. My father, Thomas Bob, Esq., stood for many years at the summit of his profession, which was that of a merchant-barber, in the city of Smug. His warehouse was the resort of all the principal people of the place, and especially of the editorial corps—a body which inspires all about it with profound veneration and awe. For my own part, I regarded them as gods, and drank in with avidity the rich wit and wisdom which continuously flowed from their august mouths during the process of what is styled ' lather '. My first moment of positive inspiration must be dated from that ever-memorable epoch, when the brilliant conductor of the ' Gad-Fly ', in the intervals of the important process just mentioned, recited aloud, before a conclave of our apprentices, an inimitable poem in honour of the ' Only Genuine Oil-of-Bob ' (so called from its talented inventor, my father), and for which effusion the editor of the ' Fly ' was remunerated with a regal liberality, by the firm of Thomas Bob and Company, merchant-barbers.

The genius of the stanzas to the ' Oil-of-Bob ' first breathed into me, I say, the divine *afflatus*. I resolved at once to become a great man and to commence by becoming a great poet. That very evening I fell upon my knees at the feet of my father.

' Father,' I said, ' pardon me !—but I have a soul above lather. It is my firm intention to cut the shop. I would be an editor—I would be a poet—I would pen stanzas to the " Oil-of-Bob ". Pardon me and aid me to be great ! '

' My dear Thingum,' replied my father (I had been christened Thingum after a wealthy relative so surnamed), ' My dear Thingum,' he said, raising me from my knees by the ears—' Thingum, my boy, you're a trump, and take after your father in having a soul. You have an immense head, too, and it must hold a great many brains. This I have long seen, and therefore had thoughts of making you a lawyer. The business, however, has grown ungenteel, and that of a politician don't pay. Upon the whole you judge wisely ;—the trade of editor is best :—and if you can be a poet at the same time,—as most of the editors are, by-the-by,—why you will kill two birds with one stone. To encourage you in the beginning of things, I will allow you a garret ; pen, ink, and paper ; a rhyming dictionary : and a copy of the " Gad-Fly ". I suppose you would scarcely demand any more.'

' I would be an ungrateful villain if I did,' I replied with enthusiasm. ' Your generosity is boundless. I will repay it by making you the father of a genius.'

Thus ended my conference with the best of men, and immediately upon its termination, I betook myself with zeal to my poetical labours ; as upon these, chiefly, I founded my hopes of ultimate elevation to the editorial chair.

In my first attempts at composition I found the stanzas to ' The Oil-of-Bob ' rather a drawback than otherwise. Their splendour more dazzled than enlightened me. The contemplation of their excellence tended, naturally, to discourage me by comparison with my own abortions ; so that for a long time I laboured in vain. At length there came into my head one of those exquisitely original ideas which now and then *will* permeate the brain of a man of genius. It was this :—or, rather, thus was it carried into execution. From the rubbish of an old book-stall, in a very remote corner of the town, I got together several antique and altogether unknown or forgotten volumes. The bookseller sold them to me for a song. From one of these, which purported to be a translation of one Dante's ' Inferno ', I copied with remarkable neatness a long passage about a man named Ugolino, who had a parcel of brats. From another which contained a good many old plays by some person whose name I forget, I extracted in the same manner, and with the same care, a great number of lines about ' angels ' and ' ministers saying grace ', and ' goblins damned ', and more besides of that sort. From a third, which was the composition of some blind man or other, either a Greek or a Choctaw—I cannot be at the pains of remembering every trifle exactly—I took about fifty verses beginning with ' Achilles' wrath ', and ' grease ', and something else. From a fourth, which I recollect was also the work of a blind man, I selected a page or two all about

' hail ' and ' holy light ' ; and although a blind man has no business to write about light, still the verses were sufficiently good in their way.

Having made fair copies of these poems I signed every one of them ' Oppodeldoc ' (a fine sonorous name), and, doing each up nicely in a separate envelope, I despatched one to each of the four principal Magazines, with a request for speedy insertion and prompt pay. The result of this well-conceived plan, however (the success of which would have saved me much trouble in after life), served to convince me that some editors are not to be bamboozled, and gave the *coup-de-grâce* (as they say in France) to my nascent hopes (as they say in the city of the transcendentals).

The fact is, that each and every one of the Magazines in question gave Mr. ' Oppodeldoc ' a complete using-up, in the ' Monthly Notices to Correspondents '. The ' Hum-Drum ' gave him a dressing after this fashion :

> ' " Oppodeldoc " (whoever he is) has sent us a long *tirade* concerning a bedlamite whom he styles " Ugolino ", who had a great many children that should have been all whipped and sent to bed without their suppers. The whole affair is exceedingly tame—not to say *flat*. " Oppodeldoc " (whoever he is) is entirely devoid of imagination—and imagination, in our humble opinion, is not only the soul of POESY, but also its very heart. " Oppodeldoc " (whoever he is) has the audacity to demand of us, for his twattle, a " speedy insertion and prompt pay ". We neither insert nor purchase any stuff of the sort. There can be no doubt, however, that he would meet with a ready sale for all the balderdash he can scribble, at the office of either the " Rowdy-Dow ", the " Lollipop ", or the " Goosetherumfoodle ".'

All this, it must be acknowledged, was very severe upon ' Oppodeldoc '—but the unkindest cut was putting the word POESY in small caps. In those five pre-eminent letters what a world of bitterness is there not involved !

But ' Oppodeldoc ' was punished with equal severity in the ' Rowdy-Dow ', which spoke thus :

> ' We have received a most singular and insolent communication from a person (whoever he is) signing himself " Oppodeldoc "—thus desecrating the greatness of the illustrious Roman Emperor so named. Accompanying the letter of " Oppodeldoc " (whoever he is) we find sundry lines of most disgusting and unmeaning rant about " angels and ministers of grace "—rant such as no madman short of a Nat Lee, or an " Oppodeldoc ", could possibly perpetrate. And for this trash of trash, we are modestly requested to " pay promptly ". No, sir—no ! We pay for nothing of *that* sort. Apply to the " Hum-Drum ", the " Lollipop ",

or the " Goosetherumfoodle ". These *periodicals* will undoubtedly accept any literary offal you may send them—and as undoubtedly *promise* to pay for it.'

This was bitter indeed upon poor ' Oppodeldoc ', but, in this instance, the weight of the satire falls upon the ' Humdrum ', the ' Lollipop ', and the ' Goosetherumfoodle ', who are pungently styled ' *periodicals* '—in italics, too—a thing that must have cut them to the heart.

Scarcely less savage was the ' Lollipop ', which thus discoursed :

' Some *individual*, who rejoices in the appellation " Oppodeldoc " (to what low uses are the names of the illustrious dead too often applied !), has enclosed us some fifty or sixty *verses* commencing after this fashion :

> Achilles' wrath, to Greece the direful spring
> Of woes unnumbered, &c., &c., &c., &c.

" Oppodeldoc " (whoever he is) is respectfully informed that there is not a printer's devil in our office who is not in the daily habit of composing better *lines*. Those of " Oppodeldoc " will not *scan*. " Oppodeldoc " should learn to *count*. But why he should have conceived the idea that *we* (of all others, *we !*) would disgrace our pages with his ineffable nonsense, is utterly beyond comprehension. Why, the absurd twattle is scarcely good enough for the " Hum-Drum ", the " Rowdy-Dow ", the " Goosetherumfoodle "—things that are in the practice of publishing " Mother Goose's Melodies " as original lyrics. And " Oppodeldoc " (whoever he is) has even the assurance to demand *pay* for this drivel. Does " Oppodeldoc " (whoever he is) know—is he aware that we could not be paid to insert it ? '

As I perused this I felt myself growing gradually smaller and smaller, and when I came to the point at which the editor sneered at the poem as ' *verses* ', there was little more than an ounce of me left. As for ' Oppodeldoc ', I began to experience *compassion* for the poor fellow. But the ' Goosetherumfoodle ' showed, if possible, less mercy than the ' Lollipop '. It was the ' Goosetherumfoodle ' that said :

' A wretched poetaster, who signs himself " Oppodeldoc ", is silly enough to fancy that *we* will print and *pay for* a medley of incoherent and ungrammatical bombast which he has transmitted to us, and which commences with the following most *intelligible* line :

> Hail, Holy Light ! Offspring of Heaven, first born.

' We say, " most *intelligible* ". " Oppodeldoc " (whoever he is) will be kind enough to tell us, perhaps, how ' *hail* ' can be ' *holy light* '. We always regarded it as *frozen rain*. Will he inform us, also, how frozen rain can be, at one and the same time, both " holy light " (whatever that is) and an " offspring " ?—which latter term (if we understand anything about English) is only employed, with propriety, in reference to small babies of about six weeks old. But it is preposterous to descant upon such absurdity—although " Oppodeldoc " (whoever he is) has the unparalleled effrontery to suppose that we will not only " insert " his ignorant ravings, but (absolutely) *pay for them !*

' Now this is fine—it is rich !—and we have half a mind to punish this young scribbler for his egotism, by really publishing his effusion, *verbatim et literatim,* as he has written it. We could inflict no punishment so severe, and we *would* inflict it, but for the boredom which we should cause our readers in so doing.

' Let " Oppodeldoc " (whoever he is) send any future *composition* of like character to the " Hum-Drum ", the " Lollipop ", or the " Rowdy-Dow ". *They* will " insert " it. *They* " insert " every month just such stuff. Send it to them. WE are not to be insulted with impunity.'

This made an end of me ; and as for the ' Hum-Drum ', the ' Rowdy-Dow ', and the ' Lollipop ', I never could comprehend how they survived it. The putting *them* in the smallest possible *minion* (that was the rub—thereby insinuating their lowness—their baseness), while WE stood looking down upon them in gigantic capitals !—oh it was *too* bitter !—it was wormwood—it was gall. Had I been either of these periodicals I would have spared no pains to have the ' Goosetherumfoodle ' prosecuted. It might have been done under the Act for the ' Prevention of Cruelty to Animals '. As for ' Oppodeldoc ' (whoever he was), I had by this time lost all patience with the fellow, and sympathized with him no longer. He was a fool, beyond doubt (whoever he was), and got not a kick more than he deserved.

The result of my experiment with the old books, convinced me, in the first place, that ' honesty is the best policy ', and, in the second, that if I could not write better than Mr. Dante, and the two blind men, and the rest of the old set, it would, at least, be a difficult matter to write worse. I took heart, therefore, and determined to prosecute the ' entirely original ' (as they say on the covers of the magazines) at whatever cost of study and pains. I again placed before my eyes, as a model, the brilliant stanzas on ' The Oil-of-Bob ' by the editor of the ' Gad-Fly ', and resolved to construct an Ode on the same sublime theme, in rivalry of what had already been done.

With my first verse I had no material difficulty. It ran thus :

> *To pen an Ode upon the ' Oil-of-Bob '.*

Having carefully looked out, however, all the legitimate rhymes to ' Bob ', I found it impossible to proceed. In this dilemma I had recourse to paternal aid ; and, after some hours of mature thought, my father and myself thus constructed the poem :

> *To pen an Ode upon the ' Oil-of-Bob '*
> *Is all sorts of a job.*
> (Signed)   SNOB.

To be sure, this composition was of no very great length —but I ' have yet to learn ', as they say in the Edinburgh Review, that the mere extent of a literary work has anything to do with its merit. As for the Quarterly cant about ' sustained effort ', it is impossible to see the sense of it. Upon the whole, therefore, I was satisfied with the success of my maiden attempt, and now the only question regarded the disposal I should make of it. My father suggested that I should send it to the ' Gad-Fly '—but there were two reasons which operated to prevent me from so doing. I dreaded the jealousy of the editor—and I had ascertained that he did not pay for original contributions. I therefore, after due deliberation, consigned the article to the more dignified pages of the ' Lollipop ', and awaited the event in anxiety, but with resignation.

In the very next published number I had the proud satisfaction of seeing my poem printed at length, as the leading article, with the following significant words, prefixed in italics and between brackets :

[We call the attention of our readers to the subjoined admirable stanzas on ' The Oil-of-Bob '. We need say nothing of their sublimity, or of their pathos :—it is impossible to peruse them without tears. Those who have been nauseated with a sad dose on the same august topic from the goose-quill of the editor of the ' Gad-Fly ', will do well to compare the two compositions.

P.S. We are consumed with anxiety to probe the mystery which envelops the evident pseudonym ' Snob '. May we hope for a personal interview ?]

All this was scarcely more than justice, but it was, I confess, rather more than I had expected :—I acknowledged this, be it observed, to the everlasting disgrace of my country and of mankind. I lost no time, however, in calling upon the editor of the ' Lollipop ', and had the good fortune to find this gentleman at home. He saluted me with an air of profound respect, slightly blended with a fatherly and patronizing admiration, wrought in him, no doubt, by my appearance of extreme youth and inexperience. Begging me to be seated, he entered at once upon the subject of my poem;—but modesty will ever forbid me to repeat the thousand compliments which he lavished upon me. The eulogies of Mr. Crab (such was the editor's name) were, however, by no means fulsomely indiscriminate. He analyzed my composition with much freedom and great ability—not hesitating to point out a few trivial defects— a circumstance which elevated him highly in my esteem. The 'Gad-Fly' was, of course, brought upon the *tapis*, and I hope never to be subjected to a criticism so searching, or to rebukes so withering, as were bestowed by Mr. Crab upon that unhappy effusion. I had been accustomed to regard the editor of the 'Gad-Fly' as something super-human; but Mr. Crab soon disabused me of that idea. He set the literary as well as the personal character of the Fly (so Mr. C. satirically designated the rival editor) in its true light. He, the Fly, was very little better than he should be. He had written infamous things. He was a penny-a-liner, and a buffoon. He was a villain. He had composed a tragedy which set the whole country in a guffaw, and a farce which deluged the universe in tears. Besides all this, he had the impudence to pen what he meant for a lampoon upon himself (Mr. Crab) and the temerity to style him 'an ass'. Should I at any time wish to express my opinion of Mr. Fry, the pages of the 'Lollipop', Mr. Crab assured me, were at my unlimited disposal. In the meantime, as it was very certain that I would be attacked in the Fly for my attempt at composing a rival poem on the 'Oil-of-Bob', he (Mr. Crab) would take it upon himself to attend, pointedly, to my private and personal interests. If I were not made a man of at once, it should not be the fault of himself (Mr. Crab).

Mr. Crab having now paused in his discourse (the latter portion of which I found it impossible to comprehend) I ventured to suggest something about the remuneration which I had been taught to expect for my poem, by an announcement on the cover of the 'Lollipop', declaring that it (the 'Lollipop') 'insisted upon being permitted to pay exorbitant prices for all accepted contributions;—

frequently expending more money for a single brief poem than the whole annual cost of the " Hum-Drum ", the " Rowdy-Dow ", and the "Goosetherumfoodle" combined '.

As I mentioned the word ' remuneration ', Mr. Crab first opened his eyes, and then his mouth, to quite a remarkable extent ; causing his personal appearance to resemble that of a highly-agitated elderly duck in the act of quacking ;— and in this condition he remained (ever and anon pressing his hands tightly to his forehead, as if in a state of desperate bewilderment) until I had nearly made an end of what I had to say.

Upon my conclusion, he sank back into his seat, as if much overcome, letting his arms fall lifelessly by his side, but keeping his mouth still rigorously open, after the fashion of the duck. While I remained in speechless astonishment at behaviour so alarming, he suddenly leaped to his feet and made a rush at the bell-rope ; but just as he reached this, he appeared to have altered his intention, whatever it was, for he dived under a table and immediately re-appeared with a cudgel. This he was in the act of uplifting (for what purpose I am at a loss to imagine), when, all at once, there came a benign smile over his features, and he sank placidly back in his chair.

' Mr. Bob,' he said (for I had sent up my card before ascending myself), ' Mr. Bob, you are a young man, I presume—*very ?* '

I assented ; adding that I had not yet concluded my third lustrum.

' Ah ! ' he replied, ' very good ! I see how it is—say no more ! Touching this matter of compensation, what you observe is very just : in fact it is excessively so. But ah— ah—the *first* contribution—the *first*, I say—it is never the Magazine custom to pay for—you comprehend, eh ? The truth is, we are usually the *recipients* in such case.' [Mr. Crab smiled blandly as he emphasized the word ' recipients '.] ' For the most part, we are *paid* for the insertion of a maiden attempt—especially in verse. In the second place, Mr. Bob, the Magazine rule is never to disburse what we term in France the *argent comptant* :—I have no doubt you understand. In a quarter or two after publication of the article—or in a year or two—we make no objection to giving our note at nine months :—provided always that we can so arrange our affairs as to be quite certain of a "burst up" in six. I really *do* hope, Mr. Bob, that you will look upon this explanation as satisfactory.' Here Mr. Crab concluded, and the tears stood in his eyes.

Grieved to the soul at having been, however innocently, the cause of pain to so eminent and so sensitive a man, I hastened to apologize, and to reassure him, by expressing my perfect coincidence with his views, as well as my entire appreciation of the delicacy of his position. Having done all this in a neat speech, I took leave.

One fine morning, very shortly afterwards, ' I awoke and found myself famous '. The extent of my renown will be best estimated by reference to the editorial opinions of the day. These opinions, it will be seen, were embodied in critical notices of the number of the ' Lollipop ' containing my poem, and are perfectly satisfactory, conclusive, and clear with the exception, perhaps, of the hieroglyphical marks, ' *Sep.* 15—1 *t.*' appended to each of the critiques.

The ' Owl ', a journal of profound sagacity, and well known for the deliberate gravity of its literary decisions— the ' Owl ', I say, spoke as follows :

' " THE LOLLIPOP ! " The October number of this delicious Magazine surpasses its predecessors, and sets competition at defiance. In the beauty of its typography and paper—in the number and excellence of its steel plates—as well as in the literary merit of its contributions —the " Lollipop " compares with its slow-paced rivals as Hyperion with a Satyr. The " Hum-Drum ", the " Rowdy-Dow ", and the " Goosetherumfoodle ", excel, it is true, in braggadocio, but, in all other points, give us the " Lollipop " ! How this celebrated journal can sustain its evidently tremendous expenses, is more than we can understand. To be sure, it has a circulation of 100,000, and its sub-scription-list has increased one-fourth during the last month ; but, on the other hand, the sums it disburses constantly for contributions are inconceivable. It is reported that Mr. Slyass received no less than thirty-seven and a half cents for his inimitable paper on " Pigs ". With Mr. CRAB, as editor, and with such names upon the list of contributors as SNOB and Slyass, there can be no such word as " fail " for the " Lolli-pop ". Go and subscribe. *Sep.* 15—1 *t.*'

I must say that I was gratified with this high-toned notice from a paper so respectable as the ' Owl '. The placing my name—that is to say, my *nom de guerre*—in priority of station to that of the great Slyass, was a compliment as happy as I felt it to be deserved.

My attention was next arrested by these paragraphs in the 'Toad'—a print highly distinguished for its uprightness, and independence — for its entire freedom from sycophancy and subserviance to the givers of dinners :

'The "Lollipop" for October is out in advance of all its contemporaries, and infinitely surpasses them, of course, in the splendour of its embellishments, as well as in the richness of its literary contents. The "Hum-Drum", the "Rowdy-Dow", and the "Goosetherumfoodle" excel, we admit, in braggadocio, but, in all other points, give us the "Lollipop". How this celebrated Magazine can sustain its evidently tremendous expenses, is more than we can understand. To be sure, it has a circulation of 200,000, and its subscription list has increased one-third during the last fortnight, but on the other hand, the sums it disburses, monthly, for contributions, are fearfully great. We learn that Mr. Mumblethumb received no less than fifty cents for his late "Monody in a Mud-Puddle".

'Among the original contributors to the present number we notice (besides the eminent editor, Mr. CRAB) such men as SNOB, Slyass, and Mumblethumb. Apart from the editorial matter, the most valuable paper, nevertheless, is, we think, a poetical gem by "Snob", on the "Oil-of-Bob"—but our readers must not suppose from the title of this incomparable *bijou*, that it bears any similitude to some balderdash on the same subject by a certain contemptible individual whose name is unmentionable to ears polite. The *present* poem "On the Oil-of-Bob", has excited universal anxiety and curiosity in respect to the owner of the evident pseudonym, "Snob"—a curiosity which, happily, we have it in our power to satisfy. "Snob" is the *nom-de-plume* of Mr. Thingum Bob, of this city,—a relative of the great Mr. Thingum (after whom he is named), and otherwise connected with the most illustrious families of the State. His father, Thomas Bob, Esq., is an opulent merchant in Smug. *Sep.* 15—1 *t.*'

This generous approbation touched me to the heart—the more especially as it emanated from a source so avowedly— so proverbially pure as the 'Toad'. The word 'balderdash', as applied to the 'Oil-of-Bob' of the Fly, I considered singularly pungent and appropriate. The words 'gem' and '*bijou*', however, used in reference to my composition, struck me as being, in some degree, feeble. They seemed to me to be deficient in force. They were not sufficiently *prononcés* (as we have it in France).

I had hardly finished reading the 'Toad', when a friend placed in my hands a copy of the 'Mole', a daily, enjoying high reputation for the keenness of its perception about matters in general, and for the open, honest, above-ground style of its editorials. The ' Mole ' spoke of the ' Lollipop ' as follows :

'We have just received the "Lollipop" for October, and *must* say that never before have we perused any single number of any periodical which afforded us a felicity so supreme. We speak advisedly. The " Hum-Drum ", the " Rowdy-Dow ", and the " Goosetherumfoodle '' must look well to their laurels. These prints, no doubt, surpass everything in loudness of pretension, but, in all other points, give us the " Lollipop " ! How this celebrated Magazine can sustain its evidently tremendous expenses, is more than we can comprehend. To be sure, it has a circulation of 300,000 ; and its subscription-list has increased one-half within the last week, but then the sum it disburses, monthly, for contributions, is astoundingly enormous. We have it upon good authority, that Mr. Fatquack received no less than sixty-two cents and a half for his late Domestic Nouvelette, the " Dish-Clout ".

' The contributors to the number before us are Mr. CRAB (the eminent editor), SNOB, Mumblethumb, Fatquack, and others ; but, after the inimitable compositions of the editor himself, we prefer a diamond-like effusion from the pen of a rising poet who writes over the signature " Snob "—a *nom de guerre* which we predict will one day extinguish the radiance of " Boz ". " SNOB ", we learn, is a Mr. THINGUM BOB, Esq., sole heir of a wealthy merchant of this city, Thomas Bob, Esq., and a near relative of the distinguished Mr. Thingum. The title of Mr. B.'s admirable poem is the " Oil-of-Bob "—a somewhat unfortunate name, by the by, as some contemptible vagabond connected with the penny press has already disgusted the town with a great deal of drivel upon the same topic. There will be no danger, however, of confounding the compositions. *Sep.* 15—1 *t.*'

The generous approbation of so clear-sighted a journal as the ' Mole ' penetrated my soul with delight. The only objection which occurred to me was, that the terms ' contemptible vagabond ' might have been better written ' *odious and* contemptible, *wretch, villain*, and vagabond '. This would have sounded more gracefully, I think. ' Diamond-like ', also, was scarcely, it will be admitted, of sufficient intensity to express what the ' Mole ' evidently *thought* of the brilliancy of the ' Oil-of-Bob '.

On the same afternoon in which I saw these notices in the ' Owl ', the ' Toad ', and the ' Mole ' I happened to meet with a copy of the ' Daddy-Long-Legs ', a periodical proverbial for the extreme extent of its understanding. And it was the ' Daddy-Long-Legs ' which spoke thus :

'The "Lollipop"!! This gorgeous Magazine is already before the public for October. The question of pre-eminence is forever put to rest, and hereafter it will be excessively preposterous in the " Hum-Drum ",

the " Rowdy-Dow ", or the " Goosetherumfoodle ", to make any farther
spasmodic attempts at competition.   These journals may excel the
" Lollipop " in outcry, but, in all other points, give us the " Lollipop " !
How this celebrated Magazine can sustain its evidently tremendous
expenses, is past comprehension.   To be sure, it has a circulation of
precisely half a million, and its subscription-list has increased seventy-
five per cent. within the last couple of days ; but then the sums it
disburses, monthly, for contributions, are scarcely credible ; we are
cognizant of the fact, that Mademoiselle Cribalittle received no less
than eighty-seven cents and a half for her late valuable Revolutionary
Tale entitled " The York-Town Katy-Did, and the Bunker-Hill Katy-
Did'nt."
  ' The most able papers in the present number, are, of course, those
furnished by the editor (the eminent Mr. CRAB), but there are numerous
magnificent contributions from such names as SNOB, Mademoiselle
Cribalittle, Slyass, Mrs. Fibalittle, Mumblethumb, Mrs. Squibalittle,
and last, though not least, Fatquack.   The world may well be challenged
to produce so rich a galaxy of genius.
  ' The poem over the signature " SNOB " is, we find, attracting universal
commendation, and, we are constrained to say, deserves, if possible,
even more applause than it has received.   The " Oil-of-Bob " is the
title of this masterpiece of eloquence and art.   One or two of our readers
may have a *very* faint, although sufficiently disgusting recollection of
a poem (?) similarly entitled, the perpetration of a miserable penny-a-
liner, mendicant, and cut-throat, connected in the capacity of scullion,
we believe, with one of the indecent prints about the purlieus of the city ;
we beg them, for God's sake, not to confound the compositions.   The
author of *the* " Oil-of-Bob " is, we hear, THINGUM BOB, Esq., a gentleman of high genius, and a scholar.   " Snob " is merely a *nom-de-guerre*.
Sept. 15—1 *t.*'

  I could scarcely restrain my indignation while I perused
the concluding portions of this diatribe.   It was clear to me
that the yea-nay manner—not to say the gentleness—the
positive forbearance with which the ' Daddy-Long-Legs '
spoke of that pig, the editor of the ' Gad-Fly '—it was
evident to me, I say, that this gentleness of speech could
proceed from nothing else than a partiality for the Fly—
whom it was clearly the intention of the ' Daddy-Long-
Legs ' to elevate into reputation at my expense.   Any one,
indeed, might perceive, with half an eye, that, had the
real design of the ' Daddy ' been what it wished to appear,
it (the ' Daddy ') might have expressed itself in terms more
direct, more pungent, and altogether more to the purpose.
The words ' penny-a-liner ', ' mendicant ', ' scullion ', and
' cut-throat ', were epithets so intentionally inexpressive
and equivocal, as to be worse than nothing when applied

to the author of the very worst stanzas ever penned by one
of the human race. We all know what is meant by ' damn-
ing with faint praise ', and, on the other hand, who could
fail seeing through the covert purpose of the ' Daddy '—
that of glorifying with feeble abuse ?

What the ' Daddy ' chose to say of the Fly, however, was
no business of mine. What it said of myself *was*. After the
noble manner in which the ' Owl ', the ' Toad ', the ' Mole '
had expressed themselves in respect to my ability, it was
rather too much to be coolly spoken of by a thing like the
' Daddy-Long-Legs ', as merely ' a gentleman of high genius,
and a scholar '. Gentleman indeed ! I made up my mind
at once, either to get a written apology from the ' Daddy-
Long-Legs ', or to call it out.

Full of this purpose, I looked about me to find a friend
whom I could entrust with a message to his Daddyship, and
as the editor of the ' Lollipop ' had given me marked tokens
of regard, I at length concluded to seek assistance upon the
present occasion.

I have never yet been able to account, in a manner
satisfactory to my own understanding, for the *very* peculiar
countenance and demeanour with which Mr. Crab listened to
me, as I unfolded to him my design. He again went through
the scene of the bell-rope and cudgel, and did not omit the
duck. At one period I thought he really intended to
quack. His fit, nevertheless, finally subsided as before,
and he began to act and speak in a rational way. He
declined bearing the cartel, however, and in fact, dissuaded
me from sending it at all ; but was candid enough to admit
that the ' Daddy-Long-Legs ' had been disgracefully in the
wrong—more especially in what related to the epithets
' gentleman and scholar '.

Towards the end of this interview with Mr. Crab, who
really appeared to take a paternal interest in my welfare,
he suggested to me that I might turn an honest penny, and,
at the same time, advance my reputation, by occasionally
playing Thomas Hawk for the ' Lollipop '.

I begged Mr. Crab to inform me who was Mr. Thomas
Hawk, and how it was expected that I should play him.

Here Mr. Crab again ' made great eyes ' (as we say in
Germany), but at length, recovering himself from a profound

attack of astonishment, he assured me that he employed the words ' Thomas Hawk ' to avoid the colloquialism, Tommy, which was low—but that the true idea was Tommy Hawk— or tomahawk—and that by ' playing tomahawk ' he referred to scalping, brow-beating, and otherwise using-up the herd of poor-devil authors.

I assured my patron that, if this was all, I was perfectly resigned to the task of playing Thomas Hawk. Hereupon Mr. Crab desired me to use-up the editor of the ' Gad-Fly ' forthwith, in the fiercest style within the scope of my ability, and as a specimen of my powers. This I did, upon the spot, in a review of the original ' Oil-of-Bob ', occupying thirty-six pages of the ' Lollipop '. I found playing Thomas Hawk, indeed, a far less onerous occupation than poetizing ; for I went upon *system* altogether, and thus it was easy to do the thing thoroughly and well. My practice was this. I bought auction copies (cheap) of ' Lord Brougham's Speeches ', ' Cobbett's Complete Works ', the ' New Slang-Syllabus ', the ' Whole Art of Snubbing ', ' Prentice's Billingsgate ' (folio edition), and ' Lewis G. Clarke on Tongue '. These works I cut up thoroughly with a curry-comb, and then, throwing the shreds into a sieve, sifted out carefully all that might be thought decent (a mere trifle) ; reserving the hard phrases, which I threw into a large tin pepper-castor with longitudinal holes, so that an entire sentence could get through without material injury. The mixture was then ready for use. When called upon to play Thomas Hawk, I anointed a sheet of foolscap with the white of a gander's egg ; then, shredding the thing to be reviewed as I had previously shredded the books,—only with more care, so as to get every word separate—I threw the latter shreds in with the former, screwed on the lid of the castor, gave it a shake, and so dusted out the mixture upon the egg'd foolscap ; where it stuck. The effect was beautiful to behold. It was captivating. Indeed, the reviews I brought to pass by this simple expedient have never been approached, and were the wonder of the world. At first, through bashfulness—the result of inexpe-rience—I was a little put out by a certain inconsistency—a certain air of the *bizarre* (as we say in France), worn by the composition as a whole. All the phrases did not *fit* (as we say in the Anglo-Saxon). Many were quite awry. Some, even, were upside-down ; and there were none of them which were not, in some measure, injured in regard to effect, by this latter species of accident, when it occurred ;—with the exception of Mr. Lewis Clarke's paragraphs, which were so vigorous, and altogether stout, that they seemed not particularly disconcerted by any extreme of position, but looked equally happy and satisfactory, whether on their heads, or on their heels.

What became of the editor of the ' Gad-Fly ', after the publication of my criticism on his ' Oil-of-Bob ', it is somewhat difficult to determine. The most reasonable conclusion is that he wept himself to death. At all events he disappeared instantaneously from the face of the earth, and no man has seen even the ghost of him since.

This matter having been properly accomplished, and the Furies appeased, I grew at once into high favour with Mr. Crab. He took me into his confidence, gave me a permanent situation as Thomas Hawk of the ' Lollipop ', and, as for the present, he could afford me no salary, allowed me to profit, at discretion, by his advice.

' My dear Thingum,' said he to me one day after dinner, ' I respect your abilities and love you as a son. You shall be my heir. When I die I will bequeath you the "Lollipop". In the meantime I will make a man of you—I *will*—provided always that you follow my counsel. The first thing to do is to get rid of the old bore.'

' Boar ? ' said I inquiringly—' pig, eh ?—*aper ?* (as we say in Latin)—who ?—where ? '

' Your father,' said he.

' Precisely,' I replied,—' pig.'

' You have your fortune to make, Thingum,' resumed Mr. Crab, ' and that governor of yours is a millstone about your neck. We must cut him at once.' [Here I took out my knife.] ' We must cut him,' continued Mr. Crab, ' decidedly and forever. He won't do—he *won't*. Upon second thoughts, you had better kick him, or cane him, or something of that kind.'

' What do you say,' I suggested modestly, ' to my kicking him in the first instance, caning him afterwards, and winding up by tweaking his nose ? '

Mr. Crab looked at me musingly for some moments, and then answered :

' I think, Mr. Bob, that what you propose would answer sufficiently well—indeed remarkably well—that is to say, as far as it went—but barbers are exceedingly hard to cut, and I think, upon the whole, that, having performed upon Thomas Bob the operations you suggest, it would be advisable to blacken, with your fists, both his eyes, very carefully and thoroughly, to prevent his ever seeing you again in fashionable promenades. After doing this, I really do not perceive that you can do any more. However—it might be just as well to roll him once or twice in the gutter, and then put him in charge of the police. Any time the next morning you can call at the watch-house and swear an assault.'

I was much affected by the kindness of feeling towards me personally, which was evinced in this excellent advice of Mr. Crab, and I did not fail to profit by it forthwith. The result was, that I got rid of the old bore, and began to feel a little independent and gentleman-like. The want of money, however, was, for a few weeks, a source of some discomfort ; but at length, by carefully putting to use my two eyes, and observing how matters went just in front of my nose, I perceived how the thing was to be brought about. I say ' thing '—be it observed—for they tell me the Latin for it is *rem*. By the way, talking of Latin, can any one tell me the meaning of *quocunque*—or what is the meaning of *modo* ?

My plan was exceedingly simple. I bought, for a song, a sixteenth of the ' Snapping-Turtle ' :—that was all. The thing was *done*, and I put money in my purse. There were some trivial arrangements afterwards, to be sure ; but these formed no portion of the plan. They were a consequence— a result. For example, I bought pen, ink, and paper, and put them into furious activity. Having thus completed a Magazine article, I gave it, for appellation, ' FOL-LOL, *by the Author of* " THE OIL-OF-BOB " ', and enveloped it to the ' Goosetherumfoodle '. That journal, however, having pronounced it ' twattle ' in the ' Monthly Notices to Correspondents ', I reheaded the paper ' " Hey-Diddle-Diddle ", by THINGUM BOB, Esq., Author of the Ode on

"The Oil-of-Bob", *and* Editor of the "Snapping-Turtle"'.
With this amendment, I re-enclosed it to the 'Goosetherumfoodle', and, while I awaited a reply, published daily,
in the 'Turtle', six columns of what may be termed
philosophical and analytical investigation of the literary
merits of the 'Goosetherumfoodle', as well as of the personal
character of the editor of the 'Goosetherumfoodle'. At
the end of a week the 'Goosetherumfoodle' discovered
that it had, by some odd mistake, 'confounded a stupid
article, headed "Hey-Diddle-Diddle" and composed by
some unknown ignoramus, with a gem of resplendent lustre
similarly entitled, the work of Thingum Bob, Esq., the
celebrated author of "The Oil-of-Bob"'. The 'Goosetherumfoodle' deeply 'regretted this very natural accident', and
promised, moreover, an insertion of the *genuine* 'Hey-
Diddle-Diddle' in the very next number of the Magazine.

The fact is, I *thought*—I *really* thought—I thought at the
time—I thought *then*—and have no reason for thinking
otherwise *now*—that the 'Goosetherumfoodle' *did* make
a mistake. With the best intentions in the world, I never
knew anything that made as many singular mistakes as
the 'Goosetherumfoodle'. From that day I took a liking
to the 'Goosetherumfoodle', and the result was I soon saw
into the very depths of its literary merits, and did not fail
to expatiate upon them, in the 'Turtle', whenever a fitting
opportunity occurred. And it is to be regarded as a very
peculiar coincidence—as one of those positively *remarkable*
coincidences which set a man to serious thinking—that
just such a total revolution of opinion—just such entire
bouleversement (as we say in French)—just such thorough
topsiturviness (if I may be permitted to employ a rather
forcible term of the Choctaws) as happened, *pro* and *con*,
between myself on the one part, and the 'Goosetherumfoodle' on the other, did actually again happen, in a brief
period afterwards, and with precisely similar circumstances,
in the case of myself and the 'Rowdy-Dow', and in the
case of myself and the 'Hum-Drum'.

Thus it was that, by a master-stroke of genius, I at
length consummated my triumphs by 'putting money in
my purse', and thus may be said really and fairly to have
commenced that brilliant and eventful career which ren-

dered me illustrious, and which now enables me to say, with Chateaubriand, ' I have made history '—' *J'ai fait l'histoire* '.

I have indeed ' made history '. From the bright epoch which I now record, my actions—my works—are the property of mankind. They are familiar to the world. It is, then, needless for me to detail how, soaring rapidly, I fell heir to the ' Lollipop '—how I merged this journal in the ' Hum-Drum '—how again I made purchase of the ' Rowdy-Dow ', thus combining the three periodicals—how, lastly, I effected a bargain for the sole remaining rival, and united all the literature of the country in one magnificent Magazine, known everywhere as the

' Rowdy-Dow, Lollipop, Hum-Drum,
and
GOOSETHERUMFOODLE.'

Yes ; I have made history. My fame is universal. It extends to the uttermost ends of the earth. You cannot take up a common newspaper in which you shall not see some allusion to the immortal THINGUM BOB. It is Mr. Thingum Bob said so, and Mr. Thingum Bob wrote this, and Mr. Thingum Bob did that. But I am meek and expire with an humble heart. After all, what is it ?—this indescribable something which men will persist in terming ' genius ' ? I agree with Buffon—with Hogarth—it is but *diligence* after all.

Look at *me !*—how I laboured—how I toiled—how I wrote ! Ye Gods, did I *not* write ? I knew not the word ' ease '. By day I adhered to my desk, and at night, a pale student, I consumed the midnight oil. You should have seen me—you *should*. I leaned to the right. I leaned to the left. I sat forward. I sat backward. I sat upon end. I sat *tête baissée* (as they have it in the Kickapoo) bowing my head close to the alabaster page. And, through all, I— *wrote*. Through joy and through sorrow, I—*wrote*. Through hunger and through thirst, I—*wrote*. Through good report and through ill report, I—*wrote*. Through sunshine and through moonshine, I—*wrote*. *What* I wrote it is un-necessary to say. The *style !*—that was the thing. I caught it from Fatquack—whizz !—fizz !—and I am giving you a specimen of it now.

HOW TO WRITE A BLACKWOOD ARTICLE

'In the name of the Prophet—figs!!'
CRY OF TURKISH FIG-PEDLER.

I PRESUME everybody has heard of me. My name is the Signora Psyche Zenobia. This I know to be a fact. Nobody but my enemies ever calls me Suky Snobbs. I have been assured that Suky is but a vulgar corruption of Psyche, which is good Greek, and means 'the soul' (that's me, I'm *all* soul) and sometimes 'a butterfly', which latter meaning undoubtedly alludes to my appearance in my new crimson satin dress, with the sky-blue Arabian *mantelet*, and the trimmings of green *agraffas*, and the seven flounces of orange-coloured *auriculas*. As for Snobbs—any person who should look at me would be instantly aware that my name wasn't Snobbs. Miss Tabitha Turnip propagated that report through sheer envy. Tabitha Turnip indeed! Oh, the little wretch! But what can we expect from a turnip? Wonder if she remembers the old adage about 'blood out of a turnip, &c.' [Mem: put her in mind of it the first opportunity.] [Mem. again—pull her nose.] Where was I? Ah! I have been assured that Snobbs is a mere corruption of Zenobia, and that Zenobia was a queen—(So am I. Dr. Moneypenny always calls me the Queen of Hearts)—and that Zenobia, as well as Psyche, is good Greek, and that my father was 'a Greek', and that consequently I have a right to our patronymic, which is Zenobia, and not by any means Snobbs. Nobody but Tabitha Turnip calls me Suky Snobbs. I am the Signora Psyche Zenobia.

As I said before, everybody has heard of me. I am that very Signora Psyche Zenobia, so justly celebrated as corresponding secretary to the '*Philadelphia, Regular, Exchange, Tea, Total, Young, Belles, Lettres, Universal, Experimental, Bibliographical, Association, To, Civilize, Humanity*'. Dr. Moneypenny made the title for us, and says he chose it because it sounded big like an empty rum-puncheon. (A vulgar man that sometimes—but he's deep.) We all sign the initials of the society after our names, in the fashion of the R. S. A., Royal Society of Arts—the S. D. U. K., Society for the Diffusion of Useful Knowledge,

&c. &c. Dr. Moneypenny says that S stands for *stale*, and that D. U. K. spells duck (but it don't), and that S. D. U. K. stands for Stale Duck, and not for Lord Brougham's society—but then Dr. Moneypenny is such a queer man that I am never sure when he is telling me the truth. At any rate, we always add to our names the initials P. R. E. T. T. Y. B. L. U. E. B. A. T. C. H.—that is to say, Philadelphia, Regular, Exchange, Tea, Total, Young, Belles, Lettres, Universal, Experimental, Bibliographical, Association, To, Civilize, Humanity—one letter for each word, which is a decided improvement upon Lord Brougham. Dr. Moneypenny will have it that our initials give our true character—but for my life I can't see what he means.

Notwithstanding the good offices of the Doctor, and the strenuous exertions of the association to get itself into notice, it met with no very great success until I joined it. The truth is, members indulged in too flippant a tone of discussion. The papers read every Saturday evening were characterized less by depth than buffoonery. They were all whipped syllabub. There was no investigation of first causes, first principles. There was no investigation of anything at all. There was no attention paid to that great point, the 'fitness of things'. In short there was no fine writing like this. It was all low—very! No profundity, no reading, no metaphysics—nothing which the learned call spirituality, and which the unlearned choose to stigmatize as cant. [Dr. M. says I ought to spell ' cant ' with a capital K—but I know better.]

When I joined the society it was my endeavour to introduce a better style of thinking and writing, and all the world knows how well I have succeeded. We get up as good papers now in the P. R. E. T. T. Y. B. L. U. E. B. A. T. C. H. as any to be found even in Blackwood. I say, Blackwood, because I have been assured that the finest writing, upon every subject, is to be discovered in the pages of that justly celebrated Magazine. We now take it for our model upon all themes, and are getting into rapid notice accordingly. And, after all, it 's not so very difficult a matter to compose an article of the genuine Blackwood stamp, if one only goes properly about it. Of course I don't speak of the political

articles. Everybody knows how *they* are managed, since
Dr. Moneypenny explained it. Mr. Blackwood has a pair
of tailor's-shears, and three apprentices who stand by him
for orders. One hands him the 'Times', another the
'Examiner', and a third a 'Gulley's New Compendium of
Slang-Whang'. Mr. B. merely cuts out and intersperses.
It is soon done—nothing but Examiner, Slang-Whang, and
Times—then Times, Slang-Whang, and Examiner—and
then Times, Examiner, and Slang-Whang.

But the chief merit of the Magazine lies in its miscellaneous articles ; and the best of these come under the
head of what Dr. Moneypenny calls the *bizarreries* (whatever that may mean) and what everybody else calls the
intensities. This is a species of writing which I have long
known how to appreciate, although it is only since my late
visit to Mr. Blackwood (deputed by the society) that I have
been made aware of the exact method of composition.
This method is very simple, but not so much so as the
politics. Upon my calling at Mr. B.'s, and making known
to him the wishes of the society, he received me with great
civility, took me into his study, and gave me a clear explanation of the whole process.

'My dear madam,' said he, evidently struck with my
majestic appearance, for I had on the crimson satin, with
the green *agraffas*, and orange-coloured *auriculas*, 'My *dear*
madam,' said he, 'sit down. The matter stands thus. In
the first place, your writer of intensities must have very
black ink, and a very big pen, with a very blunt nib. And,
mark me, Miss Psyche Zenobia !' he continued, after a
pause, with the most impressive energy and solemnity of
manner, ' mark me !—*that pen—must—never be mended !*
Herein, madam, lies the secret, the soul, of intensity. I
assume upon myself to say, that no individual, of however
great genius, ever wrote with a good pen—understand me—
a good article. You may take it for granted, that when
manuscript can be read it is never worth reading. This is
a leading principle in our faith, to which if you cannot
readily assent, our conference is at an end.'

He paused. But, of course, as I had no wish to put an
end to the conference, I assented to a proposition so very
obvious, and one, too, of whose truth I had all along been

sufficiently aware. He seemed pleased, and went on with
his instructions.

'It may appear invidious in me, Miss Psyche Zenobia,
to refer you to an article, or set of articles, in the way of
model or study ; yet perhaps I may as well call your
attention to a few cases. Let me see. There was " The
Dead Alive ", a capital thing !—the record of a gentleman's
sensations when entombed before the breath was out of his
body—full of taste, terror, sentiment, metaphysics, and
erudition. You would have sworn that the writer had been
born and brought up in a coffin. Then we had the " Con-
fessions of an Opium-eater "—fine, very fine !—glorious
imagination—deep philosophy—acute speculation—plenty
of fire and fury, and a good spicing of the decidedly unintelligible. That was a nice bit of flummery, and went
down the throats of the people delightfully. They would
have it that Coleridge wrote the paper—but not so. It
was composed by my pet baboon, Juniper, over a rummer
of Hollands and water, " hot, without sugar ".' [This I
could scarcely have believed had it been anybody but
Mr. Blackwood, who assured me of it.] 'Then there was
" The Involuntary Experimentalist ", all about a gentleman
who got baked in an oven, and came out alive and well,
although certainly done to a turn. And then there was
" The Diary of a Late Physician ", where the merit lay in
good rant, and indifferent Greek—both of them taking
things with the public. And then there was " The Man in
the Bell ", a paper by-the-by, Miss Zenobia, which I cannot
sufficiently recommend to your attention. It is the history
of a young person who goes to sleep under the clapper of
a church bell, and is awakened by its tolling for a funeral.
The sound drives him mad, and, accordingly, pulling out
his tablets, he gives a record of his sensations. Sensations
are the great things after all. Should you ever be drowned
or hung, be sure and make a note of your sensations—they
will be worth to you ten guineas a sheet. If you wish to
write forcibly, Miss Zenobia, pay minute attention to the
sensations.'

'That I certainly will, Mr. Blackwood,' said I.

'Good ! ' he replied. 'I see you are a pupil after my
own heart. But I must put you *au fait* to the details

necessary in composing what may be denominated a genuine
Blackwood article of the sensation stamp—the kind which
you will understand me to say I consider the best for all
purposes.

‘The first thing requisite is to get yourself into such a
scrape as no one ever got into before. The oven, for instance,
—that was a good hit. But if you have no oven, or big
bell, at hand, and if you cannot conveniently tumble out
of a balloon, or be swallowed up in an earthquake, or get
stuck fast in a chimney, you will have to be contented with
simply imagining some similar misadventure. I should
prefer, however, that you have the actual fact to bear you
out. Nothing so well assists the fancy, as an experimental
knowledge of the matter in hand. “Truth is strange,”
you know, “stranger than fiction ”—besides being more to
the purpose.’

Here I assured him I had an excellent pair of garters,
and would go and hang myself forthwith.

‘Good!’ he replied, ‘do so ;—although hanging is
somewhat hackneyed. Perhaps you might do better. Take
a dose of Brandreth’s pills, and then give us your sensations.
However, my instructions will apply equally well to any
variety of misadventure, and in your way home you may
easily get knocked on the head, or run over by an omnibus,
or bitten by a mad dog, or drowned in a gutter. But to
proceed.

‘Having determined upon your subject, you must next
consider the tone, or manner, of your narration. There is
the tone didactic, the tone enthusiastic, the tone natural
—all commonplace enough. But then there is the tone
laconic, or curt, which has lately come much into use. It
consists in short sentences. Somehow thus : Can’t be too
brief. Can’t be too snappish. Always a full stop. And
never a paragraph.

‘Then there is the tone elevated, diffusive, and inter-
jectional. Some of our best novelists patronize this tone.
The words must be all in a whirl, like a humming-top, and
make a noise very similar, which answers remarkably well
instead of meaning. This is the best of all possible styles
where the writer is in too great a hurry to think.

‘The tone metaphysical is also a good one. If you know

any big words this is your chance for them. Talk of the Ionic and Eleatic schools—of Archytas, Gorgias, and Alcmæon. Say something about objectivity and subjectivity. Be sure and abuse a man named Locke. Turn up your nose at things in general, and when you let slip anything a little *too* absurd, you need not be at the trouble of scratching it out, but just add a foot-note, and say that you are indebted for the above profound observation to the " Kritik der reinem Vernunft ", or to the " Metaphysische Anfangsgrunde der Naturwissenschaft ". This will look erudite and—and—and frank.

' There are various other tones of equal celebrity, but I shall mention only two more—the tone transcendental and the tone heterogeneous. In the former the merit consists in seeing into the nature of affairs a very great deal farther than anybody else. This second sight is very efficient when properly managed. A little reading of the " Dial " will carry you a great way. Eschew, in this case, big words ; get them as small as possible, and write them upside down. Look over Channing's poems and quote what he says about a " fat little man with a delusive show of Can ". Put in something about the Supernal Oneness. Don't say a syllable about the Infernal Twoness. Above all, study innuendo. Hint everything—assert nothing. If you feel inclined to say " bread and butter ", do not by any means say it outright. You may say anything and everything *approaching* to " bread and butter ". You may hint at buckwheat cake, or you may even go so far as to insinuate oatmeal porridge, but if bread and butter be your real meaning, be cautious, my *dear* Miss Psyche, not on any account to say " bread and butter " ! '

I assured him that I should never say it again as long as I lived. He kissed me and continued :

' As for the tone heterogeneous, it is merely a judicious mixture, in equal proportions, of all the other tones in the world, and is consequently made up of everything deep, great, odd, piquant, pertinent, and pretty.

' Let us suppose now you have determined upon your incidents and tone. The most important portion—in fact, the soul of the whole business, is yet to be attended to—I allude to *the filling up*. It is not to be supposed that a lady,

or gentleman either, has been leading the life of a book-
worm. And yet above all things it is necessary that your
article have an air of erudition, or at least afford evidence
of extensive general reading. Now I'll put you in the way
of accomplishing this point. See here ! ' · (pulling down
some three or four ordinary-looking volumes, and opening
them at random). ' By casting your eye down almost any
page of any book in the world, you will be able to perceive
at once a host of little scraps of either learning or *bel-
esprit-ism*, which are the very thing for the spicing of a
Blackwood article. You might as well note down a few
while I read them to you. I shall make two divisions :
first, *Piquant Facts for the Manufacture of Similes ;* and
second, *Piquant Expressions to be introduced as occasion may
require.* Write now !—' and I wrote as he dictated.

' PIQUANT FACTS FOR SIMILES. "There were originally
but three Muses—Melete, Mneme, Aœde—meditation,
memory, and singing." You may make a great deal of that
little fact if properly worked. You see it is not generally
known, and looks *recherché.* You must be careful and give
the thing with a downright improviso air.

' Again. "The river Alpheus passed beneath the sea,
and emerged without injury to the purity of its waters."
Rather stale that, to be sure, but, if properly dressed and
dished up, will look quite as fresh as ever.

' Here is something better. "The Persian Iris appears to
some persons to possess a sweet and very powerful perfume,
while to others it is perfectly scentless." Fine that, and
very delicate ! Turn it about a little, and it will do wonders.
We'll have something else in the botanical line. There's
nothing goes down so well, especially with the help of a
little Latin. Write !

' "*The Epidendrum Flos Aeris*, of Java, bears a very
beautiful flower, and will live when pulled up by the roots.
The natives suspend it by a cord from the ceiling, and enjoy
its fragrance for years." That's capital ! That will do
for the similes. Now for the Piquant Expressions.

' PIQUANT EXPRESSIONS. "*The venerable Chinese novel
Ju-Kiao-Li.*" Good ! By introducing these few words with

dexterity you will evince your intimate acquaintance with the language and literature of the Chinese. With the aid of this you may possibly get along without either Arabic, or Sanscrit, or Chickasaw. There is no passing muster, however, without Spanish, Italian, German, Latin, and Greek. I must look you out a little specimen of each. Any scrap will answer, because you must depend upon your own ingenuity to make it fit into your article. Now write!

'"*Aussi tendre que Zaïre*"—as tender as Zaïre—French. Alludes to the frequent repetition of the phrase, *la tendre Zaïre*, in the French tragedy of that name. Properly introduced, will show not only your knowledge of the language, but your general reading and wit. You can say, for instance, that the chicken you were eating (write an article about being choked to death by a chicken-bone) was not altogether *aussi tendre que Zaïre*. Write!

> *Ven muerte tan escondida,*
> *Que no te sienta venir,*
> *Porque el plazer del morir*
> *No me torne a dar la vida.*

That's Spanish—from Miguel de Cervantes. "Come quickly, O death! but be sure and don't let me see you coming, lest the pleasure I shall feel at your appearance should unfortunately bring me back again to life." This you may slip in quite *à propos* when you are struggling in the last agonies with the chicken-bone. Write!

> *Il pover' huomo che non se'n era accorto,*
> *Andava combattendo, e era morto.*

That's Italian, you perceive—from Ariosto. It means that a great hero, in the heat of combat, not perceiving that he had been fairly killed, continued to fight valiantly, dead as he was. The application of this to your own case is obvious—for I trust, Miss Psyche, that you will not neglect to kick for at least an hour and a half after you have been choked to death by that chicken-bone. Please to write!

> *Und sterb'ich doch, so sterb'ich denn*
> *Durch Sie—durch Sie!*

That's German—from Schiller. "And if I die, at least I die—for thee—for thee!" Here it is clear that you are

apostrophizing the *cause* of your disaster, the chicken.
Indeed what gentleman (or lady either) of sense, *wouldn't*
die, I should like to know, for a well-fattened capon of the
right Molucca breed, stuffed with capers and mushrooms,
and served up in a salad-bowl, with orange-jellies *en
mosaïques*. Write ! (You can get them that way at
Tortoni's).—Write, if you please !

'Here is a nice little Latin phrase, and rare too (one
can't be too *recherché* or brief in one's Latin, it's getting
so common),—*ignoratio elenchi*. He has committed an
ignoratio elenchi—that is to say, he has understood the
words of your proposition, but not the idea. The man was
a fool, you see. Some poor fellow whom you address while
choking with that chicken-bone, and who therefore didn't
precisely understand what you were talking about. Throw
the *ignoratio elenchi* in his teeth, and, at once, you have him
annihilated. If he dare to reply, you can tell him from
Lucan (here it is) that speeches are mere *anemonae verborum*,
anemone words. The anemone, with great brilliancy, has
no smell. Or, if he begin to bluster, you may be down
upon him with *insomnia Jovis*, reveries of Jupiter—a
phrase which Silius Italicus (see here !) applies to thoughts
pompous and inflated. This will be sure and cut him to the
heart. He can do nothing but roll over and die. Will you
be kind enough to write ?

'In Greek we must have something pretty—from Demos-
[thenes, for example. Ἀνὴρ ὁ φεύγων καὶ πάλιν μαχήσεται.
Aner o pheugon kai palin makesetai.] There is a tolerably
good translation of it in Hudibras—

> For he that flies may fight again,
> Which he can never do that's slain.

In a Blackwood article nothing makes so fine a show as
your Greek. The very letters have an air of profundity
about them. Only observe, madam, the astute look of that
Epsilon ! That Phi ought certainly to be a bishop ! Was
ever there a smarter fellow than that Omicron ? Just twig
that Tau ! In short, there is nothing like Greek for a
genuine sensation-paper. In the present case your application is the most obvious thing in the world. Rap out the
sentence, with a huge oath, and by way of *ultimatum* at the

good-for-nothing dunder-headed villain who couldn't understand your plain English in relation to the chicken-bone. He'll take the hint and be off, you may depend upon it.'

These were all the instructions Mr. B. could afford me upon the topic in question, but I felt they would be entirely sufficient. I was, at length, able to write a genuine Blackwood article, and determined to do it forthwith. In taking leave of me, Mr. B. made a proposition for the purchase of the paper when written ; but as he could offer me only fifty guineas a sheet, I thought it better to let our society have it, than sacrifice it for so paltry a sum. Notwithstanding this niggardly spirit, however, the gentleman showed his consideration for me in all other respects, and indeed treated me with the greatest civility. His parting words made a deep impression upon my heart, and I hope I shall always remember them with gratitude.

' My dear Miss Zenobia,' he said, while the tears stood in his eyes, ' is there *any*thing else I can do to promote the success of your laudable undertaking ? Let me reflect ! It is just possible that you may not be able, so soon as convenient, to—to—get yourself drowned, or—choked with a chicken-bone, or—or hung,—or—bitten by a—but stay ! Now I think me of it, there are a couple of very excellent bull-dogs in the yard—fine fellows, I assure you—savage, and all that—indeed just the thing for your money—they'll have you eaten up, *auriculas* and all, in less than five minutes (here 's my watch !)—and then only think of the sensations ! Here ! I say—Tom !—Peter !—Dick, you villain !—let out those '—but as I was really in a great hurry, and had not another moment to spare, I was reluctantly forced to expedite my departure, and accordingly took leave *at once*—somewhat more abruptly, I admit, than strict courtesy would have otherwise allowed.

It was my primary object upon quitting Mr. Blackwood, to get into some immediate difficulty, pursuant to his advice, and with this view I spent the greater part of the day in wandering about Edinburgh, seeking for desperate adventures—adventures adequate to the intensity of my feelings, and adapted to the vast character of the article I intended to write. In this excursion I was attended by one negro-servant Pompey, and my little lap-dog Diana.

whom I had brought with me from Philadelphia. It was not, however, until late in the afternoon that I fully succeeded in my arduous undertaking. An important event then happened of which the following Blackwood article, in the tone heterogeneous, is the substance and result.

A PREDICAMENT

What chance, good lady, hath bereft you thus ?—COMUS.

IT was a quiet and still afternoon when I strolled forth in the goodly city of Edina. The confusion and bustle in the streets were terrible. Men were talking. Women were screaming. Children were choking. Pigs were whistling. Carts they rattled. Bulls they bellowed. Cows they lowed. Horses they neighed. Cats they caterwauled. Dogs they danced. *Danced !* Could it then be possible ? *Danced !* Alas, thought I, *my* dancing days are over ! Thus it is ever. What a host of gloomy recollections will ever and anon be awakened in the mind of genius and imaginative contemplation, especially of a genius doomed to the everlasting, and eternal, and continual, and, as one might say, the—*continued*—yes, the *continued and continuous*, bitter, harassing, disturbing, and, if I may be allowed the expression, the *very* disturbing influence of the serene, and godlike, and heavenly, and exalting, and elevated, and purifying effect of what may be rightly termed the most enviable, the most *truly* enviable—nay ! the most benignly beautiful, the most deliciously ethereal, and, as it were, the most *pretty* (if I may use so bold an expression) *thing* (pardon me, gentle reader !) in the world—but I am always led away by my feelings. In *such* a mind, I repeat, what a host of recollections are stirred up by a trifle ! The dogs danced ! *I*—I *could* not ! They frisked—I wept. They capered—I sobbed aloud. Touching circumstances ! which cannot fail to bring to the recollection of the classical reader that exquisite passage in relation to the fitness of things, which is to be found in the commencement of the third volume of that admirable and venerable Chinese novel, the *Jo-Go-Slow*.

In my solitary walk through the city I had two humble

but faithful companions. Diana, my poodle ! sweetest of
creatures ! She had a quantity of hair over her one eye, and
a blue riband tied fashionably around her neck. Diana was
not more than five inches in height, but her head was somewhat bigger than her body, and her tail, being cut off
exceedingly close, gave an air of injured innocence to the
interesting animal which rendered her a favourite with all.

And Pompey, my negro !—sweet Pompey ! how shall I
ever forget thee ? I had taken Pompey's arm. He was
three feet in height (I like to be particular) and about
seventy, or perhaps eighty, years of age. He had bow-legs
and was corpulent. His mouth should not be called small,
nor his ears short. His teeth, however, were like pearl,
and his large full eyes were deliciously white. Nature had
endowed him with no neck, and had placed his ankles (as
usual with that race) in the middle of the upper portion of
the feet. He was clad with a striking simplicity. His sole
garments were a stock of nine inches in height, and a
nearly new drab overcoat which had formerly been in the
service of the tall, stately, and illustrious Dr. Moneypenny.
It was a good overcoat. It was well cut. It was well made.
The coat was nearly new. Pompey held it up out of the
dirt with both hands.

There were three persons in our party, and two of them
have already been the subject of remark. There was a
third—that third person was myself. I am the Signora
Psyche Zenobia. I am *not* Suky Snobbs. My appearance is
commanding. On the memorable occasion of which I speak
I was habited in a crimson satin dress, with a sky-blue
Arabian mantelet. And the dress had trimmings of green
agraffas, and seven graceful flounces of the orange-coloured
auricula. I thus formed the third of the party. There was
the poodle. There was Pompey. There was myself. We
were *three*. Thus it is said there were originally but three
Furies—Melty, Nimmy, and Hetty—Meditation, Memory,
and Fiddling.

Leaning upon the arm of the gallant Pompey, and
attended at a respectful distance by Diana, I proceeded
down one of the populous and very pleasant streets of the
now deserted Edina. On a sudden, there presented itself to
view a church—a Gothic cathedral—vast, venerable, and

with a tall steeple, which towered into the sky. What madness now possessed me ? Why did I rush upon my fate ? I was seized with an uncontrollable desire to ascend the giddy pinnacle, and thence survey the immense extent of the city. The door of the cathedral stood invitingly open. My destiny prevailed. I entered the ominous archway. Where then was my guardian angel ?—if indeed such angels there be. *If !* Distressing monosyllable ! what a world of mystery, and meaning, and doubt, and uncertainty is there involved in thy two letters ! I entered the ominous archway ! I entered ; and, without injury to my orange-coloured auriculas, I passed beneath the portal, and emerged within the vestibule. Thus it is said the immense river Alfred passed, unscathed, and unwetted, beneath the sea.

I thought the staircases would never have an end. *Round !* Yes, they went round and up, and round and up, and round and up, until I could not help surmising, with the sagacious Pompey, upon whose supporting arm I leaned in all the confidence of early affection—I *could* not help surmising that the upper end of the continuous spiral ladder had been accidentally, or perhaps designedly, removed. I paused for breath ; and, in the meantime, an incident occurred of too momentous a nature in a moral, and also in a metaphysical point of view, to be passed over without notice. It appeared to me—indeed I was quite confident of the fact—I could not be mistaken—no ! I had, for some moments, carefully and anxiously observed the motions of my Diana—I say that *I could not be* mistaken—Diana *smelt a rat !* At once I called Pompey's attention to the subject, and he—he agreed with me. There was then no longer any reasonable room for doubt. The rat had been smelled—and by Diana. Heavens ! shall I ever forget the intense excitement of that moment ? Alas ! what is the boasted intellect of man ? The rat !—it was there—that is to say, it was somewhere. Diana smelled the rat. I—*I could* not ! Thus it is said the Prussian Isis has, for some persons, a sweet and very powerful perfume, while to others it is perfectly scentless.

The staircase had been surmounted, and there were now only three or four more upward steps intervening between us and the summit. We still ascended, and now only one

step remained. One step ! One little, little step ! Upon
one such little step in the great staircase of human life how
vast a sum of human happiness or misery often depends !
I thought of myself, then of Pompey, and then of the
mysterious and inexplicable destiny which surrounded us.
I thought of Pompey !—alas, I thought of love ! I thought
of the many false *steps* which have been taken, and may be
taken again. I resolved to be more cautious, more reserved.
I abandoned the arm of Pompey, and, without his assistance, surmounted the one remaining step, and gained the
chamber of the belfry. I was followed immediately afterwards by my poodle. Pompey alone remained behind. I
stood at the head of the staircase, and encouraged him to
ascend. He stretched forth to me his hand, and unfortunately in so doing was forced to abandon his firm hold upon
the overcoat. Will the gods never cease their persecution ?
The overcoat it dropped, and, with one of his feet, Pompey
stepped upon the long and trailing skirt of the overcoat.
He stumbled and fell—this consequence was inevitable.
He fell forwards, and, with his accursed head, striking me
full in the—in the breast, precipitated me headlong, together with himself, upon the hard, filthy, and detestable
floor of the belfry. But my revenge was sure, sudden, and
complete. Seizing him furiously by the wool with both
hands, I tore out a vast quantity of the black, and crisp,
and curling material, and tossed it from me with every
manifestation of disdain. It fell among the ropes of the
belfry and remained. Pompey arose, and said no word.
But he regarded me piteously with his large eyes and—
sighed. Ye gods—that sigh ! It sunk into my heart. And
the hair—the wool ! Could I have reached that wool I
would have bathed it with my tears, in testimony of regret.
But alas ! it was now far beyond my grasp. As it dangled
among the cordage of the bell, I fancied it still alive. I
fancied that it stood on end with indignation. Thus the
happydandy Flos Aeris of Java, bears, it is said, a beautiful
flower, which will live when pulled up by the roots. The
natives suspend it by a cord from the ceiling and enjoy its
fragrance for years.

Our quarrel was now made up, and we looked about the
room for an aperture through which to survey the city of

Edina. Windows there were none. The sole light admitted into the gloomy chamber proceeded from a square opening, about a foot in diameter, at a height of about seven feet from the floor. Yet what will the energy of true genius not effect ? I resolved to clamber up to this hole. A vast quantity of wheels, pinions, and other cabalistic-looking machinery stood opposite the hole, close to it ; and through the hole there passed an iron rod from the machinery. Between the wheels and the wall where the hole lay, there was barely room for my body—yet I was desperate, and determined to persevere. I called Pompey to my side.

' You perceive that aperture, Pompey. I wish to look through it. You will stand here just beneath the hole—so. Now, hold out one of your hands, Pompey, and let me step upon it—thus. Now, the other hand, Pompey, and with its aid I will get upon your shoulders.'

He did everything I wished, and I found, upon getting up, that I could easily pass my head and neck through the aperture. The prospect was sublime. Nothing could be more magnificent. I merely paused a moment to bid Diana behave herself, and assure Pompey that I would be considerate and bear as lightly as possible upon his shoulders. I told him I would be tender of his feelings—*ossi tender que beefsteak*. Having done this justice to my faithful friend, I gave myself up with great zest and enthusiasm to the enjoyment of the scene which so obligingly spread itself out before my eyes.

Upon this subject, however, I shall forbear to dilate. I will not describe the city of Edinburgh. Every one has been to Edinburgh—the classic Edina. I will confine myself to the momentous details of my own lamentable adventure. Having, in some measure, satisfied my curiosity in regard to the extent, situation, and general appearance of the city, I had leisure to survey the church in which I was, and the delicate architecture of the steeple. I observed that the aperture through which I had thrust my head was an opening in the dial-plate of a gigantic clock, and must have appeared, from the street, as a large keyhole, such as we see in the face of French watches. No doubt the true object was to admit the arm of an attendant, to adjust, when necessary, the hands of the clock from within. I observed also, with surprise, the immense size of these hands, the longest of which could not have been less than ten feet in length, and, where broadest, eight or nine inches in breadth. They were of solid steel apparently, and their edges appeared to be sharp. Having noticed these particulars, and some others, I again turned my eyes upon the glorious prospect below, and soon became absorbed in contemplation.

From this, after some minutes, I was aroused by the voice of Pompey, who declared he could stand it no longer, and requested that I would be so kind as to come down. This was unreasonable, and I told him so in a speech of some length. He replied but with an evident misunderstanding of my ideas upon the subject. I accordingly grew angry, and told him in plain words, that he was a fool, that he had committed an *ignoramus e-clench-eye*, that his notions were mere *insommary Bovis*, and his words little better than *an ennemywerrybor'em*. With this he appeared satisfied, and I resumed my contemplations.

It might have been half an hour after this altercation when, as I was deeply absorbed in the heavenly scenery beneath me, I was startled by something very cold which pressed with a gentle pressure upon the back of my neck. It is needless to say that I felt inexpressibly alarmed. I knew that Pompey was beneath my feet, and that Diana was sitting, according to my explicit directions, upon her hind legs in the farthest corner of the room. What could it be ? Alas ! I but too soon discovered. Turning my head gently to one side, I perceived, to my extreme horror, that the huge, glittering, scimitar-like minute-hand of the clock, had, in the course of its hourly revolution, *descended upon my neck*. There was, I knew, not a second to be lost. I pulled back at once—but it was too late. There was no chance of forcing my head through the mouth of that terrible trap in which it was so fairly caught, and which grew narrower and narrower with a rapidity too horrible to be conceived. The agony of that moment is not to be imagined. I threw up my hands and endeavoured, with all my strength, to force upward the ponderous iron bar. I might as well have tried to lift the cathedral itself. Down, down, down it came, closer and yet closer. I screamed to Pompey for aid : but he said that I had hurt his feelings by calling him 'an ignorant old squint eye'. I yelled to Diana; but she only said 'bow-wow-wow', and that 'I had told her on no account to stir from the corner'. Thus I had no relief to expect from my associates.

Meantime the ponderous and terrific *Scythe of Time* (for I now discovered the literal import of that classical phrase) had not stopped, nor was it likely to stop, in its career. Down and still down, it came. It had already buried its sharp edge a full inch in my flesh, and my sensations grew indistinct and confused. At one time I fancied myself in Philadelphia with the stately Dr. Moneypenny, at another in the back parlour of Mr. Blackwood receiving his invaluable instructions. And then again the sweet recollection of better and earlier times came over me, and I thought of that happy period when the world was not all a desert, and Pompey not altogether cruel.

The ticking of the machinery amused me. *Amused me*, I say, for my sensations now bordered upon perfect happiness, and the most trifling circumstances afforded me pleasure. The eternal *click-clack*, *click-clack*, *click-clack*, of the clock was the most melodious of music in my ears, and occasionally even put me in mind of the grateful sermonic harangues of Dr. Ollapod. Then there were the great figures upon the dial-plate—how intelligent, how intellectual, they all looked! And presently they took to dancing the Mazurka, and I think it was the figure V who performed the most to my satisfaction. She was evidently a lady of breeding. None of your swaggerers, and nothing at all indelicate in her motions. She did the pirouette to admiration—whirling round upon her apex. I made an endeavour to hand her a chair, for I saw that she appeared fatigued with her exertions—and it was not until then that I fully perceived my lamentable situation. Lamentable indeed! The bar had buried itself two inches in my neck. I was aroused to a sense of exquisite pain. I prayed for death, and, in the agony of the moment, could not help repeating those exquisite verses of the poet Miguel De Cervantes:

> Vanny Buren, tan escondida
> Query no te senty venny
> Pork and pleasure, delly morry
> Nommy, torny, darry, widdy!

But now a new horror presented itself, and one indeed sufficient to startle the strongest nerves. My eyes, from the cruel pressure of the machine, were absolutely starting from their sockets. While I was thinking how I should possibly manage without them, one actually tumbled out of my head, and, rolling down the steep side of the steeple, lodged in the rain gutter which ran along the eaves of the main building. The loss of the eye was not so much as the insolent air of independence and contempt with which it regarded me after it was out. There it lay in the gutter just under my nose, and the airs it gave itself would have been ridiculous had they not been disgusting. Such a winking and blinking were never before seen. This behaviour on the part of my eye in the gutter was not only irritating on account of its manifest insolence and shameful ingratitude, but was also exceedingly inconvenient on account of the sympathy which always exists between two eyes of the same head, however far apart. I was forced, in a manner, to wink and to blink, whether I would or not, in exact concert with the scoundrelly thing that lay just under my nose. I was presently relieved, however, by the dropping out of the other eye. In falling it took the same direction (possibly a concerted plot) as its fellow. Both rolled out of the gutter together, and in truth I was very glad to get rid of them.

The bar was now four inches and a half deep in my neck, and there was only a little bit of skin to cut through. My sensations were those of entire happiness, for I felt that in a few minutes, at farthest, I should be relieved from my disagreeable situation. And in this expectation I was not at all deceived. At twenty-five minutes past five in the afternoon precisely, the huge minute-hand had proceeded sufficiently far on its terrible revolution to sever the small remainder of my neck. I was not sorry to see the head which had occasioned me so much embarrassment at length make a final separation from my body. It first rolled down the side of the steeple, then lodged, for a few seconds, in the gutter, and then made its way, with a plunge, into the middle of the street.

I will candidly confess that my feelings were now of the most singular—nay, of the most mysterious, the most perplexing and incomprehensible character. My senses were here and there at one and the same moment. With my head I imagined, at one time, that I the head, was the real Signora Psyche Zenobia—at another I felt convinced that myself, the body, was the proper identity. To clear my ideas upon this topic I felt in my pocket for my snuff-box, but, upon getting it, and endeavouring to apply a pinch of its grateful contents in the ordinary manner, I became immediately aware of my peculiar deficiency, and threw the box at once down to my head. It took a pinch with great satisfaction, and smiled me an acknowledgment in return. Shortly afterwards it made me a speech, which I could hear but indistinctly without ears. I gathered enough, however, to know that it was astonished at my wishing to remain alive under such circumstances. In the concluding sentences it quoted the noble words of Ariosto—

> *Il pover hommy che non sera corty*
> *And have a combat tenty erry morty ;*

thus comparing me to the hero who, in the heat of the combat, not perceiving that he was dead, continued to contest the battle with inextinguishable valour. There was nothing now to prevent my getting down from my elevation, and I did so. What it was that Pompey saw so *very* peculiar in my appearance I have never yet been able to find out. The fellow opened his mouth from ear to ear, and shut his two eyes as if he were endeavouring to crack nuts between the lids. Finally, throwing off his overcoat, he made one spring for the staircase and disappeared. I hurled after the scoundrel those vehement words of Demosthenes—

> *Andrew O'Phlegethon, you really make haste to fly,*

and then turned to the darling of my heart, to the one-eyed ! the shaggy-haired Diana. Alas ! what a horrible vision affronted my eyes ? *Was* that a rat I saw skulking into his hole ? *Are* these the picked bones of the little angel who has been cruelly devoured by the monster ? Ye Gods ! and what *do* I behold—*is* that the departed spirit, the shade, the ghost of my beloved puppy, which I perceive sitting with a grace so melancholy, in the corner ? Hearken !

for she speaks, and, heavens ! it is in the German of
Schiller—

> Unt stubby duk, so stubby dun
> Duk she ! duk she !

Alas ! and are not her words too true ?

> And if I died at least I died
> For thee—for thee.

Sweet creature ! she *too* has sacrificed herself in my behalf.
Dogless, niggerless, headless, what *now* remains for the
unhappy Signora Psyche Zenobia ? Alas—*nothing !* I
have done.

MYSTIFICATION

Slid, if these be your ' passados ' and ' montantes ', I'll have none of them.
NED KNOWLES.

THE Baron Ritzner Von Jung was of a noble Hungarian
family, every member of which (at least as far back into
antiquity as any certain records extend) was more or less
remarkable for talent of some description—the majority for
that species of *grotesquerie* in conception of which Tieck,
a scion of the house, has given some vivid, although by no
means the most vivid exemplifications. My acquaintance
with Ritzner commenced at the magnificent Chateau Jung,
into which a train of droll adventures, not to be made public,
threw me during the summer months of the year 18—.
Here it was I obtained a place in his regard, and here, with
somewhat more difficulty, a partial insight into his mental
conformation. In later days this insight grew more clear,
as the intimacy which had at first permitted it became more
close ; and when, after three years separation, we met at
G——n, I knew all that it was necessary to know of the
character of the Baron Ritzner Von Jung.

I remember the buzz of curiosity which his advent
excited within the college precincts on the night of the
twenty-fifth of June. I remember still more distinctly,
that while he was pronounced by all parties at first sight
' the most remarkable man in the world ', no person made
any attempt at accounting for this opinion. That he
was *unique* appeared so undeniable, that it was deemed

impertinent to inquire wherein the uniquity consisted. But, letting this matter pass for the present, I will merely observe that, from the first moment of his setting foot within the limits of the university, he began to exercise over the habits, manners, persons, purses, and propensities of the whole community which surrounded him, an influence the most extensive and despotic, yet at the same time the most indefinitive and altogether unaccountable. Thus the brief period of his residence at the university forms an era in its annals, and is characterized by all classes of people appertaining to it or its dependencies as 'that very extraordinary epoch forming the domination of the Baron Ritzner Von Jung'.

Upon his advent to G——n, he sought me out in my apartments. He was then of no particular age, by which I mean that it was impossible to form a guess respecting his age by any data personally afforded. He might have been fifteen or fifty, and *was* twenty-one years and seven months. He was by no means a handsome man—perhaps the reverse. The contour of his face was somewhat angular and harsh. His forehead was lofty and very fair ; his nose a snub ; his eyes large, heavy, glassy, and meaningless. About the mouth there was more to be observed. The lips were gently protruded, and rested the one upon the other after such fashion that it is impossible to conceive any, even the most complex, combination of human features, conveying so entirely, and so singly, the idea of unmitigated gravity, solemnity, and repose.

It will be perceived, no doubt, from what I have already said, that the Baron was one of those human anomalies now and then to be found, who make the science of *mystification* the study and the business of their lives. For this science a peculiar turn of mind gave him instinctively the cue, while his physical appearance afforded him unusual facilities for carrying his projects into effect. I firmly believe that no student at G——n, during that renowned epoch so quaintly termed the domination of the Baron Ritzner Von Jung, ever rightly entered into the mystery which overshadowed his character. I truly think that no person at the university, with the exception of myself, ever suspected him to be capable of a joke, verbal or practical :—

the old bull-dog at the garden-gate would sooner have been
accused—the ghost of Heraclitus—or the wig of the
Emeritus Professor of Theology. This, too, when it was
evident that the most egregious and unpardonable of all
conceivable tricks, whimsicalities, and buffooneries were
brought about, if not directly by him, at least plainly
through his intermediate agency or connivance. The
beauty, if I may so call it, of his art *mystifique*, lay in that
consummate ability (resulting from an almost intuitive
knowledge of human nature, and a most wonderful self-
possession) by means of which he never failed to make it
appear that the drolleries he was occupied in bringing to
a point, arose partly in spite, and partly in consequence of
the laudable efforts he was making for their prevention, and
for the preservation of the good order and dignity of Alma
Mater. The deep, the poignant, the overwhelming mortification, which upon each such failure of his praiseworthy
endeavours, would suffuse every lineament of his countenance, left not the slightest room for doubt of his sincerity
in the bosoms of even his most sceptical companions. The
adroitness, too, was no less worthy of observation by which
he contrived to shift the sense of the grotesque from the
creator to the created—from his own person to the absurdities to which he had given rise. In no instance before
that of which I speak, have I known the habitual mystific
escape the natural consequence of his manœuvres—an
attachment of the ludicrous to his own character and person.
Continually enveloped in an atmosphere of whim, my
friend appeared to live only for the severities of society ;
and not even his own household have for a moment
associated other ideas than those of the rigid and august
with the memory of the Baron Ritzner Von Jung.

During the epoch of his residence at G——n it really
appeared that the demon of the *dolce far niente* lay like an
incubus upon the university. Nothing at least, was done,
beyond eating and drinking, and making merry. The
apartments of the students were converted into so many
pot-houses, and there was no pot-house of them all more
famous or more frequented than that of the Baron. Our
carousals here were many, and boisterous, and long, and
never unfruitful of events.

Upon one occasion we had protracted our sitting until nearly daybreak, and an unusual quantity of wine had been drunk. The company consisted of seven or eight individuals besides the Baron and myself. Most of these were young men of wealth, of high connection, of great family pride, and all alive with an exaggerated sense of honour. They abounded in the most ultra German opinions respecting the *duello*. To these Quixotic notions some recent Parisian publications, backed by three or four desperate, and fatal rencontres at G——n, had given new vigour and impulse ; and thus the conversation, during the greater part of the night, had run wild upon the all-engrossing topic of the times. The Baron, who had been unusually silent and abstracted in the earlier portion of the evening, at length seemed to be aroused from his apathy, took a leading part in the discourse, and dwelt upon the benefits, and more especially upon the beauties, of the received code of etiquette in passages of arms with an ardour, an eloquence, an impressiveness, and an affectionateness of manner, which elicited the warmest enthusiasm from his hearers in general, and absolutely staggered even myself, who well knew him to be at heart a ridiculer of those very points for which he contended, and especially to hold the entire *fanfaronade* of duelling etiquette in the sovereign contempt which it deserves.

Looking around me during a pause in the Baron's discourse (of which my readers may gather some faint idea when I say that it bore resemblance to the fervid, chanting, monotonous, yet musical, sermonic manner of Coleridge) I perceived symptoms of even more than the general interest in the countenance of one of the party. This gentleman, whom I shall call Hermann, was an original in every respect—except, perhaps, in the single particular that he was a very great fool. He contrived to bear, however, among a particular set at the university, a reputation for deep metaphysical thinking, and, I believe, for some logical talent. As a duellist he had acquired great renown, even at G——n. I forget the precise number of victims who had fallen at his hands ; but they were many. He was a man of courage undoubtedly. But it was upon his minute acquaintance with the etiquette of the *duello,* and the *nicety* of his sense of honour, that he most especially prided himself. These things were a hobby which he rode to the death. To Ritzner, ever upon the look-out for the grotesque, his peculiarities had for a long time past afforded food for mystification. Of this, however, I was not aware ; although, in the present instance, I saw clearly that something of a whimsical nature was upon the *tapis* with my friend, and that Hermann was its especial object.

As the former proceeded in his discourse, or rather monologue, I perceived the excitement of the latter momently increasing. At length he spoke ; offering some objection to a point insisted upon by R., and giving his reasons in detail. To these the Baron replied at length (still maintaining his exaggerated tone of sentiment) and concluding, in what I thought very bad taste, with a sarcasm and a sneer. The hobby of Hermann now took the bit in his teeth. This I could discern by the studied hair-splitting *farrago* of his rejoinder. His last words I distinctly remember. ' Your opinions, allow me to say, Baron Von Jung, although in the main correct, are, in many nice points, discreditable to yourself and to the university of which you are a member. In a few respects they are even unworthy of serious refutation. I would say more than this, sir, were it not for the fear of giving you offence (here the speaker smiled blandly), I would say, sir, that your opinions are not the opinions to be expected from a gentleman.'

As Hermann completed this equivocal sentence, all eyes were turned upon the Baron. He became pale, then excessively red ; then, dropping his pocket-handkerchief, stooped to recover it, when I caught a glimpse of his countenance, while it could be seen by no one else at the table. It was radiant with the quizzical expression which was its natural character, but which I had never seen it assume except when we were alone together, and when he unbent himself freely. In an instant afterward he stood erect, confronting Hermann ; and so total an alteration of countenance in so short a period I certainly never saw before. For a moment I even fancied that I had misconceived him, and that he was in sober earnest. He appeared to be stifling with passion, and his face was cadaverously white. For a short time he remained silent, apparently

striving to master his emotion. Having at length seemingly
succeeded, he reached a decanter which stood near him,
saying as he held it firmly clenched—' The language you
have thought proper to employ, Mynheer Hermann, in
addressing yourself to me, is objectionable in so many
particulars, that I have neither temper nor time for speci-
fication. That my opinions, however, are not the opinions
to be expected from a gentleman, is an observation so
directly offensive as to allow me but one line of conduct.
Some courtesy, nevertheless, is due to the presence of this
company, and to yourself, at this moment, as my guest.
You will pardon me, therefore, if, upon this consideration,
I deviate slightly from the general usage among gentlemen
in similar cases of personal affront. You will forgive me
for the moderate tax I shall make upon your imagination,
and endeavour to consider, for an instant, the reflection of
your person in yonder mirror as the living Mynheer Hermann himself. This being done, there will be no difficulty
whatever. I shall discharge this decanter of wine at your
image in yonder mirror, and thus fulfil all the spirit, if not
the exact letter, of resentment for your insult, while the
necessity of physical violence to your real person will be
obviated.'

With these words he hurled the decanter, full of wine,
against the mirror which hung directly opposite Hermann ;
striking the reflection of his person with great precision, and
of course shattering the glass into fragments. The whole
company at once started to their feet, and, with the
exception of myself and Ritzner, took their departure. As
Hermann went out, the Baron whispered me that I should
follow him and make an offer of my services. To this I
agreed ; not knowing precisely what to make of so ridiculous a piece of business.

The duellist accepted my aid with his stiff and *ultra
recherché* air, and, taking my arm, led me to his apartment.
I could hardly forbear laughing in his face while he proceeded to discuss, with the profoundest gravity, what he
termed ' the refinedly peculiar character ' of the insult he
had received. After a tiresome harangue in his ordinary
style, he took down from his book-shelves a number of
musty volumes on the subject of the *duello*, and entertained

me for a long time with their contents ; reading aloud, and commenting earnestly as he read. I can just remember the titles of some of the works. There were the ' Ordonnance of Philip le Bel on Single Combat ' ; the ' Theatre of Honor ', by Favyn, and a treatise ' On the Permission of Duels ', by Andiguier. He displayed, also, with much pomposity, Brantome's ' Memoirs of Duels ', published at Cologne, in 1666, in the types of Elzevir—a precious and unique vellum-paper volume, with a fine margin, and bound by Derôme. But he requested my attention particularly, and with an air of mysterious sagacity, to a thick octavo, written in barbarous Latin by one Hedelin, a Frenchman, and having the quaint title, *Duelli Lex Scripta, et non ; aliterque.* From this he read me one of the drollest chapters in the world concerning *Injuriæ per applicationem, per constructionem, et per se,* about half of which, he averred, was strictly applicable to his own ' refinedly peculiar ' case, although not one syllable of the whole matter could I understand for the life of me. Having finished the chapter, he closed the book, and demanded what I thought necessary to be done. I replied that I had entire confidence in his superior delicacy of feeling, and would abide by what he proposed. With this answer he seemed flattered, and sat down to write a note to the Baron. It ran thus :

SIR,—My friend, Mr. P——, will hand you this note. I find it incumbent upon me to request, at your earliest convenience, an explanation of this evening's occurrences at your chambers. In the event of your declining this request, Mr. P. will be happy to arrange, with any friend whom you may appoint, the steps preliminary to a meeting.
With sentiments of perfect respect,
Your most humble servant,
JOHAN HERMANN.

To the Baron Ritzner Von Jung,
August 18*th,* 18—.

Not knowing what better to do, I called upon Ritzner with this epistle. He bowed as I presented it ; then, with a grave countenance, motioned me to a seat. Having perused the cartel, he wrote the following reply, which I carried to Hermann.

Sir,—Through our common friend, Mr. P., I have received your note of this evening. Upon due reflection I frankly admit the propriety of the explanation you suggest. This being admitted, I still find great difficulty (owing to the *refinedly peculiar* nature of our disagreement, and of the personal affront offered on my part) in so wording what I have to say by way of apology, as to meet all the minute exigencies, and all the variable shadows of the case. I have great reliance, however, on that extreme delicacy of discrimination, in matters appertaining to the rules of etiquette, for which you have been so long and so pre-eminently distinguished. With perfect certainty, therefore, of being comprehended, I beg leave, in lieu of offering any sentiments of my own, to refer you to the opinions of the Sieur Hedelin, as set forth in the ninth paragraph of the chapter of *Injuriæ per applicationem, per constructionem, et per se*, in his *Duelli Lex scripta, et non; aliterque*. The nicety of your discernment in all the matters here treated, will be sufficient, I am assured, to convince you *that the mere circumstance of me referring you* to this admirable passage, ought to satisfy your request, as a man of honour, for explanation.

With sentiments of profound respect,
Your most obedient servant,
Von Jung.

The Herr Johan Hermann.
  August 18*th*, 18—.

Hermann commenced the perusal of this epistle with a scowl, which, however, was converted into a smile of the most ludicrous self-complacency as he came to the rig-marole about *Injuriæ per applicationem, per constructionem, et per se*. Having finished reading, he begged me, with the blandest of all possible smiles, to be seated, while he made reference to the treatise in question. Turning to the passage specified, he read it with great care to himself, then closed the book, and desired me, in my character of confidential acquaintance, to express to the Baron Von Jung his exalted sense of his chivalrous behaviour, and, in that of second, to assure him that the explanation offered was of the fullest, the most honourable, and the most unequivocally satisfactory nature.

Somewhat amazed at all this, I made my retreat to the Baron. He seemed to receive Hermann's amicable letter as a matter of course, and after a few words of general conversation, went to an inner room and brought out the everlasting treatise *Duelli Lex scripta, et non ; aliterque.* He handed me the volume and asked me to look over some portion of it. I did so, but to little purpose, not being able to gather the least particle of meaning. He then took the book himself, and read me a chapter aloud. To my surprise, what he read proved to be a most horribly absurd account of a duel between two baboons. He now explained the mystery ; showing that the volume, as it appeared *prima facie*, was written upon the plan of the nonsense verses of Du Bartas ; that is to say, the language was ingeniously framed so as to present to the ear all the outward signs of intelligibility, and even of profundity, while in fact not a shadow of meaning existed. The key to the whole was found in leaving out every second and third word alternately, when there appeared a series of ludicrous quizzes upon a single combat as practised in modern times.

The Baron afterwards informed me that he had purposely thrown the treatise in Hermann's way two or three weeks before the adventure, and that he was satisfied, from the general tenor of his conversation, that he had studied it with the deepest attention, and firmly believed it to be a work of unusual merit. Upon this hint he proceeded. Hermann would have died a thousand deaths rather than acknowledge his inability to understand anything and everything in the universe that had ever been written about the *duello*.

X-ING A PARAGRAB

As it is well known that the 'wise men' came 'from the East', and as Mr. Touch-and-go Bullet-head came from the East, it follows that Mr. Bullet-head was a wise man; and if collateral proof of the matter be needed, here we have it—Mr. B. was an editor. Irascibility was his sole foible; for in fact the obstinacy of which men accused him was anything but his *foible*, since he justly considered it his *forte*. It was his strong point—his virtue; and it would have required all the logic of a Brownson to convince him that it was 'anything else'.

I have shown that Touch-and-go Bullet-head was a wise man; and the only occasion on which he did not prove infallible, was when, abandoning that legitimate home for all wise men, the East, he migrated to the city of Alexander-the-Great-o-nopolis, or some place of a similar title, out West.

I must do him the justice to say, however, that when he made up his mind finally to settle in that town, it was under the impression that no newspaper, and consequently no editor, existed in that particular section of the country. In establishing 'The Tea-Pot', he expected to have the field all to himself. I feel confident he never would have dreamed of taking up his residence in Alexander-the-Great-o-nopolis, had he been aware that, in Alexander-the-Great-o-nopolis, there lived a gentleman named John Smith (if I rightly remember), who, for many years, had there quietly grown fat in editing and publishing the 'Alexander-the-Great-o-nopolis Gazette'. It was solely, therefore, on account of having been misinformed, that Mr. Bullet-head found himself in Alex——suppose we call it Nopolis 'for short '—but, as he *did* find himself there, he determined to keep up his character for obst—for firmness, and remain. So remain he did; and he did more; he unpacked his press, type, etc., etc., rented an office exactly opposite to that of the 'Gazette', and, on the third morning after his arrival, issued the first number of 'The Alexan '—that is to say, of 'The Nopolis Tea-Pot ':—as nearly as I can recollect, this was the name of the new paper.

The leading article, I must admit, was brilliant—not to say severe. It was especially bitter about things in general —and as for the editor of ' The Gazette ', he was torn all to pieces in particular. Some of Bullet-head's remarks were really so fiery that I have always, since that time, been forced to look upon John Smith, who is still alive, in the light of a salamander. I cannot pretend to give *all* the ' Tea-Pot's ' paragraphs *verbatim*, but one of them ran thus:

' Oh, yes !—Oh, we perceive ! Oh, no doubt ! The editor over the way is a genius—Oh, my ! Oh, goodness, gracious !— what *is* this world coming to ? *Oh, tempora ! Oh, Moses !* '

A philippic at once so caustic and so classical, alighted like a bombshell among the hitherto peaceful citizens of Nopolis. Groups of excited individuals gathered at the corners of the streets. Everyone awaited, with heartfelt anxiety, the reply of the dignified Smith. Next morning it appeared, as follows :

' We quote from " The Tea-Pot " of yesterday the sub-joined paragraph :—" *Oh*, yes ! *Oh*, we perceive ! *Oh*, no doubt ! *Oh*, my ! *Oh*, goodness ! *Oh*, tempora ! *Oh*, Moses ! " Why, the fellow is all O ! That accounts for his reasoning in a circle, and explains why there is neither beginning nor end to him, nor to anything that he says. We really do not believe the vagabond can write a word that hasn't an O in it. Wonder if this O-ing is a habit of his? By-the-by, he came away from Down-East in a great hurry. Wonder if he *O's* as much there as he does here ? " *O !* it is pitiful ".'

The indignation of Mr. Bullet-head at these scandalous insinuations, I shall not attempt to describe. On the eel-skinning principle, however, he did not seem to be so much incensed at the attack upon his integrity as one might have imagined. It was the sneer at his *style* that drove him to desperation. What !—*he* Touch-and-go Bullet-head !—not able to write a word without an O in it ! He would soon let the jackanapes see that he was mistaken. Yes ! he would let him see how *much* he was mistaken, the puppy ! He, Touch-and-go Bullet-head, of Frogpondium, would let Mr. John Smith perceive that he, Bullet-head, could indite, if it so pleased him, a whole paragraph—ay ! a whole article—in which that contemptible vowel should not

once—not even *once*—make its appearance. But no ;—
that would be yielding a point to the said John Smith.
He, Bullet-head, would make *no* alteration in his style, to
suit the caprices of any Mr. Smith in Christendom. Perish
so vile a thought ! The O forever ! He would persist in
the O. He would be as O-wy as O-wy could be.

Burning with the chivalry of this determination, the
great Touch-and-go, in the next 'Tea-Pot', came out
merely with this simple but resolute paragraph, in reference
to this unhappy affair :

' The editor of the " Tea-Pot " has the *honour* of advising
the editor of " The Gazette " that he (the " Tea-Pot ")
will take an opportunity in to-morrow morning's paper, of
convincing him (the " Gazette ") that he (the " Tea-Pot ")
both can and will be *his own master,* as regards style ;—he
(the " Tea-Pot ") intending to show him (the " Gazette ")
the supreme, and indeed the withering contempt with which
the criticism of him (the " Gazette ") inspires the independent bosom of him (the " Tea-Pot ") by composing for the
especial gratification (?) of him (the " Gazette ") a leading
article, of some extent, in which the beautiful vowel—the
emblem of Eternity—yet so inoffensive to the hyper-
exquisite delicacy of him (the "Gazette ") shall most
certainly *not be avoided* by his (the " Gazette's ") most
obedient, humble servant, the " Tea-Pot ". " So much for
Buckingham ! " '

In fulfilment of the awful threat thus darkly intimated
rather than decidedly enunciated, the great Bullet-head,
turning a deaf ear to all entreaties for ' copy ', and simply
requesting his foreman to ' go to the d——l ', when he (the
foreman) assured him (the ' Tea-Pot ! ') that it was high
time to ' go to press ' : turning a deaf ear to everything,
I say, the great Bullet-head sat up until day-break, con-
suming the midnight oil, and absorbed in the composition
of the really unparalleled paragraph, which follows :

' So ho, John ! how now ? Told you so, you know.
Don't crow, another time, before you're out of the woods !
Does your mother *know* you're out ? Oh, no, no !—so go
home at once, now, John, to your odious old woods of
Concord ! Go home to your woods, old owl—go ! You
wont ? Oh, poh, poh, John, don't do so ! You've *got* to go.

you know ! So go at once, and don't go slow ; for nobody owns you here, you know. Oh, John, John, if you *don't* go you're no *homo*—no ! You're only a fowl, an owl ; a cow, a sow ; a doll, a poll ; a poor, old, good-for-nothing-to-nobody, log, dog, hog, or frog, come out of a Concord bog. Cool, now—cool ! *Do* be cool, you fool ! None of your crowing, old cock ! Don't frown so—don't ! Don't hollo, nor howl, nor growl, nor bow-wow-wow ! Good Lord, John, how you *do* look ! Told you so, you know—but stop rolling your goose of an old poll about so, and go and drown your sorrows in a bowl ! '

Exhausted, very naturally, by so stupendous an effort, the great Touch-and-go could attend to nothing farther that night. Firmly, composedly, yet with an air of conscious power, he handed his MS. to the devil in waiting, and then, walking leisurely home, retired, with ineffable dignity, to bed.

Meantime the devil to whom the copy was entrusted, ran up stairs to his ' case ', in an unutterable hurry, and forthwith made a commencement at ' setting ' the MS. ' up '.

In the first place, of course—as the opening word was ' So '—he made a plunge into the capital S hole and came out in triumph with a capital S. Elated by this success, he immediately threw himself upon the little-*o* box with a blindfold impetuosity—but who shall describe his horror when his fingers came up without the anticipated letter in their clutch ? who shall paint his astonishment and rage at perceiving, as he rubbed his knuckles, that he had been only thumping them to no purpose, against the bottom of an *empty* box. Not a single little-*o* was in the little-*o* hole ; and, glancing fearfully at the capital-O partition, he found *that*, to his extreme terror, in a precisely similar predica - ment. Awe-stricken, his first impulse was to rush to the foreman.

' Sir ! ' said he, gasping for breath, ' I can't never set up nothing without no o's.'

' *What* do you mean by that ? ' growled the foreman, who was in a very ill-humour at being kept up so late.

' Why, sir, there beant an *o* in the office, neither a big un nor a little un ! '

'What—what the d——l has become of all that were in the case ? '

'*I* don't know, sir,' said the boy, ' but one of them ere G'zette devils is bin prowling bout here all night, and I spect *he's* gone and cabbaged em every one.'

'Dod rot him ! I haven't a doubt of it,' replied the foreman, getting purple with rage—' but I tell you what you do, Bob, that's a good boy—you go over the first chance you get and hook every one of their i's and (d—n them !) their izzards.'

'Jist so,' replied Bob, with a wink and a frown—' *I'll* be into em, *I'll* let em know a thing or two ; but in de meantime, that ere paragrab ? *Mus* go in to-night, you know—else there'll be the d——l to pay, and—'

'And not a *bit* of pitch hot,' interrupted the foreman, with a deep sigh and an emphasis on the ' bit '. ' Is it a *very* long paragraph, Bob ? '

'Shouldn't call it a *wery* long paragrab,' said Bob.

'Ah, well, then ! do the best you can with it ! we *must* get to press,' said the foreman, who was over head and ears in work ; ' just stick in some other letter for *o*, nobody's going to read the fellow's trash, any how.'

'*Wery* well,' replied Bob, ' here goes it ! ' and off he hurried to his case ; muttering as he went—' Considdeble vell, them ere expressions, perticcler for a man as doesn't swar. So I's to gouge out all their eyes, eh ? and d——n all their gizzards ! Vell ! this here's the chap as is jist able *for* to do it.' The fact is, that although Bob was but twelve years old and four feet high, he was equal to any amount of fight, in a small way.

The exigency here described is by no means of rare occurrence in printing-offices ; and I cannot tell how to account for it, but the fact is indisputable, that when the exigency *does* occur, it almost always happens that *x* is adopted as a substitute for the letter deficient. The true reason, perhaps, is that *x* is rather the most superabundant letter in the cases, or at least *was* so in old times—long enough to render the substitution in question an habitual thing with printers. As for Bob, he would have considered it heretical to employ any other character, in a case of this kind, than the *x* to which he had been accustomed.

' I *shell* have to *x* this ere paragrab,' said he to himself, as he read it over in astonishment, ' but it's jest about the awfulest *o*-wy paragrab I ever *did* see ' : so *x* it he did, unflinchingly, and to press it went *x-ed.*

Next morning the population of Nopolis were taken all aback by reading, in ' The Tea-Pot ', the following extra-ordinary leader :

' Sx hx, Jxhn ! hxw nxw ! Txld yxu sx, yxu knxw. Dxn't crxw, anxther time, befxre yxu're xut xf the wxxds ! Dxes yxur mxther *knxw* yxu're xut ? Xh, nx, nx ! sx gx hxme at xnce, nxw, Jxhn, tx yxur xdixus xld wxxds xf Cxncxrd ! Gx hxme tx yxur wxxds, xld xwl—gx ! Yxu wxnt ? Xh, pxh, pxh, Jxhn, dxn't dx sx ! Yxu've *gxt* tx gx, yxu knxw ! sx gx at xnce, and dxn't gx slxw ; fxr nxbxdy xwns yxu here, yxu knxw. Xh, Jxhn, Jxhn, if yxu *dxn't* gx yxu're nx *hxmx*—nx ! Yxu're xnly a fxwl, an xwl ; a cxw, a sxw ; a dxll, a pxll ; a pxxr xld gxxd-fxr-nxthing-tx-nxbxdy lxg, dxg, hxg, xr frxg, cxme xut xf a Cxncxrd bxg. Cxxl, nxw—cxxl ! Dx be cxxl, yxu fxxl ! Nxne xf yxur crxwing, xld cxck ! Dxn't frxwn sx—dxn't ! Dxn't hxllx, nxr hxwl, nxr grxwl, nxr bxw-wxw-wxw ! Gxxd Lxrd, Jxhn, hxw yxu *dx* lxxk ! Txld yxu sx, yxu knxw, but stxp rxlling yxur gxxse xf an xld pxll abxut sx, and gx and drxwn yxur sxrrxws in a bxwl ! '

The uproar occasioned by this mystical and cabalistical article, is not to be conceived. The first definite idea entertained by the populace was, that some diabolical treason lay concealed in the hieroglyphics ; and there was a general rush to Bullet-head's residence, for the purpose of riding him on a rail ; but that gentleman was nowhere to be found. He had vanished, no one could tell how ; and not even the ghost of him has ever been seen since.

Unable to discover its legitimate object, the popular fury at length subsided ; leaving behind it, by way of sediment, quite a medley of opinion about this unhappy affair.

One gentleman thought the whole an X-ellent joke.

Another said that, indeed, Bullet-head had shown much X-uberance of fancy.

A third admitted him X-entric, but no more.

A fourth could only suppose it the Yankee's design to X-press, in a general way, his X-asperation.

'Say, rather, to set an X-ample to posterity,' suggested a fifth.

That Bullet-head had been driven to an extremity, was clear to all ; and in fact, since *that* editor could not be found, there was some talk about lynching the other one.

The more common conclusion, however, was, that the affair was, simply, X-traordinary and in-X-plicable. Even the town mathematician confessed that he could make nothing of so dark a problem. X, everybody knew, was an unknown quantity ; but in this case (as he properly observed), there was an unknown quantity of X.

The opinion of Bob, the devil (who kept dark ' about his having X-ed the paragrab '), did not meet with so much attention as I think it deserved, although it was very openly and very fearlessly expressed. He said that, for his part, he had no doubt about the matter at all, that it was a clear case, that Mr. Bullet-head never *could* be persvaded fur to drink like other folks, but vas *c*ontinually a-svigging o' that ere blessed XXX ale, and, as a naiteral consekvence, it just puffed him up savage, and made him X (cross) in the X-treme.

DIDDLING

CONSIDERED AS ONE OF THE EXACT SCIENCES

Hey, diddle diddle,
The cat and the fiddle.

SINCE the world began there have been two Jeremys. The one wrote a Jeremiad about usury, and was called Jeremy Bentham. He has been much admired by Mr. John Neal, and was a great man in a small way. The other gave name to the most important of the Exact Sciences, and was a great man in a *great* way—I may say, indeed, in the very greatest of ways.

Diddling—or the abstract idea conveyed by the verb to diddle—is sufficiently well understood. Yet the fact, the deed, the thing *diddling*, is somewhat difficult to define. We may get, however, at a tolerably distinct conception of the matter in hand, by defining—not the thing, diddling, in itself—but man, as an animal that diddles. Had Plato but hit upon this, he would have been spared the affront of the picked chicken.

Very pertinently it was demanded of Plato, why a picked chicken, which was clearly a ' biped without feathers ', was not, according to his own definition, a man ? But I am not to be bothered by any similar query. Man is an animal that diddles, and there is *no* animal that diddles *but* man. It will take an entire hen-coop of picked chickens to get over that.

What constitutes the essence, the nare, the principle of diddling is, in fact, peculiar to the class of creatures that wear coats and pantaloons. A crow thieves ; a fox cheats ; a weasel outwits ; a man diddles. To diddle is his destiny. ' Man was made to mourn,' says the poet. But not so :— he was made to diddle. This is his aim—his object—his *end*. And for this reason when a man's diddled we say he's ' done '.

Diddling, rightly considered, is a compound, of which the ingredients are minuteness, interest, perseverance, ingenuity, audacity, *nonchalance*, originality, impertinence, and *grin*.

Minuteness :—Your diddler is minute. His operations are upon a small scale. His business is retail, for cash, or approved paper at sight. Should he ever be tempted into magnificent speculation, he then, at once, loses his distinctive features, and becomes what we term ' financier '. This latter word conveys the diddling idea in every respect except that of magnitude. A diddler may thus be regarded as a banker *in petto*—a ' financial operation ', as a diddle at Brobdignag. The one is to the other, as Homer to ' Flaccus ' —as a Mastodon to a mouse—as the tail of a comet to that of a pig.

Interest :—Your diddler is guided by self-interest. He scorns to diddle for the mere *sake* of the diddle. He has an object in view—his pocket—and yours. He regards always the main chance. He looks to Number One. You are Number Two, and must look to yourself.

Perseverance :—Your diddler perseveres. He is not readily discouraged. Should even the banks break, he cares nothing about it. He steadily pursues his end, and

Ut canis a corio nunquam absterrebitur uncto,

so he never lets go of his game.

Ingenuity :—Your diddler is ingenious. He has constructiveness large. He understands plot. He invents and circumvents. Were he not Alexander he would be Diogenes. Were he not a diddler, he would be a maker of patent rat-traps or an angler for trout.

Audacity :—Your diddler is audacious. He is a bold man. He carries the war into Africa. He conquers all by assault. He would not fear the daggers of the Frey Herren. With a little more prudence Dick Turpin would have made a good diddler ; with a trifle less blarney, Daniel O'Connell ; with a pound or two more brains, Charles the Twelfth.

Nonchalance :—Your diddler is *nonchalant*. He is not at all nervous. He never *had* any nerves. He is never seduced into a flurry. He is never put out—unless put out of doors. He is cool—cool as a cucumber. He is calm—' calm as a smile from Lady Bury '. He is easy—easy as an old glove, or the damsels of ancient Baiæ.

Originality :—Your diddler is original—conscientiously so. His thoughts are his own. He would scorn to employ those of another. A stale trick is his aversion. He would return a purse, I am sure, upon discovering that he had obtained it by an unoriginal diddle.

Impertinence :—Your diddler is impertinent. He swaggers. He sets his arms a-kimbo. He thrusts his hands in his trowsers' pockets. He sneers in your face. He treads on your corns. He eats your dinner, he drinks your wine, he borrows your money, he pulls your nose, he kicks your poodle, and he kisses your wife.

Grin :—Your *true* diddler winds up all with a grin. But this nobody sees but himself. He grins when his daily work is done—when his allotted labours are accomplished—at night in his own closet, and altogether for his own private entertainment. He goes home. He locks his door. He divests himself of his clothes. He puts out his candle. He gets into bed. He places his head upon the pillow. All this done, and your diddler *grins*. This is no hypothesis. It is a matter of course. I reason *a priori*, and a diddle would be *no* diddle without a grin.

The origin of the diddle is referable to the infancy of the Human Race. Perhaps the first diddler was Adam. At all events, we can trace the science back to a very remote period of antiquity. The moderns, however, have brought it to a perfection never dreamed of by our thick-headed progenitors. Without pausing to speak of the 'old saws', therefore, I shall content myself with a compendious account of some of the more 'modern instances'.

A very good diddle is this. A housekeeper in want of a sofa, for instance, is seen to go in and out of several cabinet warehouses. At length she arrives at one offering an excellent variety. She is accosted, and invited to enter, by a polite and voluble individual at the door. She finds a sofa well adapted to her views, and, upon inquiring the price, is surprised and delighted to hear a sum named at least twenty per cent. lower than her expectations. She hastens to make the purchase, gets a bill and receipt, leaves her address, with a request that the article be sent home as speedily as possible, and retires amid a profusion of bows from the shop-keeper. The night arrives and no sofa. The next day passes, and still none. A servant is sent to make inquiry about the delay. The whole transaction is denied. No sofa has been sold—no money received—except by the diddler, who played shop-keeper for the nonce.

Our cabinet warehouses are left entirely unattended, and thus afford every facility for a trick of this kind. Visitors enter, look at furniture, and depart unheeded and unseen. Should any one wish to purchase, or to inquire the price of an article, a bell is at hand, and this is considered amply sufficient.

Again, quite a respectable diddle is this. A well-dressed individual enters a shop ; makes a purchase to the value of a dollar ; finds, much to his vexation, that he has left his pocket-book in another coat pocket ; and so says to the shop-keeper—

'My dear sir, never mind !—just oblige me, will you, by sending the bundle home ? But stay ! I really believe that I have nothing less than a five dollar bill, even *there*. However, you can send four dollars in change *with* the bundle, you know.'

'Very good, sir,' replies the shop-keeper, who entertains, at once, a lofty opinion of the high-mindedness of his customer. 'I know fellows', he says to himself, 'who would just have put the goods under their arm, and walked off with a promise to call and pay the dollar as they came by in the afternoon.'

A boy is sent with the parcel and change. On the route, quite accidentally, he is met by the purchaser, who exclaims: ' Ah ! this is my bundle, I see—I thought you had been home with it, long ago. Well, go on ! My wife, Mrs. Trotter, will give you the five dollars—I left instructions with her to that effect. The change you might as well give to *me*— I shall want some silver for the Post Office. Very good ! One, two, is this a good quarter ?—three, four—quite right ! Say to Mrs. Trotter that you met me, and be sure now and *do* not loiter on the way.'

The boy doesn't loiter at all—but he is a very long time in getting back from his errand—for no lady of the precise name of Mrs. Trotter is to be discovered. He consoles himself, however, that he has not been such a fool as to leave the goods without the money, and re-entering his shop with a self-satisfied air, feels sensibly hurt and indignant when his master asks him what has become of the change.

A very simple diddle, indeed, is this. The captain of a ship which is about to sail, is presented by an official-looking person, with an unusually moderate bill of city charges. Glad to get off so easily, and confused by a hundred duties pressing upon him all at once, he discharges the claim forthwith. In about fifteen minutes, another and less reasonable bill is handed him by one who soon makes it evident that the first collector was a diddler, and the original collection a diddle.

And here, too, is a somewhat similar thing. A steamboat is casting loose from the wharf. A traveller, portmanteau in hand, is discovered running towards the wharf at full speed. Suddenly, he makes a dead halt, stoops, and picks up something from the ground in a very agitated manner. It is a pocket-book, and—' Has any gentleman lost a pocket-book ? '. he cries. No one can say that he has exactly lost a pocket-book ; but a great excitement ensues, when the treasure trove is found to be of value. The boat however, must not be detained.

' Time and tide wait for no man,' says the captain.

' For God's sake, stay only a few minutes,' says the finder of the book—' the true claimant will presently appear.'

'Can't wait!' replies the man in authority; 'cast off there, d'ye hear?'

'What *am* I to do?' asks the finder, in great tribulation. 'I am about to leave the country for some years, and I cannot conscientiously retain this large amount in my possession. I beg your pardon, sir,' [here he addresses a gentleman on shore] 'but you have the air of an honest man. *Will* you confer upon me the favour of taking charge of this pocket-book—I *know* I can trust you—and of advertising it? The notes, you see, amount to a very considerable sum. The owner will, no doubt, insist upon rewarding you for your trouble—'

'*Me!*—no, *you!*—it was *you* who found the book.'

'Well, if you *must* have it so—*I* will take a small reward—just to satisfy your scruples. Let me see—why these notes are all hundreds—bless my soul! a hundred is too much to take—fifty would be quite enough, I am sure—'

'Cast off there!' says the captain.

'But then I have no change for a hundred, and upon the whole, *you* had better—'

'Cast off there!' says the captain.

'Never mind!' cries the gentleman on shore, who has been examining his own pocket-book for the last minute or so—'never mind! *I* can fix it—here is a fifty on the Bank of North America—throw me the book.'

And the over-conscientious finder takes the fifty with marked reluctance, and throws the gentleman the book, as desired, while the steamboat fumes and fizzes on her way. In about half an hour after her departure, the 'large amount' is seen to be a 'counterfeit presentment', and the whole thing a capital diddle.

A bold diddle is this. A camp-meeting, or something similar, is to be held at a certain spot which is accessible only by means of a free bridge. A diddler stations himself upon this bridge, respectfully informs all passers by of the new county law, which establishes a toll of one cent for foot passengers, two for horses and donkeys, and so forth, and so forth. Some grumble but all submit, and the diddler goes home a wealthier man by some fifty or sixty dollars well earned. This taking a toll from a great crowd of people is an excessively troublesome thing.

A neat diddle is this. A friend holds one of the diddler's promises to pay, filled up and signed in due form, upon the ordinary blanks printed in red ink. The diddler purchases one or two dozen of these blanks, and every day dips one of them in his soup, makes his dog jump for it, and finally gives it to him as a *bonne bouche*. The note arriving at maturity, the diddler, with the diddler's dog, calls upon the friend, and the promise to pay is made the topic of discussion. The friend produces it from his *escritoire*, and is in the act of reaching it to the diddler, when up jumps the diddler's dog and devours it forthwith. The diddler is not only surprised but vexed and incensed at the absurd behaviour of his dog, and expresses his entire readiness to cancel the obligation at any moment when the evidence of the obligation shall be forthcoming.

A very minute diddle is this. A lady is insulted in the street by a diddler's accomplice. The diddler himself flies to her assistance, and, giving his friend a comfortable thrashing, insists upon attending the lady to her own door. He bows, with his hand upon his heart, and most respectfully bids her adieu. She entreats him, as her deliverer, to walk in and be introduced to her big brother and her papa. With a sigh, he declines to do so. ' Is there no way, then, sir,' she murmurs, ' in which I may be permitted to testify my gratitude ? '

' Why, yes, madam, there is. Will you be kind enough to lend me a couple of shillings ? '

In the first excitement of the moment the lady decides upon fainting outright. Upon second thought, however, she opens her purse-strings and delivers the specie. Now this, I say, is a diddle minute—for one entire moiety of the sum borrowed has to be paid to the gentleman who had the trouble of performing the insult, and who had then to stand still and be thrashed for performing it.

Rather a small, but still a scientific diddle is this. The diddler approaches the bar of a tavern, and demands a couple of twists of tobacco. These are handed to him, when, having slightly examined them, he says :

' I don't much like this tobacco. Here, take it back, and give me a glass of brandy and water in its place.'

The brandy and water is furnished and imbibed, and the

diddler makes his way to the door. But the voice of the tavern-keeper arrests him.

' I believe, sir, you have forgotten to pay for your brandy and water.'

' Pay for my brandy and water !—didn't I give you the tobacco for the brandy and water ? What more would you have ? '

' But sir, if you please, I don't remember that you paid for the tobacco.'

' What do you mean by that, you scoundrel ?—Didn't I give you back your tobacco ? Isn't *that* your tobacco lying *there ?* Do you expect me to pay for what I did not take ? '

' But, sir,' says the publican, now rather at a loss what to say, ' but sir—'

' But me no buts, sir,' interrupts the diddler, apparently in very high dudgeon, and slamming the door after him, as he makes his escape.—' But me no buts, sir, and none of your tricks upon travellers.'

Here again is a very clever diddle, of which the simplicity is not its least recommendation. A purse, or pocket-book, being really lost, the loser inserts in *one* of the daily papers of a large city a fully descriptive advertisement.

Whereupon our diddler copies the *facts* of this advertisement, with a change of heading, of general phraseology, and *address*. The original, for instance, is long, and verbose, is headed ' A Pocket-Book Lost ! ' and requires the treasure, when found, to be left at No. 1 Tom street. The copy is brief, and being headed with ' Lost ' only, indicates No. 2 Dick, or No. 3 Harry street, as the locality at which the owner may be seen. Moreover, it is inserted in at least five or six of the daily papers of the day, while in point of time, it makes its appearance only a few hours after the original. Should it be read by the loser of the purse, he would hardly suspect it to have any reference to his own misfortune. But, of course, the chances are five or six to one, that the finder will repair to the address given by the diddler, rather than to that pointed out by the rightful proprietor. The former pays the reward, pockets the treasure, and decamps.

Quite an analogous diddle is this. A lady of ton has

dropped, somewhere in the street, a diamond ring of very
unusual value. For its recovery, she offers some forty or
fifty dollars reward—giving, in her advertisement, a very
minute description of the gem, and of its settings, and
declaring that, upon its restoration to No. so and so, in
such and such Avenue, the reward will be paid *instanter*,
without a single question being asked. During the lady's
absence from home, a day or two afterwards, a ring is
heard at the door of No. so and so, in such and such Avenue ;
a servant appears ; the lady of the house is asked for and
is declared to be out, at which astounding information, the
visitor expresses the most poignant regret. His business is
of importance and concerns the lady herself. In fact, he
had the good fortune to find her diamond ring. But,
perhaps it would be as well that he should call again. ' By
no means ! ' says the servant ; and ' By no means ! ' says
the lady's sister and the lady's sister-in-law, who are sum-
moned forthwith. The ring is clamorously identified, the
reward is paid, and the finder nearly thrust out of doors.
The lady returns, and expresses some little dissatisfaction
with her sister and sister-in-law, because they happen to
have paid forty or fifty dollars for a *fac-simile* of her
diamond ring—a *fac-simile* made out of real pinchbeck and
unquestionable paste.

But as there is really no end to diddling, so there would
be none to this essay, were I even to hint at half the
variations, or inflections, of which this science is susceptible.
I must bring this paper, perforce, to a conclusion, and this
I cannot do better than by a summary notice of a very
decent, but rather elaborate diddle, of which our own city
was made the theatre, not very long ago, and which was
subsequently repeated with success, in other still more
verdant localities of the Union. A middle-aged gentleman
arrives in town from parts unknown. He is remarkably
precise, cautious, staid, and deliberate in his demeanour.
His dress is scrupulously neat, but plain, unostentatious.
He wears a white cravat, an ample waistcoat, made with
an eye to comfort alone ; thick-soled cosy-looking shoes,
and pantaloons without straps. He has the whole air,
in fact, of your well-to-do, sober-sided, exact, and respectable ' man of business ', *par excellence*—one of the stern

and outwardly hard, internally soft, sort of people that we see in the crack high comedies—fellows whose words are so many bonds, and who are noted for giving away guineas, in charity, with the one hand, while, in the way of mere bargain, they exact the uttermost fraction of a farthing with the other.

He makes much ado before he can get suited with a boarding-house. He dislikes children. He has been accustomed to quiet. His habits are methodical—and then he would prefer getting into a private and respectable small family, piously inclined. Terms, however, are no object—only he must insist upon settling his bill on the first of every month (it is now the second), and begs his landlady, when he finally obtains one to his mind, *not* on any account to forget his instructions upon this point—but to send in a bill, *and* receipt, precisely at ten o'clock, on the *first* day of every month, and under no circumstances to put it off to the second.

These arrangements made, our man of business rents an office in a reputable rather than in a fashionable quarter of the town. There is nothing he more despises than pretence. 'Where there is much show,' he says, 'there is seldom anything very solid behind'—an observation which so profoundly impresses his landlady's fancy, that she makes a pencil memorandum of it forthwith, in her great family Bible, on the broad margin of the Proverbs of Solomon.

The next step is to advertise, after some such fashion as this, in the principal business sixpennies of this city—the pennies are eschewed as not 'respectable'—and as demanding payment for all advertisements in advance. Our man of business holds it as a point of his faith that work should never be paid for until done.

WANTED.—The advertisers, being about to commence extensive business operations in this city, will require the services of three or four intelligent and competent clerks, to whom a liberal salary will be paid. The very best recommendations, not so much for capacity, as for integrity, will be expected. Indeed, as the duties to be performed, involve high responsibilities, and large amounts of money must necessarily pass through the hands of those engaged, it is deemed advisable to demand a deposit of fifty dollars from each clerk employed. No person need apply, therefore, who is not prepared to leave this sum in the possession of the advertisers, and who cannot furnish the most satisfactory testimonials of morality. Young gentlemen piously inclined will be preferred. Application should be made between the hours of ten and eleven, A.M., and four and five, P.M., of Messrs.

> BOGS, HOGS, LOGS, FROGS, & CO.
> No. 110 Dog Street.

By the thirty-first day of the month, this advertisement has brought to the office of Messrs. Bogs, Hogs, Logs, Frogs, and Company, some fifteen or twenty young gentlemen piously inclined. But our man of business is in no hurry to conclude a contract with any—no man of business is *ever* precipitate—and it is not until the most rigid catechism in respect to the piety of each young gentleman's inclination, that his services are engaged and his fifty dollars receipted for, *just* by way of proper precaution, on the part of the respectable firm of Bogs, Hogs, Logs, Frogs, and Company. On the morning of the first day of the next month, the landlady does *not* present her bill, according to promise—a piece of neglect for which the comfortable head of the house ending in *ogs*, would no doubt have chided her severely, could he have been prevailed upon to remain in town a day or two for that purpose.

As it is, the constables have had a sad time of it, running hither and thither, and all they can do is to declare the man of business most emphatically, a ' hen knee high '—by which some persons imagine them to imply that, in fact, he is n. e. i.—by which again the very classical phrase *non est inventus*, is supposed to be understood. In the meantime the young gentlemen, one and all, are somewhat less piously inclined than before, while the landlady purchases a shilling's worth of the best Indian rubber, and very carefully obliterates the pencil memorandum that some fool has made in her great family Bible, on the broad margin of the Proverbs of Solomon.

THE ANGEL OF THE ODD

AN EXTRAVAGANZA

It was a chilly November afternoon. I had just consummated an unusually hearty dinner, of which the dyspeptic *truffe* formed not the least important item, and was sitting alone in the dining-room, with my feet upon the fender, and at my elbow a small table which I had rolled up to the fire, and upon which were some apologies for dessert, with some miscellaneous bottles of wine, spirit, and *liqueur*. In the morning I had been reading Glover's 'Leonidas', Wilkie's 'Epigoniad', Lamartine's 'Pilgrimage', Barlow's 'Columbiad', Tuckerman's 'Sicily', and Griswold's 'Curiosities'; I am willing to confess, therefore, that I now felt a little stupid. I made effort to arouse myself by aid of frequent Lafitte, and, all failing, I betook myself to a stray newspaper in despair. Having carefully perused the column of 'houses to let', and the column of 'dogs lost', and then the two columns of 'wives and apprentices runaway', I attacked with great resolution the editorial matter, and, reading it from beginning to end without understanding a syllable, conceived the possibility of its being Chinese, and so re-read it from the end to the beginning, but with no more satisfactory result. I was about throwing away, in disgust,

> This folio of four pages, happy work
> Which not even critics criticise,

when I felt my attention somewhat aroused by the paragraph which follows :

'The avenues to death are numerous and strange. A London paper mentions the decease of a person from a singular cause. He was playing at "puff the dart", which is played with a long needle inserted in some worsted, and blown at a target through a tin tube. He placed the needle at the wrong end of the tube, and drawing his breath strongly to puff the dart forward with force, drew the needle into his throat. It entered the lungs, and in a few days killed him.'

Upon seeing this I fell into a great rage, without exactly

knowing why. 'This thing', I exclaimed, 'is a contemptible falsehood—a poor hoax—the lees of the invention of some pitiable penny-a-liner—of some wretched concocter of accidents in Cocaigne. These fellows, knowing the extravagant gullibility of the age, set their wits to work in the imagination of improbable possibilities—of odd accidents, as they term them ; but to a reflecting intellect (like mine ', I added, in parenthesis, putting my forefinger unconsciously to the side of my nose), ' to a contemplative understanding such as I myself possess, it seems evident at once that the marvellous increase of late in these " odd accidents " is by far the oddest accident of all. For my own part, I intend to believe nothing henceforward that has anything of the " singular " about it.'

' Mein Gott, den, vat a vool you bees for dat ! ' replied one of the most remarkable voices I ever heard. At first I took it for a rumbling in my ears—such as a man sometimes experiences when getting very drunk—but, upon second thought, I considered the sound as more nearly resembling that which proceeds from an empty barrel beaten with a big stick ; and, in fact, this I should have concluded it to be, but for the articulation of the syllables and words. I am by no means naturally nervous, and the very few glasses of Lafitte which I had sipped served to embolden me a little, so that I felt nothing of trepidation, but merely uplifted my eyes with a leisurely movement, and looked carefully around the room for the intruder. I could not, however, perceive any one at all.

' Humph ! ' resumed the voice, as I continued my survey, ' you mus pe so dronk as de pig, den, for not zee me as I zit here at your zide.'

Hereupon I bethought me of looking immediately before my nose, and there, sure enough, confronting me at the table sat a personage nondescript, although not altogether indescribable. His body was a wine-pipe, or a rum-puncheon, or something of that character, and had a truly Falstaffian air. In its nether extremity were inserted two kegs, which seemed to answer all the purposes of legs. For arms there dangled from the upper portion of the carcass two tolerably long bottles, with the necks outward for hands. All the head that I saw the monster possessed of was one of those Hessian canteens which resemble a large snuff-box with a hole in the middle of the lid. This canteen (with a funnel on its top, like a cavalier cap slouched over the eyes) was set on edge upon the puncheon, with the hole toward myself; and through this hole, which seemed puckered up like the mouth of a very precise old maid, the creature was emitting certain rumbling and grumbling noises which he evidently intended for intelligible talk.

'I zay', said he, 'you mos pe dronk as de pig, vor zit dare and not zee me zit ere; and I zay, doo, you mos pe pigger vool as de goose, vor to dispelief vat iz print in de print. 'Tiz de troof—dat it iz—eberry vord ob it.'

'Who are you, pray?' said I, with much dignity, although somewhat puzzled; 'how did you get here? and what is it you are talking about?'

'As vor ow I com'd ere,' replied the figure, 'dat iz none of your pizziness; and as vor vat I be talking apout, I be talk apout vat I tink proper; and as vor who I be, vy dat is de very ting I com'd here for to let you zee for yourzelf.'

'You are a drunken vagabond,' said I, 'and I shall ring the bell and order my footman to kick you into the street.'

'He! he! he!' said the fellow, 'hu! hu! hu! dat you can't do.'

'Can't do!' said I, 'what do you mean?—I can't do what?'

'Ring de pell,' he replied, attempting a grin with his little villanous mouth.

Upon this I made an effort to get up, in order to put my threat into execution; but the ruffian just reached across the table very deliberately, and hitting me a tap on the forehead with the neck of one of the long bottles, knocked me back into the arm-chair from which I had half arisen. I was utterly astounded; and, for a moment, was quite at a loss what to do. In the meantime, he continued his talk.

'You zee,' said he, 'it iz te bess vor zit still; and now you shall know who I pe. Look at me! zee! I am te *Angel ov te Odd.*'

'And odd enough, too,' I ventured to reply; 'but I was always under the impression that an angel had wings.'

' Te wing ! ' he cried, highly incensed, ' vat I pe do mit
te wing ? Mein Gott ! do you take me vor a shicken ? '

' No—oh no ! ' I replied, much alarmed, ' you are no
chicken—certainly not.'

' Well, den, zit still and pehabe yourself, or I'll rap you
again mid me vist. It iz te shicken ab te wing, und te owl
ab te wing, und te imp ab te wing, und te head-teuffel ab te
wing. Te angel ab *not* te wing, and I am te *Angel ov te
Odd.*'

' And your business with me at present is—is— '

' My pizzness ! ' ejaculated the thing, ' vy vat a low
bred buppy you mos pe vor to ask a gentleman und an
angel apout his pizziness ! '

This language was rather more than I could bear, even
from an angel ; so, plucking up courage, I seized a salt-
cellar which lay within reach, and hurled it at the head of
the intruder. Either he dodged, however, or my aim was
inaccurate ; for all I accomplished was the demolition of
the crystal which protected the dial of the clock upon the
mantel-piece. As for the Angel, he evinced his sense of my
assault by giving me two or three hard consecutive raps
upon the forehead as before. These reduced me at once to
submission, and I am almost ashamed to confess that
either through pain or vexation, there came a few tears into
my eyes.

' Mein Gott ! ' said the Angel of the Odd, apparently
much softened at my distress ; ' mein Gott, te man is eder
ferry dronk or ferry zorry. You mos not trink it so strong—
you mos put te water in te wine. Here, trink dis, like a goot
veller, und don't gry now—don't ! '

Hereupon the Angel of the Odd replenished my goblet
(which was about a third full of port) with a colourless fluid
that he poured from one of his hand bottles. I observed
that these bottles had labels about their necks, and that
these labels were inscribed ' Kirschwasser '.

The considerate kindness of the Angel mollified me in no
little measure ; and, aided by the water with which he
diluted my port more than once, I at length regained
sufficient temper to listen to his very extraordinary discourse. I cannot pretend to recount all that he told me,
but I gleaned from what he said that he was the genius

who presided over the *contretemps* of mankind, and whose business it was to bring about the *odd accidents* which are continually astonishing the sceptic. Once or twice, upon my venturing to express my total incredulity in respect to his pretensions, he grew very angry indeed, so that at length I considered it the wiser policy to say nothing at all, and let him have his own way. He talked on, therefore, at great length, while I merely leaned back in my chair with my eyes shut, and amused myself with munching raisins and filliping the stems about the room. But, by-and-by, the Angel suddenly construed this behaviour of mine into contempt. He arose in a terrible passion, slouched his funnel down over his eyes, swore a vast oath, uttered a threat of some character which I did not precisely comprehend, and finally made me a low bow and departed, wishing me, in the language of the archbishop in Gil-Blas, ' *beaucoup de bonheur et un peu plus de bon sens* '.

His departure afforded me relief. The *very* few glasses of Lafitte that I had sipped had the effect of rendering me drowsy, and I felt inclined to take a nap of some fifteen or twenty minutes, as is my custom after dinner. At six I had an appointment of consequence, which it was quite indispensable that I should keep. The policy of insurance for my dwelling house had expired the day before ; and, some dispute having arisen, it was agreed that, at six, I should meet the board of directors of the company and settle the terms of a renewal. Glancing upward at the clock on the mantel-piece (for I felt too drowsy to take out my watch), I had the pleasure to find that I had still twenty-five minutes to spare. It was half past five ; I could easily walk to the insurance office in five minutes ; and my usual siestas had never been known to exceed five and twenty. I felt sufficiently safe, therefore, and composed myself to my slumbers forthwith.

Having completed them to my satisfaction, I again looked toward the time-piece and was half inclined to believe in the possibility of odd accidents when I found that, instead of my ordinary fifteen or twenty minutes, I had been dozing only three ; for it still wanted seven and twenty of the appointed hour. I betook myself again to my nap, and at length a second time awoke, when, to

my utter amazement, it *still* wanted twenty-seven minutes
of six. I jumped up to examine the clock, and found that
it had ceased running. My watch informed me that it was
half past seven ; and, of course, having slept two hours,
I was too late for my appointment. ' It will make no
difference,' I said : ' I can call at the office in the morning
and apologize ; in the meantime what can be the matter
with the clock ? ' Upon examining it I discovered that one
of the raisin stems which I had been filliping about the room
during the discourse of the Angel of the Odd, had flown
through the fractured crystal, and lodging, singularly
enough, in the key-hole, with an end projecting outward,
had thus arrested the revolution of the minute hand.

' Ah ! ' said I, ' I see how it is. This thing speaks for
itself. A natural accident, such as *will* happen now and
then ! '

I gave the matter no further consideration, and at my
usual hour retired to bed. Here, having placed a candle
upon a reading stand at the bed head, and having made an
attempt to peruse some pages of the ' Omnipresence of the
Deity ', I unfortunately fell asleep in less than twenty
seconds, leaving the light burning as it was.

My dreams were terrifically disturbed by visions of the
Angel of the Odd. Methought he stood at the foot of the
couch, drew aside the curtains, and, in the hollow, detestable
tones of a rum puncheon, menaced me with the bitterest
vengeance for the contempt with which I had treated him.
He concluded a long harangue by taking off his funnel-
cap, inserting the tube into my gullet, and thus deluging
me with an ocean of Kirschwasser, which he poured, in
a continuous flood, from one of the long-necked bottles
that stood him instead of an arm. My agony was at length
insufferable, and I awoke just in time to perceive that a rat
had run off with the lighted candle from the stand, but *not*
in season to prevent his making his escape with it through
the hole. Very soon, a strong suffocating odour assailed
my nostrils ; the house, I clearly perceived, was on fire.
In a few minutes the blaze broke forth with violence, and
in an incredibly brief period the entire building was wrapped
in flames. All egress from my chamber, except through
a window, was cut off. The crowd, however, quickly pro-

cured and raised a long ladder. By means of this I was descending rapidly, and in apparent safety, when a huge hog, about whose rotund stomach, and indeed about whose whole air and physiognomy, there was something which reminded me of the Angel of the Odd—when this hog, I say, which hitherto had been quietly slumbering in the mud, took it suddenly into his head that his left shoulder needed scratching, and could find no more convenient rubbing-post than that afforded by the foot of the ladder. In an instant I was precipitated and had the misfortune to fracture my arm.

This accident, with the loss of my insurance, and with the more serious loss of my hair, the whole of which had been singed off by the fire, predisposed me to serious impressions, so that, finally, I made up my mind to take a wife. There was a rich widow disconsolate for the loss of her seventh husband, and to her wounded spirit I offered the balm of my vows. She yielded a reluctant consent to my prayers. I knelt at her feet in gratitude and adoration. She blushed and bowed her luxuriant tresses into close contact with those supplied me, temporarily, by Grandjean. I know not how the entanglement took place, but so it was. I arose with a shining pate, wigless ; she in disdain and wrath, half buried in alien hair. Thus ended my hopes of the widow by an accident which could not have been anticipated, to be sure, but which the natural sequence of events had brought about.

Without despairing, however, I undertook the siege of a less implacable heart. The fates were again propitious for a brief period ; but again a trivial incident interfered. Meeting my betrothed in an avenue thronged with the *élite* of the city, I was hastening to greet her with one of my best considered bows, when a small particle of some foreign matter, lodging in the corner of my eye, rendered me, for the moment, completely blind. Before I could recover my sight, the lady of my love had disappeared—irreparably affronted at what she chose to consider my premeditated rudeness in passing her by ungreeted. While I stood bewildered at the suddenness of this accident (which might have happened, nevertheless, to any one under the sun), and while I still continued incapable of sight, I was

accosted by the Angel of the Odd, who proffered me his aid
with a civility which I had no reason to expect. He
examined my disordered eye with much gentleness and
skill, informed me that I had a drop in it, and (whatever
a 'drop' was) took it out, and afforded me relief.

I now considered it high time to die (since fortune had
so determined to persecute me), and accordingly made my
way to the nearest river. Here, divesting myself of my
clothes (for there is no reason why we cannot die as we
were born), I threw myself headlong into the current; the
sole witness of my fate being a solitary crow that had been
seduced into the eating of brandy-saturated corn, and so
had staggered away from his fellows. No sooner had
I entered the water than this bird took it into his head to
fly away with the most indispensable portion of my apparel.
Postponing, therefore, for the present, my suicidal design,
I just slipped my nether extremities into the sleeves of my
coat, and betook myself to a pursuit of the felon with all
the nimbleness which the case required and its circumstances would admit. But my evil destiny attended me
still. As I ran at full speed, with my nose up in the atmosphere, and intent only upon the purloiner of my property,
I suddenly perceived that my feet rested no longer upon
terra-firma; the fact is, I had thrown myself over a preci-
pice, and should inevitably have been dashed to pieces but
for my good fortune in grasping the end of a long guide-
rope, which depended from a passing balloon.

As soon as I sufficiently recovered my senses to comprehend the terrific predicament in which I stood or rather
hung, I exerted all the power of my lungs to make that
predicament known to the aeronaut overhead. But for a
long time I exerted myself in vain. Either the fool could
not, or the villain would not perceive me. Meantime the
machine rapidly soared, while my strength even more
rapidly failed. I was soon upon the point of resigning
myself to my fate, and dropping quietly into the sea, when
my spirits were suddenly revived by hearing a hollow voice
from above, which seemed to be lazily humming an opera
air. Looking up, I perceived the Angel of the Odd. He
was leaning with his arms folded, over the rim of the car;
and with a pipe in his mouth, at which he puffed leisurely,

seemed to be upon excellent terms with himself and the universe. I was too much exhausted to speak, so I merely regarded him with an imploring air.

For several minutes, although he looked me full in the face, he said nothing. At length removing carefully his meerschaum from the right to the left corner of his mouth, he condescended to speak.

'Who pe you,' he asked, 'und what der teuffel you pe do dare?'

To this piece of impudence, cruelty, and affectation, I could reply only by ejaculating the monosyllable 'Help!'

'Elp!' echoed the ruffian—'not I. Dare iz te pottle—elp yourself, und pe tam'd!'

With these words he let fall a heavy bottle of Kirschwasser which, dropping precisely upon the crown of my head, caused me to imagine that my brains were entirely knocked out. Impressed with this idea, I was about to relinquish my hold and give up the ghost with a good grace, when I was arrested by the cry of the Angel, who bade me hold on.

'Old on!' he said; 'don't pe in te urry—don't! Will you pe take de odder pottle, or ave you pe got zober yet and come to your zenzes?'

I made haste, hereupon, to nod my head twice—once in the negative, meaning thereby that I would prefer not taking the other bottle at present—and once in the affirmative, intending thus to imply that I *was* sober and *had* positively come to my senses. By these means I somewhat softened the Angel.

'Und you pelief, ten,' he inquired, 'at te last? You pelief, ten, in te possibility of te odd?'

I again nodded my head in assent.

'Und you ave pelief in *me*, te Angel of te Odd?'

I nodded again.

'Und you acknowledge tat you pe te blind dronk und te vool?'

I nodded once more.

'Put your right hand into your left hand preeches pocket, ten, in token ov your vull zubmizzion unto te Angel ov te Odd.'

This thing, for very obvious reasons, I found it quite

impossible to do. In the first place, my left arm had been broken in my fall from the ladder, and, therefore, had I let go my hold with the right hand, I must have let go altogether. In the second place, I could have no breeches until I came across the crow. I was therefore obliged, much to my regret, to shake my head in the negative—intending thus to give the Angel to understand that I found it inconvenient, just at that moment, to comply with his very reasonable demand ! No sooner, however, had I ceased shaking my head than—

' Go to der teuffel, ten ! ' roared the Angel of the Odd.

In pronouncing these words, he drew a sharp knife across the guide-rope by which I was suspended, and as we then happened to be precisely over my own house (which, during my peregrinations, had been handsomely rebuilt), it so occurred that I tumbled headlong down the ample chimney and alit upon the dining-room hearth.

Upon coming to my senses (for the fall had very thoroughly stunned me), I found it about four o'clock in the morning. I lay outstretched where I had fallen from the balloon. My head grovelled in the ashes of an extinguished fire, while my feet reposed upon the wreck of a small table, overthrown, and amid the fragments of a miscellaneous dessert, intermingled with a newspaper, some broken glasses and shattered bottles, and an empty jug of the Schiedam Kirschwasser. Thus revenged himself the Angel of the Odd.

MELLONTA TAUTA

On Board Balloon ' Skylark ', *April* 1, 2848.

Now, my dear friend—now, for your sins, you are to suffer the infliction of a long gossiping letter. I tell you distinctly that I am going to punish you for all your impertinences by being as tedious, as discursive, as incoherent, and as unsatisfactory as possible. Besides, here I am, cooped up in a dirty balloon, with some one or two hundred of the *canaille*, all bound on a *pleasure* excursion (what a funny idea some people have of pleasure !) and I have no

prospect of touching *terra firma* for a month at least.
Nobody to talk to. Nothing to do. When one has nothing
to do, then is the time to correspond with one's friends.
You perceive, then, why it is that I write you this letter—
it is on account of my *ennui* and your sins.

Get ready your spectacles and make up your mind to
be annoyed. I mean to write at you every day during this
odious voyage.

Heigho! when will any *Invention* visit the human peri-
cranium? Are we forever to be doomed to the thousand
inconveniences of the balloon? Will *nobody* contrive a
more expeditious mode of progress? This jog-trot movement, to my thinking, is little less than positive torture.
Upon my word we have not made more than a hundred
miles the hour since leaving home! The very birds beat
us—at least some of them. I assure you that I do not
exaggerate at all. Our motion, no doubt, seems slower
than it actually is—this on account of our having no objects
about us by which to estimate our velocity, and on account
of our going with the wind. To be sure, whenever we meet
a balloon we have a chance of perceiving our rate, and
then, I admit, things do not appear so very bad. Accustomed as I am to this mode of travelling, I cannot get over
a kind of giddiness whenever a balloon passes us in a current
directly overhead. It always seems to me like an immense
bird of prey about to pounce upon us and carry us off in
its claws. One went over us this morning about sunrise,
and so nearly overhead that its drag-rope actually brushed
the net-work suspending our car, and caused us very serious
apprehension. Our captain said that if the material of the
bag had been the trumpery varnished ' silk ' of five hundred
or a thousand years ago, we should inevitably have been
damaged. This silk, as he explained it to me, was a fabric
composed of the entrails of a species of earth-worm. The
worm was carefully fed on mulberries—a kind of fruit
resembling a water-melon—and, when sufficiently fat, was
crushed in a mill. The paste thus arising was called *papyrus*
in its primary state, and went through a variety of pro-
cesses until it finally became ' silk '. Singular to relate, it
was once much admired as an article of *female dress!*
Balloons were also very generally constructed from it

A better kind of material, it appears, was subsequently found in the down surrounding the seed-vessels of a plant vulgarly called *euphorbium*, and at that time botanically termed milk-weed. This latter kind of silk was designated as silk-buckingham, on account of its superior durability, and was usually prepared for use by being varnished with a solution of gum caoutchouc—a substance which in some respects must have resembled the *gutta percha* now in common use. This caoutchouc was occasionally called India rubber or rubber of whist, and was no doubt one of the numerous *fungi*. Never tell me again that I am not at heart an antiquarian.

Talking of drag-ropes—our own, it seems, has this moment knocked a man overboard from one of the small magnetic propellers that swarm in ocean below us—a boat of about six thousand tons, and, from all accounts, shamefully crowded. These diminutive barques should be prohibited from carrying more than a definite number of passengers. The man, of course, was not permitted to get on board again, and was soon out of sight, he and his life-preserver. I rejoice, my dear friend, that we live in an age so enlightened that no such a thing as an individual is supposed to exist. It is the mass for which the true Humanity cares. By-the-by, talking of Humanity, do you know that our immortal Wiggins is not so original in his views of the Social Condition and so forth, as his contemporaries are inclined to suppose ? Pundit assures me that the same ideas were put, nearly in the same way, about a thousand years ago, by an Irish philosopher called Furrier, on account of his keeping a retail shop for cat peltries and other furs. Pundit *knows*, you know ; there can be no mistake about it. How very wonderfully do we see verified every day, the profound observation of the Hindoo Aries Tottle (as quoted by Pundit)—' Thus must we say that, not once or twice, or a few times, but with almost infinite repetitions, the same opinions come round in a circle among men.'

April 2.—Spoke to-day the magnetic cutter in charge of the middle section of floating telegraph wires. I learn that when this species of telegraph was first put into operation by Horse, it was considered quite impossible to convey the

wires over sea ; but now we are at a loss to comprehend
where the difficulty lay ! So wags the world. *Tempora
mutantur*—excuse me for quoting the Etruscan. What
would we do without the Atlantic telegraph ? (Pundit says
Atlantic was the ancient adjective.) We lay to a few
minutes to ask the cutter some questions, and learned,
among other glorious news, that civil war is raging in
Africa, while the plague is doing its good work beautifully
both in Yurope and Ayesher. Is it not truly remarkable
that, before the magnificent light shed upon philosophy
by Humanity, the world was accustomed to regard War
and Pestilence as calamities ? Do you know that prayers
were actually offered up in the ancient temples to the end
that these *evils* (!) might not be visited upon mankind ?
Is it not really difficult to comprehend upon what principle
of interest our forefathers acted ? Were they so blind as
not to perceive that the destruction of a myriad of individuals is only so much positive advantage to the mass !

April 3.—It is really a very fine amusement to ascend the
rope-ladder leading to the summit of the balloon-bag and
thence survey the surrounding world. From the car below,
you know the prospect is not so comprehensive—you can
see little vertically. But seated here (where I write this)
in the luxuriously-cushioned open piazza of the summit,
one can see everything that is going on in all directions.
Just now, there is quite a crowd of balloons in sight, and
they present a very animated appearance, while the air is
resonant with the hum of so many millions of human
voices. I have heard it asserted that when Yellow or (as
Pundit *will* have it) Violet, who is supposed to have been
the first aeronaut, maintained the practicability of traversing
the atmosphere in all directions, by merely ascending or
descending until a favourable current was attained, he was
scarcely hearkened to at all by his contemporaries, who
looked upon him as merely an ingenious sort of madman,
because the philosophers (!) of the day declared the thing
impossible. Really now it does seem to me *quite* unaccountable how anything so obviously feasible could have
escaped the sagacity of the ancient *savants*. But in all
ages the great obstacles to advancement in Art have been
opposed by the so-called men of science. To be sure, *our*

men of science are not quite so bigoted as those of old :— oh, I have something *so* queer to tell you on this topic. Do you know that it is not more than a thousand years ago since the metaphysicians consented to relieve the people of the singular fancy that there existed but *two possible roads for the attainment of Truth !* Believe it if you can ! It appears that long, long ago, in the night of Time, there lived a Turkish philosopher (or Hindoo possibly) called Aries Tottle. This person introduced, or at all events propagated what was termed the deductive or *a priori* mode of investigation. He started with what he maintained to be *axioms* or ' self-evident truths ', and thence proceeded ' logically ' to results. His greatest disciples were one Neuclid and one Cant. Well, Aries Tottle flourished supreme until the advent of one Hog, surnamed the ' Ettrick Shepherd ', who preached an entirely different system, which he called the *a posteriori* or *inductive*. His plan referred altogether to Sensation. He proceeded by observing, analyzing, and classifying facts— *instantiæ naturæ*, as they were affectedly called—into general laws. Aries Tottle's mode, in a word, was based on *noumena* ; Hog's on *phenomena*. Well, so great was the admiration excited by this latter system that, at its first introduction, Aries Tottle fell into disrepute ; but finally he recovered ground and was permitted to divide the realm of Truth with his more modern rival. The *savants* now maintained that the Aristotelian and *Baconian* roads were the sole possible avenues to knowledge. ' Baconian,' you must know, was an adjective invented as equivalent to Hog-ian and more euphonious and dignified.

Now, my dear friend, I do assure you, most positively, that I represent this matter fairly, on the soundest authority ; and you can easily understand how a notion so absurd on its very face must have operated to retard the progress of all true knowledge—which makes its advances almost invariably by intuitive bounds. The ancient idea confined investigation to *crawling* ; and for hundreds of years so great was the infatuation about Hog especially, that a virtual end was put to all thinking properly so called. No man dared utter a truth to which he felt himself indebted to his *Soul* alone. It mattered not whether the truth was even *demonstrably* a truth, for the bullet-headed *savants* of the time regarded only *the road* by which he had attained it. They would not even *look* at the end. 'Let us see the means,' they cried, 'the means!' If, upon investigation of the means, it was found to come neither under the category Aries (that is to say Ram) nor under the category Hog, why then the *savants* went no farther, but pronounced the 'theorist' a fool, and would have nothing to do with him or his truth.

Now, it cannot be maintained, even, that by the crawling system the greatest amount of truth would be attained in any long series of ages, for the repression of *imagination* was an evil not to be compensated for by any superior *certainty* in the ancient modes of investigation. The error of these Jurmains, these Vrinch, these Inglitch, and these Amriccans (the latter, by the way, were our own immediate progenitors), was an error quite analogous with that of the wiseacre who fancies that he must necessarily see an object the better the more closely he holds it to his eyes. These people blinded themselves by details. When they proceeded Hoggishly, their 'facts' were by means always facts—a matter of little consequence had it not been for assuming that they *were* facts and must be facts because they appeared to be such. When they proceeded on the path of the Ram, their course was scarcely as straight as a ram's horn, for they *never had* an axiom which was an axiom at all. They must have been very blind not to see this, even in their own day; for even in their own day many of the long 'established' axioms had been rejected. For example—'*Ex nihilo, nihil fit*'; 'a body cannot act where it is not'; 'there cannot exist antipodes'; 'darkness cannot come out of light'—all these, and a dozen other similar propositions, formerly admitted without hesitation as axioms, were, even at the period of which I speak, seen to be untenable. How absurd in these people, then, to persist in putting faith in 'axioms' as immutable bases of Truth! But even out of the mouths of their soundest reasoners it is easy to demonstrate the futility, the impalpability of their axioms in general. Who *was* the soundest of their logicians? Let me see! I will go and ask Pundit and be back in a minute. . . . . Ah, here we have it!

Here is a book written nearly a thousand years ago and lately translated from the Inglitch—which, by the way, appears to have been the rudiment of the Amriccan. Pundit says it is decidedly the cleverest ancient work on its topic, Logic. The author (who was much thought of in his day) was one Miller, or Mill; and we find it recorded of him, as a point of some importance, that he had a mill-horse called Bentham. But let us glance at the treatise!

Ah!—'Ability or inability to conceive,' says Mr. Mill, very properly, 'is in no case to be received as a criterion of axiomatic truth'. What *modern* in his senses would ever think of disputing this truism? The only wonder with us must be, how it happened that Mr. Mill conceived it necessary even to hint at any thing so obvious. So far good—but let us turn over another page. What have we here?—'Contradictories cannot both be true—that is, cannot co-exist in nature.' Here Mr. Mill means, for example, that a tree must be either a tree or not a tree—that it cannot be at the same time a tree and not a tree. Very well; but I ask him *why*. His reply is this—and never pretends to be any thing else than this—'Because it is impossible to conceive that contradictories can both be true'. But this is no answer at all, by his own showing; for has he not just admitted as a truism that 'ability or inability to conceive is *in no case* to be received as a criterion of axiomatic truth'.

Now I do not complain of these ancients so much because their logic is, by their own showing, utterly baseless, worthless, and fantastic altogether, as because of their pompous and imbecile proscription of all *other* roads of Truth, of all *other* means for its attainment than the two preposterous paths—the one of creeping and the one of crawling—to which they have dared to confine the Soul that loves nothing so well as to *soar*.

By-the-by, my dear friend, do you not think it would have puzzled these ancient dogmaticians to have determined by *which* of their two roads it was that the most important and most sublime of *all* their truths was, in effect, attained? I mean the truth of Gravitation. Newton owed it to Kepler. Kepler admitted that his three laws were *guessed at*—these three laws of all laws which led the great Inglitch mathematician to his principle, the basis of all physical principle—to go behind which we must enter the Kingdom of Metaphysics.. Kepler guessed—that is to say *imagined*. He was essentially a ' theorist '—that word now of so much sanctity, formerly an epithet of contempt. Would it not have puzzled these old moles too, to have explained by which of the two ' roads ' a cryptographist unriddles a cryptograph of more than usual secrecy, or by which of the two roads Champollion directed mankind to those enduring and almost innumerable truths which resulted from his deciphering the Hieroglyphics ?

One word more on this topic and I will be done boring you. Is it not *passing* strange that, with their eternal prating about *roads* to Truth, these bigoted people missed what we now so clearly perceive to be the great highway—that of Consistency ? Does it not seem singular how they should have failed to deduce from the works of God the vital fact that a perfect consistency *must* be an absolute truth ! How plain has been our progress since the late announcement of this proposition ! Investigation has been taken out of the hands of the ground-moles and given, as a task, to the true and only true thinkers, the men of ardent imagination. These latter *theorize*. Can you not fancy the shout of scorn with which my words would be received by our progenitors were it possible for them to be now looking over my shoulder ? These men, I say *theorize ;* and their theories are simply corrected, reduced, systematized—cleared, little by little, of their dross of inconsistency—until, finally, a perfect consistency stands apparent which even the most stolid admit, because it *is* a consistency, to be an absolute and an unquestionable *truth*.

April 4.—The new gas is doing wonders, in conjunction with the new improvement with gutta percha. How very safe, commodious, manageable, and in every respect convenient are our modern balloons ! Here is an immense one approaching us at the rate of at least a hundred and fifty miles an hour. It seems to be crowded with people—perhaps there are three or four hundred passengers—and yet it soars to an elevation of nearly a mile, looking down upon poor us with sovereign contempt. Still a hundred or even two hundred miles an hour is slow travelling, after all. *Do* you remember our flight on the railroad across the Kanadaw continent ?—fully three hundred miles the hour —*that* was travelling. Nothing to be seen, though—nothing to be done but flirt, feast, and dance in the magnificent saloons. Do you remember what an odd sensation was experienced when, by chance, we caught a glimpse of external objects while the cars were in full flight ? Everything seemed unique—in oné mass. For my part, I cannot say but that I preferred the travelling by the slow train of a hundred miles the hour. Here we were permitted to have glass windows—even to have them open—and something like a distinct view of the country was attainable. . . . . . . Pundit says that *the route* for the great Kanadaw railroad must have been in some measure marked out about nine hundred years ago ! In fact, he goes so far as to assert that actual traces of a road are still discernible—traces referable to a period quite as remote as that mentioned. The track, it appears, was *double* only ; ours, you know, has twelve paths ; and three or four new ones are in preparation. The ancient rails were very slight, and placed so close together as to be, according to modern notions, quite frivolous, if not dangerous in the extreme. The present width of track—fifty feet—is considered, indeed, scarcely secure enough. For my part, I make no doubt that a track of some sort *must* have existed in very remote times, as Pundit asserts ; for nothing can be clearer, to my mind, than that, at some period—not less than seven centuries ago, certainly—the Northern and Southern Kanadaw continents were *united :* the Kanawdians, then, would have been driven, by necessity, to a great railroad across the continent.

April 5.—I am almost devoured by *ennui.* Pundit is the only conversible person on board ; and he, poor soul ! can speak of nothing but antiquities. He has been occupied all the day in the attempt to convince me that the ancient Amriccans *governed themselves !*—did ever anybody hear of such an absurdity ?—that they existed in a sort of every-man-for-himself confederacy, after the fashion of the ' prairie dogs ' that we read of in fable. He says that they started with the queerest idea conceivable, viz. : that all men are born free and equal—this in the very teeth of the

laws of *gradation* so visibly impressed upon all things both
in the moral and physical universe. Every man ' voted ',
as they called it—that is to say, meddled with public affairs—
until, at length, it was discovered that what is everybody's
business is nobody's, and that the ' Republic ' (so the
absurd thing was called) was without a government at all.
It is related, however, that the first circumstance which
disturbed, very particularly, the self-complacency of the
philosophers who constructed this ' Republic ', was the
startling discovery that universal suffrage gave opportunity
for fraudulent schemes, by means of which any desired
number of votes might at any time be polled, without the
possibility of prevention or even detection, by any party
which should be merely villanous enough not to be ashamed
of the fraud. A little reflection upon this discovery sufficed
to render evident the consequences, which were that
rascality *must* predominate—in a word, that a republican
government *could* never be anything but a rascally one.
While the philosophers, however, were busied in blushing
at their stupidity in not having foreseen these inevitable
evils, and intent upon the invention of new theories, the
matter was put to an abrupt issue by a fellow of the name
of *Mob*, who took everything into his own hands and set
up a despotism, in comparison with which those of the
fabulous Zeros and Hellofagabaluses were respectable and
delectable. This Mob (a foreigner, by-the-by), is said to
have been the most odious of all men that ever encumbered
the earth. He was a giant in stature—insolent, rapacious,
filthy ; had the gall of a bullock with the heart of an
hyena and the brains of a peacock. He died, at length, by
dint of his own energies, which exhausted him. Nevertheless, he had his uses, as everything has, however vile, and
taught mankind a lesson which to this day it is in no danger
of forgetting—never to run directly contrary to the natural
analogies. As for Republicanism, no analogy could be
found for it upon the face of the earth—unless we except
the case of the ' prairie dogs ', an exception which seems
to demonstrate, if anything, that democracy is a very
admirable form of government—for dogs.

April 6.—Last night had a fine view of Alpha Lyræ,
whose disk, through our captain's spy-glass, subtends an

angle of half a degree, looking very much as our sun does
to the naked eye on a misty day. Alpha Lyræ, although so
very much larger than our sun, by-the-by, resembles him
closely as regards its spots, its atmosphere, and in many
other particulars. It is only within the last century,
Pundit tells me, that the binary relation existing between
these two orbs began even to be suspected. The evident
motion of our system in the heavens was (strange to say!)
referred to an orbit about a prodigious star in the centre
of the galaxy. About this star, or at all events about a
centre of gravity common to all the globes of the Milky
Way and supposed to be near Alcyone in the Pleiades,
every one of these globes was declared to be revolving, our
own performing the circuit in a period of 117,000,000 of
years! *We*, with our present lights, our vast telescopic
improvements, and so forth, of course find it difficult to
comprehend *the ground* of an idea such as this. Its first
propagator was one Mudler. He was led, we must presume,
to this wild hypothesis by mere analogy in the first instance;
but, this being the case, he should have at least adhered to
analogy in its development. A great central orb *was*, in
fact, suggested; so far Mudler was consistent. This central
orb, however, dynamically, should have been greater than
all its surrounding orbs taken together. The question
might then have been asked—' Why do we not see it? '—
we, especially, who occupy the mid region of the cluster—
the very locality *near* which, at least, must be situated
this inconceivable central sun. The astronomer, perhaps,
at this point, took refuge in the suggestion of non-lumi-
nosity; and here analogy was suddenly let fall. But even
admitting the central orb non-luminous, how did he
manage to explain its failure to be rendered visible by
the incalculable host of glorious suns glaring in all directions about it? No doubt what he finally maintained was
merely a centre of gravity common to all the revolving
orbs—but here again analogy must have been let fall.
Our system revolves, it is true, about a common centre of
gravity, but it does this in connection with and in consequence of a material sun whose mass more than counter-
balances the rest of the system. The mathematical circle
is a curve composed of an infinity of straight lines; but

this idea of the circle—this idea of it which, in regard to all earthly geometry, we consider as merely the mathematical, in contradistinction from the practical, idea—is, in sober fact, the *practical* conception which alone we have any right to entertain in respect to those Titanic circles with which we have to deal, at least in fancy, when we suppose our system, with its fellows, revolving about a point in the centre of the galaxy. Let the most vigorous of human imaginations but attempt to take a single step towards the comprehension of a circuit so unutterable ! It would scarcely be paradoxical to say that a flash of lightning itself, travelling *forever* upon the circumference of this inconceivable circle, would still *forever* be travelling in a straight line. That the path of our sun along such a circumference—that the direction of our system in such an orbit—would, to any human perception, deviate in the slightest degree from a straight line even in a million of years, is a proposition not to be entertained ; and yet these ancient astronomers were absolutely cajoled, it appears, into believing that a decisive curvature had become apparent during the brief period of their astronomical history— during the mere point—during the utter nothingness of two or three thousand years ! How incomprehensible, that considerations such as this did not at once indicate to them the true state of affairs—that of the binary revolution of our sun and Alpha Lyræ around a common centre of gravity !

April 7.—Continued last night our astronomical amusements. Had a fine view of the five Nepturian asteroids, and watched with much interest the putting up of a huge impost on a couple of lintels in the new temple at Daphnis in the moon. It was amusing to think that creatures so diminutive as the lunarians, and bearing so little resemblance to humanity, yet evinced a mechanical ingenuity so much superior to our own. One finds it difficult, too, to conceive the vast masses which these people handle so easily, to be as light as our reason tells us they actually are.

April 8.—Eureka ! Pundit is in his glory. A balloon from Kanadaw spoke us to-day and threw on board several late papers ; they contain some exceedingly curious information relative to Kanawdian or rather to Amriccan

antiquities. You know, I presume, that labourers have
for some months been employed in preparing the ground
for a new fountain at Paradise, the emperor's principal
pleasure garden. Paradise, it appears, has been, *literally*
speaking, an island time out of mind—that is to say, its
northern boundary was always (as far back as any records
extend) a rivulet, or rather a very narrow arm of the sea.
This arm was gradually widened until it attained its present
breadth—a mile. The whole length of the island is nine
miles ; the breadth varies materially. The entire area (so
Pundit says) was, about eight hundred years ago, densely
packed with houses, some of them twenty stories high ;
land (for some most unaccountable reason) being considered as especially precious just in this vicinity. The
disastrous earthquake, however, of the year 2050, so totally
uprooted and overwhelmed the town (for it was almost too
large to be called a village) that the most indefatigable of
our antiquarians have never yet been able to obtain from
the site any sufficient data (in the shape of coins, medals, or
inscriptions) wherewith to build up even the ghost of a
theory concerning the manners, customs, &c. &c. &c., of
the aboriginal inhabitants. Nearly all that we have
hitherto known of them is, that they were a portion of
the Knickerbocker tribe of savages infesting the continent
at its first discovery by Recorder Riker, a knight of the
Golden Fleece. They were by no means uncivilized, however, but cultivated various arts and even sciences after a
fashion of their own. It is related of them that they were
acute in many respects, but were oddly afflicted with a
monomania for building what, in the ancient Amriccan,
was denominated ' churches '—a kind of pagoda instituted
for the worship of two idols that went by the names of
Wealth and Fashion. In the end, it is said, the island
became, nine-tenths of it, church. The women, too, it
appears, were oddly deformed by a natural protuberance
of the region just below the small of the back—although,
most unaccountably, this deformity was looked upon
altogether in the light of a beauty. One or two pictures of
these singular women have, in fact, been miraculously
preserved. They look very odd, *very*—like something
between a turkey-cock and a dromedary.

Well, these few details are nearly all that have descended to us respecting the ancient Knickerbockers. It seems, however, that while digging in the centre of the emperor's garden (which, you know, covers the whole island), some of the workmen unearthed a cubical and evidently chiselled block of granite, weighing several hundred pounds. It was in good preservation, having received, apparently, little injury from the convulsion which entombed it. On one of its surfaces was a marble slab with (only think of it!) *an inscription—a legible inscription*. Pundit is in ecstasies. Upon detaching the slab, a cavity appeared, containing a leaden box filled with various coins, a long scroll of names, several documents which appear to resemble newspapers, with other matters of intense interest to the antiquarian! There can be no doubt that all these are genuine Amriccan relics belonging to the tribe called Knickerbocker. The papers thrown on board our balloon are filled with fac-similes of the coins, MSS., typography, &c. &c. I copy for your amusement the Knickerbocker inscription on the marble slab :—

This Corner Stone of a Monument to the
Memory of
GEORGE WASHINGTON,
was laid with appropriate ceremonies on the
19TH DAY OF OCTOBER, 1847,
the anniversary of the surrender of
Lord Cornwallis
to General Washington at Yorktown,
A. D. 1781,
under the auspices of the
Washington Monument Association of the
city of New York.

This, as I give it, is a verbatim translation done by Pundit himself, so there *can* be no mistake about it. From the few words thus preserved, we glean several important items of knowledge, not the least interesting of which is the fact that a thousand years ago *actual* monuments had fallen into disuse—as was all very proper—the people contenting themselves, as we do now, with a mere indication of the design to erect a monument at some future time ; a corner-stone being cautiously laid by itself ' solitary and alone ' (excuse me for quoting the great Amriccan poet Benton as a guarantee of the magnanimous *intention*. We ascertain, too, very distinctly, from this admirable inscription, the how, as well as the where and the what, of the great surrender in question. As to the *where*, it was Yorktown (wherever that was), and as to the *what*, it was General Cornwallis (no doubt some wealthy dealer in corn). *He* was surrendered. The inscription commemorates the surrender of—what ?—why, ' of Lord Cornwallis '. The only question is what could the savages wish him surrendered for. But when we remember that these savages were undoubtedly cannibals, we are led to the conclusion that they intended him for sausage. As to the *how* of the surrender, no language can be more explicit. Lord Cornwallis was surrendered (for sausage) ' under the auspices of the Washington Monument Association '—no doubt a charitable institution for the depositing of corner-stones.——But, Heaven bless me ! what is the matter ? Ah, I see—the balloon has collapsed, and we shall have a tumble into the sea. I have, therefore, only time enough to add that, from a hasty inspection of the fac-similes of newspapers, &c. &c., I find that *the* great men in those days among the Amriccans, were one John, a smith, and one Zacchary, a tailor.

Good bye, until I see you again. Whether you ever get this letter or not is a point of little importance, as I write altogether for my own amusement. I shall cork the MS. up in a bottle however, and throw it into the sea.

Yours everlastingly,
Pundita.

LOSS OF BREATH

A TALE NEITHER IN NOR OUT OF ' BLACKWOOD '

O breathe not, &c.—Moore's Melodies.

The most notorious ill-fortune must in the end, yield to the untiring courage of philosophy—as the most stubborn city to the ceaseless vigilance of an enemy. Salmanezer, as we have it in the holy writings, lay three years before Samaria ; yet it fell. Sardanapalus—see Diodorus—maintained himself seven in Nineveh ; but to no purpose. Troy expired at the close of the second lustrum ; and Azoth, as

Aristæus declares upon his honour as a gentleman, opened at last her gates to Psammitticus, after having barred them for the fifth part of a century. * * *

'Thou wretch !—thou vixen !—thou shrew !' said I to my wife on the morning after our wedding, 'thou witch !—thou hag !—thou whipper-snapper !—thou sink of iniquity !—thou fiery-faced quintessence of all that is abominable !—thou—thou—' here standing upon tiptoe, seizing her by the throat, and placing my mouth close to her ear, I was preparing to launch forth a new and more decided epithet of opprobrium, which should not fail, if ejaculated, to convince her of her insignificance, when, to my extreme horror and astonishment, I discovered that *I had lost my breath*.

The phrases 'I am out of breath', 'I have lost my breath', &c., are often enough repeated in common conversation; but it had never occurred to me that the terrible accident of which I speak could *bona fide* and actually happen ! Imagine—that is if you have a fanciful turn—imagine, I say, my wonder—my consternation—my despair !

There is a good genius, however, which has never entirely deserted me. In my most ungovernable moods I still retain a sense of propriety, *et le chemin des passions me conduit*—as Lord Edouard in the 'Julie' says it did him—*à la philosophie véritable.*

Although I could not at first precisely ascertain to what degree the occurrence had affected me, I determined at all events to conceal the matter from my wife, until further experience should discover to me the extent of this my unheard of calamity. Altering my countenance, therefore, in a moment, from its bepuffed and distorted appearance, to an expression of arch and coquettish benignity, I gave my lady a pat on the one cheek, and a kiss on the other, and without saying one syllable (Furies ! I could not), left her astonished at my drollery, as I pirouetted out of the room in a *Pas de Zephyr.*

Behold me then safely ensconced in my private *boudoir*, a fearful instance of the ill consequences attending upon irascibility—alive, with the qualifications of the dead—dead, with the propensities of the living—an anomaly on the face of the earth—being very calm, yet breathless.

Yes ! breathless. I am serious in asserting that my
breath was entirely gone. I could not have stirred with it
a feather if my life had been at issue, or sullied even the
delicacy of a mirror. Hard fate !—yet there was some
alleviation to the first overwhelming paroxysm of my
sorrow. I found, upon trial, that the powers of utterance
which, upon my inability to proceed in the conversation
with my wife, I then concluded to be totally destroyed,
were in fact only partially impeded, and I discovered that
had I at that interesting crisis, dropped my voice to a
singularly deep guttural, I might still have continued to
her the communication of my sentiments ; this pitch of
voice (the guttural) depending, I find, not upon the current
of the breath, but upon a certain spasmodic action of the
muscles of the throat.

Throwing myself upon a chair, I remained for some time
absorbed in meditation. My reflections, be sure, were of no
consolatory kind. A thousand vague and lachrymatory
fancies took possession of my soul—and even the idea of
suicide flitted across my brain ; but it is a trait in the
perversity of human nature to reject the obvious and the
ready, for the far-distant and equivocal. Thus I shuddered
at self-murder as the most decided of atrocities while the
tabby cat purred strenuously upon the rug, and the very
water-dog wheezed assiduously under the table ; each
taking to itself much merit for the strength of its lungs,
and all obviously done in derision of my own pulmonary
incapacity.

Oppressed with a tumult of vague hopes and fears, I at
length heard the footsteps of my wife descending the staircase. Being now assured of her absence, I returned with
a palpitating heart to the scene of my disaster.

Carefully locking the door on the inside, I commenced
a vigorous search. It was possible, I thought that, concealed in some obscure corner, or lurking in some closet or
drawer, might be found the lost object of my inquiry. It
might have a vapoury—it might even have a tangible
form. Most philosophers, upon many points of philosophy,
are still very unphilosophical. William Godwin, however, says in his ' Mandeville ', that ' invisible things
are the only realities ', and this all will allow, is a case

in point. I would have the judicious reader pause before accusing such asseverations of an undue quantum of absurdity. Anaxagoras, it will be remembered, maintained that snow is black, and this I have since found to be the case.

Long and earnestly did I continue the investigation : but the contemptible reward of my industry and perseverance proved to be only a set of false teeth, two pairs of hips, an eye, and a bundle of *billets-doux* from Mr. Windenough to my wife. I might as well here observe that this confirmation of my lady's partiality for Mr. W. occasioned me little uneasiness. That Mrs. Lackobreath should admire anything so dissimilar to myself was a natural and necessary evil. I am, it is well known, of a robust and corpulent appearance, and at the same time somewhat diminutive in stature. What wonder then that the lath-like tenuity of my acquaintance, and his altitude, which has grown into a proverb, should have met with all due estimation in the eyes of Mrs. Lackobreath. But to return.

My exertions, as I have before said, proved fruitless. Closet after closet—drawer after drawer—corner after corner—were scrutinized to no purpose. At one time, however, I thought myself sure of my prize, having in rummaging a dressing-case, accidentally demolished a bottle of Grandjean's Oil of Archangels—which, as an agreeable perfume, I here take the liberty of recommending.

With a heavy heart I returned to my *boudoir*—there to ponder upon some method of eluding my wife's penetration, until I could make arrangements prior to my leaving the country, for to this I had already made up my mind. In a foreign climate, being unknown, I might, with some probability of success, endeavour to conceal my unhappy calamity—a calamity calculated, even more than beggary, to estrange the affections of the multitude, and to draw down upon the wretch the well-merited indignation of the virtuous and the happy. I was not long in hesitation. Being naturally quick, I committed to memory the entire tragedy of ' Metamora '. I had the good fortune to recollect that in the accentuation of this drama, or at least of such portion of it as is allotted to the hero, the tones of voice in which I found myself deficient were altogether unnecessary, and that the deep guttural was expected to reign monotonously throughout.

I practised for some time by the borders of a well-frequented marsh ;—herein, however, having no reference to a similar proceeding of Demosthenes, but from a design peculiarly and conscientiously my own. Thus armed at all points, I determined to make my wife believe that I was suddenly smitten with a passion for the stage. In this, I succeeded to a miracle ; and to every question or suggestion found myself at liberty to reply in my most frog-like and sepulchral tones with some passage from the tragedy—any portion of which, as I soon took great pleasure in observing, would apply equally well to any particular subject. It is not to be supposed, however, that in the delivery of such passages I was found at all deficient in the looking asquint—the showing my teeth—the working my knees—the shuffling my feet—or in any of those unmentionable graces which are now justly considered the characteristics of a popular performer. To be sure they spoke of confining me in a strait-jacket—but, good God ! they never suspected me of having lost my breath.

Having at length put my affairs in order, I took my seat very early one morning in the mail stage for ——, giving it to be understood, among my acquaintances, that business of the last importance required my immediate personal attendance in that city.

The coach was crammed to repletion ; but in the uncertain twilight the features of my companions could not be distinguished. Without making any effectual resistance, I suffered myself to be placed between two gentlemen of colossal dimensions ; while a third, of a size larger, requesting pardon for the liberty he was about to take, threw himself upon my body at full length, and falling asleep in an instant, drowned all my guttural ejaculations for relief, in a snore which would have put to blush the roarings of the bull of Phalaris. Happily the state of my respiratory faculties rendered suffocation an accident entirely out of the question.

As, however, the day broke more distinctly in our approach to the outskirts of the city, my tormentor arising and adjusting his shirt-collar, thanked me in a very friendly manner for my civility. Seeing that I remained motionless (all my limbs were dislocated and my head twisted on one side), his apprehensions began to be excited; and arousing the rest of the passengers, he communicated in a very decided manner, his opinion that a dead man had been palmed upon them during the night for a living and responsible fellow-traveller; here giving me a thump on the right eye, by way of demonstrating the truth of his suggestion.

Hereupon all, one after another (there were nine in company), believed it their duty to pull me by the ear. A young practising physician, too, having applied a pocket-mirror to my mouth, and found me without breath, the assertion of my persecutor was pronounced a true bill; and the whole party expressed a determination to endure tamely no such impositions for the future, and to proceed no farther with any such carcasses for the present.

I was here, accordingly, thrown out at the sign of the ' Crow ' (by which tavern the coach happened to be passing), without meeting with any farther accident than the breaking of both my arms, under the left hind wheel of the vehicle. I must besides do the driver the justice to state that he did not forget to throw after me the largest of my trunks, which, unfortunately falling on my head, fractured my skull in a manner at once interesting and extraordinary.

The landlord of the ' Crow ', who is a hospitable man, finding that my trunk contained sufficient to indemnify him for any little trouble he might take in my behalf, sent forthwith for a surgeon of his acquaintance, and delivered me to his care with a bill and receipt for ten dollars.

The purchaser took me to his apartments and commenced operations immediately. Having cut off my ears, however, he discovered signs of animation. He now rang the bell, and sent for a neighbouring apothecary with whom to consult in the emergency. In case of his suspicions with regard to my existence proving ultimately correct, he, in the meantime, made an incision in my stomach, and removed several of my viscera for private dissection.

The apothecary had an idea that I was actually dead. This idea I endeavoured to confute, kicking and plunging

with all my might, and making the most furious contortions
—for the operations of the surgeon had, in a measure,
restored me to the possession of my faculties. All, however, was attributed to the effects of a new galvanic
battery, wherewith the apothecary, who is really a man of
information, performed several curious experiments, in
which, from my personal share in their fulfilment, I could
not help feeling deeply interested. It was a source of
mortification to me nevertheless, that although I made
several attempts at conversation, my powers of speech
were so entirely in abeyance, that I could not even open
my mouth ; much less then make reply to some ingenious
but fanciful theories of which, under other circumstances,
my minute acquaintance with the Hippocratian pathology
would have afforded me a ready confutation.

Not being able to arrive at a conclusion, the practitioners
remanded me for further examination. I was taken up
into a garret ; and the surgeon's lady having accommodated
me with drawers and stockings, the surgeon himself
fastened my hands, and tied up my jaws with a pocket
handkerchief—then bolted the door on the outside as he
hurried to his dinner, leaving me alone to silence and to
meditation.

I now discovered to my extreme delight that I could
have spoken had not my mouth been tied up by the pocket
handkerchief. Consoling myself with this reflection, I was
mentally repeating some passages of the ' Omnipresence of
the Deity ', as is my custom before resigning myself to
sleep, when two cats, of a greedy and vituperative turn,
entering at a hole in the wall, leaped up with a flourish *a la
Catalani*, and alighting opposite one another on my visage,
betook themselves to indecorous contention for the paltry
consideration of my nose.

But, as the loss of his ears proved the means of elevating
to the throne of Cyrus, the Magian or Mige-Gush of Persia,
and as the cutting off his nose gave Zopyrus possession of
Babylon, so the loss of a few ounces of my countenance
proved the salvation of my body. Aroused by the pain,
and burning with indignation, I burst, at a single effort, the
fastenings and the bandage.—Stalking across the room
I cast a glance of contempt at the belligerents, and throwing

open the sash to their extreme horror and disappointment, precipitated myself, very dexterously, from the window.

The mail-robber W——, to whom I bore a singular resemblance, was at this moment passing from the city jail to the scaffold erected for his execution in the suburbs. His extreme infirmity, and long-continued ill-health, had obtained him the privilege of remaining unmanacled ; and habited in his gallows costume—one very similar to my own—he lay at full length in the bottom of the hangman's cart (which happened to be under the windows of the surgeon at the moment of my precipitation) without any other guard than the driver who was asleep, and two recruits of the sixth infantry, who were drunk.

As ill-luck would have it, I alit upon my feet within the vehicle. W——, who was an acute fellow, perceived his opportunity. Leaping up immediately, he bolted out behind, and turning down an alley, was out of sight in the twinkling of an eye. The recruits, aroused by the bustle, could not exactly comprehend the merits of the transaction. Seeing, however, a man, the precise counter-part of the felon, standing upright in the cart before their eyes, they were of opinion that the rascal (meaning W——) was after making his escape (so they expressed themselves), and, having communicated this opinion to one another, they took each a dram, and then knocked me down with the butt-ends of their muskets.

It was not long ere we arrived at the place of destination. Of course nothing could be said in my defence. Hanging was my inevitable fate. I resigned myself thereto with a feeling half stupid, half acrimonious. Being little of a cynic, I had all the sentiments of a dog. The hangman, however, adjusted the noose about my neck. The drop fell.

I forbear to depict my sensations upon the gallows ; although here, undoubtedly, I could speak to the point, and it is a topic upon which nothing has been well said. In fact, to write upon such a theme it is necessary to have been hanged. Every author should confine himself to matters of experience. Thus Mark Antony composed a treatise upon getting drunk.

I may just mention, however, that die I did not. My body *was*, but I had no breath *to be* suspended ; and but

for the knot under my left ear (which had the feel of a
military stock) I dare say that I should have experienced
very little inconvenience. As for the jerk given to my neck
upon the falling of the drop, it merely proved a corrective
to the twist afforded me by the fat gentleman in the coach.

For good reasons, however, I did my best to give the
crowd the worth of their trouble. My convulsions were
said to be extraordinary. My spasms it would have been
difficult to beat. The populace *encored*. Several gentlemen
swooned ; and a multitude of ladies were carried home in
hysterics. Pinxit availed himself of the opportunity to
retouch, from a sketch taken upon the spot, his admirable
painting of the ' Marsyas flayed alive '.

When I had afforded sufficient amusement, it was
thought proper to remove my body from the gallows ;—
this the more especially as the real culprit had in the meantime been retaken and recognized ; a fact which I was so
unlucky as not to know.

Much sympathy was, of course, exercised in my behalf,
and as no one made claim to my corpse, it was ordered
that I should be interred in a public vault.

Here, after due interval, I was deposited. The sexton
departed, and I was left alone. A line of Marston's ' Mal-
content '—

Death 's a good fellow and keeps open house—

struck me at that moment as a palpable lie.

I knocked off, however, the lid of my coffin, and stepped
out. The place was dreadfully dreary and damp, and I
became troubled with *ennui*. By way of amusement, I felt
my way among the numerous coffins ranged in order
around. I lifted them down, one by one, and breaking
open their lids, busied myself in speculations about the
mortality within.

' This,' I soliloquized, tumbling over a carcass, puffy,
bloated, and rotund—' this has been, no doubt, in every
sense of the word, an unhappy—an unfortunate man. It
has been his terrible lot not to walk, but to waddle—to pass
through life not like a human being, but like an elephant—
not like a man, but like a rhinoceros.

' His attempts at getting on have been mere abortions,

and his circumgyratory proceedings a palpable failure.
Taking a step forward, it has been his misfortune to take
two towards the right, and three towards the left. His
studies have been confined to the poetry of Crabbe. He
can have no idea of the wonder of a *pirouette*. To him a
pas de papillon has been an abstract conception. He has
never ascended the summit of a hill. He has never viewed
from any steeple the glories of a metropolis. Heat has been
his mortal enemy. In the dog-days his days have been the
days of a dog. Therein, he has dreamed of flames and
suffocation—of mountains upon mountains—of Pelion upon
Ossa. He was short of breath—to say all in a word, he
was short of breath. He thought it extravagant to play
upon wind instruments. He was the inventor of self-
moving fans, wind-sails, and ventilators. He patronized
Du Pont the bellows-maker, and died miserably in attempting to smoke a cigar. His was a case in which I feel a deep
interest—a lot in which I sincerely sympathize.

' But here,'—said I—' here '—and I dragged spitefully
from its receptacle a gaunt, tall, and peculiar-looking form
whose remarkable appearance struck me with a sense of
unwelcome familiarity—' here is a wretch entitled to no
earthly commiseration '. Thus saying, in order to obtain
a more distinct view of my subject, I applied my thumb
and fore-finger to its nose, and causing it to assume a sitting
position upon the ground, held it thus, at the length of my
arm, while I continued my soliloquy.

—' Entitled ', I repeated, ' to no earthly commiseration.
Who indeed would think of compassionating a shadow ?
Besides, has he not had his full share of the blessings of
mortality ? He was the originator of tall monuments—shot-
towers—lightning-rods—lombardy poplars. His treatise
upon ' Shades and Shadows ' has immortalized him. He
edited with distinguished ability the last edition of ' South
on the Bones '. He went early to college and studied
pneumatics. He then came home, talked eternally, and
played upon the French-horn. He patronized the bag-
pipes. Captain Barclay, who walked against Time, would
not walk against *him*. Windham and Allbreath were his
favourite writers,—his favourite artist, Phiz. He died
gloriously while inhaling gas—*levique flatu corrumpitur*, like

the *fama pudicitiæ* in Hieronymus.[1] He was indubitably a—'———

'How *can* you ?—how—*can*—you ? '—interrupted the object of my animadversions, gasping for breath, and tearing off, with a desperate exertion, the bandage around its jaws —' how *can* you, Mr. Lackobreath, be so infernally cruel as to pinch me in that manner by the nose ? Did you not see how they had fastened up my mouth—and you *must* know —if you know anything—how vast a superfluity of breath I have to dispose of ! If you do *not* know, however, sit down and you shall see.—In my situation it is really a great relief to be able to open one's mouth—to be able to expatiate —to be able to communicate with a person like yourself, who do not think yourself called upon at every period to interrupt the thread of a gentleman's discourse.—Interruptions are annoying and should undoubtedly be abolished —don't you think so ?—no reply, I beg you,—one person is enough to be speaking at a time.—I shall be done by-and-by, and then you may begin.—How the devil, sir, did you get into this place ?—not a word I beseech you—been here some time myself—terrible accident !—heard of it, I suppose—awful calamity !—walking under your windows —some short while ago—about the time you were stage-struck—horrible occurrence !—heard of ' catching one's breath,' eh ?—hold your tongue I tell you !—I caught somebody else's !—had always too much of my own—met Blab at the corner of the street—wouldn't give me a chance for a word—couldn't get in a syllable edgeways—attacked, consequently, with epilepsis—Blab made his escape—damn all fools !—they took me up for dead, and put me in this place—pretty doings all of them !—heard all you said about me—every word a lie—horrible !—wonderful !—outrageous —hideous !—incomprehensible !—et cetera—et cetera—et cetera—et cetera—'———

It is impossible to conceive my astonishment at so unexpected a discourse ; or the joy with which I became gradually convinced that the breath so fortunately caught by the gentleman (whom I soon recognized as my neighbour

[1] *Tenera res in feminis famas pudicitiæ, et quasi flos pulcherrimus, cito ad levem marcessit auram, levique flatu corrumpitur, maxime, &c.*— Hieronymus ad Salvinam.

Windenough) was, in fact, the identical expiration mislaid by myself in the conversation with my wife. Time, place, and circumstance rendered it a matter beyond question. I did not, however, immediately release my hold upon Mr. W.'s proboscis—not at least during the long period in which the inventor of lombardy poplars continued to favour me with his explanations.

In this respect I was actuated by that habitual prudence which has ever been my predominating trait. I reflected that many difficulties might still lie in the path of my preservation which only extreme exertion on my part would be able to surmount. Many persons, I considered, are prone to estimate commodities in their possession—however valueless to the then proprietor—however trouble-some, or distressing—in direct ratio with the advantages to be derived by others from their attainment, or by them-selves from their abandonment. Might not this be the case with Mr. Windenough ? In displaying anxiety for the breath of which he was at present so willing to get rid, might I not lay myself open to the exactions of his avarice ? There are scoundrels in this world, I remembered with a sigh, who will not scruple to take unfair opportunities with even a next door neighbour, and (this remark is from Epictetus) it is precisely at that time when men are most anxious to throw off the burden of their own calamities that they feel the least desirous of relieving them in others.

Upon considerations similar to these, and still retaining my grasp upon the nose of Mr. W., I accordingly thought proper to model my reply.

' Monster ! ' I began in a tone of the deepest indignation, ' monster ; and double-winded idiot !—dost *thou*, whom for thine iniquities, it has pleased heaven to accurse with a two-fold respiration—dost *thou*, I say, presume to address me in the familiar language of an old acquaintance ?—"I lie ", forsooth ! and "hold my tongue ", to be sure !—pretty conversation indeed, to a gentleman with a single breath !—all this, too, when I have it in my power to relieve the calamity under which thou dost so justly suffer—to curtail the superfluities of thine unhappy respiration.'

Like Brutus, I paused for a reply—with which, like a tornado, Mr. Windenough immediately overwhelmed me.

Protestation followed upon protestation, and apology upon apology. There were no terms with which he was unwilling to comply, and there were none of which I failed to take the fullest advantage.

Preliminaries being at length arranged, my acquaintance delivered me the respiration ; for which (having carefully examined it) I gave him afterwards a receipt.

I am aware that by many I shall be held to blame for speaking, in a manner so cursory, of a transaction so impalpable. It will be thought that I should have entered more minutely into the details of an occurrence by which—and this is very true—much new light might be thrown upon a highly interesting branch of physical philosophy.

To all this I am sorry that I cannot reply. A hint is the only answer which I am permitted to make. There were *circumstances*—but I think it much safer upon consideration to say as little as possible about an affair so delicate—*so delicate*, I repeat, and at the time involving the interests of a third party whose sulphurous resentment I have not the least desire, at this moment, of incurring.

We were not long after this necessary arrangement in effecting an escape from the dungeons of the sepulchre. The united strength of our resuscitated voices was soon sufficiently apparent. Scissors, the Whig Editor, republished a treatise upon ' the nature and origin of subterranean noises '. A reply—rejoinder—confutation—and justification—followed in the columns of a Democratic Gazette. It was not until the opening of the vault to decide the controversy, that the appearance of Mr. Windenough and myself proved both parties to have been decidedly in the wrong.

I cannot conclude these details of some very singular passages in a life at all times sufficiently eventful, without again recalling to the attention of the reader the merits of that indiscriminate philosophy which is a sure and ready shield against those shafts of calamity which can neither be seen, felt, nor fully understood. It was in the spirit of this wisdom that, among the Ancient Hebrews, it was believed the gates of Heaven would be inevitably opened to that sinner, or saint, who, with good lungs and implicit confidence, should vociferate the word ' *Amen !* ' It was in the spirit of this wisdom that, when a great plague raged at Athens, and every means had been in vain attempted for its removal, Epimenides, as Laertius relates in his second book of that philosopher, advised the erection of a shrine and temple ' to the proper God '.

LYTTLETON BARRY.

THE MAN THAT WAS USED UP

A TALE OF THE LATE BUGABOO AND KICKAPOO CAMPAIGN

*Pleurez, pleurez, mes yeux, et fondez vous en eau !
La moitié de ma vie a mis l'autre au tombeau.* CORNEILLE.

I CANNOT just now remember when or where I first made the acquaintance of that truly fine-looking fellow, Brevet Brigadier-General John A. B. C. Smith. Some one *did* introduce me to the gentleman, I am sure—at some public meeting, I know very well—held about something of great importance, no doubt—at some place or other, I feel convinced,—whose name I have unaccountably forgotten. The truth is—that the introduction was attended, upon my part, with a degree of anxious embarrassment which operated to prevent any definite impressions of either time or place. I am constitutionally nervous—this, with me, is a family failing, and I can't help it. In especial, the slightest appearance of mystery—of any point I cannot exactly comprehend—puts me at once into a pitiable state of agitation.

There was something, as it were, remarkable—yes, *remarkable*, although this is but a feeble term to express my full meaning—about the entire individuality of the personage in question. He was, perhaps, six feet in height, and of a presence singularly commanding. There was an *air distingué* pervading the whole man, which spoke of high breeding, and hinted at high birth. Upon this topic—the topic of Smith's personal appearance—I have a kind of melancholy satisfaction in being minute. His head of hair would have done honour to a Brutus ;—nothing could be more richly flowing, or possess a brighter gloss. It was of a jetty black ;—which was also the colour, or more properly

the no colour, of his unimaginable whiskers. You perceive
I cannot speak of these latter without enthusiasm ; it is
not too much to say that they were the handsomest pair
of whiskers under the sun. At all events, they encircled,
and at times partially overshadowed, a mouth utterly
unequalled. Here were the most entirely even, and the
most brilliantly white of all conceivable teeth. From
between them, upon every proper occasion, issued a voice
of surpassing clearness, melody, and strength. In the
matter of eyes, also, my acquaintance was pre-eminently
endowed. Either one of such a pair was worth a couple of
the ordinary ocular organs. They were of a deep hazel,
exceedingly large and lustrous ; and there was perceptible
about them, ever and anon, just that amount of interesting
obliquity which gives pregnancy to expression.

The bust of the General was unquestionably the finest
bust I ever saw. For your life you could not have found
a fault with its wonderful proportion. This rare peculiarity
set off to great advantage a pair of shoulders which would
have called up a blush of conscious inferiority into the
countenance of the marble Apollo. I have a passion for
fine shoulders, and may say that I never beheld them in
perfection before. The arms altogether were admirably
modelled. Nor were the lower limbs less superb. These
were, indeed, the *ne plus ultra* of good legs. Every con-
noisseur in such matters admitted the legs to be good.
There was neither too much flesh, nor too little,—neither
rudeness nor fragility. I could not imagine a more graceful
curve than that of the *os femoris*, and there was just that
due gentle prominence in the rear of the *fibula* which goes
to the conformation of a properly proportioned calf. I wish
to God my young and talented friend Chiponchipino, the
sculptor, had but seen the legs of Brevet Brigadier-General
John A. B. C. Smith.

But although men so absolutely fine-looking are neither
as plenty as reasons or blackberries, still I could not bring
myself to believe that *the remarkable* something to which
I alluded just now—that the odd air of *je ne sais quoi* which
hung about my new acquaintance—lay altogether, or
indeed at all, in the supreme excellence of his bodily endow-
ments. Perhaps it might be traced to the *manner ;*—yet

here again I could not pretend to be positive. There *was* a primness, not to say stiffness, in his carriage—a degree of measured, and, if I may so express it, of rectangular precision, attending his every movement, which, observed in a more diminutive figure, would have had the least little savour in the world, of affectation, pomposity, or constraint, but which noticed in a gentleman of his undoubted dimensions, was readily placed to the account of reserve, *hauteur*— of a commendable sense, in short, of what is due to the dignity of colossal proportion.

The kind friend who presented me to General Smith whispered in my ear some few words of comment upon the man. He was a *remarkable* man—a *very* remarkable man— indeed one of the *most* remarkable men of the age. He was an especial favourite, too, with the ladies—chiefly on account of his high reputation for courage.

' In *that* point he is unrivalled—indeed he is a perfect desperado—a down-right fire-eater, and no mistake,' said my friend, here dropping his voice excessively low, and thrilling me with the mystery of his tone.

' A downright fire-eater, and *no* mistake. Showed *that*, I should say, to some purpose, in the late tremendous swamp-fight away down South, with the Bugaboo and Kickapoo Indians.' [Here my friend opened his eyes to some extent.] ' Bless my soul!—blood and thunder, and all that!—*prodigies* of valour!—heard of him of course?— you know he's the man '——

' Man alive, how *do* you do? why how *are* ye? *very* glad to see ye, indeed!' here interrupted the General himself, seizing my companion by the hand as he drew near, and bowing stiffly, but profoundly, as I was presented. I then thought (and I think so still), that I never heard a clearer nor a stronger voice, nor beheld a finer set of teeth : but I *must* say that I was sorry for the interruption just at that moment, as, owing to the whispers and insinuations aforesaid, my interest had been greatly excited in the hero of the Bugaboo and Kickapoo campaign.

However, the delightfully luminous conversation of Brevet Brigadier-General John A. B. C. Smith soon completely dissipated this chagrin. My friend leaving us immediately, we had quite a long *tête-à-tête*, and I was not

only pleased but *really*—instructed. I never heard a more
fluent talker, or a man of greater general information.
With becoming modesty, he forebore, nevertheless, to
touch upon the theme I had just then most at heart—I
mean the mysterious circumstances attending the Bugaboo
war—and, on my own part, what I conceive to be a proper
sense of delicacy forbade me to broach the subject ;
although, in truth, I was exceedingly tempted to do so.
I perceived, too, that the gallant soldier preferred topics of
philosophical interest, and that he delighted especially in
commenting upon the rapid march of mechanical invention.
Indeed, lead him where I would, this was a point to which he
invariably came back.

' There is nothing at all like it,' he would say ; ' we are
a wonderful people, and live in a wonderful age. Para-
chutes and rail-roads—man-traps and spring-guns ! Our
steam-boats are upon every sea, and the Nassau balloon
packet is about to run regular trips (fare either way only
twenty pounds sterling) between London and Timbuctoo.
And who shall calculate the immense influence upon social
life—upon arts—upon commerce—upon literature—which
will be the immediate result of the great principles of electro
magnetics ! Nor, is this all, let me assure you ! There is
really no end to the march of invention. The most wonderful—the most ingenious—and let me add, Mr.—Mr.—
Thompson, I believe, is your name—let me add, I say, the
most *useful*—the most truly *useful* mechanical contrivances,
are daily springing up like mushrooms, if I may so express
myself, or, more figuratively, like—ah—grasshoppers—like
grasshoppers, Mr. Thompson—about us and ah—ah—ah—
around us ! '

Thompson, to be sure, is not my name ; but it is needless
to say that I left General Smith with a heightened interest
in the man, with an exalted opinion of his conversational
powers, and a deep sense of the valuable privileges we enjoy
in living in this age of mechanical invention. My curiosity,
however, had not been altogether satisfied, and I resolved
to prosecute immediate inquiry among my acquaintances
touching the Brevet Brigadier-General himself, and particularly respecting the tremendous events *quorum pars magna
fuit*, during the Bugaboo and Kickapoo campaign.

The first opportunity which presented itself, and which (*horresco referens*) I did not in the least scruple to seize, occurred at the Church of the Reverend Doctor Drum-mummupp, where I found myself established, one Sunday, just at sermon time, not only in the pew, but by the side, of that worthy and communicative little friend of mine, Miss Tabitha T. Thus seated, I congratulated myself, and with much reason, upon the very flattering state of affairs. If any person knew anything about Brevet Brigadier-General John A. B. C. Smith, that person, it was clear to me, was Miss Tabitha T. We telegraphed a few signals, and then commenced, *sotto voce*, a brisk *tête-à-tête*.

' Smith ! ' said she, in reply to my very earnest inquiry ; ' Smith !—why, not General John A. B. C. ? Bless me, I thought you *knew* all about *him* ! This is a wonderfully inventive age ! Horrid affair that !—a bloody set of wretches, those Kickapoos !—fought like a hero—prodigies of valour—immortal renown. Smith !—Brevet Brigadier-General John A. B. C. !—why, you know he's the man '—

' Man,' here broke in Doctor Drummummupp, at the top of his voice, and with a thump that came near knocking the pulpit about our ears ; ' man that is born of a woman hath but a short time to live ; he cometh up and is cut down like a flower ! ' I started to the extremity of the pew, and perceived by the animated looks of the divine, that the wrath which had nearly proved fatal to the pulpit had been excited by the whispers of the lady and myself. There was no help for it ; so I submitted with a good grace, and listened, in all the martyrdom of dignified silence, to the balance of that very capital discourse.

Next evening found me a somewhat late visitor at the Rantipole theatre, where I felt sure of satisfying my curiosity at once, by merely stepping into the box of those exquisite specimens of affability and omniscience, the Misses Arabelli and Miranda Cognoscenti. That fine tragedian, Climax, was doing Iago to a very crowded house, and I experienced some little difficulty in making my wishes understood ; especially as our box was next the slips, and completely overlooked the stage.

' Smith ? ' said Miss Arabella, as she at length comprehended the purport of my query; 'Smith?—why, not General John A. B. C.?'

'Smith?' inquired Miranda, musingly. 'God bless me, did you ever behold a finer figure?'

'Never, madam, but *do* tell me'——

'Or so inimitable grace?'

'Never, upon my word!—but pray inform me'——

'Or so just an appreciation of stage effect?'

'Madam!'

'Or a more delicate sense of the true beauties of Shakespeare? Be so good as to look at that leg!'

'The devil!' and I turned again to her sister.

'Smith?' said she, 'why, not General John A. B. C.? Horrid affair that, wasn't it?—great wretches, those Bugaboos—savage and so on—but we live in a wonderfully inventive age!—Smith!—O yes! great man!—perfect desperado—immortal renown—prodigies of valour! *Never heard!*' [This was given in a scream.] 'Bless my soul!—why, he's the man'——

'—mandragora
Nor all the drowsy syrups of the world
Shall ever medicine thee to that sweet sleep
Which thou owd'st yesterday!'

here roared out Climax just in my ear, and shaking his fist in my face all the time, in a way that I *couldn't* stand, and I *wouldn't*. I left the Misses Cognoscenti immediately, went behind the scenes forthwith, and gave the beggarly scoundrel such a thrashing as I trust he will remember to the day of his death.

At the *soirée* of the lovely widow, Mrs. Kathleen O'Trump, I was confident that I should meet with no similar disappointment. Accordingly, I was no sooner seated at the card-table, with my pretty hostess for a *vis-à-vis*, than I propounded those questions the solution of which had become a matter so essential to my peace.

'Smith?' said my partner, 'why, not General John A. B. C.? Horrid affair that, wasn't it?—diamonds, did you say?—terrible wretches those Kickapoos!—we are playing *whist*, if you please, Mr. Tattle—however, this is the age of invention, most certainly *the* age, one may say—*the* age *par excellence*—speak French?—oh, quite a hero—

perfect desperado !—*no hearts*, Mr. Tattle ? I don't believe
it !—immortal renown and all that—prodigies of valour !
Never heard ! !—why, bless me, he's the man '——

' Mann ?—*Captain* Mann ? ' here screamed some little
feminine interloper from the farthest corner of the room.
' Are you talking about Captain Mann and the duel ?—oh,
I *must* hear—do tell—go on, Mrs. O'Trump !—do now go
on ! ' And go on Mrs. O'Trump did—all about a certain
Captain Mann, who was either shot or hung, or should have
been both shot and hung. Yes ! Mrs. O'Trump, she went
on, and I—I went off. There was no chance of hearing
anything farther that evening in regard to Brevet Brigadier-
General John A. B. C. Smith.

Still I consoled myself with the reflection that the tide of
ill luck would not run against me forever, and so determined to make a bold push for information at the rout of
that bewitching little angel, the graceful Mrs. Pirouette.

' Smith ? ' said Mrs. P., as we twirled about together in
a *pas de zephyr*, ' Smith ?—why not General John A. B. C. ?
Dreadful business that of the Bugaboos, wasn't it ?—
terrible creatures, those Indians !—*do* turn out your toes !
I really am ashamed of you—man of great courage, poor
fellow !—but this is a wonderful age for invention—O dear
me, I'm out of breath—quite a desperado—prodigies of
valour—*never heard ! !*—can't believe it—I shall have to
sit down and enlighten you—Smith ! why, he's the
man '——

' Man-*Fred*, I tell you ! ' here bawled out Miss Bas-Bleu,
as I led Mrs. Pirouette to a seat. ' Did ever anybody hear
the like ? It's Man-*Fred*, I say, and not at all by any means
Man-*Friday*.' Here Miss Bas-Bleu beckoned to me in a
very peremptory manner ; and I was obliged, will I nill
I, to leave Mrs. P. for the purpose of deciding a dispute
touching the title of a certain poetical drama of Lord
Byron's. Although I pronounced, with great promptness,
that the true title was Man-*Friday*, and not by any means
Man-*Fred*, yet when I returned to seek Mrs. Pirouette she
was not to be discovered, and I made my retreat from the
house in a very bitter spirit of animosity against the whole
race of the Bas-Bleus.

Matters had now assumed a really serious aspect, and

I resolved to call at once upon my particular friend, Mr. Theodore Sinivate ; for I knew that here at least I should get something like definite information.

'Smith ? ' said he, in his well-known peculiar way of drawling out his syllables ; 'Smith ?—why, not General John A. B. C. ? Savage affair that with the Kickapo-o-o-os, wasn't it ? Say ! don't you think so ?—perfect despera-a-ado—great pity, 'pon my honour !—wonderfully inventive age !—pro-o-odigies of valour ! By the by, did you ever hear about Captain Ma-a-a-a-n ? '

'Captain Mann be d—d ! ' said I, ' please to go on with your story.'

'Hem !—oh well !—quite *la même cho-o-ose*, as we say in France. Smith, eh ? Brigadier-General John A—B—C. ? I say '—[here Mr. S. thought proper to put his finger to the side of his nose]—' I say, you don't mean to insinuate now, really and truly, and conscientiously, that you don't know all about that affair of Smith's, as well as I do, eh ? Smith ? John A—B—C. ? Why, bless me, he 's the ma-a-an '——

'*Mr.* Sinivate,' said I, imploringly, ' *is* he the man in the mask ? '

'No-o-o ! ' said he, looking wise, ' nor the man in the mo-o-on.'

This reply I considered a pointed and positive insult, and so left the house at once in high dudgeon, with a firm resolve to call my friend, Mr. Sinivate, to a speedy account for his ungentlemanly conduct and ill-breeding.

In the meantime, however, I had no notion of being thwarted touching the information I desired. There was one resource left me yet. I would go to the fountain-head. I would call forthwith upon the General himself, and demand, in explicit terms, a solution of this abominable piece of mystery. Here, at least, there should be no chance for equivocation. I would be plain, positive, peremptory—as short as pie-crust—as concise as Tacitus or Montesquieu.

It was early when I called, and the General was dressing ; but I pleaded urgent business, and was shown at once into his bed-room by an old negro valet, who remained in attendance during my visit. As I entered the chamber, I looked about, of course, for the occupant, but did not

immediately perceive him. There was a large and exceedingly odd-looking bundle of something which lay close by
my feet on the floor, and, as I was not in the best humour in
the world, I gave it a kick out of the way.

' Hem ! ahem ! rather civil that, I should say ! ' said
the bundle, in one of the smallest, and altogether the
funniest little voices, between a squeak and a whistle, that
I ever heard in all the days of my existence.

' Ahem ! rather civil that, I should observe.'

I fairly shouted with terror, and made off, at a tangent,
into the farthest extremity of the room.

' God bless me ! my dear fellow,' here again whistled
the bundle, ' what—what—what—why, what *is* the matter?
I really believe you don't know me at all.'

What *could* I say to all this—what *could* I ? I staggered
into an arm-chair, and, with staring eyes and open mouth,
awaited the solution of the wonder.

' Strange you shouldn't know me though, isn't it ? '
presently re-squeaked the nondescript, which I now perceived was performing, upon the floor, some inexplicable
evolution, very analogous to the drawing on of a stocking.
There was only a single leg, however, apparent.

' Strange you shouldn't know me, though, isn't it ?
Pompey, bring me that leg ! ' Here Pompey handed the
bundle, a very capital cork leg, already dressed, which it
screwed on in a trice ; and then it stood up before my
eyes.

' And a bloody action it *was*,' continued the thing, as if
in a soliloquy ; ' but then one musn't fight with the Bugaboos and Kickapoos, and think of coming off with a mere
scratch. Pompey, I'll thank you now for that arm.
Thomas ' [turning to me] ' is decidedly the best hand at a
cork leg ; but if you should ever want an arm, my dear
fellow, you must really let me recommend you to Bishop.'
Here Pompey screwed on an arm.

' We had rather hot work of it, that you may say. Now,
you dog, slip on my shoulders and bosom ! Pettitt makes
the best shoulders, but for a bosom you will have to go to
Ducrow.'

' Bosom ! ' said I.

' Pompey, will you *never* be ready with that wig ?

Scalping is a rough process after all; but then you can procure such a capital scratch at De L'Orme's.'

' Scratch ! '

' Now, you nigger, my teeth ! For a *good* set of these you had better go to Parmly's at once ; high prices, but excellent work. I swallowed some very capital articles, though, when the big Bugaboo rammed me down with the butt-end of his rifle.'

' Butt-end ! ram down ! ! my eye ! ! '

' O yes, by-the-by, my eye—here, Pompey, you scamp, screw it in ! Those Kickapoos are not so very slow at a gouge ; but he's a belied man, that Dr. Williams, after all ; you can't imagine how well I see with the eyes of his make.'

I now began very clearly to perceive that the object before me was nothing more nor less than my new acquaintance, Brevet Brigadier-General John A. B. C. Smith. The manipulations of Pompey had made, I must confess, a very striking difference in the appearance of the personal man. The voice, however, still puzzled me no little ; but even this apparent mystery was speedily cleared up.

' Pompey, you black rascal,' squeaked the General, ' I really do believe you would let me go out without my palate.'

Hereupon the negro, grumbling out an apology, went up to his master, opened his mouth with the knowing air of a horse-jockey, and adjusted therein a somewhat singular-looking machine, in a very dexterous manner, that I could not altogether comprehend. The alteration, however, in the entire expression of the General's countenance was instantaneous and surprising. When he again spoke, his voice had resumed all that rich melody and strength which I had noticed upon our original introduction.

' D—n the vagabonds ! ' said he, in so clear a tone that I positively started at the change, ' D—n the vagabonds ! they not only knocked in the roof of my mouth, but took the trouble to cut off at least seven-eights of my tongue. There isn't Bonfanti's equal, however, in America, for really good articles of this description. I can recommend you to him with confidence ' [here the General bowed], 'and assure you that I have the greatest pleasure in so doing.'

I acknowledged his kindness in my best manner, and took leave of him at once, with a perfect understanding of the true state of affairs—with a full comprehension of the mystery which had troubled me so long. It was evident. It was a clear case. Brevet Brigadier-General John A. B. C. Smith was the man——was *the man that was used up*.

THE BUSINESS MAN

Method is the soul of business.—OLD SAYING.

I AM a business man. I am a methodical man. Method is *the* thing, after all. But there are no people I more heartily despise, than your eccentric fools who prate about method without understanding it ; attending strictly to its letter, and violating its spirit. These fellows are always doing the most out-of-the-way things in what they call an orderly manner. Now here—I conceive—is a positive paradox. True method appertains to the ordinary and the obvious alone, and cannot be applied to the *outré*. What definite idea can a body attach to such expressions as ' methodical Jack o' Dandy ', or ' a systematical Will o' the Wisp ' ?

My notions upon this head might not have been so clear as they are, but for a fortunate accident which happened to me when I was a very little boy. A good-hearted old Irish nurse (whom I shall not forget in my will) took me up one day by the heels, when I was making more noise than was necessary, and, swinging me round two or three times, d——d my eyes for ' a skreeking little spalpeen ', and then knocked my head into a cocked hat against the bed-post. This, I say, decided my fate, and made my fortune. A bump arose at once on my sinciput, and turned out to be as pretty an organ of *order* as one shall see on a summer's day. Hence that positive appetite for system and regularity which has made me the distinguished man of business that I am.

If there is anything on earth I hate, it is a genius. Your

geniuses are all arrant asses—the greater the genius the greater the ass—and to this rule there is no exception whatever. Especially, you cannot make a man of business out of a genius, any more than money out of a Jew, or the best nutmegs out of pine-knots. The creatures are always going off at a tangent into some fantastic employment, or ridiculous speculation, entirely at variance with the ' fitness of things ', and having no business whatever to be considered as a business at all. Thus you may tell these characters immediately by the nature of their occupations. If you ever perceive a man setting up as a merchant or a manufacturer ; or going into the cotton or tobacco trade, or any of those eccentric pursuits ; or getting to be a dry-goods dealer, or soap-boiler, or something of that kind ; or pretending to be a lawyer, or a blacksmith, or a physician—anything out of the usual way—you may set him down at once as a genius, and then, according to the rule-of-three, he 's an ass.

Now I am not in any respect a genius, but a regular business man. My Day-book and Ledger will evince this in a minute. They are well kept, though I say it myself ; and, in my general habits of accuracy and punctuality, I am not to be beat by a clock. Moreover, my occupations have been always made to chime in with the ordinary habitudes of my fellow-men. Not that I feel the least indebted, upon this score, to my exceedingly weak-minded parents, who, beyond doubt, would have made an arrant genius of me at last, if my guardian angel had not come, in good time, to the rescue. In biography the truth is everything, and in autobiography it is especially so—yet I scarcely hope to be believed when I state, however solemnly, that my poor father put me, when I was about fifteen years of age, into the counting-house of what he termed ' a respectable hardware and commission merchant doing a capital bit of business ! ' A capital bit of fiddlestick ! However, the consequence of this folly was, that in two or three days, I had to be sent home to my button-headed family in a high state of fever, and with a most violent and dangerous pain in the sinciput, all round about my organ of order. It was nearly a gone case with me then—just touch-and-go for six weeks—the physicians giving me up and all that sort of thing. But, although I suffered much, I was a thankful boy in the main. I was saved from being a ' respectable hardware and commission merchant, doing a capital bit of business ', and I felt grateful to the protuberance which had been the means of my salvation, as well as to the kind-hearted female who had originally put these means within my reach.

The most of boys run away from home at ten or twelve years of age, but I waited till I was sixteen. I don't know that I should have gone, even then, if I had not happened to hear my old mother talk about setting me up on my own hook in the grocery way. The *grocery* way !—only think of that ! I resolved to be off forthwith, and try and establish myself in some *decent* occupation, without dancing attendance any longer upon the caprices of these eccentric old people, and running the risk of being made a genius of in the end. In this project I succeeded perfectly well at the first effort, and by the time I was fairly eighteen, found myself doing an extensive and profitable business in the Tailor's Walking-Advertisement line.

I was enabled to discharge the onerous duties of this profession, only by that rigid adherence to system which formed the leading feature of my mind. A scrupulous *method* characterized my actions as well as my accounts. In my case, it was method—not money—which made the man : at least all of him that was not made by the tailor whom I served. At nine, every morning, I called upon that individual for the clothes of the day. Ten o'clock found me in some fashionable promenade or other place of public amusement. The precise regularity with which I turned my handsome person about, so as to bring successively into view every portion of the suit upon my back, was the admiration of all the knowing men in the trade. Noon never passed without my bringing home a customer to the house of my employers, Messrs. Cut and Comeagain. I say this proudly, but with tears in my eyes—for the firm proved themselves the basest of ingrates. The little account about which we quarrelled and finally parted, cannot, in any item, be thought overcharged, by gentlemen really conversant with the nature of the business. Upon this point, however, I feel a degree of proud satisfaction in permitting the reader to judge for himself. My bill ran thus :

Messrs. Cut and Comeagain, Merchant Tailors.

To Peter Proffit, Walking Advertiser. Drs.

July 10. To promenade, as usual, and customer brought home,	$00 25
July 11. To do do do	25
July 12. To one lie, second class ; damaged black cloth sold for invisible green,	25
July 13. To one lie, first class, extra quality and size ; recommending milled sattinet as broadcloth,	75
July 20. To purchasing brand new paper shirt collar or dickey, to set off gray Petersham,	2
Aug. 15. To wearing double-padded bobtail frock (thermometer 706 in the shade),	25
Aug. 16. Standing on one leg three hours, to show off new-style strapped pants at 12½ cents per leg per hour,	37½
Aug. 17. To promenade, as usual, and large customer brought (fat man),	50
Aug. 18. To do do (medium size),	25
Aug. 19. To do do (small man and bad pay),	6

$2 96½

The item chiefly disputed in this bill was the very moderate charge of two pennies for the dickey. Upon my word of honour, this *was not* an unreasonable price for that dickey. It was one of the cleanest and prettiest little dickeys I ever saw ; and I have good reason to believe that it effected the sale of three Petershams. The elder partner of the firm, however, would allow me only one penny of the charge, and took it upon himself to show in what manner four of the same sized conveniences could be got out of a sheet of foolscap. But it is needless to say that I stood upon the *principle* of the thing. Business is business, and should be done in a business way. There was no *system* whatever in swindling me out of a penny—a clear fraud of fifty per cent.—no *method* in any respect. I left at once the employment of Messrs. Cut and Comeagain, and set up in the Eye-Sore line by myself—one of the most lucrative, respectable, and independent of the ordinary occupations.

My strict integrity, economy, and rigorous business habits, here again came into play. I found myself driving a flourishing trade, and soon became a marked man upon

' Change '. The truth is, I never dabbled in flashy matters, but jogged on in the good old sober routine of the calling—a calling in which I should, no doubt, have remained to the present hour, but for a little accident which happened to me in the prosecution of one of the usual business operations of the profession. Whenever a rich old hunks, or prodigal heir, or bankrupt corporation, gets into the notion of putting up a palace, there is no such thing in the world as stopping either of them, and this every intelligent person knows. The fact in question is indeed the basis of the Eye-Sore trade. As soon, therefore, as a building project is fairly afoot by one of these parties, we merchants secure a nice corner of the lot in contemplation, or a prime little situation just adjoining or right in front. This done, we wait until the palace is half-way up, and then we pay some tasty architect to run us up an ornamental mud hovel, right against it ; or a Down-East or Dutch Pagoda, or a pig-sty, or an ingenious little bit of fancy work, either Esquimau, Kickapoo, or Hottentot. Of course, we can't afford to take these structures down under a bonus of five hundred per cent. upon the prime cost of our lot and plaster. *Can* we ? I ask the question. I ask it of business men. It would be irrational to suppose that we can. And yet there was a rascally corporation which asked me to do this very thing—this *very thing !* I did not reply to their absurd proposition, of course ; but I felt it a duty to go that same night, and lamp-black the whole of their palace. For this, the unreasonable villains clapped me into jail ; and the gentlemen of the Eye-Sore trade could not well avoid cutting my connection when I came out.

The Assault and Battery business, into which I was now forced to adventure for a livelihood, was somewhat ill-adapted to the delicate nature of my constitution ; but I went to work in it with a good heart, and found my account, here as heretofore, in those stern habits of methodical accuracy which had been thumped into me by that delightful old nurse—I would indeed be the basest of men not to remember her well in my will. By observing, as I say, the strictest system in all my dealings, and keeping a well-regulated set of books, I was enabled to get over many serious difficulties, and, in the end, to establish myself very decently in the profession. The truth is, that few individuals, in any line, did a snugger little business than I. I will just copy a page or so out of my Day-Book ; and this will save me the necessity of blowing my own trumpet—a contemptible practice, of which no high-minded man will be guilty. Now, the Day-Book is a thing that don't lie.

'Jan. 1.—New Year's day. Met Snap in the street, groggy. Mem—he'll do. Met Gruff shortly afterwards, blind drunk. Mem—he'll answer too. Entered both gentlemen in my Ledger, and opened a running account with each.

'Jan. 2.—Saw Snap at the Exchange, and went up and trod on his toe. Doubled his fist and knocked me down. Good !—got up again. Some trifling difficulty with Bag, my attorney. I want the damages at a thousand, but he says that, for so simple a knock-down, we can't lay them at more than five hundred. Mem—must get rid of Bag—no *system* at all.

'Jan. 3.—Went to the theatre, to look for Gruff. Saw him sitting in a side box, in the second tier, between a fat lady and a lean one. Quizzed the whole party through an opera-glass, till I saw the fat lady blush and whisper to G. Went round, then, into the box, and put my nose within reach of his hand. Wouldn't pull it—no go. Blew it, and tried again—no go. Sat down then, and winked at the lean lady, when I had the high satisfaction of finding him lift me up by the nape of the neck, and fling me over into the pit. Neck dislocated, and right leg capitally splintered. Went home in high glee, drank a bottle of champagne, and booked the young man for five thousand. Bag says it'll do.

'Feb. 15.—Compromised the case of Mr. Snap. Amount entered in Journal—fifty cents—which 3ee.

'Feb. 16.—Cast by that villain, Gruff, who made me a present of five dollars. Costs of suit, four dollars and twenty-five cents. Nett profit—see Journal—seventy-five cents.'

Now, here is a clear gain, in a very brief period, of no less than one dollar and twenty-five cents—this is in the mere cases of Snap and Gruff ; and I solemnly assure the reader that these extracts are taken at random from my Day-Book.

It's an old saying, and a true one, however, that money is nothing in comparison with health. I found the exactions of the profession somewhat too much for my delicate state of body ; and, discovering, at last, that I was knocked all out of shape, so that I didn't know very well what to make of the matter, and so that my friends, when they met me in the street, couldn't tell that I was Peter Proffit at all, it occurred to me that the best expedient I could adopt, was to alter my line of business. I turned my attention, therefore, to Mud-Dabbling, and continued it for some years.

The worst of this occupation, is, that too many people take a fancy to it, and the competition is in consequence excessive. Every ignoramus of a fellow who finds that he hasn't brains in sufficient quantity to make his way as a walking advertiser, or an eye-sore-prig, or a salt and batter man, thinks, of course, that he'll answer very well as a dabbler of mud. But there never was entertained a more erroneous idea than that it requires no brains to mud-dabble. Especially, there is nothing to be made in this way without *method*. I did only a retail business myself, but my old habits of *system* carried me swimmingly along. I selected my street-crossing, in the first place, with great deliberation, and I never put down a broom in any part of the town *but that*. I took care, too, to have a nice little puddle at hand, which I could get at in a minute. By these means I got to be well known as a man to be trusted ; and this is one-half the battle, let me tell you, in trade. Nobody ever failed to pitch *me* a copper, and got over *my* crossing with a clean pair of pantaloons. And, as my business habits, in this respect, were sufficiently understood, I never met with any attempt at imposition. I wouldn't have put up with it, if I had. Never imposing upon anyone myself, I suffered no one to play the possum with me. The frauds of the banks of course I couldn't help. Their suspension put me to ruinous inconvenience. These, however, are not individuals, but corporations ; and corporations, it is very well known, have neither bodies to be kicked, nor souls to be damned.

I was making money at this business, when, in an evil moment, I was induced to merge in the Cur-Spattering—a somewhat analogous, but, by no means, so respectable a profession. My location, to be sure, was an excellent one, being central, and I had capital blacking and brushes. My little dog, too, was quite fat and up to all varieties of snuff. He had been in the trade a long time, and, I may say, understood it. Our general routine was this ;—Pompey, having rolled himself well in the mud, sat upon end at the shop door, until he observed a dandy approaching in bright boots. He then proceeded to meet him, and gave the Wellingtons a rub or two with his wool. Then the dandy swore very much, and looked about for a boot-black. There I was, full in his view, with blacking and brushes. It was only a minute's work, and then came a sixpence. This did moderately well for a time ;—in fact, I was not avaricious, but my dog was. I allowed him a third of the profit, but he was advised to insist upon half. This I couldn't stand—so we quarrelled and parted.

I next tried my hand at the Organ-grinding for a while, and may say that I made out pretty well. It is a plain, straightforward business, and requires no particular abilities. You can get a music-mill for a mere song, and, to put it in order, you have but to open the works, and give them three or four smart raps with a hammer. It improves the tone of the thing, for business purposes, more than you can imagine. This done, you have only to stroll along, with the mill on your back, until you see tan-bark in the street, and a knocker wrapped up in buckskin. Then you stop and grind ; looking as if you meant to stop and grind till doomsday. Presently a window opens, and somebody pitches you a sixpence, with a request to ' Hush up and go on ', &c. I am aware that some grinders have actually afforded to ' go on ' for this sum ; but for my part, I found the necessary outlay of capital too great, to permit of my ' going on ' under a shilling.

At this occupation I did a good deal ; but, somehow, I was not quite satisfied, and so finally abandoned it. The truth is, I laboured under the disadvantage of having no monkey—and American streets are so muddy, and a Democratic rabble is so obtrusive, and so full of demnition mischievous little boys.

I was now out of employment for some months, but at length succeeded, by dint of great interest, in procuring a

situation in the Sham-Post. The duties, here, are simple,
and not altogether unprofitable. For example :—very early
in the morning I had to make up my packet of sham letters.
Upon the inside of each of these I had to scrawl a few
lines—on any subject which occurred to me as sufficiently
mysterious—signing all the epistles Tom Dobson, or Bobby
Tompkins, or anything in that way. Having folded and
sealed all, and stamped them with sham postmarks—New
Orleans, Bengal, Botany Bay, or any other place a great
way off—I set out, forthwith, upon my daily route, as if in
a very great hurry. I always called at the big houses to
deliver the letters, and receive the postage. Nobody
hesitates at paying for a letter—especially for a double
one—people are *such* fools—and it was no trouble to get
round a corner before there was time to open the epistles.
The worst of this profession was, that I had to walk so
much and so fast ; and so frequently to vary my route.
Besides, I had serious scruples of conscience. I can't bear
to hear innocent individuals abused—and the way the whole
town took to cursing Tom Dobson and Bobby Tompkins,
was really awful to hear. I washed my hands of the matter
in disgust.

My eighth and last speculation has been in the Cat-
Growing way. I have found this a most pleasant and lucrative business, and, really, no trouble at all. The country, it
is well-known, has become infested with cats—so much so
of late, that a petition for relief, most numerously and
respectably signed, was brought before the legislature at
its late memorable session. The assembly, at this epoch,
was unusually well-informed, and, having passed many
other wise and wholesome enactments, it crowned all with
the Cat-Act. In its original form, this law offered a pre-
mium for cat-*heads* (fourpence a-piece), but the Senate
succeeded in amending the main clause, so as to substitute
the word ' *tails* ' for ' heads '. This amendment was so
obviously proper, that the house concurred in it *nem. con.*

As soon as the Governor had signed the bill, I invested
my whole estate in the purchase of Toms and Tabbies. At
first, I could only afford to feed them upon mice (which are
cheap), but they fulfilled the Scriptural injunction at so
marvellous a rate, that I at length considered it my best

policy to be liberal, and so indulged them in oysters and turtle. Their tails, at a legislative price, now bring me in a good income ; for I have discovered a way, in which, by means of Macassar oil, I can force three crops in a year. It delights me to find, too, that the animals soon get accustomed to the thing, and would rather have the appendages cut off than otherwise. I consider, myself, therefore, a made man, and am bargaining for a country seat on the Hudson.

PENGUIN POPULAR CLASSICS

Published or forthcoming

Charles and Mary Lamb	Tales from Shakespeare
D. H. Lawrence	The Rainbow
	Sons and Lovers
	Women in Love
Edward Lear	Book of Nonsense
Gaston Leroux	The Phantom of the Opera
Jack London	White Fang *and* The Call of the Wild
Captain Marryat	The Children of the New Forest
Herman Melville	Moby Dick
John Milton	Paradise Lost
Edith Nesbit	Five Children and It
	The Railway Children
Francis Turner Palgrave	The Golden Treasury
Edgar Allan Poe	Selected Tales
Sir Walter Scott	Ivanhoe
	Rob Roy
	Waverley
Saki	The Best of Saki
Anna Sewell	Black Beauty
William Shakespeare	Antony and Cleopatra
	As You Like It
	Hamlet
	Henry V
	Julius Caesar
	King Lear
	Macbeth
	The Merchant of Venice
	A Midsummer Night's Dream
	Othello
	Romeo and Juliet
	The Tempest
	Twelfth Night

PENGUIN POPULAR CLASSICS

PENGUIN POPULAR POETRY